CHILD'S PLOY

MACMILLAN · MIDNIGHT · LIBRARY

An Anthology of Mystery
and Suspense Stories

CHILD'S PLOY

EDITED BY

MARCIA MULLER

AND

BILL PRONZINI

MACMILLAN PUBLISHING COMPANY
New York

Copyright © 1984
by Bill Pronzini and Marcia Muller

Macmillan Publishing Company
866 Third Avenue, New York, N.Y. 10022
Collier Macmillan Canada, Inc.

Library of Congress Cataloging in Publication Data
Main entry under title:

Child's ploy.

(Macmillan midnight library)
1. Detective and mystery stories, American. 2. Detective and
mystery stories, English. I. Muller, Marcia. II. Pronzini, Bill
III. Series
PS648.D4C47 1984   813'.01'08   83-26711
ISBN: 0-02-599250-3

10   9   8   7   6   5   4   3   2   1

Printed in the United States of America

Acknowledgments

The editors gratefully acknowledge permission to reprint the following:

"The Rocking-Horse Winner," by D. H. Lawrence. From *The Complete Stories of D. H. Lawrence*, Volume III. Copyright © 1933 by The Estate of D. H. Lawrence. Copyright renewed © 1961 by Angelo Ravagli and C. M. Weekley, Executors of the Estate of Frieda Lawrence Ravagli. Reprinted by permission of Viking Penguin, Inc.

"The Beautiful White Horse," by William Saroyan. Copyright © 1938, 1966 by William Saroyan. Reprinted from *My Name is Aram* by permission of Harcourt Brace Jovanovich, Inc.

"Little Boy Lost," by Q. Patrick. Copyright © 1946 by The American Mercury, Inc. First published in *Ellery Queen's Mystery Magazine*. Reprinted by permission of Hugh Wheeler.

"Too Early Spring," by Stephen Vincent Benét. Copyright © 1933 by The Butterick Company; renewed © 1961 by Rosemary Carr Benet. Reprinted by permission of Brandt & Brandt Literary Agents, Inc.

"The Threatening Three," by Wiliam Campbell Gault. Copyright © 1948 by Periodical House, Inc. First published in *10-Story Detective* as "The Threatening Trio." Reprinted by permission of the author.

"The End of the Party," by Graham Greene. From *21 Stories* by Graham Greene. Copyright © 1947 by Graham Greene. Copyright renewed 1975 by Graham Greene. Reprinted by permission of Viking Penguin, Inc.

"The Landscape of Dreams," by John Lutz. Copyright © 1982 by John Lutz. First published in *Ellery Queen's Mystery Magazine*. Reprinted by permission of the author.

"Fire Escape," by Cornell Woolrich. Copyright © 1947 by Mystery Club, Inc., under the title "The Boy Cried Murder." Reprinted by permission of Scott Meredith Literary Agency, Inc., 845 Third Avenue, New York, N.Y. 10022.

"Ludmila," by Jean L. Backus. Copyright © 1973 by Jean L. Backus. First published in *Alfred Hitchcock Presents: Stories To Be Read With the Lights On*, under the pseudonym David Montross. Reprinted by permission of the author.

"Day for a Picnic," by Edward D. Hoch. Copyright © 1963 by Fiction Publishing Co. First published in *The Saint* as by Pat McMahon. Reprinted by permission of the author.

"Carnival Day," by Nedra Tyre. Copyright © 1957 by Davis Publications, Inc. First published in *Ellery Queen's Mystery Magazine*. Reprinted by permission of the author and her agents, Scott Meredith Literary Agency, Inc., 845 Third Avenue, New York, N.Y. 10022.

"Good Man, Bad Man," by Jerome Weidman. Copyright © 1967 by The Curtis Publishing Company. First published in *The Saturday Evening Post*. Reprinted by permission of Brandt & Brandt Literary Agents, Inc.

"Looie Follows Me," by John D. MacDonald. Copyright © 1949 by Crowell-Collier Publishing Co.; renewed © 1977 by John D. Mac-Donald Publishing, Inc. First published in *Collier's*. Reprinted by permission of the author.

"Here Lies Another Blackmailer," by Bill Pronzini. Copyright © 1974 by H.S.D. Publications, Inc. First published in *Alfred Hitchcock's Mystery Magazine*. Reprinted by permission of the author.

"Morning Song," by Betty Ren Wright. Copyright © 1982 by Renown Publications, Inc. First published in *Mike Shayne Mystery Magazine*. Reprinted by permission of Larry Sternig Literary Agency.

"The Hedge Between," by Charlotte Armstrong. Copyright © 1953 by Charlotte Armstrong. Copyright renewed © 1981 by Jeremy A. Lewi, Peter A. Lewi and Jacquelin Lewi Bynagta. Reprinted by permission of Brandt & Brandt Literary Agents, Inc.

"Uncle Max," by Pat McMahon. Copyright © 1965 by Fiction Publishing Co. First published in *The Saint*. Reprinted by permission of the author.

Contents

Contents

CHILD'S PLOY

Introduction

MURDER and mayhem are not child's play, of course. Fictionally, however, they may become child's *ploy*—when they are allowed to invade the otherwise happy and innocent world of children.

In adult tales of suspense, the child appears in various guises—often as a pawn of corrupt adults or as an unwitting catalyst for a crime; occasionally as the perpetrator of a misdeed; more rarely, as a detective. But in spite of this wide range of roles, many readers tend to think of youthful protagonists only in terms of the boy and girl sleuths who have become so popular during this century. (Boy sleuths were also popular during the latter half of the last century; the adventures of such dime-novel heroes as Young King Brady and Young Sleuth were read by millions in the late 1800s.)

Indeed, some juvenile detectives have become household names, and many an adult mystery reader will proudly proclaim that he first encountered clues and red herrings in the pages of a Nancy Drew or Hardy Boys adventure. These intrepid youngsters—as well as the more realistically drawn creations of Margaret Sutton (Judy Bolton) and Bruce Campbell (Ken Holt and Sandy Allen)—have become role models for generations of children around the world. It might, in fact, be argued that while browsing among today's adult mystery titles, many of us are really searching for Ken or Judy or Nancy in grown-up form.

The child's role in adult suspense fiction, however, has largely been ignored. This is due in part to the fact that although there are many short stories featuring young people, there are but few novels.

French writer Maurice Leblanc invented the earliest of the young detective heroes, Isidore Beautrelet, in *The Hollow Needle* (1910); but this novel is virtually unknown among today's readers. The same is true of Isidore's female counterpart, named only Dorothy, who appeared in an even more obscure Leblanc work, *The Secret Tomb*, in 1923. In this country, newsboy sleuth Eddie Parks of George Ade's *Bang! Bang!* (1928) is more a vehicle for parody of the Horatio Alger tradition than a convincing character. And while Harvey J. O'Higgins' Barney Cook is a more believable creation, and somewhat better known as a result, he only appears in a collection of seven short stories, *The Adventures of Detective Barney* (1915), which has long been out of print.

The best American novel featuring young sleuths has also been out of print for many years. This is Craig Rice's *Home Sweet Homicide* (1944), in which the three Carstairs children—ten-year-old Archie, thirteen-year-old April, and fifteen-year-old Dinah (all patterned after the author's offspring)—are given full prominence as they astonish their elders and dismay the police with their fresh and amusing approach to crime detection.

The portrait of a child which William March presents in his 1954 novel, *The Bad Seed*, is the complete antithesis of that of the charming Carstairs children. Rhoda Penmark is a wicked, calculating child—the one in millions who, for no evident genetic reason, is born evil. March's novel is compelling and frightening; unfortunately, its great popularity, first as a book, then as a play and film, set a trend which persists to this day—that of the "child monster." The recent spate of horror novels capitalizing on the presence of a germ of evil in the young, be it inherent or induced by some sort of demonic possession, merely serves to dull the impact of what, in March's hands, was a powerful and meaningful theme.

Other present-day novelists have used the ploy of an imperiled child to much better advantage. Mary Higgins Clark's finely crafted novels, *Where Are the Children?* (1975) and *A Stranger is Watching* (1979) depict the child as the target of evil, and were immediate bestsellers as a result of their intelligent and sympathetic handling of a difficult theme. A number of Margaret Millar's superior novels also make use of menaced children in a similarly intelligent and sympathetic fashion. In *The Fiend* (1964), the lives of nine adults are caught up in an atmosphere of terror surrounding a threat to a little girl; and in Margaret Millar's most recent work, *Banshee* (1983), the death of a child has a devastating impact on the lives of both her playmates and the adults who knew her.

Young people as detectives are almost as rare in suspense short stories as they are in novels; Charlotte Armstrong's "The Hedge Between" (included here) is one of the best of these. Much more prevalent, unhappily enough, are stories concerning child murderers or would-be murderers, children with a criminal bent, misguided children, and just-plain-evil children; and stories in which youngsters are the victims of corrupt adults, affected by circumstances which they cannot begin to understand. Still others deal with children who become involved in crime as a result of their own inquisitiveness, or by accident, or through an error in youthful judgment.

No matter what their theme, the best of these short stories concern awakenings: The child starts out an innocent, viewing the world with the unquestioning acceptance he has from birth. Events, however, force that first, fateful confrontation with reality, and the child begins to perceive his surroundings with a new, and often sadder, clarity. This implied or actual realization gives the characters greater depth, brings them alive, and we are able to catch glimpses of the adults they will one day be.

The stories we have selected for inclusion in these pages are all told from the point of view of children (in some cases retrospectively by the adults they have become). They encompass the full range of types and themes; some have happy endings and some don't, just as is the case in real life. Their authors are not only those well-known in the category of mystery fiction (Cornell Woolrich, John D. MacDonald, Charlotte Armstrong, Q. Patrick, William Campbell Gault, Edward D. Hoch), but those well known in the literary mainstream (D. H. Lawrence, Willa Cather, Katherine Mansfield, William Saroyan, Graham Greene, Stephen Vincent Benét, Jerome Weidman). And they all, we believe, have two important things in common: they treat their subject matter with compassion and understanding; and they are as entertaining as they are expertly written.

We hope you like these children's ploys. And we suspect that when you've finished reading them, you'll be as relieved as we are that they are only fictional . . .

—Marcia Muller and Bill Pronzini

San Francisco, California
July 1983

The Rocking-Horse Winner

D. H. LAWRENCE

D. H. Lawrence (1885–1930) is generally considered to be one of the most important novelists of the early twentieth century; he can also be considered one of the most controversial. While Sons and Lovers, published in 1913, is thought by many critics to be his masterpiece, he is more widely known for the sexually explicit Lady Chatterley's Lover (1928). Lawrence's frank depictions of the physical and psychological aspects of sexual relations, as well as his use of the principles of psychoanalysis, set him apart from his more staid contemporaries. In "The Rocking-Horse Winner," a very different type of story, the author establishes a delicate psychological balance within a family, and gives the reader a glimpse of a child with a rare and unbearable gift.

THERE was a woman who was beautiful, who started with all the advantages, yet she had no luck. She married for love, and the love turned to dust. She had bonny children, yet she felt they had been thrust upon her, and she could not love them. They looked at her coldly, as if they were finding fault with her. And hurriedly she felt she must cover up some fault in herself. Yet what it was that she must cover up she never knew. Nevertheless, when her children were present, she always felt the center of her heart go hard. This troubled her, and in her manner she was all the more gentle and anxious for her children, as if she loved them very much. Only she herself knew that at the center of her heart was a hard little place that could not feel love, no, not for anybody. Everybody else said of her: "She is such a good mother. She adores her children." Only she herself, and her children themselves, knew it was not so. They read it in each other's eyes.

There were a boy and two little girls. They lived in a pleasant house, with a garden, and they had discreet servants, and felt themselves superior to anyone in the neighborhood.

Although they lived in style, they felt always an anxiety in the house. There was never enough money. The mother had a small income, and the father had a small income, but not nearly enough for the social position which they had to keep up. The father went in to town to some office. But though he had good prospects, these prospects never materialized. There was always the grinding sense of the shortage of money, though the style was always kept up.

At last the mother said, "I will see if I can't make something." But she did not know where to begin. She racked her brains, and tried this thing and the other, but could not find anything successful. The failure made deep lines come into her face. Her children were growing up, they would have to go to school. There must be more money, there must be more money. The father, who was always very handsome and expensive in his tastes, seemed as if he never would be able to do anything worth doing. And the mother, who had a great belief in herself, did not succeed any better, and her tastes were just as expensive.

And so the house came to be haunted by the unspoken phrase: There must be more money! There must be more money! The children could hear it all the time, though nobody said it aloud. They heard it at Christmas, when the expensive and splendid toys filled the nursery. Behind the shining modern rocking horse, behind the smart doll's house, a voice would start whispering: "There must be more money! There must be more money!" And the children would stop playing, to listen for a moment. They would look into each other's eyes, to see if they had all heard. And each one saw in the eyes of the other two that they too had heard. "There must be more money! There must be more money!"

It came whispering from the springs of the still-swaying rocking horse, and even the horse, bending his wooden, champion head, heard it. The big doll, sitting so pink and smirking in her new pram, could hear it quite plainly, and seemed to be smirking all the more self-consciously because of it. The foolish puppy, too, that took the place of the Teddy bear, he was looking so extraordinarily foolish for no other reason but that he heard the secret whisper all over the house: "There must be more money!"

Yet nobody ever said it aloud. The whisper was everywhere, and therefore, no one spoke it. Just as no one ever says: "We are breathing!" in spite of the fact that breath is coming and going all the time.

"Mother," said the boy Paul one day, "why don't we keep a car of our own? Why do we always use Uncle's, or else a taxi?"

"Because we're the poor members of the family," said the mother.

"But why are we, Mother?"

"Well—I suppose," she said slowly and bitterly, "it's because your father has no luck."

The boy was silent for some time.

"Is luck money, Mother?" he asked, rather timidly.

"No, Paul. Not quite. It's what causes you to have money."

"Oh!" said Paul vaguely. "I thought when Uncle Oscar said filthy lucker, it meant money."

"Filthy lucre does mean money," said the mother. "But it's lucre, not luck."

"Oh!" said the boy. "Then what is luck, Mother?"

"It's what causes you to have money. If you're lucky you have money. That's why it's better to be born lucky than rich. If you're rich, you may lose your money. But if you're lucky, you will always get more money."

"Oh! Will you? And is Father not lucky?"

"Very unlucky, I should say," she said bitterly.

The boy watched her with unsure eyes.

"Why?" he asked.

"I don't know. Nobody ever knows why one person is lucky and another unlucky."

"Don't they? Nobody at all? Does nobody know?"

"Perhaps God. But He never tells."

"He ought to, then. And aren't you lucky either, Mother?"

"I can't be, if I married an unlucky husband."

"But by yourself, aren't you?"

"I used to think I was, before I married. Now I think I am very unlucky indeed."

"Why?"

"Well—never mind! Perhaps I'm not really," she said.

The child looked at her, to see if she meant it. But he saw, by the lines of her mouth, that she was only trying to hide something from him.

"Well, anyhow," he said stoutly, "I'm a lucky person."

"Why?" said his mother, with a sudden laugh.

He stared at her. He didn't even know why he had said it.

"God told me," he asserted, brazening it out.

"I hope He did, dear!" she said, again with a laugh, but rather bitter.

"He did, Mother!"

"Excellent!" said the mother, using one of her husband's exclamations.

The boy saw she did not believe him; or rather, that she paid no attention to his assertions. This angered him somewhere, and made him want to compel her attention.

He went off by himself, vaguely, in a childish way, seeking for the clue to "luck." Absorbed, taking no heed of other people, he went about with a sort of stealth, seeking inwardly for luck. He wanted it. When the two girls were playing dolls in the nursery, he wanted luck, he wanted it, he would sit on his big rocking horse, charging madly into space, with a frenzy that made the little girls peer at him uneasily. Wildly the horse careered, the waving dark hair of the boy tossed, his eyes had a strange glare in them. The little girls dared not speak to him.

When he had ridden to the end of his mad little journey, he climbed down and stood in front of his rocking horse, staring fixedly into its lowered face. Its red mouth was slightly open, its big eye was wide and glassy-bright.

"Now!" he would silently command the snorting steed. "Now, take me to where there is luck! Now take me!"

And he would slash the horse on the neck with the little whip he had asked Uncle Oscar for. He knew the horse could take him to where there was luck, if only he forced it. So he would mount again, and start on his furious ride, hoping at last to get there. He knew he could get there.

"You'll break your horse, Paul!" said the nurse.

"He's always riding like that! I wish he'd leave off!" said his sister Joan.

But he only glared down on them in silence. Nurse gave him up. She could make nothing of him. Anyhow, he was growing beyond her.

One day his mother and his Uncle Oscar came in when he was on one of his furious rides. He did not speak to them.

"Hallo, you young jockey! Riding a winner?" said his uncle.

"Aren't you growing too big for a rocking horse? You're not a very little boy any longer, you know," said his mother.

But Paul only gave a blue glare from his big, rather close-set eyes. He would speak to nobody when he was in full tilt. His mother watched him with an anxious expression on her face.

At last he suddenly stopped forcing his horse into the mechanical gallop, and slid down.

"Well, I got there," he announced fiercely, his blue eyes still flaring, and his sturdy long legs straddling apart.

"Where did you get to?" asked his mother.

"Where I wanted to go," he flared back at her.

"That's right, son!" said Uncle Oscar. "Don't you stop till you get there. What's the horse's name?"

"He doesn't have a name," said the boy.

"Gets on without all right?" asked the uncle.

"Well, he has different names. He was called Sansovino last week."

"Sansovino, eh? Won the Ascot. How did you know his name?"

"He always talks about horse races with Bassett," said Joan.

The uncle was delighted to find that his small nephew was posted with all the racing news. Bassett, the young gardener, who had been wounded in the left foot in the war and had got his present job through Oscar Cresswell, whose batman he had been, was a perfect blade of the "turf." He lived in the racing events, and the small boy lived with him.

Oscar Cresswell got it all from Bassett.

"Master Paul comes and asks me, so I can't do more than tell him, sir," said Bassett, his face terribly serious, as if he were speaking of religious matters.

"And does he ever put anything on a horse he fancies?"

"Well—I don't want to give him away—he's a young sport, a fine sport, sir. Would you mind asking him himself? He sort of takes a pleasure in it, and perhaps he'd feel I was giving him away, sir, if you don't mind."

Bassett was serious as a church.

The uncle went back to his nephew, and took him off for a ride in the car.

"Say, Paul, old man, do you ever put anything on a horse?" the uncle asked.

The boy watched the handsome man closely.

"Why, do you think I oughtn't to?" he parried.

"Not a bit of it! I thought perhaps you might give me a tip for the Lincoln."

The car sped on into the country, going down to Uncle Oscar's place in Hampshire.

"Honor bright?" said the nephew.

"Honor bright, son!" said the uncle.

"Well, then, Daffodil."

"Daffodil! I doubt it, sonny. What about Mirza?"

"I only know the winner," said the boy. "That's Daffodil."

"Daffodil, eh?"

There was a pause. Daffodil was an obscure horse comparatively.

"Uncle!"

"Yes, son?"

"You won't let it go any further, will you? I promised Bassett."

"Bassett be damned, old man! What's he got to do with it?"

"We're partners. We've been partners from the first. Uncle, he lent me my first five shillings, which I lost. I promised him, honor bright, it was only between me and him; only you gave me that ten-shilling note I started winning with, so I thought you were lucky. You won't let it go any further, will you?"

The boy gazed at his uncle from those big, hot, blue eyes, set rather close together. The uncle stirred and laughed uneasily.

"Right you are, son! I'll keep your tip private. Daffodil, eh? How much are you putting on him?"

"All except twenty pounds," said the boy. "I keep that in reserve."

The uncle thought it a good joke.

"You keep twenty pounds in reserve, do you, you young romancer? What are you betting, then?"

"I'm betting three hundred," said the boy gravely.

"But it's between you and me, Uncle Oscar! Honor bright?"

The uncle burst into a roar of laughter.

"It's between you and me all right, you young Nat Gould," he said, laughing. "But where's your three hundred?"

"Bassett keeps it for me. We're partners."

"You are, are you! And what is Bassett putting on Daffodil?"

"He won't go quite as high as I do, I expect. Perhaps he'll go a hundred and fifty."

"What, pennies?" laughed the uncle.

"Pounds," said the child, with a surprised look at his uncle. "Bassett keeps a bigger reserve than I do."

Between wonder and amusement Uncle Oscar was silent. He pursued the matter no further, but he determined to take his nephew with him to the Lincoln races.

"Now, son," he said, "I'm putting twenty on Mirza, and I'll put five for you on any horse you fancy. What's your pick?"

"Daffodil, Uncle."

"No, not the fiver on Daffodil!"

"I should if it was my own fiver," said the child.

"Good! Good! Right you are! A fiver for me and a fiver for you on Daffodil."

The child had never been to a race meeting before, and his eyes were blue fire. He pursed his mouth tight, and watched. A Frenchman just in front had put his money on Lancelot. Wild with excitement, he flayed his arms up and down, yelling, "Lancelot! Lancelot!" in his French accent.

Daffodil came in first, Lancelot second, Mirza third. The child, flushed with eyes blazing, was curiously serene. His uncle brought him four five-pound notes, four to one.

"What am I to do with these?" he cried, waving them before the boy's eyes.

"I suppose we'll talk to Bassett," said the boy. "I expect I have fifteen hundred now; and twenty in reserve; and this twenty."

His uncle studied him for some moments.

"Look here, son!" he said. "You're not serious about Bassett and that fifteen hundred, are you?"

"Yes, I am. But it's between you and me, Uncle. Honor bright!"

"Honor bright all right, son! But I must talk to Bassett."

"If you'd like to be a partner, Uncle, with Bassett and me, we could all be partners. Only, you'd have to promise, honor bright, Uncle, not to let it go beyond us three. Bassett and I are lucky, and you must be lucky, because it was your ten shillings I started winning with. . . ."

Uncle Oscar took both Bassett and Paul into Richmond Park for an afternoon, and there they talked.

"It's like this, you see, sir," Bassett said. "Master Paul would get me talking about racing events, spinning yarns, you know, sir. And he was always keen on knowing if I'd made or if I'd lost. It's about a year since, now, that I put five shillings on Blush of Dawn for him: and we lost. Then the luck turned, with that ten shillings he had from you: that we put on Singhalese. And since that time, it's been pretty steady, all things considering. What do you say, Master Paul?"

"We're all right when we're sure," said Paul. "It's when we're not quite sure that we go down."

"Oh, but we're careful then," said Bassett.

"But when are you sure?" smiled Uncle Oscar.

"It's Master Paul, sir," smiled Bassett, in a secret, religious voice. "It's as if he had it from heaven. Like Daffodil, now, for the Lincoln. That was as sure as eggs."

"Did you put anything on Daffodil?" asked Oscar Cresswell.

"Yes, sir. I made my bit."

"And my nephew?"

Bassett was obstinately silent, looking at Paul.

"I made twelve hundred, didn't I, Bassett? I told uncle I was putting three hundred on Daffodil?"

"That's right," said Bassett, nodding.

"But where's the money?" asked the uncle.

"I keep it safe locked up, sir. Master Paul he can have it any minute he likes to ask for it."

"What, fifteen hundred pounds?"

"And twenty! And forty, that is, with the twenty he made on the course."

"It's amazing!" said the uncle.

"If Master Paul offers you to be partners, sir, I would, if I were you: if you'll excuse me," said Bassett.

Oscar Cresswell thought about it.

"I'll see the money," he said.

They drove home again, and, sure enough, Bassett came round to the gardenhouse with fifteen hundred pounds in notes. The twenty pounds' reserve was left with Joe Glee, in the Turf Commission deposit.

"You see, it's all right, Uncle, when I'm sure! Then we go strong for all we're worth. Don't we, Bassett?"

"We do that, Master Paul."

"And when are you sure?" said the uncle, laughing.

"Oh, well, sometimes I'm absolutely sure, like about Daffodil," said the boy; "and sometimes I have an idea; and sometimes I haven't even an idea, have I, Bassett? Then we're careful, because we mostly go down."

"You do, do you! And when you're sure, like about Daffodil, what makes you sure, sonny?"

"Oh, well, I don't know," said the boy uneasily. "I'm sure, you know, Uncle, that's all."

"It's as if he had it from heaven, sir," Bassett reiterated.

"I should say so!" said the uncle.

But he became a partner. And when the Leger was coming on, Paul was "sure" about Lively Spark, which was a quite inconsiderable horse. The boy insisted on putting a thousand on the horse, Bassett went for five hundred, and Oscar Cresswell two hundred. Lively Spark came in first, and the betting had been ten to one against him. Paul had made ten thousand.

"You see," he said, "I was absolutely sure of him."

Even Oscar Cresswell had cleared two thousand.

"Look here, son," he said, "this sort of thing makes me nervous."

"It needn't, Uncle! Perhaps I shan't be sure again for a long time."

"But what are you going to do with your money?" asked the uncle.

"Of course," said the boy, "I started it for Mother. She said she had no luck, because Father is unlucky, so I thought if I was lucky, it might stop whispering."

"What might stop whispering?"

"Our house. I hate our house for whispering."

"What does it whisper?"

"Why—why"—the boy fidgeted—"why, I don't know. But it's always short of money, you know, Uncle."

"I know it, son, I know it."

"You know people send Mother writs, don't you, Uncle?"

"I'm afraid I do," said the uncle.

"And then the house whispers, like people laughing at you behind your back. It's awful, that is! I thought if I was lucky—"

"You might stop it," added the uncle.

The boy watched him with big blue eyes, that had an uncanny cold fire in them, and he said never a word.

"Well, then!" said the uncle. "What are we doing?"

"I shouldn't like Mother to know I was lucky," said the boy.

"Why not, son?"

"She'd stop me."

"I don't think she would."

"Oh!"—and the boy writhed in an odd way—"I don't want her to know, Uncle."

"All right, son! We'll manage it without her knowing."

They managed it very easily. Paul, at the other's suggestion, handed over five thousand pounds to his uncle, who deposited it with the family lawyer, who was then to inform Paul's mother that a relative had put five thousand pounds into his hands, which sum was to be paid out a thousand pounds at a time, on the mother's birthday, for the next five years.

"So she'll have a birthday present of a thousand pounds for five successive years," said Uncle Oscar. "I hope it won't make it all the harder for her later."

Paul's mother had her birthday in November. The house had been "whispering" worse than ever lately, and, even in spite of his luck, Paul could not bear up against it. He was very anxious to see the effect of the birthday letter, telling his mother about the thousand pounds.

When there were no visitors, Paul now took his meals with his parents, as he was beyond the nursery control. His mother went into town nearly every day. She had discovered that she had an odd knack of sketching furs and dress materials, so she worked secretly in the studio of a friend who was the chief "artist" for the leading drapers. She drew the figures of ladies in furs and ladies in silk and sequins for the newspaper advertisements. This young woman artist earned several thousand pounds a year, but Paul's mother only made several hundreds, and she was again dissatisfied. She so wanted to be first in something, and she did not succeed, even in making sketches for drapery advertisements.

She was down to breakfast on the morning of her birthday. Paul watched her face as she read her letters. He knew the lawyer's letter. As his mother read it, her face hardened and became more expressionless. Then a cold, determined look came on her mouth. She hid the letter under the pile of others, and said not a word about it.

"Didn't you have anything nice in the post for your birthday, Mother?" asked Paul.

"Quite moderately nice," she said, her voice cold and absent.

She went away to town without saying more.

But in the afternoon Uncle Oscar appeared. He said Paul's mother had had a long interview with the lawyer, asking if the whole five thousand could not be advanced at once, as she was in debt.

"What do you think, Uncle?" said the boy.

"I leave it to you, son."

"Oh, let her have it, then! We can get some more with the other," said the boy.

"A bird in the hand is worth two in the bush, laddie!" said Uncle Oscar.

"But I'm sure to know for the Grand National; or the Lincolnshire; or else the Derby. I'm sure to know for one of them," said Paul.

So Uncle Oscar signed the agreement, and Paul's mother touched the whole five thousand. Then something very curious happened. The voices in the house suddenly went mad, like a chorus of frogs on a spring evening. There were certain new furnishings, and Paul had a tutor. He was really going to Eton, his father's school, in the following autumn. There were flowers in the winter, and blossoming of the luxury Paul's mother had been used to. And yet the voices in the house, behind the sprays of mimosa and almond blossom, and from under the piles of iridescent cushions, simply trilled and screamed in a sort of ecstasy: "There must be more money; O-h-h-h; there must be more money. Oh, now now-w! Now-w-w—there must be more money!—more than ever! More than ever!"

It frightened Paul terribly. He studied away at his Latin and Greek with his tutors, but his intense hours were spent with Bassett. The Grand National had gone by: he had not "known," and had lost a hundred pounds. Summer was at hand. He was in agony for the Lincoln. But even for the Lincoln he didn't "know," and he lost fifty pounds. He became wild-eyed and strange, as if something were going to explode in him.

"Let it alone, son! Don't you bother about it!" urged Uncle Oscar. But it was as if the boy couldn't really hear what his uncle was saying.

"I've got to know for the Derby! I've got to know for the Derby," the child reiterated, his big blue eyes blazing with a sort of madness.

His mother noticed how over-wrought he was.

"You'd better go to the seaside. Wouldn't you like to go now to the seaside, instead of waiting? I think you'd better," she said, looking down at him anxiously, her heart curiously heavy because of him.

But the child lifted his uncanny blue eyes.

"I couldn't possibly go before the Derby, Mother!" he said. "I couldn't possibly go before the Derby, Mother!" he said. "I couldn't possibly!"

"Why not?" she said, her voice becoming heavy when she was opposed. "Why not? You can still go from the seaside to see the Derby with your Uncle Oscar, if that's what you wish. No need for you to wait here. Besides, I think you care too much about these races. It's a bad sign. My family has been a gambling family, and you won't know till you grow up how much damage it has done. But it has done damage. I shall have to send Bassett away, and ask Uncle Oscar not to talk racing to you, unless you promise to be reasonable about it: go away to the seaside and forget it. You're all nerves!"

"I'll do what you like, Mother, so long as you don't send me away till after the Derby," the boy said.

"Send you away from where? Just from this house?"

"Yes," he said, gazing at her.

"Why, you curious child, what makes you care about this house so much, suddenly? I never knew you loved it."

He gazed at her without speaking. He had a secret within a secret, something he had not divulged, even to Bassett or to his Uncle Oscar.

But his mother, after standing undecided and a little bit sullen for some moments, said:

"Very well, then! Don't go to the seaside till after the Derby, if you don't wish it. But promise me you won't let your nerves go to pieces. Promise you won't think so much about horse racing and events, as you call them!"

"Oh, no," said the boy casually. "I won't think much about them, Mother. You needn't worry. I wouldn't worry, Mother, if I were you."

"If you were me and I were you," said his mother, "I wonder what we should do!"

"But you know you needn't worry, Mother, don't you?" the boy repeated.

"I should be awfully glad to know it," she said wearily.

"Oh, well, you can, you know. I mean, you ought to know you needn't worry," he insisted

"Ought I? Then I'll see about it," she said.

Paul's secret of secrets was his wooden horse, that which had no name. Since he was emancipated from a nurse and a nursery governess, he had had his rocking horse removed to his own bedroom at the top of the house.

"Surely, you're too big for a rocking horse!" his mother had remonstrated.

"Well, you see, Mother, till I can have a real horse, I like to have some sort of animal about," had been his quaint answer.

"Do you feel he keeps you company?" she laughed.

"Oh, yes!" He's very good, he always keeps me company, when I'm there," said Paul.

So, the horse, rather shabby, stood in an arrested prance in the boy's bedroom.

The Derby was drawing near, and the boy grew more and more tense. He hardly heard what was spoken to him, he was very frail, and his eyes were really uncanny. His mother had sudden strange seizures of uneasiness about him. Sometimes, for half-an-hour, she would feel a sudden anxiety about him that was almost anguish. She wanted to rush to him at once, and know he was safe.

Two nights before the Derby, she was at a big party in town, when one of her rushes of anxiety about her boy, her firstborn, gripped her heart till she could hardly speak. She fought with the feeling, might and main, for she believed in common sense. But it was too strong. She had to leave the dance and go downstairs to telephone to the country. The children's nursery governess was terribly surprised and startled at being rung up in the night.

"Are the children all right, Miss Wilmot?"

"Oh, yes, they are quite all right."

"Master Paul? Is he all right?"

"He went to bed as right as a trivet. Shall I run up and look at him?"

"No," said Paul's mother reluctantly. "No! Don't trouble. It's all right. Don't sit up. We shall be home fairly soon." She did not want her son's privacy intruded upon.

"Very good," said the governess.

It was about one o'clock when Paul's mother and father drove up to their house. All was still. Paul's mother went to her room and slipped off her white fur cloak. She had told her maid not to wait up for her. She heard her husband downstairs, mixing a whisky and soda.

And then, because of the strange anxiety at her heart, she stole upstairs to her son's room. Noiselessly she went along the upper corridor. Was there a faint noise? What was it?

She stood, with arrested muscles, outside his door, listening. There was a strange, heavy, and yet not loud noise. Her heart stood still. It was a soundless noise, yet rushing and powerful. Something huge, in violent, hushed motion. What was it? What in God's name was it? She ought to know. She felt that she knew the noise. She knew what it was.

Yet she could not place it. She couldn't say what it was. And on and on it went, like a madness.

Softly, frozen with anxiety and fear, she turned the door handle.

The room was dark. Yet in the space near the window, she heard and saw something plunging to and fro. She gazed in fear and amazement.

Then suddenly she switched on the light, and saw her son, in his green pajamas, madly surging on the rocking horse. The blaze of light suddenly lit him up, as he urged the wooden horse, and lit her up, as she stood, blonde, in her dress of pale green and crystal, in the doorway.

"Paul!" she cried. "Whatever are you doing?"

"It's Malabar!" he screamed, in a powerful strange voice. "It's Malabar!"

His eyes blazed at her for one strange and senseless second, as he ceased urging his wooden horse. Then he fell with a crash to the ground, and she, all her tormented motherhood flooding upon her, rushed to gather him up.

But he was unconscious, and unconscious he remained, with some brain fever. He talked and tossed, and his mother sat stonily by his side.

"Malabar! It's Malabar! Bassett, Bassett, I know! It's Malabar!"

So the child cried, trying to get up and urge the rocking horse that gave him his inspiration.

"What does he mean by Malabar?" asked the heart-frozen mother.

"I don't know," said the father stonily.

"What does he mean by Malabar?" she asked her brother Oscar.

"It's one of the horses running for the Derby," was the answer.

And, in spite of himself, Oscar Cresswell spoke to Bassett, and himself put a thousand on Malabar; at fourteen to one.

The third day of the illness was critical; they were waiting for a change. The boy, with his rather long curly hair, was tossing ceaselessly on the pillow. He neither slept nor regained consciousness, and his eyes were like blue stones. His mother sat, feeling her heart had gone, turned actually into a stone.

In the evening, Oscar Cresswell did not come, but Bassett sent a message saying could he come up for one moment, just one moment? Paul's mother was very angry at the intrusion, but on second thought she agreed. The boy was the same. Perhaps Bassett might bring him to consciousness.

The gardener, a shortish fellow with a little brown mustache, and sharp little brown eyes, tiptoed into the room, touched his imaginary cap to Paul's mother, and stole to the bedside, staring with glittering, smallish eyes at the tossing, dying child.

"Master Paul!" he whispered. "Master Paul! Malabar came in first all right, a clean win. I did as you told me. You've made over seventy thousand pounds, you have; you've got over eighty thousand. Malabar came in all right, Master Paul."

"Malabar! Malabar! Did I say Malabar, Mother? Did I say Malabar? Do you think I'm lucky, Mother? I knew Malabar, didn't I? Over eighty thousand pounds! I call that lucky, don't you Mother? Over eighty thousand pounds! I knew, didn't I know I knew? Malabar came in all right. If I ride my horse till I'm sure, then I tell you, Bassett, you can go as high as you like. Did you go for all you were worth, Bassett?"

"I went a thousand on it, Master Paul."

"I never told you, Mother, that if I can ride my horse, and get there, then I'm absolutely sure—oh, absolutely! Mother, did I ever tell you? I am lucky!"

"No, you never did," said the mother.

But the boy died in the night.

And even as he lay dead, his mother heard her brother's voice saying to her: "My God, Hester, you're eighty-odd thousand to the good, and a poor devil of a son to the bad. But, poor devil, poor devil, he's best gone out of a life where he rides his rocking horse to find a winner."

How Pearl Button Was Kidnapped

KATHERINE MANSFIELD

New Zealander Katherine Mansfield (1888–1923) was one of the finest and most prolific short story writers of the early twentieth century. Before her death of tuberculosis at the age of thirty-five, she produced a large body of work which was collected, both during her lifetime and posthumously, in such volumes as In a German Pension *(1911),* Bliss *(1920), and* The Little Girl *(1924). Many of these evoke the culture and conflicts of her native New Zealand. In addition to stories, Mansfield also wrote poetry and published a journal. The setting and events depicted in "How Pearl Button Was Kidnapped" are a reflection of an earlier, less complicated age; and the implications of what happens to young Pearl are perhaps more frightening by contrast.*

PEARL Button swung on the little gate in front of the House of Boxes. It was the early afternoon of a sunshiny day with little winds playing hide-and-seek in it. They blew Pearl Button's pinafore frill into her mouth, and they blew the street dust all over the House of Boxes. Pearl watched it—like a cloud—like when Mother peppered her fish and the top of the pepper-pot came off. She swung on the little gate, all alone, and she sang a small song.

Two big women came walking down the street. One was dressed in red and the other was dressed in yellow and green. They had pink handkerchiefs over their heads, and both of them carried a big flax basket of ferns. They had no shoes and stockings on, and they came walking along, slowly, because they were so fat, and talking to each other and always smiling. Pearl stopped swinging, and when they saw her they stopped walking. They looked and looked at her and then they talked to each other, waving their arms and clapping their hands together. Pearl began to laugh.

The two women came up to her, keeping close to the hedge and looking in a frightened way toward the House of Boxes.

"Hallo, little girl!" said one.

Pearl said, "Hallo!"

"You all alone by yourself?"

Pearl nodded.

"Where's your mother?"

"In the kitchen, ironing-because-it's-Tuesday."

The women smiled at her and Pearl smiled back. "Oh," she said, "haven't you got very white teeth indeed! Do it again."

The dark women laughed, and again they talked to each other with funny words and wavings of the hands. "What's your name?" they asked her.

"Pearl Button."

"You coming with us, Pearl Button? We got beautiful things to show you," whispered one of the women.

So Pearl got down from the gate and she slipped out into the road. And she walked between the two dark women down the windy road, taking little running steps to keep up, and wondering what they had in their House of Boxes.

They walked a long way. "You tired?" asked one of the women, bending down to Pearl. Pearl shook her head. They walked much farther. "You not tired?" asked the other woman. And Pearl shook her head again, but tears shook from her eyes at the same time and her lips trembled.

One of the women gave over her flax basket of ferns and caught Pearl Button up in her arms, and walked with Pearl Button's head against her shoulder and her dusty little legs dangling. She was softer than a bed and she had a nice smell—a smell that made you bury your head and breathe and breathe it . . .

They set Pearl Button down in a log room full of other people the same color as they were—and all these people came close to her and looked at her, nodding and laughing and throwing up their eyes. The woman who had carried Pearl took off her hair ribbon and shook her curls loose. There was a cry from the other women, and they crowded close and some of them ran a finger through Pearl's yellow curls, very gently, and one of them, a young one, lifted all Pearl's hair and kissed the back of her little white neck. Pearl felt shy but happy at the same time.

There were some men on the floor, smoking, with rugs and feather mats round their shoulders. One of them made a funny face at her and he pulled a great big peach out of his pocket and set it on the floor, and flicked it with his finger as though it were a marble. It rolled right over to her. Pearl picked it up. "Please can I eat it?" she asked.

At that they all laughed and clapped their hands, and the man with the funny face made another at her and pulled a pear out of his pocket and sent it bobbling over the floor. Pearl laughed. The women sat on the floor and Pearl sat down too. The floor was very dusty. She carefully pulled up her pinafore and dress and sat on her petticoat as she had been taught to sit in dusty places, and she ate the fruit, the juice running all down her front.

"Oh!" she said in a very frightened voice to one of the women, "I've spilt all the juice!"

"That doesn't matter at all," said the woman, patting her cheek. A man came into the room with a long whip in his hand. He shouted something. They all got up, shouting, laughing, wrapping themselves up in rugs and blankets and feather mats. Pearl was carried again, this time into a great cart, and she sat on the lap of one of her women with the driver beside her.

It was a green cart with a red pony and a black pony. It went very fast out of the town. The driver stood up and waved the whip round his head. Pearl peered over the shoulder of her woman. Other carts were behind like a procession. She waved at them. Then the country came. First fields of short grass with sheep on them and little bushes of white flowers and pink briar-rose baskets—then big trees on both sides of the road—and nothing to be seen except big trees. Pearl tried to look through them but it was quite dark. Birds were singing. She nestled closer in the big lap. The woman was warm as a cat, and she moved up and down when she breathed, just like purring.

Pearl played with a green ornament round her neck, and the woman took the little hand and kissed each of her fingers and then turned it over and kissed the dimples. Pearl had never been happy like this before. On the top of a big hill they stopped. The driving man turned to Pearl and said, "Look, look!" and pointed with his whip.

And down at the bottom of the hill was something perfectly different—a great big piece of blue water was creeping over the land. She screamed and clutched at the big woman, "What is it, what is it?"

"Why," said the woman, "it's the sea."

"Will it hurt us—is it coming?"

"Ai-e, no, it doesn't come to us. It's very beautiful. You look again."

Pearl looked. "You're sure it can't come," she said.

"Ai-e, no. It stays in its place," said the big woman. Waves with white tops came leaping over the blue. Pearl watched them break on a long piece of land covered with garden-path shells. They drove round a corner.

There were some little houses down close to the sea, with wood fences round them and gardens inside. They comforted her. Pink and red and blue washing hung over the fences, and as they came near more people came out, and five yellow dogs with long thin tails. All the people were fat and laughing, with little naked babies holding on to them or rolling about in the gardens like puppies.

Pearl was lifted down and taken into a tiny house with only one room and a veranda. There was a girl there with two pieces of black hair down to her feet. She was setting the dinner on the floor.

"It *is* a funny place," said Pearl, watching the pretty girl while the woman unbuttoned her little drawers for her. She was very hungry. She ate meat and vegetables and fruit and the woman gave her milk out of a green cup. And it was quite silent except for the sea outside and the laughs of the two women watching her. "Haven't you got any Houses of Boxes?" she said. "Don't you all live in a row? Don't the men go to offices? Aren't there any nasty things?"

They took off her shoes and stockings, her pinafore and dress. She walked about in her petticoat and then she walked outside with the grass pushing between her toes. The two women came out with different sorts of baskets. They took her hands. Over a little paddock, through a fence, and then on warm sand with brown grass in it they went down to the sea. Pearl held back when the sand grew wet, but the women coaxed, "Nothing to hurt, very beautiful. You come."

They dug in the sand and found some shells which they threw

into the baskets. The sand was set as mud pies. Pearl forgot her fright and began digging too. She got hot and wet, and suddenly over her feet broke a little line of foam. "Oo, oo!" she shrieked, dabbling with her feet, "Lovely, lovely!" She paddled in the shallow water. It was warm. She made a cup of her hands and caught some of it. But it stopped being blue in her hands. She was so excited that she rushed over to her woman and flung her little thin arms around the woman's neck, hugging her, kissing . . .

Suddenly the girl gave a frightful scream. The woman raised herself and Pearl slipped down on the sand and looked toward the land. Little men in blue coats—little blue men came running, running toward her with shouts and whistlings—a crowd of little blue men to carry her back to the House of Boxes.

The Beautiful White Horse

WILLIAM SAROYAN

It has been said that William Saroyan's fiction has a wondering, almost childlike quality. Indeed it does, in the best sense of that description. "The Beautiful White Horse," in which the Armenian lad named Aram becomes involved in a rather benign case of horse thievery, is a perfect example—an amusing, simple but not simplistic, delightful little tale. Saroyan (1908–1982) published his first story, "Daring Young Man on the Flying Trapeze," in 1934, and went on to write numerous plays (The Time of Your Life was awarded a Pulitzer Prize in 1940); collections of short stories (My Name is Aram); novels (The Human Comedy); and his autobiography, Here Comes, There Goes, You Know Who (1961). Some have speculated that it was because he led a troubled personal life that Saroyan's fictional world was a relatively calm and innocent place.

ONE day back there in the good old days when I was nine and the world was full of every imaginable kind of magnificence, and life was still a delightful and mysterious dream, my cousin Mourad, who was considered crazy by everybody who knew him except me, came to my house at four in the morning and woke me up by tapping on the window of my room.

Aram, he said.

I jumped out of bed and looked out the window.

I couldn't believe what I saw.

It wasn't morning yet, but it was summer and with daybreak not many minutes around the corner of the world it was light enough for me to know I wasn't dreaming.

My cousin Mourad was sitting on a beautiful white horse.

I stuck my head out of the window and rubbed my eyes.

Yes, he said in Armenian. It's a horse. You're not dreaming. Make it quick if you want to ride.

I knew my cousin Mourad enjoyed being alive more than anybody else who had ever fallen into the world by mistake, but this was more than even I could believe.

In the first place, my earliest memories had been memories of horses and my first longings had been longings to ride.

This was the wonderful part.

In the second place, we were poor.

This was the part that wouldn't permit me to believe what I saw.

We were poor. We had no money. Our whole tribe was poverty-stricken. Every branch of the Garoghlanian family was living in the most amazing and comical poverty in the world. Nobody could understand where we ever got money enough to keep us with food in our bellies, not even the old men of the family. Most important of all, though, we were famous for our honesty. We had been famous for our honesty for something like eleven centuries, even when we had been the wealthiest family in what we liked to think was the world. We were proud first, honest next, and after that we believed in right and wrong. None of us would take advantage of anybody in the world, let alone steal.

Consequently, even though I could *see* the horse, so magnificent; even though I could *smell* it, so lovely; even though I could *hear* it breathing, so exciting; I couldn't *believe* the horse had anything to do with my cousin Mourad or with me or with any of the other members of our family, asleep or awake, because I *knew* my cousin Mourad couldn't have *bought* the horse, and if he couldn't have bought it he must have *stolen* it, and I refused to believe he had stolen it.

No member of the Garoghlanian family could be a thief.

I stared first at my cousin and then at the horse. There was a pious stillness and humor in each of them which on the one hand delighted me and on the other frightened me.

Mourad, I said, where did you steal this horse?

Leap out of the window, he said, if you want to ride.

It was true, then. He *had* stolen the horse. There was no question about it. He had come to invite me to ride or not, as I chose.

Well, it seemed to me stealing a horse for a ride was not the same thing as stealing something else, such as money. For all I knew, maybe it wasn't stealing at all. If you were crazy about horses the way my cousin Mourad and I were, it wasn't stealing. It wouldn't become stealing until we offered to sell the horse, which of course I knew we would never do.

Let me put on some clothes, I said.

All right, he said, but hurry.

I leaped into my clothes.

I jumped down to the yard from the window and leaped up onto the horse behind my cousin Mourad.

That year we lived at the edge of town, on Walnut Avenue. Behind our house was the country: vineyards, orchards, irrigation ditches, and country roads. In less than three minutes we were on Olive Avenue, and then the horse began to trot. The air was new and lovely to breathe. The feel of the horse running was wonderful. My cousin Mourad who was considered one of the craziest members of our family began to sing. I mean, he began to roar.

Every family has a crazy streak in it somewhere, and my cousin Mourad was considered the natural descendant of the crazy streak in our tribe. Before him was our uncle Khosrove, an enormous man with a powerful head of black hair and the largest mustache in the San Joaquin Valley, a man so furious in temper, so irritable, so impatient that he stopped anyone from talking by roaring, *It is no harm; pay no attention to it.*

That was all, no matter what anybody happened to be talking about. Once it was his own son Arak running eight blocks to the barber shop where his father was having his mustache trimmed to tell him their house was on fire. This man Khosrove sat up in the chair and roared, It is no harm; pay no attention to it. The barber said, But the boy says your house is on fire. So Khosrove roared, Enough, it is no harm, I say.

My cousin Mourad was considered the natural descendant of this man, although Mourad's father was Zorab, who was practical and nothing else. That's how it was in our tribe. A man could be the father of his son's flesh, but that did not mean that he was also the father of his spirit. The distribution of the various kinds of spirit of our tribe had been from the beginning capricious and vagrant.

We rode and my cousin Mourad sang. For all anybody knew we were still in the old country where, at least according to some of our neighbors, we belonged. We let the horse run as long as it felt like running.

At last my cousin Mourad said, Get down. I want to ride alone.

Will you let me ride alone? I said.

That is up to the horse, my cousin said. Get down.

The *horse* will let me ride, I said.

We shall see, he said. Don't forget that I have a way with a horse.

Well, I said, any way you have with a horse, I have also.

For the sake of your safety, he said, let us hope so. Get down.

All right, I said, but remember you've got to let me try to ride alone.

I got down and my cousin Mourad kicked his heels into the horse and shouted, *Vazire*, run. The horse stood on its hind legs, snorted, and burst into a fury of speed that was the loveliest thing I had ever seen. My cousin Mourad raced the horse across a field of dry grass to an irrigation ditch, crossed the ditch on the horse, and five minutes later returned, dripping wet.

The sun was coming up.

Now it's my turn to ride, I said.

My cousin Mourad got off the horse.

Ride, he said.

I leaped to the back of the horse and for a moment knew the awfulest fear imaginable. The horse did not move.

Kick into his muscles, my cousin Mourad said. What are you waiting for? We've got to take him back before everybody in the world is up and about.

I kicked into the muscles of the horse. Once again it reared and snorted. Then it began to run. I didn't know what to do. Instead of running across the field to the irrigation ditch the horse ran down the road to the vineyard of Dikran Halabian where it began to leap over vines. The horse leaped over seven vines before I fell. Then it continued running.

My cousin Mourad came running down the road.

I'm not worried about you, he shouted. We've got to get that horse. You go this way and I'll go this way. If you come upon him, be kindly. I'll be near.

I continued down the road and my cousin Mourad went across the field toward the irrigation ditch.

It took him half an hour to find the horse and bring him back.

All right, he said, jump on. The whole world is awake now.

What will we do? I said.

Well, he said, we'll either take him back or hide him until tomorrow morning.

He didn't sound worried and I knew he'd hide him and not

take him back. Not for a while, at any rate.

Where will we hide him? I said.

I know a place, he said.

How long ago did you steal this horse? I said.

It suddenly dawned on me that he had been taking these early morning rides for some time and had come for me this morning only because he knew how much I longed to ride.

Who said anything about stealing a horse? he said.

Anyhow, I said, how long ago did you begin riding every morning?

Not until this morning, he said.

Are you telling the truth? I said.

Of course not, he said, but if we are found out, that's what you're to say. I don't want both of us to be liars. All you know is that we started riding this morning.

All right, I said.

He walked the horse quietly to the barn of a deserted vineyard which at one time had been the pride of a farmer named Fetvajian. There were some oats and dry alfalfa in the barn.

We began walking home.

It wasn't easy, he said, to get the horse to behave so nicely. At first it wanted to run wild, but, as I've told you, I have a way with a horse. I can get it to want to do anything I want it to do. Horses understand me.

How do you do it? I said.

I have an understanding with a horse, he said.

Yes, but what sort of an understanding? I said.

A simple and honest one, he said.

Well, I said, I wish I knew how to reach an understanding like that with a horse.

You're still a small boy, he said. When you get to be thirteen you'll know how to do it.

I went home and ate a hearty breakfast.

That afternoon my uncle Khosrove came to our house for coffee and cigarettes. He sat in the parlor, sipping and smoking and remembering the old country. Then another visitor arrived, a farmer named John Byro, an Assyrian who, out of loneliness, had learned to speak Armenian. My mother brought the lonely visitor coffee and tobacco and he rolled a cigarette and sipped and smoked, and then at last, sighing sadly, he said, My white horse which was stolen last month is still gone. I cannot understand it.

My uncle Khosrove became very irritated and shouted, It's no harm. What is the loss of a horse? Haven't we all lost the homeland? What is this crying over a horse?

That may be all right for you, a city dweller, to say, John Byro said, but what of my surrey? What good is a surrey without a horse?

Pay no attention to it, my uncle Khosrove roared.

I walked ten miles to get here, John Byro said.

You have legs, my uncle Khosrove shouted.

My left leg pains me, the farmer said.

Pay no attention to it, my uncle Khosrove roared.

That horse cost me sixty dollars, the farmer said.

I spit on money, my uncle Khosrove said.

He got up and stalked out of the house, slamming the screen door.

My mother explained.

He has a gentle heart, she said. It is simply that he is homesick and such a large man.

The farmer went away and I ran over to my cousin Mourad's house.

He was sitting under a peach tree, trying to repair the hurt wing of a young robin which could not fly. He was talking to the bird.

What is it? he said.

The farmer John Byro, I said. He visited our house. He wants his horse. You've had it a month. I want you to promise not to take it back until I learn to ride.

It will take you *a year* to learn to ride, my cousin Mourad said.

We could keep the horse a year, I said.

My cousin Mourad leaped to his feet.

What? he roared. Are you inviting a member of the Garogh-lanian family to steal? The horse must go back to its true owner.

When? I said.

In six months at the latest, he said.

He threw the bird into the air. The bird tried hard, almost fell twice, but at last flew away, high and straight.

Early every morning for two weeks my cousin Mourad and I took the horse out of the barn of the deserted vineyard where we were hiding it and rode it, and every morning the horse, when it was my turn to ride alone, leaped over grape vines and small trees and threw me and ran away. Nevertheless, I hoped in time to learn to ride the way my cousin Mourad rode.

One morning on the way to Fetvajian's deserted vineyard we ran into the farmer John Byro who was on his way to town.

Let me do the talking, my cousin Mourad said. I have a way with farmers.

Good morning, John Byro, my cousin Mourad said to the farmer.

The farmer studied the horse eagerly.

Good morning, sons of my friends, he said. What is the name of your horse?

My Heart, my cousin Mourad said in Armenian.

A lovely name, John Byro said, for a lovely horse. I could swear it is the horse that was stolen from me many weeks ago. May I look into its mouth?

Of course, Mourad said.

The farmer looked into the mouth of the horse.

Tooth for tooth, he said. I would swear it *is* my horse if I didn't know your parents. The fame of your family for honesty is well known to me. Yet the horse is the twin of my horse. A suspicious man would believe his eyes instead of his heart. Good day, my young friends.

Good day, John Byro, my cousin Mourad said.

Early the following morning we took the horse to John Byro's vineyard and put it in the barn. The dogs followed us around without making a sound.

The dogs, I whispered to my cousin Mourad. I thought they would bark.

They would at somebody else, he said. I have a way with dogs.

My cousin Mourad put his arms around the horse, pressed his nose into the horse's nose, patted it, and then we went away.

That afternoon John Byro came to our house in his surrey and showed my mother the horse that had been stolen and returned.

I do not know what to think, he said. The horse is stronger than ever. Better-tempered, too. I thank God.

My uncle Khosrove, who was in the parlor, became irritated and shouted, Quiet, man, quiet. Your horse has been returned. Pay no attention to it.

Paul's Case

WILLA CATHER

Willa Cather (1873–1947) is widely known, of course, for her novels of midwestern prairie life—My Antonia, One of Ours (for which she won the Pulitzer Prize in 1922), A Lost Lady—and for Death Comes for the Archbishop (1927), a moving novel about the missionary experiences of a Roman Catholic bishop working with the Indians of New Mexico. "Paul's Case" is one of her few excursions into the realm of crime and suspense, but we think you'll agree that it's a memorable one. In this haunting tale, Cather creates a powerful portrait of a boy who does not belong in the world into which he was born—and skillfully leads us to the tragic outcome of his romantic yearnings.

I T was Paul's afternoon to appear before the faculty of the Pittsburgh High School to account for his various misdemeanors. He had been suspended a week ago, and his father had called at the Principal's office and confessed his perplexity about his son. Paul entered the faculty room suave and smiling. His clothes were a trifle outgrown, and the tan velvet on the collar of his open overcoat was frayed and worn; but for all that there was something of the dandy about him, and he wore an opal pin in his neatly knotted black four-in-hand, and a red carnation in his buttonhole. This latter adornment the faculty somehow felt was not properly significant of the contrite spirit befitting a boy under the ban of suspension.

Paul was tall for his age and very thin, with high, cramped shoulders and a narrow chest. His eyes were remarkable for a certain hysterical brilliancy, and he continually used them in a conscious, theatrical sort of way, peculiarly offensive in a boy. The pupils were abnormally large, as though he were addicted to belladonna, but there was a glassy glitter about them which that drug does not produce.

When questioned by the Principal as to why he was there, Paul stated, politely enough, that he wanted to come back to school. This was a lie, but Paul was quite accustomed to lying; found it, indeed, indispensable for overcoming friction. His teachers were asked to state their respective charges against him, which they did with such a rancor and aggrievedness as evinced that this was not a usual case. Disorder and impertinence were among the offenses named, yet each of his instructors felt that it was scarcely possible to put into words the real cause of the trouble, which lay in a sort of hysterically defiant manner of the boy's; in the contempt which they all knew he felt for them, and which he seemingly made not the least effort to conceal. Once, when he had been making a synopsis of a paragraph at the blackboard, his English teacher had stepped to his side and attempted to guide his hand. Paul had started back with a shudder and thrust his hands violently behind him. The astonished woman could scarcely have been more hurt and embarrassed had he struck at her. The insult was so involuntary and definitely personal as to be unforgettable. In one way and another, he had made all his teachers, men and women alike, conscious of the same feeling of physical aversion. In one class he habitually sat with his hand shading his eyes; in another he always looked out of the window during the recitation; in another he made a running commentary on the lecture, with humorous intent.

His teachers felt this afternoon that his whole attitude was symbolized by his shrug and his flippantly red carnation flower, and they fell upon him without mercy, his English teacher leading the pack. He stood through it smiling, his pale lips parted over his white teeth. (His lips were continually twitching, and he had a habit of raising his eyebrows that was contemptuous and irritating to the last degree). Older boys than Paul had broken down and shed tears under the ordeal, but his set smile did not once desert him, and his only sign of discomfort was the nervous trembling of the fingers that toyed with the buttons of his overcoat, and an occasional jerking of the other hand which held his hat. Paul was always smiling, always glancing about him, seeming to feel that people might be watching him and trying to detect something. This conscious expression, since it was as far as possible from boyish mirthfulness, was usually attributed to insolence or "smartness."

As the inquisition proceeded, one of his instructors repeated an impertinent remark of the boy's, and the Principal asked him whether he thought that a courteous speech to make to a woman. Paul shrugged his shoulder slightly and his eyebrows twitched.

"I don't know," he replied. "I didn't mean to be polite or impolite, either. I guess it's a sort of way I have, of saying things regardless."

The Principal asked him whether he didn't think that a way it would be well to get rid of. Paul grinned and said he guessed so. When he was told that he could go, he bowed gracefully and went out. His bow was like a repetition of the scandalous red carnation.

His teachers were in despair, and his drawing master voiced the feeling of them all when he declared there was something about the boy which none of them understood. He added: "I don't really believe that smile of his comes altogether from insolence; there's something sort of haunted about it. The boy is not strong, for one thing. There is something wrong about the fellow."

The drawing master had come to realize that, in looking at Paul, one saw only his white teeth and the forced animation of his eyes. One warm afternoon the boy had gone to sleep at his drawing board, and his master had noted with amazement what a white, blue-veined face it was; drawn and wrinkled like an old man's about the eyes, the lips twitching even in his sleep.

His teachers left the building dissatisfied and unhappy; humiliated to have felt so vindictive toward a mere boy, to have uttered this feeling in cutting terms, and to have set each other on, as it were, in the gruesome game of intemperate reproach. One of them remembered having seen a miserable street cat set at bay by a ring of tormentors.

As for Paul, he ran down the hill whistling the Soldiers' Chorus from *Faust*, looking wildly behind him now and then to see whether some of his teachers were not there to witness his lightheartedness. As it was now late in the afternoon and Paul was on duty that evening as usher at Carnegie Hall, he decided that he would not go home to supper.

When he reached the concert hall the doors were not yet open. It was chilly outside, and he decided to go up into the picture gallery—always deserted at this hour—where there were some of Raffelli's gay studies of Paris streets and an airy blue Venetian scene or two that always exhilarated him. He was delighted to find no one in the gallery but the old guard, who sat in the corner, a newspaper on his knee, a black patch over one eye and the other closed. Paul possessed himself of the place and walked confidently up and down, whistling under his breath. After a while he sat down before a blue Rico and lost himself. When he bethought him to look at his watch, it was after seven o'clock, and he rose with a start and ran downstairs, making a face at Augustus Caesar, peering out from the castroom, and an evil gesture at the Venus of Milo as he passed her on the stairway.

When Paul reached the ushers' dressing room half a dozen boys were there already, and he began excitedly to tumble into his uniform. It was one of the few that at all approached fitting, and Paul thought it very becoming—though he knew the tight, straight coat accentuated his narrow chest, about which he was exceedingly sensitive. He was always excited while he dressed, twangling all over to the tuning of the strings and the preliminary flourishes of the horns in the music room; but tonight he seemed quite beside himself, and he teased and plagued the boys until, telling him that he was crazy, they put him down on the floor and sat on him.

Somewhat calmed by his suppression, Paul dashed out to the front of the house to seat the early comers. He was a model usher. Gracious and smiling he ran up and down the aisles. Nothing was too much trouble for him; he carried messages and brought programs as though it were his greatest pleasure in life, and all the people in his section thought him a charming boy, feeling that he remembered and admired them. As the house filled, he grew more and more vivacious and animated, and the color came to his cheeks and lips. It was very much as though this were a great reception and Paul were the host. Just as the musicians came out to take their places, his English teacher arrived with checks for the seats which a prominent manufacturer had taken for the season. She betrayed some embarrassment when she handed Paul the tickets, and a *hauteur* which subsequently made her feel very foolish. Paul was startled for a moment, and had the feeling of wanting to put her out; what business had she here among all these fine people and gay colors? He looked her over and decided that she was not appropriately dressed and must be a fool to sit downstairs in such togs. The tickets had probably been sent her out of kindness, he reflected, as he put down a seat for her, and she had about as much right to sit there as he had.

When the symphony began Paul sank into one of the rear seats with a long sigh of relief, and lost himself as he had done before the Rico. It was not that symphonies, as such, meant anything in particular to Paul, but the first sigh of the instruments seemed to free some hilarious spirit within him; something that struggled there like the Genius in the bottle found by the Arab fisherman. He felt a sudden zest of life; the lights danced before his eyes and the concert hall blazed into unimaginable splendor. When the soprano soloist came on, Paul forgot even the nastiness of his teacher's being there, and gave himself up to the peculiar intoxication such personages always had for him. The soloist chanced to be a German woman, by no means in her first youth, and the mother of many children; but she wore a satin gown and a tiara, and she had that indefinable air of achievement, that world-shine upon her, which always blinded Paul to any possible defects.

After a concert was over, Paul was often irritable and wretched until he got to sleep—and tonight he was even more than usually restless. He had the feeling of not being able to let down; of its being impossible to give up this delicious excitement which was the only thing that could be called living at all. During the last number he withdrew and, after hastily changing his clothes in the dressing room, slipped out to the side door where the singer's carriage stood. Here he began pacing rapidly up and down the walk, waiting to see her come out.

Over yonder the Schenley, in its vacant stretch, loomed big and square through the fine rain, the windows of its twelve stories glowing like those of a lighted cardboard house under a Christmas tree. All the actors and singers of any importance stayed there when they were in the city, and a number of the big manufacturers of the place lived there in the winter. Paul had often hung about the hotel, watching the people go in and out, longing to enter and leave schoolmasters and dull care behind him forever.

At last the singer came out, accompanied by the conductor, who helped her into her carriage and closed the door with a cordial *auf wiedersehen*—which set Paul to wondering whether she were not an old sweetheart of his. Paul followed the carriage over to the hotel, walking so rapidly as not to be far from the entrance when the singer alighted and disappeared behind the swinging glass doors which were opened by a Negro in a tall hat and a long coat. In the moment that the door was ajar, it seemed to Paul that he, too, entered. He seemed to feel himself go after her up the steps, into the warm, lighted building, into an exotic, a tropical world of shiny, glistening surfaces and basking ease. He reflected upon the mysterious dishes that were brought into the dining room, the green bottles in buckets of ice, as he had seen them in the supper party pictures of the Sunday supplement. A quick gust of wind brought the rain down with sudden vehemence, and Paul was startled to find that he was still outside in the slush of the gravel driveway; that his boots were letting in the water and his scanty overcoat was clinging wet about him; that the lights in front of the concert hall were out, and that the rain was driving in sheets between him and the orange glow of the windows above him. There it was, what he wanted—tangibly before him, like the fairy world of a Christmas pantomime; as the rain beat in his face, Paul wondered whether he were destined always to shiver in the black night outside, looking up at it.

He turned and walked reluctantly toward the car tracks. The end had to come some time; his father in his night-clothes at the top of the stairs, explanations that did not explain, hastily improvised fictions that were forever tripping him up, his upstairs room and its horrible yellow wallpaper, the creaking bureau with the greasy plush collarbox, and over his painted wooden bed the pictures of George Washington and John Calvin, and the framed motto, "Feed my Lambs," which had been worked in red worsted by his mother, whom Paul could not remember.

Half an hour later, Paul alighted from the Negley Avenue car and went slowly down one of the side streets off the main thoroughfare. It was a highly respectable street, where all the houses were exactly alike, and where business men of moderate means begot and reared large families of children, all of whom went to Sabbath school and learned the shorter catechism, and were interested in arithmetic; all of whom were as exactly alike as their homes, and of a piece with the monotony in which they lived. Paul never went up Cordelia Street without a shudder of loathing. His home was next to the house of the Cumberland minister. He approached it tonight with the nerveless sense of defeat, the hopeless feeling of sinking back forever into ugliness and commonness that he had always had when he came home. The moment he turned into Cordelia Street he felt the waters close above his head. After each of these orgies of living, he experienced all the physical depression which follows a debauch; the loathing of respectable beds, of common food, of a house permeated by kitchen odors; a shuddering repulsion for the flavorless, colorless mass of everyday existence; a morbid desire for cool things and soft lights and fresh flowers.

The nearer he approached the house, the more absolutely unequal Paul felt to the sight of it all; his ugly sleeping chamber; the cold bathroom with the grimy zinc tub, the cracked mirror, the dripping spigots; his father, at the top of the stairs, his hairy legs sticking out from his nightshirt, his feet thrust into carpet slippers. He was so much later than usual that there would certainly be inquiries and reproaches. Paul stopped short before the door. He felt that he could not be accosted by his father tonight; that he would not toss again on that miserable bed. He would not go in. He would tell his father that he had no car fare, and it was raining so hard he had gone home with one of the boys and stayed all night.

Meanwhile, he was wet and cold. He went around to the back of the house and tried one of the basement windows, found it open, raised it cautiously, and scrambled down the cellar wall to the floor. There he stood, holding his breath, terrified by the noise he had made; but the floor above him was silent, and there was no creak on the stairs. He found a soap-box, and carried it over to the soft ring of light that streamed from the furnace door, and sat down. He was horribly afraid of rats, so he did not try to sleep, but sat looking distrustfully at the dark, still terrified lest he might have awakened his father. In such reactions, after one of the experiences which made days and nights out of the dreary blanks of the calendar, when his senses were deadened, Paul's head was always singularly clear. Suppose his father had heard him getting in at the window and had come down and shot him for a burglar? Then, again, suppose his father had come down, pistol in hand, and he had cried out in time to save himself, and his father had been horrified to think how nearly he had killed him? Then, again, suppose a day should come when his father would remember that night, and wish there had been no warning cry to stay his hand? With this last supposition Paul entertained himself until daybreak.

The following Sunday was fine; the sodden November chill was broken by the last flash of autumnal summer. In the morning Paul had to go to church and Sabbath school, as always. On seasonable Sunday afternoons the burghers of Cordelia Street usually sat out on their front "stoops," and talked to their neighbors on the next stoop, or called to those across the street in neighborly fashion. The men sat placidly on gay cushions placed upon the steps that led down to the sidewalk, while the women, in their Sunday "waists," sat in rockers on the cramped porches, pretending to be greatly at their ease. The children played in the streets; there were so many of them that the place resembled the recreation grounds of a kindergarten. The men on the steps—all in their shirt sleeves, their vests unbuttoned—sat with their legs well apart, their stomachs comfortably protruding, and talked of the prices of things, or told anecdotes of the sagacity of their various chiefs and overlords. They occasionally looked over the multitude of squabbling children, listened affectionately to their high-pitched, nasal voices, smiling to see their own proclivities reproduced in their offspring, and interspersed their legends of the iron kings with remarks about their sons' progress at school, their grades in arithmetic, and the amounts they had saved in their toy banks. On this last Sunday of November, Paul sat all the afternoon on the lowest step of his "stoop," staring into the street, while his sisters, in their rockers, were talking to the minister's daughters next door about how many shirtwaists they had made in the last week, and how many waffles someone had eaten at the last church supper. When the weather was warm, and his father was in a particularly jovial frame of mind, the girls made lemonade, which was always brought out in a red-glass pitcher, ornamented with forget-me-nots in blue enamel. This the girls thought very fine, and the neighbors joked about the suspicious color of the pitcher.

Today Paul's father, on the top step, was talking to a young man who shifted a restless baby from knee to knee. He happened to be the young man who was daily held up to Paul as a model, and after whom it was his father's dearest hope that he would pattern. This young man was of a ruddy complexion, with a compressed, red mouth, and faded nearsighted eyes, over which he wore thick spectacles, with gold bows that curved about his ears. He was clerk to one of the magnates of a great steel corporation, and was looked upon in Cordelia Street as a young man with a future. There was a story that, some five years ago—he was now barely twenty-six—he had been a trifle "dissipated," but in order to curb his appetites and save the loss of time and strength that a sowing of wild oats might have entailed, he had taken his chief's advice, oft reiterated to his employees, and at twenty-one had married the first woman whom he could persuade to share his fortunes. She happened to be an angular schoolmistress, much older than he, who also wore thick glasses, and who had now borne him four children, all nearsighted, like herself.

The young man was relating how his chief, now cruising in the Mediterranean, kept in touch with all the details of the business, arranging his office hours on his yacht just as though he were at home, and "knocking off work enough to keep two stenographers busy." His father told, in turn, the plan his corporation was considering, of putting in an electric railway plant at

Cairo. Paul snapped his teeth; he had an awful apprehension that they might spoil it all before he got there. Yet he rather liked to hear these legends of the iron kings, that were told and retold on Sundays and holidays; these stories of palaces in Venice, yachts on the Mediterranean, and high play at Monte Carlo appealed to his fancy, and he was interested in the triumphs of cash boys who had become famous, though he had no mind for the cash-boy stage.

After supper was over, and he had helped to dry the dishes, Paul nervously asked his father whether he could go to George's to get some help in his geometry, and still more nervously asked for car fare. This latter request he had to repeat, as his father, on principle, did not like to hear requests for money, whether much or little. He asked Paul whether he could not go to some boy who lived nearer, and told him that he ought not to leave his school work until Sunday; but he gave him the dime. He was not a poor man, but he had a worthy ambition to come up in the world. His only reason for allowing Paul to usher was that he thought a boy ought to be earning a little.

Paul bounded upstairs, scrubbed the greasy odor of the dishwater from his hands with the ill-smelling soap he hated, and then shook over his fingers a few drops of violet water from the bottle he kept hidden in his drawer. He left the house with his geometry conspicuously under his arm, and the moment he got out of Cordelia Street and boarded a downtown car, he shook off the lethargy of two deadening days, and began to live again.

The leading juvenile of the permanent stock company which played at one of the downtown theaters was an acquaintance of Paul's, and the boy had been invited to drop in at the Sunday night rehearsals whenever he could. For more than a year Paul had spent every available moment loitering about Charley Edwards's dressing room. He had won a place among Edwards's following not only because the young actor, who could not afford to employ a dresser, often found him useful, but because he recognized in Paul something akin to what churchmen termed "vocation."

It was at the theater and at Carnegie Hall that Paul really lived; the rest was but a sleep and a forgetting. This was Paul's fairy tale, and it had for him all the allurement of a secret love. The moment he inhaled the gassy, painty, dusty odor behind the scenes, he breathed like a prisoner set free, and felt within him the possibility of doing or saying splendid, brilliant things. The moment the cracked orchestra beat out the overture from *Martha*, or jerked at the serenade from *Rigoletto*, all stupid and ugly things slid from him, and his senses were deliciously, yet delicately fired.

Perhaps it was because, in Paul's world, the natural nearly always wore the guise of ugliness, that a certain element of artificiality seemed to him necessary in beauty. Perhaps it was because his experience of life elsewhere was so full of Sabbath-school picnics, petty economies, wholesome advice as to how to succeed in life, and the unescapable odors of cooking, that he found this existence so alluring, these smartly clad men and women so attractive, that he was so moved by these starry apple orchards that bloomed perennially under the limelight.

It would be difficult to put it strongly enough how convincingly the stage entrance of that theater was for Paul the actual portal of Romance. Certainly none of the company ever suspected it, least of all Charley Edwards. It was very like the old stories that used to float about London of fabulously rich Jews, who had subterranean halls, with palms, and fountains, and soft lamps and richly apparelled women who never saw the disenchanting light of London day. So, in the midst of that smoke-palled city, enamored of figures and grimy toil, Paul had his secret temple, his wishing-carpet, his bit of blue-and-white Mediterranean shore bathed in perpetual sunshine.

Several of Paul's teachers had a theory that his imagination had been perverted by garish fiction; but the truth was, he scarcely ever read at all. The books at home were not such as would either tempt or corrupt a youthful mind, and as for reading the novels that some of his friends urged upon him—well, he got what he wanted much more quickly from music; any sort of music, from an orchestra to a barrel organ. He needed only the spark, the indescribable thrill that made his imagination master of his senses, and he could make plots and pictures enough of his own. It was equally true that he was not stage-struck—not, at any rate, in the usual acceptation of that expression. He had no desire to become an actor, any more than he had to become a musician. He felt no necessity to do any of these things; what he wanted was to see, to be in the atmosphere, float on the wave of it, to be carried out, blue league after blue league, away from everything.

After a night behind the scenes, Paul found the schoolroom more than ever repulsive; the bare floors and naked walls; the prosy men who never wore frock coats, or violets in their button-holes; the women with their dull gowns, shrill voices, and piti-ful seriousness about prepositions that govern the dative. He could not bear to have the other pupils think, for a moment, that he took these people seriously; he must convey to them that he considered it all trivial, and was there only by way of a joke, anyway. He had autographed pictures of all the members of the stock company which he showed his classmates, telling them the most incredible stories of his familiarity with these people, of his acquaintance with the soloists who came to Carnegie Hall, his suppers with them and the flowers he sent them. When these stories lost their effect, and his audience grew listless, he would bid all the boys good-by, announcing that he was going to travel for a while; going to Naples, to California, to Egypt. Then, next Monday, he would slip back, conscious and nervously smiling, his sister was ill, and he would have to defer his voyage until spring.

Matters went steadily worse with Paul at school. In the itch to let his instructors know how heartily he despised them, and how thoroughly he was appreciated elsewhere, he mentioned once or twice that he had no time to fool with theorems; adding—with a twitch of the eyebrows and a touch of that ner-vous bravado which so perplexed them—that he was helping the people down at the stock company; they were old friends of his.

The upshot of the matter was, that the Principal went to Paul's father, and Paul was taken out of school and put to work. The manager at Carnegie Hall was told to get another usher in his stead; the doorkeeper at the theater was warned not to admit him to the house; and Charley Edwards remorsefully promised the boy's father not to see him again.

The members of the stock company were vastly amused when some of Paul's stories reached them—especially the women. They were hard-working women, most of them supporting indolent husbands or brothers, and they laughed rather bitterly at having stirred the boy to such fervid and florid inventions. They agreed with the faculty and with his father, that Paul's was a bad case.

The east-bound train was plowing through a January snowstorm, the dull dawn was beginning to show gray when the engine whistled a mile out of Newark. Paul started up from the seat where he had lain curled in uneasy slumber, rubbed the breath-misted window glass with his hand, and peered out. The snow was whirling in curling eddies above the white bottom-lands, and the drifts lay already deep in the fields and along the fences, while here and there the long dead grass and dried weed stalks protruded black above it. Lights shone from the scattered houses, and a gang of laborers who stood beside the track waved their lanterns.

Paul had slept very little, and he felt grïmy and uncomfortable. He had made the all-night journey in a day coach because he was afraid if he took a Pullman he might be seen by some Pittsburgh businessman who had noticed him in Denny & Carson's office. When the whistle woke him, he clutched quickly at his breast pocket, glancing about him with an uncertain smile. But the little, clay-bespattered Italians were still sleeping, the slatternly women across the aisle were in open-mouthed oblivion, and even the crumby, crying babies were for the nonce stilled. Paul settled back to struggle with his impatience as best he could.

When he arrived at the Jersey City station, he hurried through his breakfast, manifestly ill at ease and keeping a sharp eye about him. After he reached the Twenty-third Street station, he consulted a cabman, and had himself driven to a men's furnishing establishment which was just opening for the day. He spent upward of two hours there, buying with endless reconsidering and great care. His new street suit he put on in the fitting room; the frock coat and dress clothes he had bundled into the cab with his new shirts. Then he drove to a hatter's and a shoe house. His next errand was at Tiffany's, where he selected silver-mounted brushes and a scarfpin. He would not wait to have his silver marked, he said. Lastly, he stopped at a trunk shop on Broadway, and had his purchases packed into various traveling bags.

It was a little after one o'clock when he drove up to the Waldorf, and, after settling with the cabman, went into the office. He registered from Washington; said his mother and father had been abroad, and that he had come down to await the arrival of their steamer. He told his story plausibly and had no trouble, since he offered to pay for them in advance, in engaging his rooms; a sleeping room, sitting room and bath.

Not once, but a hundred times Paul had planned his entry into New York. He had gone over every detail of it with Charley Edwards, and in his scrapbook at home there were pages of description about New York hotels, cut from the Sunday papers.

When he was shown to his sitting room on the eighth floor, he saw at a glance that everything was as it should be; there was but one detail in his mental picture that the place did not realize, so he rang for the bellboy and sent him down for flowers. He moved about nervously until the boy returned, putting away his new linen and fingering it delightedly as he did so. When the flowers came, he put them hastily into water, and then tumbled into a hot bath. Presently he came out of his white bathroom, resplendent in his new silk underwear, and playing with the tassels of his red robe. The snow was whirling so fiercely outside his windows that he could scarcely see across the street; but within, the air was deliciously soft and fragrant. He put the violets and jonquils on the tabouret beside the couch, and threw himself down with a long sigh, covering himself with a Roman blanket. He was thoroughly tired; he had been in such haste, he had stood up to such a strain, covered so much ground in the last twenty-four hours, that he wanted to think how it had all come about. Lulled by the sound of the wind, the warm air, and the cool fragrance of the flowers, he sank into deep, drowsy retrospection.

It had been wonderfully simple; when they had shut him out of the theater and concert hall, when they had taken away his bone, the whole thing was virtually determined. The rest was a mere matter of opportunity. The only thing that at all surprised him was his own courage—for he realized well enough that he had always been tormented by fear, a sort of apprehensive dread that, of late years, as the meshes of the lies he had told closed about him, had been pulling the muscles of his body tighter and tighter. Until now, he could not remember a time when he had not been dreading something. Even when he was a little boy, it was always there—behind him, or before, or on either side. There had always been the shadowed corner, the dark place into which he dared not look, but from which something seemed always to be watching him—and Paul had done things that were not pretty to watch, he knew.

But now he had a curious sense of relief, as though he had at last thrown down the gauntlet to the things in the corner.

Yet it was but a day since he had been sulking in the traces; but yesterday afternoon that he had been sent to the bank with Denny & Carson's deposit, as usual—but this time he was instructed to leave the book to be balanced. There was above two thousand dollars in checks, and nearly a thousand in the bank notes which he had taken from the book and quietly transferred to his pocket. At the bank he had made out a new deposit slip. His nerves had been steady enough to permit his returning to the office, where he had finished his work and asked for a full day's holiday tomorrow, Saturday, giving a perfectly reasonable pretext. The bank book, he knew, would not be returned before Monday or Tuesday, and his father would be out of town for the next week. From the time he slipped the bank notes into his pocket until he boarded the night train for New York, he had not known a moment's hesitation.

How astonishingly easy it had all been; here he was, the thing done; and this time there would be no awakening, no figure at the top of the stairs. He watched the snowflakes whirling by his window until he fell asleep.

When he awoke, it was four o'clock in the afternoon. He bounded up with a start; one of his precious days gone already! He spent nearly an hour in dressing, watching every stage of his toilet carefully in the mirror. Everything was quite perfect; he was exactly the kind of boy he had always wanted to be.

When he went downstairs, Paul took a carriage and drove up Fifth Avenue toward the Park. The snow had somewhat abated; carriages and tradesmen's wagons were hurrying soundlessly to and fro in the winter twilight; boys in woolen mufflers were shoveling off the doorsteps; the avenue stages made fine spots of color against the white street. Here and there on the corners whole flower gardens blooming behind glass windows, against which the snowflakes stuck and melted; violets, roses, carnations, lilies of the valley—somehow vastly more lovely and alluring that they blossomed thus unnaturally in the snow. The Park itself was a wonderful stage winter-piece.

When he returned, the pause of the twilight had ceased, and the tune of the streets had changed. The snow was falling faster, lights streamed from the hotels that reared their many stories fearlessly up into the storm, defying the raging Atlantic winds. A long, black stream of carriages poured down the avenue, intersected here and there by other streams, tending horizontally. There were a score of cabs about the entrance of his hotel, and his driver had to wait. Boys in livery were running in and out of the awning stretched across the sidewalk, up and down the red velvet carpet laid from the door to the street. Above, about, within it all, were the rumble and roar, the hurry and toss of thousands of human beings as hot for pleasure as himself, and on every side of him towered the glaring affirmation of the omnipotence of wealth.

The boy set his teeth and drew his shoulders together in a spasm of realization; the plot of all dramas, the text of all romances, the nerve-stuff of all sensations was whirling about him like the snowflakes. He burnt like a faggot in a tempest.

When Paul came down to dinner, the music of the orchestra floated up the elevator shaft to greet him. As he stepped into the thronged corridor, he sank back into one of the chairs against the wall to get his breath. The lights, the chatter, the perfumes, the bewildering medley of color—he had, for a moment, the feeling of not being able to stand it. But only for a moment; these were his own people, he told himself. He went slowly about the corridors, through the writing rooms, smoking rooms, reception rooms, as though he were exploring the chambers of an enchanted palace, built and peopled for him alone.

When he reached the dining room he sat down at a table near a window. The flowers, the white linen, the many-colored wine glasses, the gay toilettes of the women, the low popping of corks, the undulating repetitions of the *Blue Danube* from the orchestra, all flooded Paul's dream with bewildering radiance. When the roseate tinge of his champagne was added—that cold, precious, bubbling stuff that creamed and foamed in his glass— Paul wondered that there were honest men in the world at all. This was what all the world was fighting for, he reflected; this was what all the struggle was about. He doubted the reality of his past. Had he ever known a place called Cordelia Street, a place where fagged-looking business men boarded the early car? Mere rivets in a machine they seemed to Paul—sickening men, with combings of children's hair always hanging to their coats, and the smell of cooking in their clothes. Cordelia Street—Ah, that belonged to another time and country! Had he not always been thus, had he not sat here night after night, from as far back as he could remember, looking pensively over just such shimmering textures, and slowly twirling the stem of a glass like this one between his thumb and middle finger? He rather thought he had.

He was not in the least abashed or lonely. He had no especial desire to meet or to know any of these people; all he demanded was the right to look on and conjecture, to watch the pageant. The mere stage properties were all he contended for. Nor was he lonely later in the evening, in his loge at the Opera. He was entirely rid of his nervous misgivings, of his forced aggressiveness, of the imperative desire to show himself different from his surroundings. He felt now that his surroundings explained him. Nobody questioned the purple; he had only to wear it passively. He had only to glance down at his dress coat to reassure himself that here it would be impossible for anyone to humiliate him.

He found it hard to leave his beautiful sitting room to go to bed that night, and sat long watching the raging storm from his turret window. When he went to sleep, it was with the lights turned on in his bedroom; partly because of his old timidity, and partly so that, if he should wake in the night, there would be no wretched moment of doubt, no horrible suspicion of yellow wallpaper, or of Washington and Calvin above his bed.

On Sunday morning the city was practically snowbound. Paul breakfasted late, and in the afternoon he fell in with a wild San Francisco boy, a freshman at Yale, who said he had run down for a "little flyer" over Sunday. The young man offered to show Paul the night side of the town, and the two boys went off together after dinner, not returning to the hotel until seven o'clock the next morning. They had started out in the confiding warmth of a champagne friendship, but their parting in the elevator was singularly cool. The freshman pulled himself together to make his train, and Paul went to bed. He awoke at two o'clock in the afternoon, very thirsty and dizzy, and rang for ice water, coffee and the Pittsburgh papers.

On the part of the hotel management, Paul excited no suspicion. There was this to be said for him, that he wore his spoils with dignity and in no way made himself conspicuous. His chief greediness lay in his ears and eyes, and his excesses were not offensive ones. His dearest pleasures were the gray winter twilights in his sitting room; his quiet enjoyment of his flowers, his clothes, his wide divan, his cigarette and his sense of power. He could not remember a time when he had felt so at peace with himself. The mere release from the necessity of petty lying, lying every day and every day, restored his self-respect. He had never lied for pleasure, even at school; but to make himself noticed and admired, to assert his difference from other Cordelia Street boys; and he felt a good deal more manly, more honest, even, now that he had no need for boastful pretensions, now that he could, as his actor friends used to say, "dress the part." It was characteristic that remorse did not occur to him. His golden days went by without a shadow, and he made each as perfect as he could.

On the eighth day after his arrival in New York, he found the whole affair exploited in the Pittsburgh papers, exploited with a wealth of detail which indicated that local news of a sensational nature was at a low ebb. The firm of Denny & Carson announced that the boy's father had refunded the full amount of his theft, and that they had no intention of prosecuting. The Cumberland minister had been interviewed, and expressed his hope of yet reclaiming the motherless lad, and Paul's Sabbath-school teacher declared that she would spare no effort to that end. The rumor had reached Pittsburgh that the boy had been seen in a New York hotel, and his father had gone East to find him and bring him home.

Paul had just come in to dress for dinner; he sank into a chair, weak in the knees, and clasped his head in his hands. It was to be worse than jail, even; the tepid waters of Cordelia Street were to close over him finally and forever. The gray monotony stretched before him in hopeless, unrelieved years; Sabbath school, Young Peoples' Meeting, the yellow-papered room, the damp dish-towels; it all rushed back upon him with sickening vividness. He had the old feeling that the orchestra had suddenly stopped, the sinking sensation that the play was over. The sweat broke out on his face, and he sprang to his feet, looked about him with his white, conscious smile, and winked at himself in the mirror. With something of the childish belief in miracles with which he had so often gone to class, all his lessons unlearned, Paul dressed and dashed whistling down the corridor to the elevator.

He had no sooner entered the dining room and caught the measure of the music, than his remembrance was lightened by his old elastic power of claiming the moment, mounting with it, and finding it all sufficient. The glare and glitter about him, the mere scenic accessories had again, and for the last time, their old potency. He would show himself that he was game, he would finish the thing splendidly. He doubted, more than ever, the existence of Cordelia Street, and for the first time he drank his wine recklessly. Was he not, after all, one of these fortunate beings? Was he not still himself, and in his own place? He drummed a nervous accompaniment to the music and looked about him, telling himself over and over that it had paid.

He reflected drowsily, to the swell of the violin and the chill sweetness of his wine, that he might have done it more wisely. He might have caught an outbound steamer and been well out of their clutches before now. But the other side of the world had seemed too far away and too uncertain then; he could not have waited for it; his need had been too sharp. If he had to choose over again, he would do the same thing tomorrow. He looked affectionately about the dining room, now gilded with a soft mist. Ah, it had paid indeed!

Paul was awakened next morning by a painful throbbing in his head and feet. He had thrown himself across the bed without undressing, and had slept with his shoes on. His limbs and hands were lead heavy, and his tongue and throat were parched. There came upon him one of those fateful attacks of clear-headedness that never occurred except when he was physically exhausted and his nerves hung loose. He lay still and closed his eyes and let the tide of realities wash over him.

His father was in New York; "stopping at some joint or other," he told himself. The memory of successive summers on the front stoop fell upon him like a weight of black water. He had not a hundred dollars left; and he knew now, more than ever, that money was everything, the wall that stood between all he loathed and all he wanted. The thing was winding itself up; he had thought of that on his first glorious day in New York, and had even provided a way to snap the thread. It lay on his dressing table now; he had got it out last night when he came blindly up from dinner—but the shiny metal hurt his eyes, and he disliked the look of it, anyway.

He rose and moved about with a painful effort, succumbing now and again to attacks of nausea. It was the old depression exaggerated; all the world had become Cordelia Street. Yet somehow he was not afraid of anything, was absolutely calm; perhaps because he had looked into the dark corner at last, and knew. It was bad enough, what he saw there; but somehow not so bad as his long fear of it had been. He saw everything clearly now. He had a feeling that he had made the best of it, that he had lived the sort of life he was meant to live, and for half an hour he sat staring at the revolver point. But he told himself that was not the way, so he went downstairs and took a cab to the ferry.

When Paul arrived at Newark, he got off the train and took another cab, directing the driver to follow the Pennsylvania tracks out of the town. The snow lay heavy on the roadways and had drifted deep in the open fields. Only here and there the dead grass or dried weed stalks projected, singularly black, above it. Once well into the country, Paul dismissed the carriage and walked, floundering along the tracks, his mind a medley of irrelevant things. He seemed to hold in his brain an actual picture of everything he had seen that morning. He remembered every feature of both his drivers, the toothless old woman from whom he had bought the red flowers in his coat, the agent from whom he had got his ticket, and all of his fellow passengers on the ferry. His mind, unable to cope with vital matters near at hand, worked feverishly and deftly at sorting and grouping these images. They made for him a part of the ugliness of the world, of the ache in his head, and the bitter burning on his tongue. He stooped and put a handful of snow into his mouth as he walked, but that, too, seemed hot. When he reached a little hillside, where the tracks ran through a cut some twenty feet below him, he stopped and sat down.

The carnations in his coat were drooping with the cold, he noticed; all their red glory over. It occurred to him that all the flowers he had seen in the show windows that first night must have gone the same way, long before this. It was only one splendid breath they had, in spite of their brave mockery at the winter outside the glass. It was a losing game in the end, it seemed, this revolt against the homilies by which the world is run. Paul took one of the blossoms carefully from his coat and scooped a little hole in the snow, where he covered it up. Then he dozed a while, from his weak condition, seeming insensible to the cold.

The sound of an approaching train woke him, and he started to his feet, remembering only his resolution, and afraid lest he should be too late. He stood watching the approaching locomotive, his teeth chattering, his lips drawn away from them in a frightened smile; once or twice he glanced nervously sidewise, as though he were being watched. When the right moment came, he jumped. As he fell, the folly of his haste occurred to him with merciless clearness, the vastness of what he had left undone. There flashed through his brain, clearer than ever before, the blue of Adriatic water, the yellow of Algerian sands.

He felt something strike his chest—his body was being thrown swiftly through the air, on and on, immeasurably far and fast, while his limbs gently relaxed. Then, because the picture-making mechanism was crushed, the disturbing visions flashed into black, and Paul dropped back into the immense design of things.

Little Boy Lost

Q. PATRICK

The stories and novels of Q. Patrick (or Patrick Quentin) are
the creation of several individuals who collaborated at different
times with one another during the 1930s, 1940s, and 1950s. The
first Q. Patrick collaborations were the work of Richard Wilson
Webb and Martha Mott Kelley; Webb then collaborated with
Mary Louise Aswell and later with Hugh Callingham Wheeler. It
is the team of Webb and Wheeler that was most long-lasting and
prolific, creating numerous stories and the novels in the Peter
Duluth and Lieutenant Timothy Trant series. They also used a
third pseudonym, Jonathan Stagge. Although Richard Webb left
the collaboration in the early 1950s, Hugh Wheeler continued to
use the Patrick Quentin pseudonym on much of his work until
1965. In "Little Boy Lost," a creation of the Webb/Wheeler team,
we are taken into an English girls' school, as seen through the
eyes of a misfit—a young boy, son of the headmistress. Perhaps
it is no wonder that such surroundings make him strange, if not
a little dangerous.

THE day his father died was chiefly memorable to Branson Foster because he was allowed to sleep in the small dressing-room off his mother's bedroom. An end was thus made to the nights in the fourth-storey attic where the little boy had lain obdurately awake, afraid of the hostile darkness, resenting the adult injustice that separated him from the mother who adored and spoiled him. It was his father who had been responsible for his exile, and now that formidable presence, whose black mustache smelt of mouthwash and the top of breakfast eggs, was gone.

His father's death brought Branson not only comfort but freedom from the fear that had haunted him since his eighth birthday. The question of his departure to a boys' boarding school had lapsed. Branny's mother had given him tearful reassurance on that point as she kissed him goodnight and tucked him under the delicious warmth of the quilted eiderdown.

"You are the man of the house now, darling. You must stay and help your poor mummie run this silly old girls' school."

Almost certainly, the vague, bewildered Constance Foster never dreamed that her passionate adoration might be harmful for a son of nearly nine. In 1915, small English seaside resorts had not heard of mother-fixations. Nor was Dr. Sigmund Freud even a name at Oaklawn School for Girls in Littleton-on-Sea. With the death of her husband it seemed only natural to her that mother and son, sharing a common grief, should cling even closer together.

After the funeral, at which the wheezing voice of the vicar had consigned the mustache to eternal rest, Branny's bed was put permanently in the little room adjoining his mother's. Attics, Mrs. Foster argued, were dangerous in wartime. From then on, going to bed became a pleasure rather than a terror for Branny. He could read as long as he liked and when his mother came upstairs, he could hear her gentle movements through the

quarter-opened door and bask in the warm certainty of her near-
ness and safety. And during her frequent spells of poorliness—
for Mrs. Foster considered herself frail—he could tiptoe into her
room when his anxiety for her goaded him too painfully, and
satisfy himself that the fragile, cherished figure in the bed was
actually alive and breathing.

Almost every day of this new life brought a major or minor
delight. The older girls made much of their headmistress's only
son in his bereavement. The younger girls constituted a respect-
ful audience for whose benefit he could strut as the only male in
a household of women. And as a symbol of his importance, he
was permitted full use of the front stairs, strictly forbidden to
housemaids, girls, and even to junior mistresses.

Each golden day reached its climax in the evening when instead of taking plain supper in the school dining-room, he had
light tea alone with his mother in his father's erstwhile study.
Often the meagre wartime fare would be augmented by a boiled
egg, a tin of sardines, or some similar delicacy.

His mother would watch him devour these with a smile half-
excited, half-guilty, murmuring:

"It's naughty of me, I know, in wartime, but a growing boy
really does need it."

Luckily for the finances of Oaklawn School, she did not enter-
tain a similar sentiment with regard to the forty or fifty growing
girls under her care.

The middle weeks of the summer term passed for mother and
son as an idyl. Mrs. Foster looked prettier than ever in her widow's weeds which lent an air of pathos to the soft brown eyes
and heightened the ethereal pallor of her perfect skin. She was
careful to present the world with a decorous show of grief. But
inwardly she, like her son, was happier than she had been in
years. Her husband's hand, heavy as his mustache, was no
longer there to suppress her natural volatility. Branny spoiled
her as she spoiled him. With her son she could yield to her
moods of almost childish gaiety. She could also indulge the tendency to poorliness which Mr. Foster had so unimaginatively

discouraged. When the responsibilities of her position became too irksome, it was delightful to pamper a mild headache in a darkened room while Branny hovered with solicitude and *eau de cologne*.

As sole principal of Oaklawn School, Mrs. Foster dreamily muddled the accounts, allowed the servants and tradespeople to lead her by the nose, and let institutional discipline slide.

But, halcyon as this period was, it carried in it, unknown to Branny, the seed of its own destruction. The late George Foster had bought Oaklawn School for Girls with his wife's money and had made her joint principal. But he himself had owned two-thirds of the goodwill and knowing his Constance, had anticipated just such a situation as had now arisen. He had loved the school, built it up through his own labors, and had made testamentary precautions to preserve it.

Hence the invasion of the Aunts. This started by what, in the Second World War, would have been termed "infiltration."

Aunt Nellie was the first to come. There seemed nothing particularly ominous about her arrival since she appeared toward the end of the summer term, wearing dark glasses as the result of a visit to an oculist in the nearby town of Bristol. Branny had seen Aunt Nellie only once before and connected her pleasantly with strawberries and cream for tea on the lawn and a "silver penny" on her departure for India. In the dim past, an amorous purser on a P and O liner had called her a "dashed pretty woman" and the epithet had stuck, although it had long since lost any semblance of accuracy.

Aunt Nellie was discovered in the drawing room just before lunch one day. Branny's mother said:

"Come in, darling, and say how d'you do to your pretty aunt."

Branny stared at Aunt Nellie solemnly. She said, giggling:

"Not pretty with these awful glasses on, Constance. There, I'll take them off."

Branny was still unimpressed. He saw a massive woman with

fluffy pinkish hair, a great deal of jewelry, light bloodshot eyes, and a high color. Since he was in love with a small, dark woman with large eyes and ivory cheeks, he had every reason to remain unimpressed. When his aunt had removed the glasses, he said gravely:

"You aren't so very pretty even now, are you?"

Aunt Nellie laughed again and said: "Now is that a gallant thing for a little pukka sahib to say?"

And being a woman, she never forgave him.

There was no silver penny this time—and no departure.

Aunt Nellie was currently without occupation or domicile. She had made the war an excuse to get away from India where she had left a dyspeptic colonel husband to his curries and concubines. Abandoning India, however, had not made her abandon its vocabulary. Everything around Oaklawn School became pukka or not pukka. Lunch became tiffin. Mrs. Foster was a memsahib, and Aunt Nellie drove the servants almost crazy by addressing them as ayahs and giving capricious orders in bastard Hindustani. Also, owing to the demands of her elaborate toilet, she spent an indecent amount of time in the bathroom.

But at first Aunt Nellie's visit was rather a joke to Branny. Her garrulous intrusion upon his private teas with his mother was tiresome, but she brought compensatory delights. For example, he discovered the joys of exploring her bedroom and made the younger pupils goggle incredulously at the report of his discoveries there. Once, thinking Aunt Nellie safely in the bathroom, he had bedizened himself with her cosmetics, wrapped himself in her satin peignoir, and attaching a pinkish false front to his head, had run down to the second form classroom to the hysterical delight of a bevy of little girls.

But he had paid dearly for this short-lived accolade. Aunt Nellie was lying in wait for him behind the bathroom door as he sneaked upstairs. She swooped out, a bald, outraged condor, and seized him. Snatching her property, she shook Branny till his teeth chattered, slapped his painted face several times, and banged his head against the bathroom wall so hard that Mrs. Foster, attracted by her beloved's outcries, hovered ineffectually, screaming:

"*Pas sa tête*, Nellie. *Pas sa tête.*"

Nor did Branny's punishment end there. For a whole week Aunt Nellie refused implacably to eat at the same table with him and he was obliged for seven days to forego his teas with his mother and to partake once again of thick slices of bread without even jam at the "kids" table in the school dining-room.

These tribulations, however, did not greatly disturb Branny for Aunt Nellie, despite the length of her stay, was a visitor and must, surely, depart in time. Soon he and his mother would be alone again and life would reassume its untarnished bloom.

He wrote Aunt Nellie a polite little note of apology which was frigidly accepted. In due course the teas were resumed.

It was on the second evening of his rehabilitation that Branny began to suspect Aunt Nellie was not a visitor after all. Over the teacups his aunt and his mother were discussing the French Mademoiselle who had been recalled by a telegram to her native Paris.

"It's about time, Constance," remarked Aunt Nellie, "that I started to do my war bit, *n'est ce pas?*"

And sure enough, when it came to the period for French next morning, there was Aunt Nellie to give the lesson, Aunt Nellie insisting on a far too-French French accent from her pupils and making herself ridiculous by singing little French songs which no one understood.

From that day on Aunt Nellie gave up Hindustani and interlarded every sentence with a French word or phrase and embellished them with pretty Gallic gestures.

But Anglo-Indian or Anglo-French, she seemed to have become a permanency.

As the summer term drew to a close Branny continually begged his mother to deny this dreadful possibility but she put him off by references to the school's goodwill which were meaningless to him.

The blow really fell about the middle of the summer holidays. For several days his mother had been busy with correspondence. The zeppelin raids over London had started and parents were rushing their children from the east to safer schools in the west. It had been necessary to have a new stock of prospectuses printed.

Idly Branny picked up one of these as he stood by his mother waiting for her to finish a letter. The front page riveted his attention. Under the heading:

OAKLAWN SCHOOL
FOR GIRLS

in place of the familiar Principals, Mr. and Mrs. George H. Foster, he read:

Principals: Mrs. George H. Foster
Mrs. John Delaney
Miss Hilda Foster

Mrs. John Delaney was Aunt Nellie. Under other circumstances, that would have been sufficiently terrible. But Miss Hilda Foster was Aunt Hilda, the fabulous, almost mythical Aunt Hilda of whom the very memory was panic.

And she was coming here to Oaklawn to be joint headmistress with Aunt Nellie and his mother. The idea was beyond contemplation.

"But, mummy," he wailed, "she can't come here. This is your school. It was yours and daddy's."

Mrs. Foster kissed him a trifle wistfully and explained that his father had wished and willed things so.

"You'll see, Branny," she concluded, "with your aunts here we'll have more time together. Time for walks in the country, picnics."

But Branny felt desolation like a stone in the pit of his stomach. He locked himself in the lavatory and cried until he was violently sick.

Aunt Hilda arrived with the first days of September, about two weeks before the beginning of the winter term. She was even more terrifying than Branny's memory of her.

Having been paid companion to a difficult lady of title, she had waited for her death and its consequent small annuity before descending on Oaklawn. She immediately showed that there is no female tyrant so absolute as one who has herself been under tyranny.

In appearance she was almost the exact opposite of Aunt Nellie. There was no false front about Aunt Hilda, either actual or metaphorical. A short, heavy woman, she wore her grayish hair back uncompromisingly from her forehead. Her manner was as uncompromising as a steam shovel. She creaked like one, too, as she moved heavily about, clucking at the inefficiencies of the establishment. She clucked over the school accounts, the tradesmen's bills. She clucked over the laxity of the domestics, and several of Branny's friends among the kitchen staff—especially those on whom he could rely for snatches of food at illicit hours—were sent away in tears. Aunt Hilda clucked disapprovingly over Mrs. Foster too, whisking away all her sister-in-law's faint protests with an abrupt:

"Nonsense, Constance."

When the more important things in the establishment had been clucked into a state of dull efficiency, Aunt Hilda turned her attention to Branny, who, she decided, was a shockingly coddled child. First of all she banished him once again to the fear-inhabited attic bedroom. Having neither the strength of will nor the command of vocabulary to defy her sister-in-law, Mrs. Foster tried at least to soften this blow for her son by providing him with a night-light. But Aunt Hilda snapped:

"Nonsense, Constance, stop pampering the child. Besides, it's unpatriotic to waste tallow in wartime."

It was unpatriotic, apparently, to waste quite a few things on Branny. The teas stopped almost immediately and his diet was rigidly overhauled. Meat, which he loved, was almost forbidden. In place of warm slices from a new cottage loaf with butter

or jam, he had to make out with thick slices of yesterday's bread
scraped by Aunt Hilda's own hands with a thin film of marga-
rine. And at breakfast, even in holiday time when there were no
pupils to consider, he had to endure the agony of lumpy por-
ridge swimming in hot milk while his aunts, good trencher-
women both, partook liberally of ham, sausages, or poached
eggs and bacon.

Exasperated one morning when Constance furtively slipped a
sausage to Branny from her own plate, Aunt Hilda pronounced
the dreaded words:

"Constance, you are hopeless with that child. There is only
one thing to do. He must go to a boys' boarding school. He needs
the discipline of boys of his own age. You are turning him into a
milksop."

There followed a heated argument at the end of which Constance dissolved in tears and Branny, goaded beyond endurance
called his aunts "Two fat old pigs."

Oddly enough in this impasse it was Aunt Nellie who came
forward with a solution which more or less proved satisfactory
to all parties. She approached Constance some hours later in her
bedroom where she had taken her poorliness and Branny after
the storm in the breakfast teacups. Aunt Nellie argued with
sweet persuasiveness. No one wanted to get rid of dear Branson,
of course, but Constance must admit it was not good for a child
to be the only little boy in a school for girls. Now she, Aunt
Nellie, had been writing to her friends in Mysore; indeed, she
flattered herself she had worked up quite a neat little Anglo-
Indian connection for the school. In some cases parents had not
wanted their children to be separated, it being wartime and India being so far away, and several girls could be snared for the
school provided their little brothers could also be admitted. The
introduction of boys into the school would not only solve the
problem of Branny, it would bring the sisters proportionate financial benefits.

It was this last consideration which won the nod of approval
from Aunt Hilda, and the winter term was not too far advanced

by the time Branny was sharing his attic—now pretentiously called the boys' dormitory—with the first harbinger of the male contingent.

Branny might almost have been at boarding school, so far had he been severed from his mother. They had to scheme for their meetings like guilty lovers. Since Branny could no nothing, it was Mrs. Foster who developed craft. She persuaded one of the junior governesses that she was not "strong" enough and substituted herself as director of the younger children's afternoon walk. She imagined ailments for the solitary male boarder so that she could sneak up to the dormitory for a surreptitious squeeze of Branny's hand before "Lights out."

These were, however, frugal crumbs of comfort for Branny. Life had become even bleaker than in the most flourishing days of the mustache. And with the stubborn simplification of the very young, Branny viewed the causes of this new régime and affixed all the blame for it on Aunt Hilda.

From then on he hated Aunt Hilda with a hatred that was the more bitter because there was no one with whom he could share it.

Although the admission of boys to Oaklawn had brought him no positive advantages, it did bring him a friend and ally who influenced him profoundly. This was the male boarder, a youngster of Branny's own age, who was afflicted with the name of Marmaduke Cattermole. His father was the Vice-vice something-or-other of something-or-other in India and the son was Vice and Sophistication personified. A degenerate imp, as Aunt Hilda was to call him later, not without a certain approximation to essential truth.

Branny was a trifle overawed when this angelic-looking child first appeared. In fact everyone was overawed by Marmalade, as he himself chose to be called. Aunt Hilda, observing his ethereal complexion and remembering the alphabetic distinctions following his father's name, decreed an extra blanket for him and a glass of milk at midday.

This milk, intended by Aunt Hilda as a special mark of favor, produced an unexpected result. For Marmalade had a passionate and whimsical hatred for milk and when it became plain that milk was to be forced upon him willynilly, this hatred transferred itself to Aunt Hilda as the instigator of his misery. In a short time his loathing outrivalled and outshone even that of Branny.

Indeed, Marmalade was obsessed with Aunt Hilda. He brewed malice against her with every breath and being a talented boy both with pencil and in doggerel rhythm, he mightily convulsed Branny with his verses and sketches. Outwardly he was honey-sweet to her but behind her back the angel was transformed into a monster. He invented innumerable names for her, among which the few printable ones were "blackbeetle," "hellwitch," and "the female gorilla."

There is nothing like hatred to breed hatred in others. Branny and Marmalade fanned each other to a pitch of frenzy and in this new alliance with a boy of his own age against the Arch-Enemy, Branny forgot some of his hunger for his mother.

Gradually and imperceptibly Marmalade led the more timid Branny into action. It started with a terrifying, tiptoed investigation of Aunt Hilda's bedroom. The yield was less exotic than that of Aunt Nellie's room. There were some severe black dresses with whalebone collar-supports which Marmalade promptly removed; a coroneted handkerchief sachet, doubtless the gift of the titled lady whose declining years had been cheered; some entrancing thick bloomers over which the two boys giggled; and several pair of formidable stays.

The nearest approach to feminine daintiness was a bottle of *eau de cologne*. Following Marmalade's lead, Branny spat into it long and dribblingly.

The most intriguing object was a key hidden in a small drawer. After frantic detective work it was found to open a small medicine closet on the shelf above Aunt Hilda's bed. Its contents were disappointing too. Apart from a few household medicaments, there was an enema tube, whose purpose was unknown even to the sophisticated Marmalade, and a small bottle labeled brandy.

Marmalade pointed to it in delight. "Look, man. I bet the old blackbeetle guzzles brandy all night. Bet she gets drunk as a geyser, man."

This allegation, though fascinating, was incidentally quite unfounded. Aunt Hilda was the soberest of mortals and kept a small supply of brandy as an emergency measure against sickness in others of less iron constitution.

Marmalade pointed excitedly to another bottle of approximately the same size and shape. It was labeled TINCTURE OF IODINE—POISON, and there was a red skull and crossbones.

"Coo, man, let's pour some of that into the brandy," he said daringly, "so next time the old witch takes a swig—"

"Gosh, no, man. You'd get put in prison or hanged." Branny's voice was awestruck. He had a wholesome terror of the forces of law and justice.

Marmalade snorted. "Who cares for the rotten old police? If old blackbeetle was out in India, we'd do her in easy, man. One of my Dad's houseboys pushed his wife off a cliff into the river and a crocodile ate her. Never found out either till someone killed the crocodile and found her bracelet inside. He didn't get into any kind of a row." Marmy's saintlike face puckered in a simian grin. "Pity the poor crocodile that ate old hellwitch."

But since there were no cliffs and no crocodiles at the Oaklawn School, little that was productive could be gleaned from this lurid reminiscence. Satisfying themselves with a last dribble in the *eau de cologne* bottle, the two boys stole away to safety.

Apparently nothing was suspected and the conspirators exchanged ecstatic grins every time Aunt Hilda took out her handkerchief and a faint whiff of *eau de cologne* assailed their nostrils.

Not long content with past triumphs, Marmalade's fertile mind soon conceived a new plan of attack. Pleading scientific experiments, he made a surreptitious deal with Ruby, the most amenable of the scullery maids, whereby for the sum of one half-penny apiece she would hand over to him every live mouse caught in the kitchen traps. They soon had quite a flourishing family which they kept in a biscuit tin and fed on crusts from their supper.

At last the hour to strike came. Aunt Hilda's only real self-indulgence was an hour of "forty winks" after tea. It was an immutable law and one could absolutely count upon it. Plans were duly laid. Branny was to stand guard at the foot of the front stairs while Marmalade stole up the back way with his biscuit tin and planted the mice in Aunt Hilda's bed.

Branny waited breathlessly at his post. He could hear the clink of cups where his mother and aunts were taking their tea. Every-thing was running smoothly. Marmalade reappeared, his golden face beautiful with anticipation.

"Right between the sheets, man. All four of 'em. I bet the old—"

"Cave," whispered Branny, for at that moment the study door opened and Aunt Hilda appeared. They withdrew into the shadows where they could not be seen but from whence they could watch the broad black back as it camelled its way ponder-ously upward over the drugget and stair rods.

The two children waited in the darkness, hardly daring to breathe.

At last it came—that faint scream which was probably the most feminine act ever perpetrated by Aunt Hilda. They heard her door open, they saw her appear, clad in a gray woolen dress-ing gown, at the top of the stairs.

Then, for all her bulk, Aunt Hilda ran down the front stairs as swiftly as a young doe, calling to no one in particular.

"The cat, quick! Mouse in my bed!"

The cat was duly obtained and shut in Aunt Hilda's room where it allegedly left a half-eaten carcass under the bed.

Though the two boys hovered around, they never discovered the fate of the other mice. Whether they were squashed by the bulk of Aunt Hilda or whether they escaped to plague her further was forever shrouded in mystery.

But the reason for the mice's presence in her bed did not long remain a mystery to the astute Aunt Hilda. The truth was made plain after a rigorous cross-examination of the scullery maid, Ruby, and Branny and Marmy received the Wages of Sin.

They were ordered to spend the rest of the day locked in their room, where they were to write one hundred times in their best copperplate hand the laudable sentence:

"Do unto others as you would be done by."

No food would be served until Aunt Hilda was satisfied with their task.

They wasted considerable time trying to tie two nibs on to a single pen and thus do two lines at once. Finally they abandoned this and settled to their work, which they finished about an hour after their normal dinner time. They were, of course, ravenous, but they were too proud to signal their distress. However, they had a friend at court, for a faint rustling under the door attracted their attention and they saw six thin bars of milk chocolate appear under the crack. They fell on them and devoured them avidly without speculation as to their source.

It was typical of Branny's love for his mother that he never subsequently caused her embarrassment by thanking her. In some respects he was a very tactful and gallant gentleman.

As the afternoon lengthened with no sign from their jailer, Satan inevitably entered to find mischief for idle hands. He started innocently enough, goading Marmalade to write a number of lyrics all beginning with the line of their imposition.

But after a while this palled and the poet turned artist. Since they had used up all their paper, Marmalade adorned the end-leaves of Branny's copy of *Black Beauty* with caricatures of Aunt Hilda's ample figure, which became increasingly anatomical. By the time they heard Aunt Hilda's footsteps on the stairs, the end-papers of Miss Sewell's innocuous little opus were in a condition which would have caused the cheeks of its authoress to turn deep scarlet. Quickly *Black Beauty* was hidden behind the other books on the shelf and forgotten.

Although Marmalade remained the only male boarder, Oaklawn School for Girls prospered financially—an undeniable fact of which the aunts made capital, attributing it, of course, to their own efficiency and overlooking the geographical and chronological aspects of the case.

Branny, as far divorced as ever from his mother, dreamed of the holidays for which he and his mother had secretly planned a trip to Weston-Super-Mare.

But when the holidays came his dreams were shattered, for Aunt Nellie's Anglo-Indian connection had been all too successful and there were several unwanted, homeless girls who had nowhere to go and had to remain under the school's care.

So Constance was required to stay at home and Branny stayed too, eating the same uninteresting food as during term time and denied even the use of the front stairs.

But life was not too impossible—at least not until the day that Aunt Hilda started, unbeknown to anyone else, to collect items for a local Church bazaar for the Belgian Refugee Fund. During the course of her probings, she came upon Branny's books and it was not long before *Black Beauty* was discovered. Unfortunately there was a duplicate copy and she picked on the one in which Marmalade, now vacationing with an aunt in Chapstow, had made his recognizable drawings.

It went to the vicarage along with other books, a faded lampshade, two broken parasols, a wilted pair of chintz curtains, and a supernumerary pair of andirons.

Branny was in the garden the next day when the vicar's wife arrived. With the sure instinct of childhood, he knew that there was trouble brewing even before he saw *Black Beauty* clasped to an indignant bosom.

He gave her one of his slowest, sweetest smiles, but she hardly responded. Then his heart went sick because he saw what she was carrying.

She was shown to the drawing-room to see Aunt Hilda, and soon Branny's mother and Aunt Nellie were sent for. Branny hovered around but acoustically the drawing-room was poor— that is, for people listening outside the door. He heard nothing but later, when the vicar's wife left and the conference was transferred to the study, his eavesdropping was more successful.

"It's entirely your fault, Constance," Aunt Hilda was speaking. "You've raised the child without the first principles of discipline."

"He needs a good whipping," this from Aunt Nellie.

"It's not his fault and you're not to touch him." Branny could hear his mother's voice, tearful but determined. Then he caught the mention of Marmalade's name.

"That degenerate imp . . . he'll have to go . . . wouldn't have had Mrs. Jackson . . . for the world . . . scandal . . . ruin the school . . . of course, Branny must go too."

It was more than Branny could bear. He pushed open the door and marched in.

The three women were sitting around the center table. His mother held a handkerchief up to her face. Aunt Hilda's arms were folded across a broad intransigent chest. Aunt Nellie drummed jeweled fingers. On the table lay *Black Beauty*, open at the end-pages, the broad caricatures glaringly displayed.

Branny's eyes were riveted on them in horrified fascination. Then some strange impulse seized him and he started to laugh, helplessly, hysterically.

"Branson Foster." Aunt Hilda's voice thundered through the room. But it was Aunt Nellie's ringed hand that delivered the sharp slap to the boy's face.

"Stop it—at once!"

Branny's laughter ended as abruptly as it had begun.

He moved toward his mother, seeking her face. But it was hidden behind her handkerchief.

Aunt Hilda demanded: "Branson, did you—er—perpetrate these—these—?"

Branson was still looking at his mother, paying no attention to Aunt Hilda.

"Speak up, you wicked child," rapped Aunt Nellie.

But Branny did not answer. The aunts started talking, both at once. Branny had found his mother's hand and was squeezing it. His touch seemed to give her courage because she spoke at last.

"Hilda, Nellie," she faltered. "Leave us alone, will you, please?"

"Very well, Constance. He's *your* son." Aunt Hilda rose ponderously. "But if you find he isn't innocent—and I can't believe he is . . ."

"Innocent," snorted Aunt Nellie. "He must have a good whipping."

Aunt Hilda took a ruler from the desk and pushed it across the table towards Constance. The two aunts withdrew.

Alone with his mother, Branny did not speak for a moment. His eyes turned again to the dreadful book on the table. Then suddenly, almost fiercely, he picked it up and threw it in the fire. The sight of the flames curling around the images of Aunt Hilda gave him a strange satisfaction.

His mother's large brown eyes were staring at him inquiringly.

"Oh, Branny, did you. . . . Oh, if only I knew what to do . . . if your father were alive."

His eyes downcast, Branny said:

"I didn't do it but—but I don't want Them to know I didn't."

"But Branny . . ."

"I'll take a whipping." He took the ruler from the table and held it out.

"But Branny . . . if you're innocent—"

"I'll take a whipping," he repeated doggedly.

"Oh, Branny, I know what it is. You don't want to tell on Marmy."

Still Constance did not move. Her large brown eyes filled with tears. With sudden determination Branny seized the ruler from her with his right hand and brought it down on his own left palm with hard, painful whacks. After each blow he uttered a realistic howl. He changed hands, striking at his right hand. With the sixth blow he gave vent to a burst of caterwauling which, for all its violence, was almost sincere.

Then he rushed from the room, past his listening aunts who looked at each other and nodded in satisfaction. He could almost hear them saying:

"I didn't know poor Constance had it in her."

He ran up the front stairs to his room and stayed there almost all day.

When next he saw his mother alone, he learned that Aunt Hilda was adamant about his going away to a boys' boarding school next term. Marmy would have to leave, too.

And when he went up to bed in his lonely attic, Aunt Hilda forbade him once again the use of the front stairs. That night he dreamed of Marmy's Indian crocodile, but the woman toppling over the cliff into the reptile's jaws was not the houseboy's wife, it was Aunt Hilda. And when he awoke, a strange quivering of excitement was in him. If Aunt Hilda were gone, life could be golden again. Accidents did happen. Why couldn't an accident happen to Aunt Hilda?

Once his mind had leaped this terrific hurdle, the idea was never out of his thoughts. He nursed it like a secret joy. An accident had happened to the wife of Marmy's father's houseboy and nothing had happened to the houseboy. Marmy had said so. The profundity of Marmy's influence on him was beginning to show. Timid, unassertive, he would never have imagined what he was imagining if the other boy had not taught him that one can fight even the most formidable foe.

His dreamings were at first thrilling but vague. He remembered the blue bottle of iodine in Aunt Hilda's room with its red skull and marked with the word POISON, and wondered what would happen if by chance some of it got into Aunt Hilda's brandy. Iodine tasted bad. Branny knew that because he had licked some off once after it had been applied to a cut finger. Probably Aunt Hilda would taste the iodine and not drink the brandy. No, the accident wouldn't happen that way.

Branny's mind dwelt constantly and caressingly on Marmy's Indian reminiscence of the unwanted wife, the cliff, and the crocodile. His days and nights were exalted with an image of Aunt Hilda falling from a high place, while below, its jaws gaping to receive its prey, squatted a monstrous but cooperative crocodile. In Branny's secret dream world, Aunt Hilda gradually stopped being a human being. She became a symbol of Injustice. If something happened to her, it would not be something happening to a real person of real flesh and blood.

He brooded more and more, yearning for the old days of closeness and safety with his beloved. He grew so pale with brooding that his mother became quite worried about him. However, she ascribed his vapors to his dread of going away to boarding school, for arrangements were already being made with a gentlemanly but inexpensive establishment in Kent and his departure was scheduled for the beginning of the Easter term.

It was the Germans who brought Branny's secret desire out of the realms of dream and into reality. The zeppelin raids had now begun in earnest and it was rumored that they would not concentrate upon London alone but were planning to destroy the industrial cities of the midlands, even the nearby city of Bristol. These rumors were confirmed by a solemn visit from the vicar who, in his role of special constable, was responsible for seeing that all regulations were observed concerning the safety of Littletonians.

England was not yet blacked-out as it was to be later in the War and the street lamps had not yet been painted that bluish purple which, though picturesque, was to make the towns and villages so gloomy at night. The menace from the air—especially in the west—was nowhere near as great as in the Second World holocaust. Nevertheless, each little town in England was beginning to take itself seriously as a target especially picked by the Kaiser himself, and black cloth for curtains was at a premium.

The menace, however inconsiderable, was there. And the vicar, a resourceful and conscientious man, felt responsible for the safety of his flock, in particular for the young lambs entrusted to the care of the principals of Oaklawn School for Girls.

Consequently, he evolved a plan and called on Mrs. Foster and the Aunts for a solemn conference.

It had been arranged by the local authorities that the approach of zeppelins should be signaled by the ringing of the church bell. At the first peal it behooved everybody to extinguish all lights and betake themselves to the security of their cellars. But the vicar realized that in a house of some sixty or seventy persons—mostly young persons—there might be panic or confusion resulting in serious accidents.

He suggested that the three Principals should divide up the duties among themselves or their appointees and having decided on their battle stations, they should hold a practice or two during daylight hours. In this way the girls and mistresses would get accustomed to the routine and then—when the fatal hour struck—they would hurry to the safety of the cellar like trained soldiers with the minimum of disorder. He further suggested that an air of jollity or "larkishness" should be given to the whole proceeding so that the children would not be unduly intimidated or alarmed.

"If I can be of any service," he concluded mildly, "you can count on me."

But that was sending coals to Newcastle. Aunt Hilda had grasped the idea perfectly. And her superb generalship was more than equal to it. In fact, it was exactly the task she relished.

After dinner the next day she addressed the whole school, including the staff and servants, allotting specific duties.

She tried, unsuccessfully, to give to the project an air of holiday or treat—a special amusement designed by herself for the delectation of the whole school. While attempting to make light of any possible danger, she managed to make her discourse sound like Pericles's Funeral Oration.

The girls and mistresses smiled half-heartedly as they trooped out of the dining-hall.

However, the actual practice alert did prove to be more fun than had been expected. Aunt Hilda scheduled it for the second hour of afternoon school. She handled it with impressive thoroughness. Girls, governesses, even the servants were instructed to go upstairs to their rooms, to undress and get right into bed, just as if it were their normal bedtime. At the sound of the whistle, things were to begin.

It was far, far better than the algebra or French of afternoon school.

The girls loved it, especially the little ones. And how they giggled when—the whistle having sounded—Aunt Nellie appeared in a cerise peignoir and lighting the candle in broad daylight, advised them, half in English and half in French: "Look sharp, children, and prenny garde."

Squeaking and tittering could be heard from every room, particularly from the senior dormitory where Miss Earle—who had a flair for the dramatic—had appeared in a Japanese kimono with her hair actually done up in a full panoply of curl papers.

Branny enjoyed it all, too. He had, as the only possessor of a flashlight, been given a special assignment. His job was to stand at the top of the back stairs, flashing on his light when needed and shooing off any one who made a turn toward the front stairs. He entertained himself by flashing his light into the girls' eyes as they scuttled down the stairs with a "boo, look out for the zeppelins" or a surreptitious pinch for those with whom he knew he could take liberties.

After the last girl and junior staff member had been shepherded down, Branny stood at his post and watched, fascinated, as Aunt Hilda emerged from her room in a snuff-colored dressing gown and conscientiously went through the motions of turning out the unlighted gaslights in each passage. Then, carrying a lit candle, she made her portentous way down the front stairs towards the gas bracket in the hall. She was moving fast and purposefully but on the last stair but one she stumbled and the candle fell from her hand.

As Branny scurried away to join the others in the cellar he suddenly knew what was going to happen.

A minute later, when Aunt Hilda came down, he heard her say to Ruby: "One of the rods is loose on the front stairs. See to it at once or someone will break her neck."

Branny's pulses were racing as he heard these words from the dark corner of the cellar where he was holding his mother's hand.

The stair rod is loose . . . someone will break her neck . . .

Next time, perhaps, it wouldn't be daylight. A stair rod might be loose at the top of the stairs rather than at the bottom. Then someone going down hurriedly in the darkness might easily fall all the way from the top and—break her neck. . . .

That night, when going through the stereotyped formula of his prayers: "And bless mother and all kind friends and make me a good boy. Amen," he added a rider:

"And please, God, make the zeppelins come here soon."

During the ensuing days while he was waiting for his prayers to be answered, Branny was a model boy. He was good, so obedient, that everyone thought he must be sickening from some infectious disease.

He was particularly polite to Aunt Hilda, for he had inspected the front stairs very carefully. The carpet was overlaid by a drugget of thick, patterned linen. This was held in place by stair rods which fitted into rings at both ends. By pushing the rod an inch or two out of its rung on the banister side and by loosening the drugget, he found he achieved a surface almost as slippery and hazardous as a toboggan slide. Only a quick grab at the banister with the right hand could save anyone. And Aunt Hilda had held the candle in her right hand during the practice. After the fall, when the drugget would automatically be more loosened, no one could ever guess that the stair rods had been deliberately pushed out of their ringsockets.

He decided on loosening the rods on two stairs—the third and fourth from the top—and practiced several times, even doing it with his eyes closed, since the final deed would have to be done in darkness.

With a child's implacability he trained himself to the task as thoroughly and impersonally as a guerrilla, but he never really assessed what he was doing. There was going to be an accident. That was all.

Waiting was hard, especially at night when he lay sleepless in bed, his senses tingling in expectation of the sound of the church bell. That there might be any real danger from zeppelins to himself or to his mother never even occurred to him. Branny feared no straightforward menace.

He was asleep when the church bell finally sounded at two o'clock on a bitter cold night in early December. He jumped out of bed shivering, put on his trousers and jersey, picked up his flashlight, and made his way to his appointed place between the front and back stairs.

From the girls' bedrooms he could hear twitterings, less gay and giggly now that the real thing had come. He watched the governesses moving, candles in hand, from dormitory to dormitory. Then he slipped to his mother's room and escorted her to the servants' wing, whence she was to conduct the maids down the kitchen stairs into the distant safety of the cellar.

Before the procession started was his time for action. Very quickly, and quite calmly, he ran to the front stairs and loosened the rods and the drugget on the third and fourth stairs.

Soon afterwards the girls and governesses began to troop from their dormitories. The children, for the most part, looked frightened and bewildered. Branny didn't tease them or pretend to be a zeppelin this time, but—as befitted the only male in the house—said cheerful and encouraging things.

"The old zeps won't get this far. We'll shoot 'em all down over London. You see if we don't. . . ."

Then, when everyone had dispersed—including Aunt Nellie

in her cerise wrap—Branny made his way down the back stairs and to the far end of the hall where he could keep the front stairs under observation.

He did not exactly want to witness Aunt Hilda's downfall. There was no element of sadism or gloating in his scrutiny. It was simply a ruthless sense of efficiency which made him wish to reassure himself that the accident would happen.

The church bell had stopped tolling and the minutes seemed endless. In the near-darkness he could hear the grandfather clock near him ticking off the seconds like drum beats.

Then there was the opening of a door upstairs and he recognized Aunt Hilda's heavy tread as she moved along the upstairs passages, turning out the gas. As he waited breathless, he heard another sound. Someone was running with light, swift tread up the back stairs. It must, he reflected, be one of the governesses who had forgotten something. He heard Aunt Hilda's voice saying:

"Forgotten your coat? Well, hurry up and get it. It's very cold in the cellar and I hope none of the girls . . .''

The sound of the light scurrying footsteps retreated. A door opened and closed. For a second or two there was no sound except the rhythmic ticking of the grandfather clock and the pounding of Branny's own heart.

Then footsteps again and—as he peered unseeingly into the darkness upstairs—Branny was conscious of someone approaching the top of the front stairs. Aunt Hilda must be coming down, but without her candle.

Now he could see her dimly as she moved. She had reached the small landing at the crest of the stairs.

She started down. He watched in a kind of appalled fascination.

Then there was the metallic rattle of stair rods. A scream . . . a crash . . . as she fell forward and hurtled down the stairs, landing on the tiles of the front hall.

A little moan . . . then silence . . .

For a moment Branny stood motionless. One impulse urged him to move forward, another held him back. A sense of triumph warred with a feeling of fear for what he had done.

In the dim light from the gas by the front door he could see the dark figure lying still—very still—at the foot of the stairs.

He felt nothing—only the certainty that Aunt Hilda was there—dead.

Then he heard a sound that made his blood turn to ice. There were heavy footsteps above him and a voice came from the upstairs landing: "Good God, what has happened? Did you have an accident?"

It was a horribly familiar voice. *Aunt Hilda's voice!* He became conscious that his Aunt, holding her candle high above her head, was making her way down the stairs, skirting the perilous third and fourth steps.

Aunt Hilda was coming down the stairs. Then it could not be Aunt Hilda who was lying there, a dark pool on the tiles of the hall.

Through his agony of remorse and terror Branny heard Aunt Hilda's voice again:

"Constance, Constance, are you hurt?"

There was no need for Branny to move closer. In the nearing light from his aunt's candle, he could make out quite clearly the outlines of that figure lying there, could see the aureole of dark hair framing the beloved face, paler now than death.

"Mother!"

The word came in a groan of agony. Then Branny turned away and disappeared into the darkness.

There is a degree of suffering beyond which the human mind cannot go, even in childhood where suffering is so acute. It is beyond the realm of sanity and verges on the outer darkness beyond which there is no thought, no reason.

Luckily for Branny he reached that point of narcosis immediately. His only instinct was a blind desire to hide—somewhere far away, to fade and quite forget. Up in the attic there was a cupboard whose door he could lock from the inside. It was musty and dirty but he didn't care. It was dark and as far away from the front hall as possible.

For hours he crouched there in the darkness, his mind mercifully blank. If any conscious thought came to him it was simply that he had killed his mother and if he stayed hidden up there long enough he'd die too and that would be that.

Somewhere in the house were voices and footsteps, the girls returning from their cellar and trooping back to their dormitories. And then someone was calling his name:

"Branny . . . Branny . . ."

But he didn't move. He'd never come out of his hiding place . . . never . . . and when they found him, if they ever did, he'd be dead and they could bury him by his mother.

He sat there, dry-eyed, and immobile as a rock. He had no sense of time or place any more. He slept. He was dimly conscious of that when he awoke. He was dimly conscious too of faint light creeping through the cracks in the door which told him it was day. Then the daylight went again. It never occurred to him that he might be hungry. He did not even feel the aching of his body. Noises sounded occasionally, infinitely remote. He heard them but he didn't try to interpret them. He slept again and awoke again to his stubborn grief.

At some point, it might have been aeons later, he heard Aunt Nellie's voice and he knew that she was near, actually in the attic.

"The cupboard, Miss Snellgrove. When Miss Foster searched up here yesterday, she never thought of the cupboard. It is just possible . . ."

And then Miss Snellgrove's tearful voice. "Oh, Mrs. Delaney, hasn't there been any new word from the police station?"

"Not a word, but it's hopeless. They have searched everywhere, all over the countryside. I am convinced, Miss Snellgrove that the boy is . . ."

At that moment the door handle of the cupboard was vigorously shaken.

"See? It's locked. Branny." Aunt Nellie's voice was kind but strained with anxiety. "Branny, I know you are there. Do come out, there's a good boy."

Branny crouched deeper into the cupboard and pulled some musty curtains over him. They were not going to get him out by any trick of kindness or anxiety.

They were both tugging at the unyielding door.

"He must be there. Oh, Branny, do come out. . . ."

At last they went away. It seemed a long time before anyone came again and then there was the sound of footsteps and a man's voice. Branny recognized it at once as that of the doctor who had attended his father during his final illness.

"Branny—" this time it was Aunt Hilda speaking—"Dr. Berry is here to talk to you. He has something to tell you." She added hurriedly: "I'm going away so you can talk to him alone."

Branny heard her heavy footsteps departing and the doctor's voice:

"Branson, my boy, won't you come out? I want to talk to you about your mother."

Branny did not answer. They were speaking softly and gently to him now, but as soon as they got him out, they'd be harsh with him. Perhaps they had guessed what he had done on the stairs and he would be sent to prison.

Then Doctor Berry spoke again. "Branson," he said quietly, "I want you to come with me and see your mother. She's asking for you. She needs you very badly, my boy."

Branny's heart missed a beat. Through all those long hours in the darkness it had never occurred to him that his mother might still be alive.

Slowly his hand went up to the lock. Then he withdrew it again. No, this might be a trap—to lure him out so they could pounce on him.

"Branson, she's down in the drawing-room waiting. You wouldn't want to be unkind to her, would you? She's had a terrible accident. . . ."

Branny could bear it no longer. He crashed open the cupboard door and stood there facing Dr. Berry. For a moment the physician stared in astonishment at the child. Branny was covered with grime and dust. His hair was full of cobwebs and the expression on his pale face held in it all the misery of the world.

Dr. Berry was strangely touched and, dirty as Branson was, he drew him towards him. The kindness of a stranger was too much for the boy and the pent-up flow of unshed tears broke loose in a torrent.

For a moment Dr. Berry said nothing. He just held the quivering child close and patted his head while Branny wept his heart out. Then the doctor produced a handkerchief, wiped Branny's eyes, and said cheerfully:

"Come on, now, old boy. You've got to be a man. Your mother needs a man to look after her and you're the only one in the house, you know."

Then in answer to an unspoken question, he went on: "She's going to live, Branson, but she may never be able to walk again. That's why she'll need a man like you to look after her."

He took Branny's hand and led him from the attic. "Now, go on down and have a good scrub and then we'll take you to see her. Come on, let's see a clean smiling face and look sharp."

Aunt Hilda and Aunt Nellie were waiting for him downstairs. They kissed him and Aunt Hilda said "poor little boy" as she produced the best Brown Windsor soap. Aunt Nellie got his Sunday suit and used her own comb and brush to brush the dust and cobwebs from his hair.

And then, when he looked clean and neat, Aunt Hilda said: "Your mother's in the drawing-room, dear. Her bed is down there now and you can have the little study next door all for your own. So you can look after her. And you can have all your meals together."

"And," put in Aunt Nellie with a grim attempt at cheerfulness, "after a few weeks when your mother's a little stronger, she'll need you to push her wheel-chair. So you won't be going to boarding school next term after all . . ."

Dr. Berry led him then into the drawing-room where his mother's bed was placed near the window. She lay in it, frail and beautiful, her soft hair about her face.

"Well, here's your new nurse, Mrs. Foster."

Branny moved to his mother's bedside and took the slender hand that she held out to him. They looked long into each other's eyes like lovers.

"Branny," she breathed. "Oh, Branny, darling . . ."

After the doctor had left, they stayed there, fingers intertwined. There was a faint fall of snow outside the windows and through an open door Branny could see his own bed in the little room that had been prepared for him. There was even a fire.

Soon Aunt Hilda came in, carrying a tea tray with two cups only. There was a boiled egg for Branny and muffins to be toasted.

"Now, Nurse Branson," she said, "I'm going to leave you to take care of your patient."

Branny felt his heart would burst with joy.

Too Early Spring

STEPHEN VINCENT BENÉT

"Too Early Spring" tells a poignant and suspenseful tale of young love and how its innocence can be corrupted—not by the lovers themselves, but by the unjust actions of their not-so-innocent elders. At first you may feel there is no crime in this story, but upon reflection you may wonder. There are many different kinds of crimes, after all. . . . Stephen Vincent Benét (1898–1943), produced a large body of literary work during his all-too-brief career. His talents extended from short stories to novels to poetry, and he was twice the recipient of the Pulitzer Prize for poetry—in 1929 for John Brown's Body, *a narrative poem about the Civil War, and in 1944 for the posthumously published* Western Star. *His novels include* Spanish Bayonet *and* Young People's Pride.

I 'M writing this down because I don't ever want to forget the way it was. It doesn't seem as if I could, now, but they all tell you things change. And I guess they're right. Older people must have forgotten or they couldn't be the way they are. And that goes for even the best ones, like Dad and Mr. Grant. They try to understand but they don't seem to know how. And the others make you feel dirty or else they make you feel like a goof. Till, pretty soon, you begin to forget yourself—you begin to think, "Well, maybe they're right and it was that way." And that's the end of everything. So I've got to write this down. Because they smashed it forever—but it wasn't the way they said.

Mr. Grant always says in comp. class: "Begin at the beginning." Only I don't know quite where the beginning was. We had a good summer at Big Lake but it was just the same summer. I worked pretty hard at the practice basket I rigged up in the barn, and I learned how to do the back jackknife. I'll never dive like Kerry but you want to be as all-around as you can. And, when I took my measurements, at the end of that summer, I was 5 ft. 9¾ and I'd gained 12 lbs. 6 oz. That isn't bad for going on sixteen and the old chest expansion was O.K. You don't want to get too heavy, because basketball's a fast game, but the year before was the year when I got my height, and I was so skinny, I got tired. But this year, Kerry helped me practice, a couple of times, and he seemed to think I had a good chance for the team. So I felt pretty set up—they'd never had a Sophomore on it before. And Kerry's a natural athlete, so that means a lot from him. He's a pretty good brother too. Most Juniors at State wouldn't bother with a fellow in High.

It sounds as if I were trying to run away from what I have to write down, but I'm not. I want to remember that summer, too, because it's the last happy one I'll ever have. Oh, when I'm an old man—thirty or forty—things may be all right again. But that's a long time to wait and it won't be the same.

And yet, that summer was different, too, in a way. So it must have started then, though I didn't know it. I went around with the gang as usual and we had a good time. But, every now and then, it would strike me we were acting like awful kids. They thought I was getting the big head, but I wasn't. It just wasn't much fun—even going to the cave. It was like going on shooting marbles when you're in High.

I had sense enough not to try to tag after Kerry and his crowd. You can't do that. But when they all got out on the lake in canoes, warm evenings, and somebody brought a phonograph along, I used to go down to the Point, all by myself, and listen and listen. Maybe they'd be talking or maybe they'd be singing, but it all sounded mysterious across the water. I wasn't trying to hear what they said, you know. That's the kind of thing Tot Pickens does. I'd just listen, with my arms around my knees—and somehow it would hurt me to listen—and yet I'd rather do that than be with the gang.

I was sitting under the four pines, one night, right down by the edge of the water. There was a big moon and they were singing. It's funny how you can be unhappy and nobody know it but yourself.

I was thinking about Sheila Coe. She's Kerry's girl. They fight but they get along. She's awfully pretty and she can swim like a fool. Once Kerry sent me over with her tennis racket and we had quite a conversation. She was fine. And she didn't pull any of this big sister stuff, either, the way some girls will with a fellow's kid brother.

And when the canoe came along, by the edge of the lake, I thought for a moment it was her. I thought maybe she was looking for Kerry and maybe she'd stop and maybe she'd feel like talking to me again. I don't know why I thought that—I didn't have any reason. Then I saw it was just the Sharon kid, with a new kind of bob that made her look grown-up, and I felt sore. She didn't have any business out on the lake at her age. She was just a Sophomore in High, the same as me.

I chunked a stone in the water and it splashed right by the

canoe, but she didn't squeal. She just said, "Fish," and chuck-led. It struck me it was a kid's trick, trying to scare a kid.

"Hello, Helen," I said. "Where did you swipe the gunboat?"

"They don't know I've got it," she said. "Oh, hello, Chuck Peters. How's Big Lake?"

"All right," I said. "How was camp?"

"It was peachy," she said. "We had a peachy counselor, Miss Morgan. She was on the Wellesley field-hockey team."

"Well," I said, "we missed your society." Of course we hadn't, because they're across the lake and don't swim at our raft. But you ought to be polite.

"Thanks," she said. "Did you do the special reading for English? I thought it was dumb."

"It's always dumb," I said. "What canoe is that?"

"It's the old one," she said. "I'm not supposed to have it out at night. But you won't tell anybody, will you?"

"Be your age," I said. I felt generous. "I'll paddle a while, if you want," I said.

"All right," she said, so she brought it in and I got aboard. She went back in the bow and I took the paddle. I'm not strong on carting kids around, as a rule. But it was better than sitting there by myself.

"Where do you want to go?" I said.

"Oh, back towards the house," she said in a shy kind of voice. "I ought to, really. I just wanted to hear the singing."

"K.O.," I said. I didn't paddle fast, just let her slip. There was a lot of moon on the water. We kept around the edge so they wouldn't notice us. The singing sounded as if it came from a different country, a long way off.

She was a sensible kid, she didn't ask fool questions or giggle about nothing at all. Even when we went by Petters' Cove. That's where the lads from the bungalow colony go and it's pretty well populated on a warm night. You can hear them talk-ing in low voices and now and then a laugh. Once Tot Pickens and a gang went over there with a flashlight, and a big Bohunk chased them for half a mile.

I felt funny, going by there with her. But I said, "Well, it's certainly Old Home Week"—in an offhand tone, because, after all, you've got to be sophisticated. And she said, "People are funny," in just the right sort of way. I took quite a shine to her after that and we talked. The Sharons have only been in town three years and somehow I'd never really noticed her before. Mrs. Sharon's awfully good-looking but she and Mr. Sharon fight. That's hard on a kid. And she was a quiet kid. She had a small kind of face and her eyes were sort of like a kitten's. You could see she got a great kick out of pretending to be grown-up— and yet it wasn't all pretending. A couple of times, I felt just as if I were talking to Sheila Coe. Only more comfortable, because, after all, we were the same age.

Do you know, after we put the canoe up, I walked all the way back home, around the lake? And most of the way, I ran. I felt swell too. I felt as if I could run forever and not stop. It was like finding something. I hadn't imagined anybody could ever feel the way I did about some things. And here was another person, even if it was a girl.

Kerry's door was open when I went by and he stuck his head out, and grinned.

"Well, kid," he said. "Stepping out?"

"Sure. With Greta Garbo," I said, and grinned back to show I didn't mean it. I felt sort of lightheaded, with the run and everything.

"Look here, kid—" he said, as if he was going to say something. Then he stopped. But there was a funny look on his face.

And yet I didn't see her again till we were both back in High. Mr. Sharon's uncle died, back East, and they closed the cottage suddenly. But all the rest of the time at Big Lake, I kept remembering that night and her little face. If I'd seen her in daylight, first, it might have been different. No, it wouldn't have been.

All the same, I wasn't even thinking of her when we bumped into each other, the first day of school. It was raining and she had on a green slicker and her hair was curly under her hat. We grinned and said hello and had to run. But something happened to us, I guess.

I'll say this now—it wasn't like Tot Pickens and Mabel Palmer. It wasn't like Junior David and Betty Page—though they've been going together ever since kindergarten. It wasn't like any of those things. We didn't get sticky and sloppy. It wasn't like going with a girl.

Gosh, there'd be days and days when we'd hardly see each other, except in class. I had basketball practice almost every afternoon and sometimes evenings and she was taking music lessons four times a week. But you don't have to be always twosing with a person, if you feel that way about them. You seem to know the way they're thinking and feeling, the way you know yourself.

Now let me describe her. She had that little face and the eyes like a kitten's. When it rained, her hair curled all over the back of her neck. Her hair was yellow. She wasn't a tall girl but she wasn't chunky—just light and well made and quick. She was awfully alive without being nervous—she never bit her fingernails or chewed the end of her pencil, but she'd answer quicker than anyone in the class. Nearly everybody liked her, but she wasn't best friends with any particular girl, the mushy way they get. The teachers all thought a lot of her, even Miss Eagles. Well, I had to spoil that.

If we'd been like Tot and Mabel, we could have had a lot more time together, I guess. But Helen isn't a liar and I'm not a snake. It wasn't easy, going over to her house, because Mr. and Mrs. Sharon would be polite to each other in front of you and yet there'd be something wrong. And she'd have to be fair to both of them and they were always pulling at her. But we'd look at each other across the table and then it would be all right.

I don't know when it was that we knew we'd get married to each other, some time. We just started talking about it, one day, as if we always had. We were sensible, we knew it couldn't happen right off. We thought maybe when we were eighteen. That was two years but we knew we had to be educated. You don't get as good a job, if you aren't. Or that's what people say.

We weren't mushy either, like some people. We got to kissing each other good-by, sometimes, because that's what you do when you're in love. It was cool, the way she kissed you, it was like leaves. But lots of the time we wouldn't even talk about getting married, we'd just play checkers or go over the old Latin, or once in a while go to the movies with the gang. It was really a wonderful winter. I played every game after the first one and she'd sit in the gallery and watch and I'd know she was there. You could see her little green hat or her yellow hair. Those are the class colors, green and gold.

And it's a queer thing, but everybody seemed to be pleased. That's what I can't get over. They liked to see us together. The grown people, I mean. Oh, of course, we got kidded too. And old Mrs. Withers would ask me about "my little sweetheart," in that awful damp voice of hers. But, mostly, they were all right. Even Mother was all right, though she didn't like Mrs. Sharon. I did hear her say to Father, once, "Really, George, how long is this going to last? Sometimes I feel as if I just couldn't stand it."

Then Father chuckled and said to her. "Now, Mary, last year you were worried about him because he didn't take any interest in girls at all."

"Well," she said, "he still doesn't. Oh, Helen's a nice child— no credit to Eva Sharon—and thank heaven she doesn't giggle. Well, Charles is mature for his age too. But he acts so solemn about her. It isn't natural."

"Oh, let Charlie alone," said Father. "The boy's all right. He's just got a one-track mind."

But it wasn't so nice for us after the spring came.

In our part of the state, it comes pretty late, as a rule. But it was early this year. The little kids were out with scooters when usually they'd still be having snowfights and, all of a sudden, the radiators in the classrooms smelt dry. You'd got used to that smell for months—and then, there was a day when you hated it again and everybody kept asking to open the windows. The monitors had a tough time, that first week—they always do when spring starts—but this year it was worse than ever because it came when you didn't expect it.

Usually, basketball's over by the time spring really breaks, but this year it hit us while we still had three games to play. And it certainly played hell with us as a team. After Bladesburg nearly licked us, Mr. Grant called off all practice till the day before the St. Matthew's game. He knew we were stale—and they've been state champions two years. They'd have walked all over us, the way we were going.

The first thing I did was telephone Helen. Because that meant there were six extra afternoons we could have, if she could get rid of her music lessons any way. Well, she said, wasn't it wonderful, her music teacher had a cold? And that seemed just like Fate.

Well, that was a great week and we were so happy. We went to the movies five times and once Mrs. Sharon let us take her little car. She knew I didn't have a driving license but of course I've driven ever since I was thirteen and she said it was all right. She was funny—sometimes she'd be awfully kind and friendly to you and sometimes she'd be like a piece of dry ice. She was that way with Mr. Sharon too. But it was a wonderful ride. We got stuff out of the kitchen—the cook's awfully sold on Helen—and drove way out in the country. And we found an old house, with the windows gone, on top of a hill, and parked the car and took the stuff up to the house and ate it there. There weren't any chairs or tables but we pretended there were.

We pretended it was our house, after we were married. I'll never forget that. She'd even brought paper napkins and paper plates and she set two places on the floor.

"Well, Charles," she said, sitting opposite me, with her feet tucked under, "I don't suppose you remember the days we were both in school."

"Sure," I said—she was always much quicker pretending things than I was— "I remember them all right. That was before Tot Pickens got to be President." And we both laughed.

"It seems very distant in the past to me—we've been married

so long," she said, as if she really believed it. She looked at me.

"Would you mind turning off the radio, dear?" she said. "This modern music always gets on my nerves."

"Have we got a radio?" I said.

"Of course, Chuck."

"With television?"

"Of course, Chuck."

"Gee, I'm glad," I said. I went and turned it off.

"Of course, if you *want* to listen to the late market reports—" she said just like Mrs. Sharon.

"Nope," I said. "The market—uh—closed firm today. Up twenty-six points."

"That's quite a long way up, isn't it?"

"Well, the country's perfectly sound at heart, in spite of this damfool Congress," I said, like Father.

She lowered her eyes a minute, just like her mother, and pushed away her plate.

"I'm not very hungry tonight," she said. "You won't mind if I go upstairs?"

"Aw, don't be like that," I said. It was too much like her mother.

"I was just seeing if I could," she said. "But I never will, Chuck."

"I'll never tell you you're nervous, either," I said. "I—oh, gosh!"

She grinned and it was all right. "Mr. Ashland and I have never had a serious dispute in our wedded lives," she said—and everybody knows who runs *that* family. "We just talk things over calmly and reach a satisfactory conclusion, usually mine."

"Say, what kind of house have we got?"

"It's a lovely house," she said. "We've got radios in every room and lots of servants. We've got a regular movie projector and a library full of good classics and there's always something in the icebox. I've got a shoe closet."

"A what?"

"A shoe closet. All my shoes are on tipped shelves, like Mother's. And all my dresses are on those padded hangers. And I say to the maid, 'Elise, Madam will wear the new French model today.' ''

"What are my clothes on?" I said. "Christmas trees?"

"Well " she said. "You've got lots of clothes and dogs. You smell of pipes and the open and something called Harrisburg tweed."

"I do not," I said. "I wish I had a dog. It's a long time since Jack."

"Oh, Chuck, I'm sorry," she said.

"Oh, that's all right," I said. "He was getting old and his ear was always bothering him. But he was a good pooch. Go ahead."

"Well," she said, "of course we give parties—"

"Cut the parties," I said.

"Chuck! They're grand ones!"

"I'm a homebody," I said. "Give me—er—my wife and my little family and—say, how many kids have we got, anyway?"

She counted on her fingers. "Seven."

"Good Lord," I said.

"Well, I always wanted seven. You can make it three, if you like."

"Oh, seven's all right, I suppose," I said. "But don't they get awfully in the way?"

"No," she said. "We have governesses and tutors and send them to boarding school."

"O.K.," I said. "But it's a strain on the old man's pocketbook, just the same."

"Chuck, will you ever talk like that? Chuck, this is when we're rich." Then suddenly, she looked sad. "Oh, Chuck, do you suppose we ever will?" she said.

"Why, sure," I said.

"I wouldn't mind if it was only a dump," she said. "I could cook for you. I keep asking Hilda how she makes things."

I felt awfully funny. I felt as if I were going to cry.

"We'll do it," I said. "Don't you worry."

"Oh, Chuck, you're a comfort," she said.

I held her for a while. It was like holding something awfully precious. It wasn't mushy or that way. I know what that's like too.

"It takes so long to get old," she said. "I wish I could grow up tomorrow. I wish we both could."

"Don't you worry," I said. "It's going to be all right."

We didn't say much, going back in the car, but we were happy enough. I thought we passed Miss Eagles at the turn. That worried me a little because of the driving license. But, after all, Mrs. Sharon had said we could take the car.

We wanted to go back again, after that, but it was too far to walk and that was the only time we had the car. Mrs. Sharon was awfully nice about it but she said, thinking it over, maybe we'd better wait till I got a license. Well, Father didn't want me to get one till I was seventeen but I thought he might come around. I didn't want to do anything that would get Helen in a jam with her family. That shows how careful I was of her. Or thought I was.

All the same, we decided we'd do something to celebrate if the team won the St. Matthew's game. We thought it would be fun if we could get a steak and cook supper out somewhere— something like that. Of course we could have done it easily enough with a gang, but we didn't want a gang. We wanted to be alone together, the way we'd been at the house. That was all we wanted. I don't see what's wrong about that. We even took home the paper plates, so as not to litter things up.

Boy, that was a game! We beat them 36–34 and it took an extra period and I thought it would never end. That two-goal lead they had looked as big as the Rocky Mountains all the first half. And they gave me the full school cheer with nine Peters when we tied them up. You don't forget things like that.

Afterwards, Mr. Grant had a kind of spread for the team at his house and a lot of people came in. Kerry had driven down from State to see the game and that made me feel pretty swell. And what made me feel better yet was his taking me aside and saying, "Listen, kid, I don't want you to get the swelled head, but you did a good job. Well, just remember this. Don't let anybody kid you out of going to State. You'll like it up there." And Mr. Grant heard him and laughed and said, "Well, Peters, I'm not proselytizing. But your brother might think about some of the Eastern colleges." It was all like the kind of dream you have when you can do anything. It was wonderful.

Only Helen wasn't there because the only girls were older girls. I'd seen her for a minute, right after the game, and she was fine, but it was only a minute. I wanted to tell her about that big St. Matthew's forward and—oh, everything. Well, you like to talk things over with your girl.

Father and Mother were swell but they had to go on to some big shindy at the country club. And Kerry was going there with Sheila Coe. But Mr. Grant said he'd run me back to the house in his car and he did. He's a great guy. He made jokes about my being the infant phenomenon of basketball, and they were good jokes too. I didn't mind them. But, all the same, when I'd said good night to him and gone into the house, I felt sort of let down.

I knew I'd be tired the next day but I didn't feel sleepy yet. I was too excited. I wanted to talk to somebody. I wandered around downstairs and wondered if Ida was still up. Well, she wasn't, but she'd left half a chocolate cake, covered over, on the kitchen table, and a note on top of it, "Congratulations to Mister Charles Peters." Well, that was awfully nice of her and I ate some. Then I turned the radio on and got the time signal— eleven—and some snappy music. But still I didn't feel like hitting the hay.

So I thought I'd call up Helen and then I thought—probably she's asleep and Hilda or Mrs. Sharon will answer the phone and be sore. And then I thought—well, anyhow, I could go over and walk around the block and look at her house. I'd get some fresh air out of it, anyway, and it would be a little like seeing her.

So I did—and it was a swell night—cool and a lot of stars— and I felt like a king, walking over. All the lower part of the

Sharon house was dark but a window upstairs was lit. I knew it was her window. I went around back of the driveway and whistled once—the whistle we made up. I never expected her to hear.

But she did, and there she was at the window, smiling. She made motions that she'd come down to the side door.

Honestly, it took my breath away when I saw her. She had on a kind of yellow thing over her night clothes and she looked so pretty. Her feet were so pretty in those slippers. You almost expected her to be carrying one of those animals kids like—she looked young enough. I know I oughtn't to have gone into the house. But we didn't think anything about it—we were just glad to see each other. We hadn't had any sort of chance to talk over the game.

We sat in front of the fire in the living room and she went out to the kitchen and got us cookies and milk. I wasn't really hungry, but it was like that time at the house, eating with her. Mr. and Mrs. Sharon were at the country club, too, so we weren't disturbing them or anything. We turned off the lights because there was plenty of light from the fire and Mr. Sharon's one of those people who can't stand having extra lights burning. Dad's that way about saving string.

It was quiet and lovely and the firelight made shadows on the ceiling. We talked a lot and then we just sat, each of us knowing the other was there. And the room got quieter and quieter and I'd told her about the game and I didn't feel excited or jumpy any more—just rested and happy. And then I knew by her breathing that she was asleep and I put my arm around her for just a minute. Because it was wonderful to hear that quiet breathing and know it was hers. I was going to wake her in a minute. I didn't realize how tired I was myself.

And then we were back in that house in the country and it was our home and we ought to have been happy. But something was wrong because there still wasn't any glass in the windows and a wind kept blowing through them and we tried to shut the doors but they wouldn't shut. It drove Helen distracted and we were both running through the house, trying to shut the doors, and we were cold and afraid. Then the sun rose outside the windows, burning and yellow and so big it covered the sky. And with the sun was a horrible, weeping voice. It was Mrs. Sharon's saying, "Oh, my God, oh my God."

I didn't know what had happened, for a minute, when I woke. And then I did and it was awful. Mrs. Sharon was saying "Oh, Helen—I trusted you . . ." and looking as if she were going to faint. And Mr. Sharon looked at her for a minute and his face was horrible and he said, "Bred in the bone," and she looked as if he'd hit her. Then he said to Helen—

I don't want to think of what they said. I don't want to think of any of the things they said. Mr. Sharon is a bad man. And she is a bad woman, even if she is Helen's mother. All the same, I could stand the things he said better than hers.

I don't want to think of any of it. And it is all spoiled now. Everything is spoiled. Miss Eagles saw us going to that house in the country and she said horrible things. They made Helen sick and she hasn't been back at school. There isn't any way I can see her. And if I could, it would be spoiled. We'd be thinking about the things they said.

I don't know how many of the people know, at school. But Tot Pickens passed me a note. And, that afternoon. I caught him behind his house. I'd have broken his nose if they hadn't pulled me off. I meant to. Mother cried when she heard about it and Dad took me into his room and talked to me. He said you can't lick the whole town. But I will anybody like Tot Pickens. Dad and Mother have been all right. But they say things about Helen and that's almost worse. They're for me because I'm their son. But they don't understand.

I thought I could talk to Kerry but I can't. He was nice but he looked at me in such a funny way. I don't know—sort of impressed. It wasn't the way I wanted him to look. But he's been decent. He comes down almost every weekend and we play catch in the yard.

You see, I just go to school and back now. They want me to go with the gang, the way I did, but I can't do that. Not after Tot. Of course my marks are a lot better because I've got more time to study now. But it's lucky I haven't got Miss Eagles though Dad made her apologize. I couldn't recite to her.

I think Mr. Grant knows because he asked me to his house once and we had a conversation. Not about that, though I was terribly afraid he would. He showed me a lot of his old college things and the gold football he wears on his watch chain. He's got a lot of interesting things.

Then we got talking, somehow, about history and things like that and how times had changed. Why, there were kings and queens who got married younger than Helen and me. Only now we lived longer and had a lot more to learn. So it couldn't happen now. "It's civilization," he said. "And all civilization's against nature. But I suppose we've got to have it. Only sometimes it isn't easy." Well, somehow or other, that made me feel less lonely. Before that I'd been feeling that I was the only person on earth who'd ever felt that way.

I'm going to Colorado, this summer, to a ranch, and next year, I'll go East to school. Mr. Grant says he thinks I can make the basketball team, if I work hard enough, though it isn't as big a game in the East as it is with us. Well, I'd like to show them something. It would be some satisfaction. He says not to be too fresh at first, but I won't be that.

It's a boys' school and there aren't even women teachers. And, maybe, afterwards, I could be a professional basketball player or something, where you don't have to see women at all. Kerry says I'll get over that; but I won't. They all sound like Mrs. Sharon to me now, when they laugh.

They're going to send Helen to a convent—I found out that. Maybe they'll let me see her before she goes. But, if we do, it will be all wrong and in front of people and everybody pretending. I sort of wish they don't—though I want to, terribly. When her mother took her upstairs that night—she wasn't the same Helen. She looked at me as if she was afraid of me. And no matter what they do for us now, they can't fix that.

The Threatening Three

WILLIAM CAMPBELL GAULT

If you like good old-fashioned stories about good old-fashioned kids, you'll love "The Threatening Three"—a trio of snoopy junior crimefighters who decide to ferret out the truth about political chicanery in their small midwestern town. Their methods and misadventures, reminiscent of those of the Carstairs kids in Craig Rice's Home Sweet Homicide, are bound to produce a smile or two. William Campbell Gault has been entertaining readers of all ages for close to fifty years, ever since his first professional sale to a pulp magazine in 1936. More than half of his sixty novels are juveniles with sports backgrounds; the rest are adult mysteries. He has also published upwards of three hundred short stories. His first adult novel, Don't Cry For Me, was awarded the Mystery Writers of America Edgar as the Best First Mystery of 1951; one of his most recent books, The Cana Diversion, received the Private Eye Writers of America Shamus as the Best Paperback Original of 1982.

I WAS listening to the Secret Six when Pop came home that day. He came into the living room and said, "Where's your mother, Joe?"

"She's next door talking to Mrs. Marcus," I told him. "What's the matter, Pop?"

He frowned at me. "What do you mean—what's the matter?"

"You never come home at this time and you look like something's the matter," I said.

He started to say something and then Mom came in the front door and into the living room. "You're home early, Don," she said. "Is something wrong?"

"Plenty," he said, and looked at me. Then he looked at my mother. "Let's go out to the kitchen."

They went out to the kitchen and I knew they were going to talk about something they didn't want me to hear. But I wasn't even interested. Because Sturtevant Strong, who is head of the Secret Six, had just discovered the mysterious power by which Gentleman Jack Jethroe had killed seven fear-crazed victims in his fiendish plan to gain control of Atom, Incorporated. It was a new kind of radar Gentleman Jack had used, a killing, distance-defying horror which was the product of the brilliant but twisted brain of Gentleman Jack.

Anyway, that's what Sturtevant Strong said when he explained it to the FBI. I wasn't sure just how it worked, but the FBI understood, all right. They've got all kinds of different experts and they understand everything. Smart as they are, though, they sure seem to need a lot of help from Sturtevant Strong and his five able assistants.

Me and Sam Marcus and Nick Anzotti all have the Secret Six badge, and compass, and six-in-one jackknife and secret code. It took a lot of box tops to get all that stuff.

Now the announcer was saying, "And here, for the benefit of all our young allies around this great country, is the president of the Junior Secret Six clubs, the stalwart son of Sturtevant Strong—Sturdian Strong, whose unusual name is derived from the fact that he never fails to enjoy the—"

From the doorway Pop said, "Will you turn that off now, Joe? I've something to tell you."

He came over to sit in the chair across from mine. He just sat there at first, studying me, and then he said, "I'm going to be out of town for a little while, Joe. I don't want you to give your mother any trouble while I'm gone."

"I won't," I promised. "But Pop, remember about the eighteenth?"

"I remember," he said. "That's the opening game."

"Do you think you—*might* be back in time?"

"I can't be sure," he said.

"You'll try, though, won't you?"

"I'll try," he said. "But don't bank on it, Joe. And remember, now, help your mother all you can, won't you?"

"Sure," I told him. "Don't worry, Pop."

He gave me that funny grin again. "I'll try not to."

Then Mom called him from upstairs and he went up the steps.

I had the funniest feeling that something was wrong, that there was trouble coming up, and Pop was running away from it.

I don't know why I should think that, because Pop's a reporter and he's gone out of town before.

When he came downstairs again, Mom was with him. Pop had a suitcase in his hand and Mom looked like she'd been crying. He kissed her and winked at me, and we both stood watching him go down the steps.

"Sometimes," she said, "I think your dad is too smart for his own good, Joey."

That's what was the matter with Gentleman Jack Jethroe, too. I said, "Pop never acts smart. He never shows off."

"No, he doesn't. But he meddles in things. He's not satisfied with the *status quo*."

"What's that?"

"That means the state in which anything is." She shook her head. "I mean, things as they are. He wants to change things."

"Why is he leaving us now, Mom?" I asked. "There's something wrong, isn't there?"

She didn't answer me right away. She just looked at me, then she reached over to muss my hair. "Don't bother your head about it," she said. "It's grown-up monkeyshines."

"If Pop's in trouble I want to help," I said. "I can call out the Threatening Three."

She looked scared but I knew she was just kidding me. "What a horrible name!" she said.

"It's just me and Sam Marcus and Nick Anzotti," I explained. "We couldn't get six fellows who wanted to join a Junior Secret Six so we made up that name. I'm the chief."

She was smiling now, and you couldn't tell she'd been crying before. "And how did you get to be the chief?"

"Well," I said, "I can beat Nick at wrestling but he can beat me at boxing, and both of us can beat Sam at wrestling and boxing. So it had to be between me and Nick."

"A natural leader of men," Mom said. "I always knew it, Joe. Do you think you could leave the executive mansion long enough to get me a loaf of bread?"

I met Sam on the way over to get the bread. "Your dad taking a trip?" he asked me.

I nodded.

"My dad says he's the best reporter in town," Sam went on. "My dad says we'll have honest government in this town yet if your dad keeps working at it." Sam didn't say anything for a second. Then he went on, "He said he can't understand why that City Hall crowd hasn't shut him up by this time."

I didn't say anything but I felt good.

"What's the City Hall crowd?" Sam asked.

"I'm not sure," I said, "but I'll bet they're a gang of crooks."

"Must be," Sam said. "Like Gentleman Jack's gang, huh?"

"Sure," I said. And then I looked around to see if any spies were listening. "Meeting tonight," I said. "Call Nick. We ought to investigate that City Hall crowd."

"We could go down there Saturday," Sam said. "I could make up some bombs."

Sam's our chemist and can make stink bombs. He's got a Dandy Deluxe Chemistry Set. Sam's smart but kind of small.

"All right," I agreed. "And we'd better take our Pulverizers." Our Pulverizers are just water guns, but we add ammonia.

Sam left me at the store and went over to tell Nick about the meeting tonight. When I came back home again Mom was already setting the table, and I helped her.

She said, "If anybody should ask you where your dad is, you don't know, do you, Joey?"

"No, I don't," I said. "Aren't you going to tell me, Mom?" She shook her head. "If you don't know, you can't let it slip."

"Is he running away from that City Hall crowd?" I asked her.

She stopped what she was doing and just stared at me. "What do you know about the City Hall crowd, Joe Wells?"

"Oh, a fellow hears things around," I said.

"Well," she told me, "one thing you'll never hear around is that your dad runs from anybody or anything. Just remember that, chief."

"Sure," I said. "I'll bet he really went to get help from the FBI, didn't he?"

She started to laugh then. "Joey, Joey . . ." she said. Then she shook her head. "It was a bad day for this household when Sturtevant Strong entered it."

I didn't argue with her because it's hard to make grownups understand about the Secret Six. It's hard to make them understand about a lot of important things.

Nick and Sam came over just as I was finishing drying the dishes.

"We'll go upstairs to my room," I said, "if that's all right, Mom."

She smiled at me. "There's some soda water in the refrigerator, if you boys want any."

"Maybe later," I said. "We've got some things to talk about first."

What we talked about mostly was the City Hall crowd and whether we should go down there or not. Sam said, "My dad says that anybody who pays taxes or not has a right to know what's going on at the city hall."

Nick said, "My dad says the further he can get from the city hall, the better off he'll be. There sure must be something funny going on down there."

"Then we ought to go down there Saturday," I decided. "Should we take a vote?"

We took a vote and it was three to nothing for going down on Saturday. We decided we wouldn't need any bombs but we would use some Formula X in our Pulverizers. We would add water to it so it wouldn't be too strong.

Then we went down and had some soda water and cookies Mom had ready for us in the kitchen.

"Did you arrive at any momentous decisions?" she asked us.

"I'm not allowed to say," I answered, and the others nodded.

Sam and I met Nick at Ellsworth and Vine on Saturday morning, and we took a street car downtown from there. We all had our Pulverizers and we had them loaded. We sat together in the back of the car, not saying much so as not to reveal our plans.

We got off on Water Street and walked the rest of the way. Before we went in, through the Water Street entrance, Nick said, "Let's remember the code words now in case we have trouble. Let's be ready all the time."

He put his hand in his pocket where the Pulverizer was. Sam and I kept our right hands in our pockets, too.

I'm supposed to be the leader but Nick led the way into the city hall. The first floor is about three stories high, with balconies running around it where the second and third floors would be in a regular building. The *Register of Deeds*, it said over one door, and *License Bureau* over another, and *Comptroller*, but we couldn't see any signs that read *City Hall Crowd*.

Sam said, "Let's go over to the dime store and see if they've got any cheap flashlights. We can't do anything here."

"Okay," I said but Nick shook his head.

"I'm going to ask somebody," he said. "You guys are chicken."

Right next to the *Register of Deeds* sign there was another one—*Information*. Nick went in.

Sam looked at me and I looked at Sam, and then we followed him. There was a man sitting behind a counter in there, and a couple of ladies working typewriters.

Nick said to the man, "Could you tell me where I could find the City Hall crowd?"

The man was big and fat and he didn't answer right away. The two ladies looked at each other and smiled. Finally the man said, "What's that, son?" He got up and came over to the counter.

Nick said, "We're looking for the City Hall crowd. We thought they had a room down here somewhere."

The ladies were giggling now but the man wasn't even smiling. "What gave you that idea, boy?"

Nick didn't say anything for a second, but Sam said, "My dad says the City Hall crowd is trying to shut up Joe's pa so we came down here to investigate them."

The man looked at Sam. "He did, eh? And who's your dad?"

"Sidney Marcus," Sam said proudly.

The man just nodded. "And who's Joe?"

"I am," I said. "I'm Joe Wells, and my dad's a reporter."

The ladies weren't laughing any more and the fat man was frowning.

"I see," he said, and looked at Nick. "And how about you, junior? What's your name?"

"Sturdian Strong," Nick said, and the ladies laughed.

The fat man got red in the face. "Don't be smart, brown eyes," he said. "When I ask you a question I want a straight answer."

"We're not running the information desk," Nick said.

This fat man got a mean look in his eyes, and he said, "Listen, you little greaseball—" And that's as far as he got.

Because Nick had his Pulverizer out in a jiffy and he shot a stream of Formula X right at the man's necktie. The man started to cough as we ran out of the office.

I was going lickety-split for the River Street doorway when the fat man came out of his office yelling, "Stop those hoodlums!"

Sam passed me up while I was still about fifteen feet from the doorway, and Nick was right behind me. A broad, tall man in a light suit was standing near the doorway, a briefcase in his hand.

He jumped toward the door to block us off, and Sam let go with his Pulverizer. The man turned his head to one side as he twisted away from the doorway. We all made it through the door, Sam in the lead.

He kept gaining on us as we chased up River Street and cut into an alley. Halfway through, another alley crossed this one and we took that. Sam waited for us there on First Street, where this second alley came out.

He looked as scared as I felt. But Nick didn't look scared; he just looked mad.

Sam said, "Golly, and he knows our names, too. Will my dad ever give me blazes!"

"He knows my name, too," I said.

"He doesn't know mine," Nick said.

We were walking down First Street now, toward the car line.

"I'm going over to my pa's office," Nick said.

"I'm going home," Sam said. "If I'm going to catch it, I might as well get it right away."

"Me, too," I said. "See you later, Nick. I'll phone you tonight. Okay?"

Nick just nodded, not looking at either of us.

On the street car Sam said, "You haven't anything to worry about. You didn't shoot your Pulverizer."

"It was my idea, though," I said. "The whole thing was my

idea. Don't forget, one for all and all for one." That's our motto.

"I wonder what Nick's going to do," Sam said.

"He'll probably tell his dad about it," I said. "He won't mention our names, though, not Nick."

"Not Nick," Sam agreed. "His dad's a sort of promoter, isn't he?"

I nodded. "He used to be a fighter and now he bought the Vikings." The Vikings are a professional football team.

We didn't say any more all the way home.

Nobody was home when I got there. There was a note from Mom, which read:

> *Am meeting your dad downtown.*
> *Will be home around lunchtime.*
>   Mother

I should have been glad to know Pop was home again, but I knew that if the cops came out to tell him about what happened, he'd be a lot tougher on me than Mom would.

I was standing in the living room, looking out of the front window, when I saw the policeman walk up the steps of the Marcus house next door. There was a squad car across the street and another cop was getting out now and looking over this way.

I went to the kitchen. I could hear my heart beating and I felt winded, like I'd been running.

The front doorbell rang.

It sounded awful loud because the house was so quiet. I didn't move. I was as scared as I'd ever been in my life. I knew I'd never be able to go to the door while that policeman stood out there.

It rang about three more times before it stopped. And long after the ringing had stopped I stayed out in the kitchen, not moving, breathing quietly.

I was still standing there when Mom and Pop came home.

I went out into the hallway, and Mom said, "Well, here you are."

Pop said, "What's the matter next door, Joe?"

"I guess Sam's in trouble," I said. Then I took a big gulp of air. "I guess I am, too, Pop."

I was shaking now. If I was younger, I'd have been crying. Pop and Mom were just staring at me.

"Serious trouble, Joe?" Pop asked.

I didn't tell them about Nick being along, then, but I told them all the rest. Some of the trouble I tell Pop he just laughs at. He didn't laugh this time.

He looked at Mom and then out at the squad car. He said, "I'm going next door. You two stay here."

When he'd left, Mom said, "This came at a bad time, Joey. Your dad can't afford any trouble with the law right now."

She didn't have to say any more and she didn't. She couldn't make me feel any worse than I did, no matter what she said.

I was in the kitchen when Pop came back. He and Mom went into the living room. I heard him say, "One of the men they squirted was Ritter. Wouldn't you know it?"

"The District Attorney?" Mom asked.

"That's right. He and the Registrar of Deeds. They'll make a case, all right, and the *Courier* will blow it into a major scandal. Delinquent youth . . . The fact that I'm a *Star* reporter will be mentioned. And they'll take it in front of Judge Arliss. He's in with them. Those kids could be sent to a home, you know that?"

"No?" Mom said. "Don, you're not serious?"

"I wonder who that other kid was," Pop said.

"I think I know," Mom said. "That Anzotti boy."

"Nick Anzotti's son?"

"That's right."

"Well. I'll be . . ." Pop said, and no more.

Then they came out to the kitchen. Pop said, "You look sick, Joey."

"I'm all right," I said. "I'm sorry, Pop, about—what happened. That—" And then I didn't know what to say.

He put his fist up against my jaw and grinned at me. "It's okay. You're a pretty good boy, generally. This is the first time you've ever had any trouble with the law. It's going to be the last, isn't it?''

"That's a promise," I said.

He studied me for a few seconds. "This young Anzotti have much of a temper, Joe?''

I nodded.

"His father's son," Pop said, and looked at Mom.

"Maybe you should phone him," Mom said. "You can use all the allies you can get, Don."

Pop sort of grinned. "I think I will. I think that's a good idea, honey.''

He went out into the hall to phone and Mom said, "I seem to be out of butter, Joe. See how fast you can bring back a pound and I'll start making lunch."

When I came back from the store, Mom had lunch almost ready. Pop was talking on the telephone, saying, "There's a chance, chief, that Nick will have something to tell me about that Butler girl. He hinted that he might have something along that line.''

I felt kind of strange. Here I'd expected all the trouble we'd caused would turn everything topsy-turvy at home, and they were so excited with their own troubles I didn't even get bawled out.

When Pop came in to eat I asked him, "Who's the Butler girl, Pop?''

He sighed and looked at Mom. Then he said, "Joe, you have exceptional hearing. Sally Butler is a very attractive women who was formerly married to our district attorney. She knows all about that City Hall crowd you and your stalwart crew went down to battle with. I heard she was out of town, and that's where I've been, out of town, looking for her. Now, Nick Anzotti as much as told me he knows where she is.''

"I see," I said. "So maybe it was all for the best, after all, huh, Pop?''

"I'm not ready to admit that," he said. "Do you know who that fat man in the Registrar of Deeds office was?''

"The Registrar of Deeds," I said.

"Officially," Pop said. "But he got the job through his services to the organization. He's been indicted for murder twice but never convicted. That's the kind of man you went after with water pistols."

"What does *indicted* mean, Pop?"

"It means *charged*. It means that certain people of authority thought he had committed the crime and they had papers drawn up, making the charge. But he was cleared both times. Sally Butler, or Sally Butler Ritter, I should say, knows about both of those murders, I feel sure. That's why I want to see her. Now you know everything I do, almost."

Mom said, "Do you think it's wise, Don, telling him all those horrible things?"

"I think so," Pop said. "I don't think the truth can hurt anyone excepting those who should be hurt." Pop looked all wound up.

"How does Mr. Anzotti know Sally Butler Ritter?" I asked.

"Mr. Anzotti knows about everybody in town," Pop says. "Sally Butler used to be a singer in a night club, and Mr. Anzotti, before his marriage, knew lots of singers and entertainers. Next question?"

"I can't think of any right now," I said.

"Then we can eat," Mom said and looked sadly at both of us. "Two Don Quixotes in one family." She shook her head.

Pop went down to the paper right after we ate, and Mom upstairs to clean. I was sitting in the living room reading Ned Stanton's Secret Cave, when the phone rang.

It was Nick. "Got to see you right away," he said. "Sam, too. Meet you at the Kelsey Street Library."

The way Nick had looked when I left him, I had a hunch meeting him might just get us into more trouble. But if it was important, I had to go, and he sounded like it was important.

I told Mom, "I'm going down to the library," and then went out to see if Sam was around.

He was looking out the front window so I went up on his

porch and gave him the sign for an important meeting. He came out onto the porch and I told him about Nick's call.

"Gosh," Sam said, "I don't know." He looked back at the door behind him.

"It's just down to the library," I said. "Nick's going to meet us there."

"I'll ask," Sam said. "Wait here."

In a couple of minutes he came out again. "I've got to be back in an hour," he said. "Dad's downtown, talking to the district attorney now."

Nick was waiting for us when we got to the Kelsey Street Library. He was looking just the way he'd been looking when we left him. He motioned us outside.

He said to me, "I know where that lady is your pa's looking for. That Sally Butler."

"Let's go down and tell my pop," I said.

Nick shook his head. "My pa says he isn't ready to tell anybody anything yet. I was with him when he went to see her. She won't talk, he says. She's plenty sour on Ritter now but she won't talk. But I was out in the car, and I put the address down."

"What can we do?" I said.

"Maybe she'll talk to us. My pa says she knows plenty about Ritter and about Tullgren."

"Who's Tullgren?" Sam asked.

"That fat guy, that mean guy," Nick answered. Nick looked kind of mean himself when he said that.

Sam said, "I don't think we ought to get mixed up in this. This is for our folks."

"We are mixed up in it," Nick said. "We started it. I'll bet that Sally Butler would talk to us." He looked at me questioningly.

Maybe I can help Pop, I thought. *I owe him some help after the trouble I caused him this morning.*

"We can try," I said.

Sam shrugged then. "You're the chief," he said.

But I wasn't, not really. Nick was taking over, I knew. Nick was wound up like my pop gets, only in a different way. Nick was burning. Nick wasn't ever going to forget that fat man.

He had the address down on a slip of paper. It was only about three blocks from the library and we walked over.

It was a small house with a picket fence in front, a low, white house. We stopped at the gate for a second. Sam said, "Maybe she isn't home."

That's what I was hoping.

But Nick pushed the gate open. "We'll know after we ring," he said.

He led the way up the walk. He pushed the bell button. The door seemed to open right away and this lady stood there.

She was about as old as Mom, and Mom's thirty. She was almost as pretty as Mom, and she had a smile that made me feel right at home.

Nobody said anything and finally she said, "Well, you must have had something to say or you wouldn't have rung my bell."

"Are you Mrs. Sally Ritter?" Nick asked.

"I'm not a Mrs., I'm a Miss," she answered. "Why do you want to know my name?"

"Because if you're who we think you are, we want to help you," I told her. "We're the Threatening Three and we're here on official business."

She smiled, then frowned and shook her head. "You don't look very threatening to me."

"We don't threaten good people, only bad people," I explained. "We think you're good people."

She stared at us, not smiling now. "Come in," she said. "I—don't like to stand in open doorways."

We went in, through a hall and into a small, bright living room.

Nick said, "We wanted to ask you about Mr. Tullgren."

She seemed to freeze right where she was standing. Her face got pale and she sat down quickly in a chair near the door. Her voice was hardly louder than a whisper.

"What—are you boys talking about?"

"We're investigating the City Hall crowd," Nick said. "When my pa was over here before, I sat out in front in the car. You wouldn't talk to my pa, but I thought you would tell us."

She said, "You're Nick Anzotti's boy?"

Nick nodded, "Nick, Junior. And that's Joe Wells, the reporter's son. I guess his pa has been looking for you."

"I guess he has," she said, and looked at me. Then she asked Sam, "And who are you?"

"Sam Marcus," he said. "My father is a lawyer."

She smiled, but there wasn't any happiness in it. "The Threatening Three . . ." she said. "Well, you very nearly were, at that." She got up again.

"You mean," Nick said, "you're not going to tell us anything?"

She turned to face him. "That's what I mean. Nor your fathers, either. If this was their idea it was a bad one."

"It wasn't their idea." I said. "It was our idea, ma'am. And I think you're making a mistake."

"Oh," she said. "In what way, young man?"

"All citizens should fight evil," I said. "All citizens should be interested in good government."

She looked like she was going to smile again but she didn't. "And where did you read that?" she asked me.

"I didn't read it," I said. "I heard it over the radio."

"A political speech? You listen to political speeches?"

"No, ma'am. It was Sturtevant that said it."

"I've never heard of him," she said. "And I wouldn't want to tarnish your dreams, young Mr. Wells, but don't believe everything you hear on the radio, will you?"

"I never listen to the ads," I said, "especially the singing ones."

"That's a good start," she said.

The doorbell rang. Again she seemed to freeze, and then she asked quietly, "Does anybody know you boys are here? Could that be one of your parents?"

We all shook our heads.

"Don't move," she said, and started for the door. Then she seemed to change her mind. "Maybe you'd better go back into the kitchen."

We went out to the kitchen and closed the door as the bell rang again.

We could hear her open the front door and we could hear her say, "Well, Art, this is a surprise!"

"A *pleasant* surprise, Sally?" a man's voice said.

"I wouldn't make that broad a statement," she answered. "What's on your mind, Art?"

I knew I should recognize the voice but I couldn't quite. Not until Nick said, "Tullgren—the fat man."

I nodded, and so did Sam.

"You're on my mind," he answered.

"That's flattering," she said. "Though I never would have suspected it." She was trying to sound unworried but she wasn't making it.

"Maybe it's not the way you think," his heavy voice went on. "I hear the *Star's* hot-shot crime man's been looking for you."

"I hear so, too," she said, "but I've nothing to tell him, Art." Her voice was higher now. "Not a thing. You don't have to worry about anything like that."

"But I do worry, Sally. I hear Nick Anzotti was here to see you today, and I learned Nick's on the warpath because of what I called his kid. I've been doing nothing but worry all day, Sally."

There was a silence, then, one awful silence.

Nick whispered to Sam, "Call the police. Or your pa. Call somebody, quick. I'm going to sneak through the hall and lock that front door." Nick's eyes were bright, and his face was tight and thin-looking.

He started quietly down the hall after he locked the back door.

He never did get to the front door. From the living room came a terrible scream, not loud, muffled, but it seemed even worse than if it had been loud. I heard a loud thump from there.

Then Nick was shouting from the front hall. "Call the cops!"

I opened the door to the living room as Sam picked up the phone in the back hall.

Miss Sally Butler was lying on the floor in the living room, and there was blood all over her. I started to get weak and sick. From the front hall, I could hear Nick hollering for help.

I was scared but Nick was my friend.

The only thing I could see was a little end table, and I took that with me through the living room and toward the front hall.

Nick was up against the corner in there. About five feet from him the big man stood, his back to me. He had a knife in his hand and he was just staring at Nick, the way it seemed to me.

Then he started to walk toward Nick.

My knees were weak, but I ran as well as I could. I was about three feet from him when I threw the end table.

It caught him on the head and shoulders, and he turned as it crashed to the floor.

I couldn't move for a second. I thought I was going to faint. I saw Nick scrambling for the end table, but the big man heard him and he turned back.

Then a big mixing bowl came sailing down the hall and smashed into the man's side. That was Sam helping out.

The bowl threw the man off balance for a second and I saw Nick kick at the man's face. I picked up a lamp from a table and got as close as I could.

As the man reached for Nick's foot, I let him have the lamp right on the head. It was pottery and it smashed all to pieces, and he went all the way down.

Sam came running along the hall, carrying a rolling pin, as the man started to get up.

Sam swung that rolling pin with all his might, and it made an awful noise as it hit the man's skull.

Outside we could hear the sirens, now. Sam said, "I'm going to call my dad's office. I don't want to see any cops unless my dad's around."

Nick was standing over the fat man, looking down. Nick wasn't saying a word. He didn't even seem to be breathing.

Well, Miss Sally Butler didn't die. She testified against the City Hall crowd, and all but one of them went to jail, and that one wasn't important at all. But I guess she was still scared, because she left town right after the trial. She didn't have to do that; the Threatening Three would have protected her from the one guy that was left.

Anyhow, we got our names in the paper and on the radio, and Pop says we deserve it because we gave this town good government at last. He and Nick's dad and Sam's dad are in the club now, and we can really call it the Secret Six.

But they won't listen to the radio with us. They say that's more than any son has a right to expect.

The End of the Party

GRAHAM GREENE

The strange symbiosis often present between twins, and the pain which a rupture of that partnership can bring, is the theme of this powerful story by acclaimed novelist Graham Greene. Born in England in 1904, Greene has created a diverse body of literary work, ranging from thrillers such as Orient Express *(1932) and* Our Man in Havana *(1958), to deeply introspective novels such as* The Power and the Glory *(1940) and* The Comedians *(1965). His* The End of the Affair, *which delves into the conflict between traditional religious belief and secular desire, was awarded the Catholic Literary Award for 1951. No matter what literary form it takes, Greene's work is noted for its fine characterization and masterful craftsmanship.*

PETER Morton woke with a start to face the first light. Through the window he could see a bare bough dropping across a frame of silver. Rain tapped against the glass. It was January the fifth.

He looked across a table, on which a night-light had guttered into a pool of water, at the other bed. Francis Morton was still asleep, and Peter lay down again with his eyes on his brother. It amused him to imagine that it was himself whom he watched, the same hair, the same eyes, the same lips and line of cheek. But the thought soon palled, and the mind went back to the fact which lent the day importance. It was the fifth of January. He could hardly believe that a year had passed since Mrs. Henne-Falcon had given her last children's party.

Francis turned suddenly upon his back and threw an arm across his face, blocking his mouth. Peter's heart began to beat fast, not with pleasure now but with uneasiness. He sat up and called across the table, "Wake up." Francis's shoulders shook and he waved a clenched fist in the air, but his eyes remained closed. To Peter Morton the whole room seemed suddenly to darken, and he had the impression of a great bird swooping. He cried again, "Wake up," and once more there was silver light and the touch of rain on the windows.

Francis rubbed his eyes. "Did you call out?" he asked.

"You are having a bad dream," Peter said with confidence. Already experience had taught him how far their minds reflected each other. But he was the elder, by a matter of minutes, and that brief extra interval of light, while his brother still struggled in pain and darkness, had given him self-reliance and an instinct of protection toward the other who was afraid of so many things.

"I dreamed that I was dead," Francis said.

"What was it like?" Peter asked with curiosity.

"I can't remember," Francis said, and his eyes turned with

relief to the silver of day, as he allowed the fragmentary memories to fade.

"You dreamed of a big bird."

"Did I?" Francis accepted his brother's knowledge without question, and for a little the two lay silent in bed facing each other, the same green eyes, the same nose tilting at the tip, the same firm lips parted, and the same premature modeling of the chin. The fifth of January, Peter thought again, his mind drifting idly from the image of cakes to the prizes which might be won. Egg-and-spoon races, spearing apples in basins of water, blindman's buff.

"I don't want to go," Francis said suddenly. "I suppose Joyce will be there . . . Mabel Warren." Hateful to him, the thought of a party shared with those two. They were older than he. Joyce was eleven and Mabel Warren thirteen. Their long pigtails swung superciliously to a masculine stride. Their sex humiliated him, as they watched him fumble with his egg, from under lowered scornful lids. And last year . . . he turned his face away from Peter, his cheeks scarlet.

"What's the matter?" Peter asked.

"Oh, nothing. I don't think I'm well. I've got a cold. I oughtn't to go to the party."

Peter was puzzled. "But, Francis, is it a bad cold?"

"It will be a bad cold if I go to the party. Perhaps I shall die."

"Then you mustn't go," Peter said with decision, prepared to solve all difficulties with one plain sentence, and Francis let his nerves relax in a delicious relief, ready to leave everything to Peter. But though he was grateful he did not turn his face towards his brother. His cheeks still bore the badge of a shameful memory, of the game of hide-and-seek last year in the darkened house, and of how he had screamed when Mabel Warren put her hand suddenly upon his arm. He had not heard her coming. Girls were like that. Their shoes never squeaked. No boards whined under their tread. They slunk like cats on padded claws. When the nurse came in with hot water Francis lay tranquil, leaving everything to Peter. Peter said, "Nurse, Francis has got a cold."

The tall starched woman laid the towels across the cans and said, without turning, "The washing won't be back till tomorrow. You must lend him some of your handkerchiefs."

"But, Nurse," Peter asked, "hadn't he better stay in bed?"

"We'll take him for a good walk this morning," the nurse said. "Wind'll blow away the germs. Get up now, both of you," and she closed the door behind her.

"I'm sorry," Peter said, and then, worried at the sight of a face creased again by misery and foreboding, "Why don't you just stay in bed? I'll tell mother you felt too ill to get up." But such a rebellion against destiny was not in Francis's power. Besides, if he stayed in bed they would come up and tap his chest and put a thermometer in his mouth and look at his tongue, and they would discover that he was malingering. It was true that he felt ill, a sick empty sensation in his stomach and a rapidly beating heart, but he knew that the cause was only fear, fear of the party, fear of being made to hide by himself in the dark, uncompanioned by Peter and with no night-light to make a blessed breach.

"No, I'll get up," he said, and then with sudden desperation, "But I won't go to Mrs. Henne-Falcon's party. I swear on the Bible I won't." Now surely all would be well, he thought. God would not allow him to break so solemn an oath. He would show him a way. There was all the morning before him and all the afternoon until four o'clock. No need to worry now when the grass was still crisp with the early frost. Anything might happen. He might cut himself or break his leg or really catch a bad cold. God would manage somehow.

He had such confidence in God that when at breakfast his mother said, "I hear you have a cold, Francis," he made light of it. "We should have heard more about it," his mother said with irony, "if there was not a party this evening," and Francis smiled uneasily, amazed and daunted by her ignorance of him. His happiness would have lasted longer if, out for a walk that morning, he had not met Joyce. He was alone with his nurse, for

Peter had leave to finish a rabbit-hutch in the woodshed. If Peter had been there he would have cared less; the nurse was Peter's nurse also, but now it was as though she were employed only for his sake, because he could not be trusted to go for a walk alone. Joyce was only two years older and she was by herself.

She came striding towards them, pigtails flapping. She glanced scornfully at Francis and spoke with ostentation to the nurse. "Hello, Nurse. Are you bringing Francis to the party this evening? Mabel and I are coming." And she was off again down the street in the direction of Mabel Warren's home, consciously alone and self-sufficient in the long empty road. "Such a nice girl," the nurse said. But Francis was silent, feeling again the jump-jump of his heart, realizing how soon the hour of the party would arrive. God had done nothing for him, and the minutes flew.

They flew too quickly to plan any evasion, or even to prepare his heart for the coming ordeal. Panic nearly overcame him when, all unready, he found himself standing on the doorstep, with coat-collar turned up against a cold wind, and the nurse's electric torch making a short luminous trail through the darkness. Behind him were the lights of the hall and the sound of a servant laying the table for dinner, which his mother and father would eat alone. He was nearly overcome by a desire to run back into the house and call out to his mother that he would not go to the party, that he dared not go. They could not make him go. He could almost hear himself saying those final words, breaking down for ever, as he knew instinctively, the barrier of ignorance that saved his mind from his parents' knowledge. "I'm afraid of going. I won't go. I daren't go. They'll make me hide in the dark, and I'm afraid of the dark. I'll scream and scream and scream." He could see the expression of amazement on his mother's face, and then the cold confidence of a grown-up's retort. "Don't be silly. You must go. We've accepted Mrs. Henne-Falcon's invitation."

But they couldn't make him go; hesitating on the doorstep while the nurse's feet crunched across the frost-covered grass to the gate, he knew that. He would answer, "You can say I'm ill. I won't go. I'm afraid of the dark." And his mother, "Don't be silly. You know there's nothing to be afraid of in the dark." But he knew the falsity of that reasoning; he knew how they taught also that there was nothing to fear in death, and how fearfully they avoided the idea of it. But they couldn't make him go to the party. "I'll scream. I'll scream."

"Francis, come along." He heard the nurse's voice across the dimly phosphorescent lawn and saw the small yellow circle of her torch wheel from tree to shrub and back to tree again. "I'm coming," he called with despair, leaving the lighted doorway of the house; he couldn't bring himself to lay bare his last secrets and end reserve between his mother and himself, for there was still in the last resort a further appeal possible to Mrs. Henne-Falcon. He comforted himself with that, as he advanced steadily across the hall, very small, towards her enormous bulk. His heart beat unevenly, but he had control now over his voice, as he said with meticulous accent, "Good evening, Mrs. Henne-Falcon. It was very good of you to ask me to your party." With his strained face lifted towards the curve of her breasts, and his polite set speech, he was like an old withered man. For Francis mixed very little with other children. As a twin he was in many ways an only child. To address Peter was to speak to his own image in a mirror, an image a little altered by a flaw in the glass, so as to throw back less a likeness of what he was than of what he wished to be, what he would be without his unreasoning fear of darkness, footsteps of strangers, the flight of bats in dusk-filled gardens.

"Sweet child," said Mrs. Henne-Falcon absent-mindedly, before, with a wave of her arms, as though the children were a flock of chickens, she whirled them into her set programme of entertainments: egg-and-spoon races, three-legged races, the spearing of apples, games which held for Francis nothing worse than humiliation. And in the frequent intervals when nothing was required of him and he could stand alone in corners as far removed as possible from Mabel Warren's scornful gaze, he was

able to plan how he might avoid the approaching terror of the
dark. He knew there was nothing to fear until after tea, and not
until he was sitting down in a pool of yellow radiance cast by the
ten candles on Colin Henne-Falcon's birthday cake did he become fully conscious of the imminence of what he feared.
Through the confusion of his brain, now assailed suddenly by a
dozen contradictory plans, he heard Joyce's high voice down the
table. "After tea we are going to play hide-and-seek in the dark."

"Oh, no," Peter said, watching Francis's troubled face with
pity and an imperfect understanding, "don't let's. We play that
every year."

"But it's on the programme," cried Mabel Warren. "I saw it
myself. I looked over Mrs. Henne-Falcon's shoulder. Five
o'clock, tea. A quarter to six to half-past, hide-and-seek in the
dark. It's all written down in the programme."

Peter did not argue, for if hide-and-seek had been inserted in
Mrs. Henne-Falcon's programme, nothing which he could say
could avert it. He asked for another piece of birthday cake and
sipped his tea slowly. Perhaps it might be possible to delay the
game for a quarter of an hour, allow Francis at least a few extra
minutes to form a plan, but even in that Peter failed, for children
were already leaving the table in twos and threes. It was his third
failure, and again, the reflection of an image in another's mind,
he saw a great bird darken his brother's face with its wings. But
he upbraided himself silently for his folly, and finished his cake
encouraged by the memory of that adult refrain, "There's nothing to fear in the dark." The last to leave the table, the brothers
came together to the hall to meet the mustering and impatient
eyes of Mrs. Henne-Falcon.

"And now," she said, "we will play hide-and-seek in the
dark."

Peter watched his brother and saw, as he had expected, the
lips tighten. Francis, he knew, had feared this moment from the
beginning of the party, had tried to meet it with courage and had
abandoned the attempt. He must have prayed desperately for
cunning to evade the game, which was now welcomed with

cries of excitement by all the other children. "Oh, do let's." "We must pick sides." "Is any of the house out of bounds?" Where shall home be?"

"I think," said Francis Morton, approaching Mrs. Henne-Falcon, his eyes unwaveringly on her exuberant breasts, "it will be no use my playing. My nurse will be calling for me very soon."

"Oh, but your nurse can wait, Francis," said Mrs. Henne-Falcon absent-mindedly, while she clapped her hands together to summon to her side a few children who were already straying up the wide staircase to upper floors. "Your mother will never mind."

That had been the limit of Francis's cunning. He had refused to believe that so well prepared an excuse could fail. All that he could say now, still in the precise tone which other children hated, thinking it a symbol of conceit, was, "I think I had better not play." He stood motionless, retaining, though afraid, unmoved features. But the knowledge of his terror, or the reflection of the terror itself, reached his brother's brain. For the moment, Peter Morton could have cried aloud with the fear of bright lights going out, leaving him alone in an island of dark surrounded by the gentle lapping of strange footsteps. Then he remembered that the fear was not his own, but his brother's. He said impulsively to Mrs. Henne-Falcon, "Please. I don't think Francis should play. The dark makes him jump so." They were the wrong words. Six children began to sing, "Cowardly, cowardly custard," turning torturing faces with the vacancy of wide sunflowers towards Francis Morton.

Without looking at his brother, Francis said, "Of course I will play. I am not afraid. I only thought . . ." But he was already forgotten by his human tormentors and was able in loneliness to contemplate the approach of the spiritual, the more unbounded, torture. The children scrambled round Mrs. Henne-Falcon, their shrill voices pecking at her with questions and suggestions. "Yes, anywhere in the house. We will turn out all the lights. Yes, you can hide in the cupboards. You must stay hidden as long as you can. There will be no home."

Peter, too, stood apart, ashamed of the clumsy manner in which he had tried to help his brother. Now he could feel, creeping in at the corners of his brain, all Francis's resentment of his championing. Several children ran upstairs, and the lights on the top floor went out. Then darkness came down like the wings of a bat and settled on the landing. Others began to put out the lights at the edge of the hall, till the children were all gathered in the central radiance of the chandelier, while the bats squatted round on hooded wings and waited for that, too, to be extinguished.

"You and Francis are on the hiding side," a tall girl said, and then the light was gone, and the carpet wavered under his feet with the sibilance of footfalls, like small cold draughts, creeping away into corners.

"Where's Francis?" he wondered. "If I join him he'll be less frightened of all these sounds." "These sounds" were the casing of silence. The squeak of a loose board, the cautious closing of a cupboard door, the whine of a finger drawn along polished wood.

Peter stood in the center of the dark deserted floor, not listening but waiting for the idea of his brother's whereabouts to enter his brain. But Francis crouched with fingers on this ears, eyes uselessly closed, mind numbed against impressions, and only a sense of strain could cross the gap of dark. Then a voice called "Coming," and as though his brother's self-possession had been shattered by the sudden cry, Peter Morton jumped with fear. But it was not his own fear. What in his brother was a burning panic, admitting no ideas except those which added to the flame, was in him an altruistic emotion that left the reason unimpaired. "Where, if I were Francis, should I hide?" Such, roughly, was his thought. And because he was, if not Francis himself, at least a mirror to him, the answer was immediate. "Between the oak

bookcase on the left of the study door and the leather settee.''
Peter Morton was unsurprised by the swiftness of the response.
Between the twins there could be no jargon of telepathy. They
had been together in the womb, and they could not be parted.

Peter Morton tiptoed towards Francis's hiding place. Occasionally a board rattled, and because he feared to be caught by
one of the soft questers through the dark, he bent and untied his
laces. A tag struck the floor and the metallic sound set a host of
cautious feet moving in his direction. But by that time he was in
his stockings and would have laughed inwardly at the pursuit
had not the noise of someone stumbling on his abandoned shoes
made his heart trip in the reflection of another's surprise. No
more boards revealed Peter Morton's progress. On stockinged
feet he moved silently and unerringly towards his object. Instinct told him that he was near the wall, and, extending a hand,
he laid the fingers across his brother's face.

Francis did not cry out, but the leap of his own heart revealed
to Peter a proportion of Francis's terror. "It's all right," he whispered, feeling down the squatting figure until he captured a
clenched hand. "It's only me. I'll stay with you." And grasping
the other tightly, he listened to the cascade of whispers his utter-
ance had caused to fall. A hand touched the bookcase close to
Peter's head and he was aware of how Francis's fear continued
in spite of his presence. It was less intense, more bearable, he
hoped, but it remained. He knew that it was his brother's fear
and not his own that he experienced. The dark to him was only
an absence of light; the groping hand that of a familiar child.
Patiently he waited to be found.

He did not speak again, for between Francis and himself touch
was the most intimate communion. By way of joined hands
thought could flow more swiftly than lips could shape themselves round words. He could experience the whole progress of
his brother's emotion, from the leap of panic at the unexpected
contact to the steady pulse of fear, which now went on and on
with the regularity of a heart-beat. Peter Morton thought with

intensity, "I am here. You needn't be afraid. The lights will go on again soon. That rustle, that movement is nothing to fear. Only Joyce, only Mabel Warren." He bombarded the drooping form with thoughts of safety, but he was conscious that the fear continued. "They are beginning to whisper together. They are tired of looking for us. The lights will go on soon. We shall have won. Don't be afraid. That was only someone on the stairs. I believe it's Mrs. Henne-Falcon. Listen. They are feeling for the lights." Feet moving on a carpet, hands brushing a wall, a curtain pulled apart, a clicking handle, the opening of a cupboard door. In the case above their heads a loose book shifted under a touch. "Only Joyce, only Mabel Warren, only Mrs. Henne-Falcon," a crescendo of reassuring thought before the chandelier burst, like a fruit tree, into bloom.

The voices of the children rose shrilly into the radiance. "Where's Peter?" "Have you looked upstairs?" "Where's Francis?" but they were silenced again by Mrs. Henne-Falcon's scream. But she was not the first to notice Francis Morton's stillness, where he had collapsed against the wall at the touch of his brother's hand. Peter continued to hold the clenched fingers in an arid and puzzled grief. It was not merely that his brother was dead. His brain, too young to realize the full paradox, yet wondered with an obscure self-pity why it was that the pulse of his brother's fear went on and on, when Francis was now where he had been always told there was no more terror and no more darkness.

The Landscape of Dreams
JOHN LUTZ

While the actual events of "The Landscape of Dreams" are happening to an adult, it is the voice of the child, speaking from her subconscious, which sets them in motion. And it is the awakening of the childhood memories which provides a final, chilling twist to this haunting story. Born in 1939, John Lutz is the author of such mystery and suspense novels as The Truth of the Matter *(1971),* Bonegrinder *(1977),* Lazarus Man *(1979), and* The Shadow Man *(1981). His more than one hundred short stories have appeared regularly in* Ellery Queen's Mystery Magazine *and* Alfred Hitchcock's Mystery Magazine.

ELECTRIC-SHOCK therapy does odd things to the memory. It causes periods of forgetfulness, with total disregard for the order in which events happened. And in that same random order it causes periods of remembrance.

Memories are imbedded something like fossils in the rock strata of our years. Dr. Melinger told me that once. Or did he only agree when I suggested that analogy? The thing is, mental therapy is like conducting an archeological dig, only when you reach the fossils, sometimes they seem to come to life. And there are plenty of interesting memories buried in everyone's layers of years, even in those of a forty-year-old Indianapolis housewife like me.

There's no point in telling you about what caused my problems—about Jeff leaving me, or our son Billy dying of a drug overdose. Maybe the misery of the present is what makes me think more and more, awake and in dreams, about my childhood on an Illinois farm less than two hundred miles from here. About the willow tree that grew outside my bedroom window.

Willows are the most beautiful of trees, the most graceful. And the saddest, which is why they're known as weeping willows. This one, which grew too near our two-story white-frame farmhouse, was one of the largest willows I've ever seen—unless I'm just remembering it through the eyes of a ten-year-old girl. It was higher than the roof, and its long drooping branches draped to the ground and waved gently in the flatland winds, reacting to every soft current as if it were some lonesome plant that grew on the bottom of the sea.

Its spreading branches formed a sort of shelter, a quiet still point of the universe that I could reach by climbing out my bedroom window onto a thick limb that paralleled the house. I could move inside the concealing branches of the huge tree, secretly observing the rest of the world through a soft green veil. I got into the habit of spending time in the tree on warm summer nights, embraced by its thick branches in the soft moonlight that filtered in through the dense foliage.

Sometimes I'd go into the tree during the daytime. Once, when I was lying unseen on one of the big limbs, I heard my bedroom window close. There was no way out of the tree. The branches that reached ground level were too slender to support even my ten-year-old body. I had to call for help. I remember my mother, beautiful then, pushing through the lower branches with her own arms like graceful limbs, looking up at me and smiling a tolerant, loving smile, reaching to help me down. It is one of those crystallized moments of childhood, precious ever after in my memory.

Mother believed I climbed into the tree from the ground, I'm sure. I never told her about how I often went there from my window when everyone thought I was asleep. She would have forbidden that, of course, and I would have obeyed. Now I know that if I had confessed that day, everything would be different.

The willow tree figures in my dream, but that's not surprising. Willows are ideally suited to the landscape of dreams.

In the dream, which occurs about every third night, I see through the tree's delicate green veil two people moving in the moonlit yard. My mother and father, talking softly, unintelligibly, in some foreign language, perhaps. They enter the barn and leave the wide door open so they can see each other in the yellow moonlight. Their words become louder. Father yells something about a phone call. Then he is on the ground. In the ground! A hole, a grave, has been readied in the barn's dirt floor. Mother raises her right arm to her forehead. She turns and drops something long and silver, and picks up a shovel. I can hear her sobbing as she fills in the grave.

Dr. Melinger was interested in the dream. My father, you see, ran away with my mother's sister, my Aunt Verna, when I was ten. Aunt Verna had been afraid to face Mother and had taken the train to Louisville, where Father later joined her. My mother never got over that. Religion and family were one and the same to her. Mother was a fourth-generation Corbet, a descendant of the town's founders. Family honor was her life.

We never mentioned Father or Aunt Verna after they ran away together. Not once. Not even when Mother was a frail gray woman in her sixties, still living on the farm.

I've been back to the farm a few times during the past ten years. It's the same, only most of the surrounding fields have been parceled off and sold to neighbors. And the willow tree was cut down long ago. It got diseased and had to be removed so it wouldn't rot and fall on the house. A tree that big could cause a lot of damage.

I had discussed the dream with Dr. Melinger the day before he introduced me to a swarthy man in a light gray suit, a Mr. Edwards.

Mr. Edwards smiled a nice smile and we shook hands. His hand was as dry as wheat chaff. I'd given Dr. Melinger permission to phone Mr. Edwards. I had loved my father, who was a tall man who thrived on hard work and listening to the radio.

"Mr. Edwards is the F.B.I. agent I told you about, Doris," Dr. Melinger said to me. "He wants you to help him get to the truth. And getting to the truth is what would help you."

"It seems that your father and Verna Corbet weren't heard of after they left Homesville," Mr. Edwards said.

"Everybody knew they ran away together," I told him. "They were ashamed. Things were different thirty years ago. Maybe they even changed their names."

"That's possible. In fact, it's likely. Still, Dr. Melinger and I think we should check into the matter further. For the sake of everyone involved."

"You think what I dreamed really happened," I said.

"Not necessarily."

"I think it did," I told him. I saw him glance at Dr. Melinger. I didn't care. I loved my father. I loved both my parents, and still do. But I understood my mother. She couldn't bear the thought of Father running away with her own sister. That struck not only at her, but at her sense of family honor. She was a Corbet; Aunt

Verna was a Corbet. Mother had lost her mind for a while and killed Father. I loved her, but I couldn't forgive her for that. And there was such a thing as justice.

"I've talked to the sheriff in Homesville," Mr. Edwards said. "I'd like you to make a phone call to your mother, a call that will be recorded. The tape might provide the justification for digging up the floor of the barn where you saw your father buried in your dream."

I agreed to do that, and watched while Mr. Edwards and a bureau technician set up the recorder near the phone. Then I dialed Mother's number at the farm. She'd be home, probably watching a TV soap opera.

The phone rang twice.

"Mother, this is Doris."

"Why, Dorie . . ." She sounded surprised. I only phoned on holidays, usually. "It's good to hear from you. Nothing's wrong, is it?"

"I don't know, Mother."

Long silence. "What do you mean, you don't know?"

I felt a funny lump in my throat. I could hear soap-opera theme music in the background. "Mother," I said, "I think Father is dead. I think you had something to do with it. In the barn. I think he's under the barn."

Her intake of breath was like a harsh wind. She didn't say anything. Mr. Edwards had earphones on and was staring sober-faced down at the desk.

"Can you tell me it isn't true, Mother?" I asked.

"The barn's been torn down for years," she said. "There's a new barn."

"Then he's under where the old barn was," I said. "Can you tell me it isn't true, Mother?"

"What's gotten into you, Dorie?"

"Can you tell me it isn't true, Mother?" I pleaded.

"Dorie . . ." She was crying.

"Please, Mother!" And I was crying too. I hung up. I was afraid of what might happen if I didn't.

Mr. Edwards peeled off his earphones. "Thank you, Doris," he said. "I think this is what we needed. I can get the court order immediately. Do you want to drive to Homesville with us later today, to show us where the old barn was?"

Dr. Melinger nodded and smiled at me. A reassuring smile.

"I want to be with my mother," I said.

"Certainly," Mr. Edwards said. He shook hands with Dr. Melinger.

Mother was dead when we reached the farm. She had turned Father's old shotgun on herself. They wouldn't let me see her. Sheriff Hunicutt and Mr. Edwards held me on the porch.

Beside the body there had been a note in Mother's handwriting, a confession that she had murdered Father because she couldn't bear the thought of him living with her sister Verna. Their relationship would be a constant embarrassment, a permanent dishonor to the Corbet name. Mother was too proud to accept that, so she had killed him.

I showed Mr. Edwards where the old barn used to be, then a deputy took me back to town while the rest of the men started to dig. As the patrol car pulled from the driveway, I saw the wide flat stump of the willow tree. There were a few graceful shoots rising from it, swaying in the breeze. Young growth, the way I was in the dream.

Later that day they told me they found Father's bones four feet under the ground. The sternum still bore the mark of a long-ago knife thrust. The vision from the willow had been true.

Dr. Melinger explained to me back in Indianapolis that I had suppressed the dark knowledge of my mother's murder of my father, because I didn't want to believe it happened. It wasn't uncommon, he said, for his patients to have blocked such occurrences from their conscious minds. The shock treatments had jogged my memory and brought things to the surface, like the firing of a cannon over a deep lake. I would be better now, he assured me, despite tho tragedy of my mother's suicide.

For a while I believed him. Until I had the second dream.

Time plays tricks. Memories aren't like a slide show, in sharp focus and neat chronological order.

I was in the willow tree again, on a warm summer night thirty years ago, watching two figures through the sad green veil of branches, and listening.

"You can't be pregnant!" Father said to Verna.

"Precautions don't always work, Carl," Verna said patiently, though a little fearfully. "I'm going to have a child. Your child. Nothing can change that."

Below me my father seemed to become smaller, as if Verna's words had released a weight that suddenly descended on him. A wind ruffled Verna's flower-print dress that seemed strangely luminous in the moonlight and in the glare from the downstairs windows.

"My God!" Father said. "My God, what now?"

"We have to tell Myra when she comes back from town," Verna said. "There's nothing else to do."

"That's crazy!"

"There's nothing else to do, Carl!"

But Father thought of something else, and in his panic he couldn't stop himself from doing it. They were standing near the corner of the house, where several tools were leaning against the porch rail. One of the tools was a pitchfork that father had intended to equip with a new handle. He jabbed Verna in the stomach with the pitchfork, and she squatted down with one hand on the ground, kind of like she was going to shoot marbles. Either Father or Verna let out a soft, desperate whine.

The pitchfork moved again, a familiar motion I'd seen Father make with it a thousand times to gather hay. Verna said, "Carl," and fell over backward.

Father was still standing, leaning on the pitchfork and staring down at Verna, when Mother drove up in the car. She got out and walked toward him, moving slower as she got nearer.

"Verna's dead," Father told her, not looking away from the body.

"I can see that." I had never heard Mother so calm. Her voice made me think of lemonade and shelling peas, and the wheat-field on a clear, still day.

"She told me she was pregnant," Father said.

Mother seemed to straighten, even as she stared down at Verna. "I suspected, Carl."

"How could you?"

"I'm not the fool either of you thought I was."

"I lost my head, Myra. I don't know how it happened. I killed her." He dropped the pitchfork and took a heavy step toward the porch.

"Where are you going, Carl?" Mother asked curtly.

"To phone the sheriff."

"No, you're not."

"I have to, Myra. Do you understand that I killed Verna? I killed your sister. I killed her baby."

"Turning yourself in won't change that," Mother said.

"I *have* to, Myra!"

"Carry her to the barn, Carl. I'll bring the shovel."

"What?"

"We're going to bury Verna. We have to get her out of the way before Dorie wakes up tomorrow. Then you can think about things, and if you still want to phone the sheriff, he'll still be there to answer the phone."

Father stood for a while with his hands on his hips.

"Pick her up and bring her, Carl. Damn you, you owe me *that*, after what you've done! You owe the Corbets that!"

He shook his head, but he did what Mother said. He lifted Verna and carried her toward the barn.

Mother followed with the shovel.

All this must have happened on the same night that was in my first dream. But whether it did or not, I'll never tell Dr. Melinger about the second willow-tree dream. Mr. Edwards will never go digging for another body beneath the old barn floor, where Aunt Verna had been with Father all these years, but not in the way she'd planned.

I understand what happened now, and I understand Mother's pride, the Corbet pride. She could endure even the public knowledge that her husband had gone away with her sister, but not that he had impregnated Verna, then murdered her. A Corbet might marry a philanderer, but not a killer of a woman and her unborn. Mother would never rest if people knew that about her.

That's why she became a murderess herself. And though anyone who might have been hurt by father's crime is now beyond all harm, no one will ever learn the truth from me. Despite what's happened, I owe Mother and the other Corbets that much. I loved her and still do. That's in the blood, Corbet blood, and there's no changing it, not ever.

And me? I'm willing to accept what remaining silent means for me. I know I'll continue to dream, to be trapped within the branches of the weeping willow tree. Until my mother helps me down.

Fire Escape

CORNELL WOOLRICH

Cornell Woolrich was one of the few writers able to sustain a high pitch of pulse-pounding, edge-of-the-chair suspense; in fact, no writer past or present has done it better or more consistently. "Fire Escape" is among his most harrowing stories. This tale of twelve-year-old Buddy and his flight into terror after witnessing a brutal murder is so vivid and cinematic that it was filmed as The Window (1949), starring Bobby Driscoll, Arthur Kennedy, and Barbara Hale, a minor film noir classic in its own right. A tragic figure who lived most of his life in hotel rooms, Woolrich (1903-1968) has been called "the Poe of the twentieth century and the poet of its shadows." The best of his novels, including the tours-de-force The Bride Wore Black (1940) and Phantom Lady (1942), are currently in print in paperback—a revival and recognition that are long overdue.

THE kid was twelve, and his name was Buddy. His real name wasn't that, it was Charlie, but they called him Buddy.

He was small for his age. The world he lived in was small too. Or rather, one of them was. He lived in two worlds at once. One of them was a small, drab, confined world; just two squalid rooms, in the rear of a six-story tenement, 20 Holt Street; stifling in summer, freezing in winter. Just two grownups in it, Mom and Pop. And a handful of other kids like himself, that he knew from school and from playing on the streets.

The other world had no boundaries, no limits. You could do anything in it. You could go anywhere. All you had to do was just sit still and think hard. Make it up as you went along. The world of the imagination. He did a lot of that. But he was learning to keep it to himself. They told him he was getting too big now for that stuff. They swatted him, and called it lies. The last time he'd tried telling them about it, Pop had threatened: "I'm going to wallop you good next time you make up any more of them fancy lies of yours!"

"It comes from them Sat'day-afternoon movies he's been seeing," Mom said. "I told him he can't go any more."

And then this night came along. It felt as if it were made of boiling tar, poured all over you. July was hot everywhere, but on Holt Street it was hell. He kept trying and he kept trying, and it wouldn't work; the bedding on his cot got all soggy and streaked with damp. Pop wasn't home; he worked nights. The two rooms were like the chambers of an oven, with all the gas burners left on full tilt. Buddy took his pillow with him finally and climbed out the window onto the fire-escape landing just outside, and tried it out out there. It wasn't the first time; he'd done it lots before. You couldn't fall off, the landing was railed around. Well, you could if you were unlucky, but it hadn't happened yet. He sort of locked his arm through the rail uprights, and that kept him from rolling in his sleep.

It wouldn't work, it was just as bad out there. It was still like an oven, only now with the burners out maybe. He decided maybe it would be better if he tried it a little higher up. Sometimes there was a faint stirring of breeze skimming along at roof level. It couldn't bend and get down in here behind the tenements. He picked up the pillow and went up the iron slats one flight, to the sixth-floor landing, and tried it there.

It wasn't very much better. But it had to do, you couldn't go up any higher than that. He'd learned by experience you couldn't sleep on the roof itself, because it was covered with gravel, and that got into you and hurt. And underneath it was tar-surfaced, and in the hot weather that got soft and stuck to you all over.

He wriggled around a little on the hard-bitten iron slats, with empty spaces in-between, that were like sleeping on a grill, and then finally he dozed off. The way you can even on a fire escape, when you're only twelve.

Morning came awfully fast. It seemed to get light only about a minute later. The shine tickled his eyelids and he opened them. Then he saw that it wasn't coming down from above, from the sky, the way light should. It was still dark, it was still night up there. It was coming in a thin bar, down low, even with his eyes, running along the bottom of the window he was lying outside of, on a level with the fire-escape landing he was lying on. If he'd been standing up instead of stretched out flat, it would have run over his feet instead of across his eyes. It was only about an inch high. A dark shade unrolled nearly to the bottom, but that had slipped back maybe a half turn on its roller, cut the rest of it off. But with his eyes up close against it like they were, it was nearly as good as the whole window being lit up. He could see the whole inside of the room.

There were two people in it, a man and a woman. He would have closed his eyes again and gone right back to sleep—what did he care about watching grownups?—except for the funny, sneaky way they were both acting. That made him keep on watching, wondering what they were up to.

The man was asleep on a chair, by a table. He'd been drinking or something. There was a bottle and two glasses on the table in front of him. His head was down on the table, and his hand was in front of his eyes, to protect them from the light.

The woman was moving around on tiptoes, trying not to make any noise. She was carrying the man's coat in her hands, like she'd just taken it off the back of the chair, where he'd hung it before he fell asleep. She had on a lot of red and white stuff all over her face, but Buddy didn't think she looked very pretty. When she got around the other side of the table from him, she stopped, and started to dip her hand in and out of all the pockets of the coat. She kept her back to him while she was doing it. But Buddy could see her good from the side, he was looking right in at her.

That was the first sneaky thing he saw that made him keep on watching them. And the second was, he saw the fingers of the man's hand, the one that was lying in front of his eyes, split open, and the man stole a look through them at what she was doing.

Then when she turned her head, to make sure he was asleep, he quickly closed his fingers together again, just in time.

She turned her head the other way again and went ahead doing what she was doing.

She came up with a big fat roll of money from the coat, all rolled up tight, and she threw the coat aside, and bent her head close, and started to count it over. Her eyes got all bright, and Buddy could see her licking her lips while she was doing it.

All of a sudden he held his breath. The man's arm was starting to crawl along the top of the table toward her, to reach for her and grab her. It moved very slow and quiet, like a big thick snake inching along after somebody, and she never noticed it. Then when it was out straight and nearly touching her, the man started to come up off his chair after it and crouch over toward her, and she never heard that either. He was smiling, but it wasn't a very good kind of a smile.

Buddy's heart was pounding. He thought, "You better look

around, lady, you better look around!" But she didn't. She was too busy counting the money.

All of a sudden the man jumped and grabbed her. His chair went over flat, and the table nearly did too, but it recovered and stayed up. His big hand, the one that had been reaching out all along, caught her around the back of the neck, and held on tight, and he started to shake her from head to foot. His other hand grabbed the wrist that was holding the money; she tried to jam it down the front of her dress, but she wasn't quick enough; he twisted her wrist slowly around, to make her let go of it.

She gave a funny little squeak like a mouse, but not very loud; at least it didn't come out the window very loud, where Buddy was.

"No you don't!" Buddy heard the man growl. "I figured something like this was coming! You gotta get up pretty early in the morning to put anything like that over on me!"

"Take your hands off me!" she panted. "Let go of me!"

He started to swing her around from side to side. "You won't ever try anything like this again, by the time I get through with you!" Buddy heard the man grunt.

All of a sudden she screamed, "Joe! Hurry up in here! I can't handle him any longer by myself!" But she didn't scream it out real loud, just in a sort of a smothered way, as if she didn't want it to carry too far.

The door flew open, and a second man showed up. He must have been standing right outside it waiting the whole time, to come in that fast. He ran up behind the man who was being robbed. She held on tight and kept him from turning around to meet him.

The second man waited until his head was in the right position, and then he locked both his own hands together in a double fist, and smashed them down with all his might on the back of the other man's neck.

The other man dropped to the floor like a stone and lay there quiet for a minute.

The woman scrambled down and started to pick up all the

money that was lying around on the floor. "Here!" she said,
handing it to the man.

"Hurry up, let's get out of here!" he snarled. "What'd you
have to bungle it up like that for? Why didn't you fix his drink
right?"

"I did, but it didn't work on him. He musta seen me do it."

"Come on!" he said, and started for the door. "When he
comes to, he'll bring the cops down on us."

All of a sudden the man lying on the floor wrapped his arm
tight around both legs of the second man, pinning them together. The second man tripped and fell down flat, full length.
The other man scrambled on top of him before he could get up,
held him that way, and it started in all over again.

The man they were robbing was the better fighter of the two.
He swung punches at the second man's head, while he had him
under him like that. In another minute he would have punched
him cold, even Buddy could tell that. His arms spread out limp
on the floor, and his fists started to open up lazy.

But the woman went running all around the place hunting for
something to help with. All of a sudden she threw open a drawer
in a bureau and took out something that flashed in the light.
Buddy couldn't see what it was for a minute, she was so fast
with it. She darted in close to them and put it in the outstretched
hand of the man who was lying underneath, being knocked
silly.

Then when it swept up high over both their heads a second
later, Buddy could see what it was by that time all right! It was a
short, sharp knife. Buddy's eyes nearly came out of his head.

The man swung it and buried it in the other's back. Right up
to the hilt; you couldn't see the blade any more.

The fight stopped cold on the instant, but not the stabbing. He
wrenched it out with a sawing motion from side to side, and
swung it again, and buried it again, in a different place this time.
The other man wasn't moving any more, just sort of recoiling
with the stab itself.

He wasn't satisfied even yet. He freed it a third time, with a lot of trouble, and it came up and went back in again. Then they both lay there still, one of them getting his breath, the other not breathing any more.

Finally he rolled the crumpled weight off him, and picked himself up, and felt his jaw. Then they both stood looking down at what lay there, he and the woman.

"Is he dead?" Buddy heard her ask in a scared voice.

"Wait a minute, I'll see." He got down by him, and put his hand underneath him, where his heart was. Then he pulled it out. Then he pulled the knife out of his back. Then he stood up.

He looked at her and shook his head a little.

"Holy smoke!" she gasped. "We've killed him! Joe, what'll we do?" She didn't say it very loud, but it was so quiet in the room now, Buddy could hear everything they said.

The man grabbed her arm and squeezed it tight. "Take it easy. There's plenty of people killed, that they never find out who done it. Just don't lose your head, that's all. We'll get by with it."

He held her until he was sure she was steady, then he let go of her again.

He looked all around the room. "Gimme some newspapers. I want to keep this stuff from getting on the floor."

He got down and stuffed them underneath the body on all sides.

Then he said, "Case the door, see if there's anyone out there that heard us. Open it slow and careful, now."

She went over to it on tiptoe, and moved it open just on a crack, and looked out with one eye. Then she made it a little wider, and stuck her whole head out, and turned it both ways. Then she pulled it in again, and closed up, and came back to him.

"Not a soul around," she whispered.

"All right. Now case the window. See if it's all right out in the back there. Don't pull up the shade, just take a squint out the side of it."

She started to come over to where Buddy's eyes were staring

in, and she got bigger and bigger every minute, the closer she got. Her head went way up high out of sight, and her waist blotted out the whole room. He couldn't move, he was like paralyzed. The little gap under the shade must have been awfully skinny for her not to see it, but he knew in another minute she was going to look right out on top of him, from higher up.

He rolled over flat on his back, it was only a half-roll because he'd been lying on his side until now, and that was about all the moving there was time for him to do. There was an old blanket over the fire-escape rail, hung out to air. He clawed at it and pulled it down on top of him. He only hoped it covered all of him, but there wasn't time to tuck it around evenly. About all he could do was hunch himself up and make himself as small as possible, and pray none of him stuck out. A minute later, even with his head covered, he could tell, by a splash of light that fell across the blanket, like a sort of stripe, that she'd tipped the shade back and was staring out the side of it.

"There's something white down here," Buddy heard her say, and he froze all over. He even stopped breathing, for fear his breath would show up against the blanket, make it ripple.

"Oh, I know!" she explained, in relief. "It's that blanket I left out there yesterday. It must have fallen down. Gee, for a minute I thought it was somebody lying there!"

"Don't stand there all night," the man growled.

The stripe of light went out, and Buddy knew she'd let the shade go back in place.

He was still afraid to move for a minute, even after that. Then he worked his head clear of the blanket and looked again.

Even the gap was gone now. She must have pulled the shade down even, before she turned away. He couldn't see them any more, but he could still hear them.

But he didn't want to. All he wanted to do was get down off there! He knew, though, that if he could hear them, they could hear him just as easy. He had to do it slow. The fire-escape was old and rickety, it might creak. He started to stretch out his legs, backward, toward the ladder steps going down. Then when he had them out straight, he started to palm himself along backward on the flats of his hands, keeping his head and shoulders down. It was a little bit like swimming the breast stroke on dry land. Or rather on iron slats, which was worse still.

But he could still keep on hearing them the whole time he was doing it.

"Here's his identification papers," the man said. "Cliff Bristol. Mate on a merchant ship. That's good. Them guys disappear awfully easy. Not too many questions asked. We want to make sure of getting everything out of his pockets, so they won't be able to trace who he was."

The woman said, like she was almost crying, "Oh, what do we care what his name is. We've done it, that's all that matters. Come on, Joe, for God's sake let's get out of here!"

"We don't have to get out now," the man said. "Why should we? All we have to do is get him out. Nobody seen him come up here with you. Nobody knows it happened. If we lam out now and leave him here, they'll be after us in five seconds. If we just stay here like we are, nobody'll be any the wiser."

"But how you going to do it, Joe? How you going to get him out?"

"I'll show you. Bring out them two valises of yours, and empty the stuff out of them."

Buddy was worming his way down the fire-escape steps backward now, but his face and chin was still balanced above the landing.

"But he won't go into one of them, a great big guy like him," the woman protested.

"He will the way I'll do it," the man answered. And then he said, "Go in the bathroom and get me my razor."

Buddy's chin went down flat on the landing for a minute, and he felt like he wanted to throw up. The fire escape creaked a little, but the woman had groaned just then, and that covered it up.

"You don't have to watch," the man said. "You go outside the door and wait, if you feel that way about it. Come in again if you hear anyone coming."

Buddy began to move again, spilling salt water from his mouth.

"Hand me all the rest of the newspapers we got in here, before you go," he heard the man say. "And bring in that blanket you said was outside the window, that'll come in handy too. I'm going to need it for a lining."

Buddy wriggled the rest of the way down, like a snake in reverse. He felt his feet touch bottom on his own landing, outside his own windows, and he was safe! But there was something soft clinging to them. He looked, and it was the blanket. It had gotten tangled around his foot while he was still up above there, and he'd trailed it down with him without noticing in his excitement.

He kicked it clear of himself, but there was no time to do anything else with it. He squirmed across the sill and toppled back into his own flat, and left it lying out there. An instant later a shot of light doused the fire escape and he heard the window above go up, as she reached out for it.

Then he heard her whisper in a frightened, bated voice: "It blew down! I see it, there it is down below. It was right out here a minute ago, and now it's down below!"

The man must have told her to go after it and bring it up. The light went out, he must have put the light out in the room, so she'd have a chance to climb down and get it without being seen. Buddy could hear the wooden window frame ease the rest of the way up in the dark, then a stealthy scrape on the iron ladder stairs.

He pressed himself up flat against the wall, under his own sill. He was small enough to fit in there. He saw the white of the blanket flick upward and disappear from sight.

Then he heard her whisper, just as she went in her own window again, "That's funny; and there's not a breath of air stirring either! How did it come to get blown down there?"

Then the window rustled closed, and it was over.

Buddy didn't get up and walk to his own bed. He couldn't lift himself that high. He crawled to it on his hands and knees.

He pulled the covers all over him, even past the top of his head, and as hot as the night had seemed only a little while ago, he shook as if it were the middle of December and goose-pimples came out all over him.

He was still shaking for a long time after. He could hear someone moving around right over him once in a while, even with the covers over his head, and just picturing what was going on up there, that would start him in to shaking all over again.

It took a long time. Then everything got quiet. No more creaks on the ceiling, like somebody was rocking back and forth, sawing away at something. He was all covered with sweat now, and the sheets were damp.

Then he heard a door open, and someone moved softly down the stairs outside. Past his own door and down to the bottom. Once something scraped a little against the wall, like a valise. He started in shaking again, worse than ever.

He didn't sleep all the rest of the night. Hours later, after it was already light, he heard someone coming quietly up the stairs. This time nothing scraped against the walls. Then the door closed above, and after that there was no more sound of anything.

Then in a little while his mother got up in the next room and got breakfast started and called in to him.

He got dressed and dragged himself in to her, and when she turned around and saw him she said, "You don't look well, Buddy. You feel sick?"

He didn't want to tell her, he wanted to tell his father.

His father came home from work a few minutes after that, and they sat down to the table together like they did every morning, Buddy to his breakfast and his father to his before-bedtime supper.

Ho waited till his mother was out of the room, then he whispered: "Pop, I want to tell you something."

"Okay, shoot," his father grinned.

"Pop, there's a man and a woman livin' over us—"

"Sure, I know that," his father said, helping himself to some bacon. "That's no news to me. I've seen them, coming and going. I think the name's Scanlon or Hanlon, something like that."

Buddy shifted his chair closer and leaned nearer his father's ear. "But Pop," he breathed, "last night they killed a man up there, and they cut up his body into small pieces, and stuck it into two valises."

His father stopped chewing. Then he put down his knife and fork. Then he turned around slowly in his chair and looked at him hard. For a minute Buddy thought he felt sick and scared about it, like he had himself. But then he saw that he was only sore. Sore at Buddy himself.

"Mary, come in here," he called out grimly.

Buddy's mother came to the door and looked in at them.

"He's at it again," his father said. "I thought I told you not to let him go to any more of them Sat'day movies."

She gnawed her lip worriedly. "Making things up again?"

"I didn't make—" Buddy started to protest.

"I wouldn't even repeat to you the filthy trash he's just been telling me, it would turn your blood cold." His father whacked him across the mouth with the back of his hand. "Shut up," he said. "If there's one thing I can't stand it's a liar. One of them congenial liars."

"What'd he say?" his mother asked troubledly.

"It's not fit for you to hear," his father said indignantly. But then he went ahead and told her anyway. "He said they done someone in up there, over us, and then chopped him up into small pieces and carted him off in two valises."

His mother touched her apron to her mouth nauseatedly. "The Kellermans?" she gasped in horrified disbelief. "Oh Buddy, when are you going to stop that? Why, they're the last people in the world—She seems like a very nice woman. Why she was right down here at the door only the other day, to borrow a cup of sugar from me. She always has a smile and a nice word, whenever you pass her on the stairs. Why, they're the *last* ones—!''

"Well, he'll grow up fine," his father said darkly. "There's something wrong with a boy like that. This had to happen to me! I don't know where he gets it from. I wasn't that way, in my whole life. My brother Ed, rest his soul, wasn't that way. You were never that way, nor anyone on your side of the family. But I'm going to take it out of him if it's the last thing I do." He started to roll up his shirt sleeve. He pushed his chair back. "You come in here with me."

Then at the door he gave him one more chance. "Are you going to say it's not true?"

"But I *saw* them. I watched through the window and *saw* them," Buddy wailed helplessly.

His father's jaw set tight. "All right, come in here." He closed the door after the two of them.

It didn't hurt very much. Well, it did, but just for a minute; it didn't last. His father wasn't a man with a vicious temper; he was just a man with a strong sense of what was right and what was wrong. His father just used half-strength on him; just enough to make him holler out satisfactorily, not enough to really bruise him badly.

Then when he got through, he rolled down his shirt sleeve and said to the sniffling Buddy: "Now are you going to make up any more of them fancy lies of yours?"

There was an out there, and Buddy was smart enough to grab it. "No, sir," he said submissively. "I'm not going to make up any lies." And he started for the door.

But his father added quickly, too quickly, "Then you're ready to admit now that wasn't true, what you told me in there at the table?"

Buddy swallowed hard and stood still, with freedom just within reach. He didn't answer.

"Answer me," his father said severely. "Was it or wasn't it?"

There was a dilemma here, and Buddy couldn't handle it. He'd been walloped for telling what they thought was a lie. Now they wanted him to do the very thing they'd punished him for doing in the first place. If he told the truth it would be called a lie, and if he told a lie he'd only be repeating what he knew they were walloping him for.

He tried to side-step it by asking a question of his own. "When you—when you *see* a thing yourself, with your own eyes, is it true *then?*" he faltered.

"Sure," his father said impatiently. "You're old enough to know that! You're not two years old."

"Then I saw it, and it has to be true."

This time his father got real sore. He hauled him back from the door by the scruff of his neck, and for a minute he acted as if he were going to give him another walloping, all over again. But he didn't. Instead he took the key out of the door, opened it, and put the key in the front. "You're going to stay in here until you're ready to admit that whole thing was a dirty, rotten lie!" he said wrathfully. "You'll stay in here all day, if you have to!"

He went out, slammed the door after him, and locked Buddy in from the outside. Then he took the key out of the lock, so Buddy's mother wouldn't weaken while he was asleep.

Buddy went over and slumped down gloomily onto a chair, and hung his head, and tried to puzzle it out. He was being punished for doing the very thing they were trying to lace into him: sticking to the truth.

He heard his father moving around out there getting ready for bed; heard his shoes drop heavily one after the other, then the bedsprings creak. Then after that nothing. He'd sleep all day now, until dark. But maybe his mother would let him out, before she went to work for the day.

He went over to the door and started to jiggle the knob back and forth, to try and attract her attention with as little noise as he could. "Mom," he whispered close to the keyhole. "Hey, mom."

After a while he heard her tiptoe up on the other side.

"Mom, are you there? Let me out."

"It's for your own good, Buddy," she whispered back. "I can't do it unless you take back that sinful lie you told. He told me not to." She waited patiently. "Do you take it back, Buddy? Do you?"

"No," he sighed. He went back to the chair and disheartenedly sat down once more.

What was a fellow to do, when even his own people wouldn't believe him? Who was he to turn to? You had to tell *somebody* about a thing like that. If you didn't, it was just as bad as—just as bad as if you were one of the ones that did it. He wasn't as scared any more as he'd been last night, because it was daylight now, but he still felt a little sick at his stomach whenever he thought of it. You *had* to tell somebody.

Suddenly he turned his head and looked at the window. Why hadn't he thought of that before? Not about getting out through the window; he'd known he could all along, it was latched on the inside. But he hadn't tried to get out that way until now, because he wanted to stay here and get them to believe him here, where he was. As long as they wouldn't believe him here, there was another place where maybe they *would* believe him.

That's what grownups did the first thing, whenever they were in his predicament. Why shouldn't a kid do it? The police. They were the ones had to be told. They were the ones you were supposed to tell, anyway. Even his father, if he'd only believed him, was supposed to tell them. Well, if his father wouldn't, then he'd tell them himself.

He got up and softshoed over to the window and eased it up. He slung himself over onto the fire escape. It was easy, of course; nothing to it. At his age it was just as easy as going out a door. Then he eased it down again. But not all the way, he left just a little crack open underneath, so he could get his fingers in and get it up again when he came back.

He'd tell the police, and then he'd come back and sneak in again through the window, and be there when his father woke up and unlocked the door. That would get it off his mind; then he wouldn't have to worry any more.

He went down the fire escape, dropped off where the last sec-

tion of ladder was hoisted clear of the ground, went in through
the basement, and came out the front, up the janitor's steps without meeting anybody. He beat it away from in front of the house
fast, so he wouldn't be seen by anyone who knew him, any of
the neighbors for instance, who might later accidentally tell on
him. Then as soon as he was safely around the corner he slowed
up and tried to figure out how you went about it. Telling the
police.

It was better to go to a station house, for anything as important
as this, instead of just telling a stray neighborhood cop you met
on the sidewalk. He was a little bit in awe of station houses, but
as long as you hadn't done anything yourself it was probably
safe enough to go into one.

He didn't know where one was exactly, but he knew there
must be one somewhere close around, there had to be. He saw a
storekeeper sweeping the sidewalk, and he got up his courage
and went up to him.

"Where's the station house, mister?" he asked.

"How should I know?" said the man gruffly. "What am I, a
telephone book? Look out with your feet, can't you see I'm
busy?"

He backed away. That gave him an idea. He turned and went
looking for a drugstore, and when he found one, he went in and
looked in the telephone books they had in the back, chained to
the wall.

He picked the nearest one to where he was, and he headed for
it. When he got there, all his instinctive fear of that kind of
place, left over from when he was a kid of six or eight and cops
were the natural enemies of small boys, came back again for a
minute. He hung around outside for a short while, and then finally he saw the station house cat go in, and that gave him courage, and he went in himself.

The man at the desk didn't pay any attention to him for a long
time. He was looking over some papers or something. Buddy
just stood there and waited, afraid to speak first.

Finally he said, kindly, "What is it, son? Lost your dog or something?"

"No sir," Buddy said spasmodically. "I—I got something I want to tell someone."

The desk sergeant grinned absently, continuing to look at what he was looking at. "And what would that be, now?"

Buddy glanced apprehensively behind him, at the street outside, as though fearful of being overheard from there. "Well, it's pretty serious," he gulped. "It's about a man that was killed."

The sergeant gave him his full attention for the first time. "You know something about a man that was killed?"

"Yessir," said Buddy breathlessly. "Last night. And I thought I better tell you." He wondered if that was enough, and he could go now. No, they had to have the name and address; they couldn't just guess.

The sergeant clawed his chin. "You're not trying to be a smart aleck, now, or anything like that?" he asked warningly. One look at Buddy's face, however, seemed to reassure him on that point.

"No sir," Buddy said strenuously.

"Well, I'll tell you. That's not my department, exactly. You see that hall there, over next to the clock? You go down that to the second door you come to. There's a man in there, you tell him about it. Don't go in the first door, now, or he'll have your life; he eats kids your age for breakfast."

Buddy went over the mouth of the corridor, looked back from there for reassurance.

"Second door," the sergeant reassured him.

He went on. He made a wide loop around the dread first door, pressing himself flat against the opposite wall to get safely by it. Then he knocked on the one after that, and felt as scared as if it were the principal's office at school. Even more scared, in fact.

" 'Min,' " a voice said.

He couldn't move for a minute.

"Well?" the voice repeated with a touch of annoyance.

To stay out, now, was worse than to go in. Buddy took a deep breath, held it, caving in his middle, and went in. Then he remembered to close the door after him. When you didn't close the door after you in the principal's office, you had to go outside and come in all over again.

There was another man, at another desk. His eyes had been fixed in readiness at a point about six feet up the door. When it opened and closed, and they still met nothing, they dropped down to Buddy's four-foot level.

"What is this?" he growled. "How'd you get in here?" The first part of the question didn't seem to be addressed to Buddy himself, but to the ceiling light or something like that.

Buddy had to go through the thing a second time, and repetition didn't make it come any easier than the first.

The man just looked at him. In his imagination, Buddy had pictured a general rising-up and an excited, pell-mell rushing out on the part of everyone in the station house, when he delivered his news; patrol cars wailing into high gear and orders being barked around. That was what always happened in pictures. Everyone always jumped up and rushed out, whenever somebody came in and told them something like this. But now, in real life: the man just looked at him.

He said, "What's your name, son?" He said, "What's your address?"

Buddy told him.

He said, "D'y'ever have a nightmare, son? You know, a pretty bad dream that scares the life out of you?"

"Oh, sure," Buddy said incautiously. "I've had 'em, lots of times."

The man said, into a boxlike thing on his desk, "Ross, come in here."

Another man came in. He didn't have on a uniform either; neither of them did. Which made them a little déclassé in Buddy's esteem. They conferred in low voices; he couldn't hear a word they said. He knew it was about himself, though; he could tell by the way they'd look over at him every now and then.

They didn't look in the right way. They should have looked sort of—well, sort of concerned, worried about what he'd told them, or something. Instead, they looked sort of amused; like men who are trying to keep straight faces.

Then the first one spoke up again. "So you saw them cut him up and—"

This was a distortion, and Buddy scotched it quick. He wasn't here to make things up, although only a few short weeks ago, he would have grabbed at the chance this gave him, it was a wonderful opening. "No, sir," he said, "I didn't see *that* part of it; I just heard them say they were going to do it. But—"

But then before he could reaffirm that he had seen the man fall and the knife go home three times, as he was about to, the detective cut in with another question, without waiting. So he was left with the appearance of having made a whole retraction, instead of just a partial one.

"Did you tell your parents about this?"

This was a bad one, and nobody knew it better than Buddy.

"Yes," he mumbled unwillingly.

"Then why didn't they come and tell us about it, why'd they send you instead?"

He tried to duck that by not answering.

"Speak up, son."

You had to tell the truth to cops; that was serious, not telling the truth to cops. Even *civilian* cops, like these. "They didn't believe me," he breathed.

"Why didn't they believe you?"

"They—they think I'm always making up things."

He saw the look they gave one another, and he knew what it meant. He'd already lost the battle. They were already on his father's side.

"Oh, they do, hunh? Well, *do* you make up things?"

You had to tell the truth to cops. "I used to. I used to a lot. But not any more. Not this time. This time I'm not making it up."

He saw one of them tap a finger to his forehead, just once. He wasn't meant to see it, it was done very quickly, but he saw it.

"Well, do you know for sure when you are and when you're not making things up, son?"

"I do, honest!" he protested. "I *know* I'm not this time! I *know* I'm not!"

But it wasn't a very good answer, he knew that. It was the only one he had, though. They got you in corners where you hardly knew what you were saying any more.

"We'll send somebody around, son, and check up," the first man reassured him. He turned to the other man. "Ross, go over there and take a look around. Don't put your foot down too hard, it's not official. Sell them a magazine subscription or something—No, an electric razor, that'll tie in with the story. There's one in my locker, you can take that with you for a sample. It's the—" He glanced at Buddy inquiringly.

"The sixth floor, right over us."

"That's all I've got to do," Ross said disgruntledly. But he went out.

"You wait out in the hall, son," the first man said to Buddy. "Sit down on the bench out there."

Buddy went out and sat. About half an hour went by, not much more. Then he saw Ross come back and go in again. He waited hopefully for the rushing out and shouting of orders to come. Nothing happened. Nobody stirred. All he could hear was Ross swearing and complaining in a low voice, through the frosted glass inset of the door, and the other man laughing, like you do when there's a joke at somebody's expense. Then they sent for him to come in again.

Ross gave Buddy a dirty look. The other man tried to straighten his face. He passed his hand slowly in front of his mouth, and it came out serious at the other side of it.

"Son," he said, "you can hear things quite easily through that ceiling of yours, can't you? The one between you and them. Pretty thin?"

"Y'yes," Buddy faltered, wondering what was coming next.

"Well, what you heard was a program on their radio."

"There wasn't any. They didn't have a radio in the room."

Ross gave him quite an unfriendly look. "Yes they do," he said sourly. "I was just over there, and I saw it myself. You could hear it all the way down the stairs to the third floor, when I came away. I been on the force fourteen years, and this kid's going to tell me what *is* in a room I case and what isn't!"

"All right, Ross," the other man tried to soothe him.

"But I saw it through the *window!*" Buddy wailed.

"It could have still been the radio, son," he explained pacifyingly. "Remember, you can't *see* something that's said, you can only hear it. You could have been looking square at them, and still hearing what the radio was saying.

"What time was it you were out there?" Ross growled at Buddy.

"I don't know. Just—just nighttime. We only got an alarm clock and you can't see it in the dark."

Ross shrugged angrily at the other man, as if to say: See what I mean? "It was the Crime-Smashers Program," he said bitterly. "It's on from eleven to twelve. And last night was Wednesday. Or don't you know that either?" he flared in an aside to Buddy. "She told me herself it was a partic'ly gruesome one this time. Said her husband wouldn't talk to her for an hour afterward, because he can't stand hearing that kind of stuff and she dotes on it. She admits she had it on too loud, just to spite him. Fair enough?"

The other man just looked at Buddy, quizzically. Buddy just looked at the floor.

Ross finished rubbing it in, with vengeful relish. "*And* her husband uses a safety razor. She brought it out and showed it to me herself when I tried to peddle the prop to her. Did you ever try cutting up anybody with one of them? *And* there are two valises still right there in the room with them. I saw them when I pretended to fumble my pencil and stooped down to pick it up from the floor. With their lids left ajar and nothing worse in them than a mess of shirts and women's undies. And not brand-new replacements, either; plenty grubby and battered from years of knocking around with them. Even papered all over with faded hotel labels. I don't think cheapskates like them would be apt to own four valises, two apiece. And if they did, I don't think they'd pack the stiff in the two best ones and keep the two worst ones for themselves; it would most likely be the other way around. And, finally, they've got newspapers still kicking around from two weeks back; I spotted the date-lines on a few of them myself. What were they supposed to have used to clean up the mess, Kleenex?''

And he backed his arm toward Buddy, as if to let one fly at him across the ear. The other man, laughing, had to reach over quickly and hold him back. "A little practice-work won't hurt you.''

"On level ground maybe; not up six flights of stairs.'' He stalked out and gave the door a clout behind him.

The other man sent for a cop; this time one of the kind in uniform. For a minute Buddy thought he was going to be arrested then and there, and his stomach went down to about his feet, nearly.

"Where do you live, son? You better take him back with you, Lyons.''

"Not the *front* way,'' Buddy pleaded, aghast. "I can get in like I got out.''

"Just to make sure you get safely back, son. You've done enough damage for one day.'' And the man at the desk waved him, and the whole matter he'd tried to tell them about, out the door.

He knew better than to fight a policeman. That was about the worst thing you could do, fight back at a policeman. He went along with him tractably, his head hanging down in shame.

They went inside and up the stairs. The Carmody kid on the second floor peeked out the door and shrieked to her sister, "Ooh, they've arrested Buddy!''

"They have not!'' he denied indignantly. "They're just bringing me home special!''

They stopped in front of his own door. "Here, son?''

Buddy quailed. *Now* he was going to get it!

The policeman tapped, and his mother, not his father, opened the door. She must have been late leaving for work today, to still be there. Her face got white for a minute.

The policeman winked at her to reassure her. "Nothing to get frightened about, lady. He just came over and gave us a little story, and we thought we better bring him back here where he belongs."

"Buddy!" she said, horrified. "You went and told *them?*"

"Does he do it very often?" the policeman asked.

"All the time. All the time. But never anything as bad as this."

"Getting worse, hunh? Well, you ought to talk to the principal of his school, or maybe a doctor."

There was a stealthy creak on the stairs, and the Kellerman woman had paused on her way down, was standing looking at them. Curiously, but with cold composure.

The cop didn't even turn his head. "Well, I gotta be getting back," he said, and touched the visor of his cap to Buddy's mother.

Buddy got panicky. "Come in, quick!" he whispered frantically. "Come in quick, before she sees us!" And tried to drag his mother in out of the doorway.

She resisted, held him there in full view. "There she is now. You apologize. You say you're sorry, hear me?"

The woman came the rest of the way down. She smiled affably, in neighborly greeting. Buddy's mother smiled in answering affability.

"Nothing wrong, is there?"

"No, nothing wrong," Buddy's mother murmured deprecatingly.

"I thought I saw a policeman at the door here, as I was coming down."

"Buddy did something he shouldn't." Without taking her eyes off the woman, she shook Buddy in an aside. Meaning, pantomimically, "Apologize." He hung back, tried to efface himself behind her.

"He *looks* like a good little boy," the woman said patronizingly. "What'd he do?"

"He's not a good boy," Buddy's mother said firmly. "He makes things up. He tells things on people. Horrible things. Things that aren't so. It can cause a lot of trouble, especially when the people are living in the same house with us—" She didn't finish it.

The woman's eyes rested speculatively on Buddy for a long cool moment. Speculation ended and conviction entered them. They never wavered. She might have been thinking of a blanket that suddenly fell down the fire escape from one floor to the next when there was no wind. She might have been thinking of a razor salesman that asked too many questions.

Something about that look, it went right through you. It crinkled you all up. It was like death itself looking at you. Buddy'd never met a look like that before. It was so still, so deep, so cold, so dangerous.

Then she smiled. The look in her eyes didn't go out, but her mouth smiled. "Boys will be boys," she said sweetly. She reached out to try and playfully pull his hair or something like that, but he swerved his head violently aside, with something akin to horror, and she failed to reach him.

She turned away and left them. But she went up, not down. She had been coming from above just now, now she went back that way again. "I'm always forgetting something," she murmured as if to herself. "That letter I wanted to mail."

Buddy knew, with an awful certainty. She wanted to tell *him*. The man. She wanted to tell him right away, without losing a minute.

The politeness forced on her by the spectator at an end, Buddy's mother resumed her flurried handling of him where she had left off. She wrestled him violently into their flat and closed the door. But he wasn't aware of anything that she said to him; he could only think of one thing.

"Now you told her!" he sobbed in mortal anguish. "Now they *know!* Now they know *who!*"

His mother misunderstood, beautifully and completely. "Oh, now you're ashamed of yourself, is that it? I should think you would be!" She retrieved the key from his sleeping father's pillow, unlocked the door, thrust him in, and relocked it. "I was going to let you out, but now you'll stay in there the rest of the day!"

He didn't hear her, didn't know what she was saying at all.

"Now you told her!" he said over and over. "Now they'll get me for it!"

He heard her leave for work. He was left alone there, in the stifling flat, with just his father's heavy breathing in the outside room to keep him company.

Fear didn't come right away. He knew he was safe while his father was out there. They couldn't get at him. That's why he didn't mind being in there, he didn't even try to get out through the window a second time. He was all right as long as he stayed where he was. It was tonight he was worried about, when his father was away at work and just his mother was asleep in the flat with him.

The long hot day burned itself out. The sun started to go down, and premonitory fear came with the creeping, deepening blue shadows. He'd never felt this way before. The night was going to be bad, the night was going to be his enemy, and he didn't have anyone he could tell it to, so they'd help him. Not his father, not his mother, not even the police. And if you didn't have the police on your side, you might as well give up, there was no hope for you. They were on the side of everyone in the whole world, who wasn't a crook or murderer. *Everyone.* But not him. He was left out.

His mother came back from work. He heard her start to get supper ready, then call to his father, to wake him. He heard his father moving around getting dressed. Then the key was inserted, the door unlocked. He jumped up from the chair he'd been huddled on. His father motioned him to come out. "Now you going to behave yourself?'' he asked gruffly. "You going to cut that stuff out?''

"Yes sir," he said docilely. "Yes sir.''

"Sit down and have your supper."

They sat down to eat.

His mother didn't mean to give way on him, he could tell that; it came out accidentally, toward the end of the meal. She incautiously said something about her employer having called her down.

"Why?" his father asked.

"Oh, because I was five or ten minutes late."

"How'd you happen to be late? You *seemed* to be ready on time."

"I was *ready*, but by the time I got through talking to that policeman that came to the do—" She stopped short, but the damage was already done.

"What policeman that came to the door?"

She didn't want to, but he finally made her tell him. "Buddy sneaked out. One of them brought him back here with him. Now, Charlie, don't, you just finished eating."

Buddy's father hauled him off his chair by the shoulder.

"I belted you once today. How many times am I going to have to—"

There was a knock at the door, and that saved Buddy for a minute. His father let go of him, went over and opened it. He stood out there a minute with someone, then he closed it, came back, and said in surprise: "It's a telegram. And for *you*, Mary."

"Who on earth—?" She tore it open tremulously. Then she gave him a stricken look. "It's from Emma. She must be in some kind of trouble. She says to come out there at once, she needs me. 'Please come without delay as soon as you get this.' "

Emma was Buddy's aunt, his mother's sister. She lived all the way out on Staten Island.

"It must be the children," his mother said. "They must be both taken sick at once or something."

"Maybe it's her herself," his father said. "That would be even worse."

"If I could only reach her! That's what comes of not having telephones."

She started to get her things together. Buddy pleaded, terrified, "Don't go. Mom! It's a trick. It's from them. They want you out of the way. They want to get me."

"Still at it," his father said, giving him a push. "Get inside there. Go ahead, Mary. You'll be half the night getting there as it is. I'll take care of him. Gimme a hammer and a couple of long nails," he added grimly. "He'll stay put, I'll see to that."

He drove them through the two sash joints of the window in there, riveting it inextricably closed. "That oughta keep you. Now you can tell your stories to the four walls, to your heart's content!"

His mother patted his head tearfully, "Please be a good boy, listen to your father," and was gone.

He only had one protector left now. And a protector who had turned against him. He tried to reason with him, win him over.

"Pop, don't leave me here alone. They're going to come down and get me. Pop, take me with you to the plant; I won't get in your way. Honest, I won't."

His father eyed him balefully. "Keep it up. Just keep it up. You're going to a doctor tomorrow. I'm going to take you to one myself and find out what's the matter with you."

"Pop, don't lock the door. Don't. *Don't!* At least give me a chance so I can get out." He tried to hang on to the knob with both hands, but his father's greater strength dragged it slowly around in a closing arc.

"So you can run around to the police again and disgrace us? Well, if you're so afraid of *them*, whoever they are, then you ought to be glad I'm locking the door, that'll keep you safe from them. You confounded little liar!"

Cluck! went the key in the lock.

He pressed his face close to the door seam and pleaded agonizedly, "Pop, don't leave the key in. If you gotta lock me up, at least take the key with you."

"The key stays in. I ain't taking a chance on dropping it somewhere and losing it."

He began to pound with his fists, frantic now and beyond all control. "Pop, come back! Take me with you! Don't leave me here alone! Pop, I take it back. It wasn't so."

His father was thoroughly exasperated by now, nothing could have made him relent.

"I'll see you when I come back from work, young fellow!" he rasped. "You've got something coming to you!"

The outer door slammed, and he was gone beyond recall.

He was alone now. Alone with crafty enemies, alone with imminent death.

He stopped his outcries at once. Now they were risky. Now they could no longer help him, now they might even bring on the danger all the quicker.

He put out the light. It made it more scary without it, but he knew it was safer to be in the dark than in the light. Maybe he could fool them into thinking nobody was there, if he stayed in the dark like this. Maybe, but he didn't have much hope. They must have watched down the stairs, seen his father go alone.

Silence, then. Not a sound. Not a sound of menace, at least; from overhead, or from the outside room. Plenty of sounds outside in the back; the blurred harmless sounds of a summer night. Radios, and dishes being washed, and a baby crying somewhere, then going off to sleep.

Too early yet, he had a little time yet. That almost made it worse, to have to sit and *wait* for it to come.

A church bell began to toll. St. Agnes', the little neighborhood church a couple of blocks over. You could always hear it from here. He counted the strokes. Nine. No, there was another one. Ten already. Gee, time had gone fast. In the dark you couldn't keep track of it very easy.

It would take Mom a full hour and a half to get over to Aunt

Emma's, even if she made good connections. She'd have to cross over to lower Manhattan first, and then go by ferry down the bay, and then take the bus out to where the place was. And another hour and a half to get back, even if she left right away. But she wouldn't leave right away. She'd stay on there for a while, even after she found out the message was a fake. She wouldn't think there was any danger, she trusted everyone so. She always saw the good in everyone. She'd think it was just a harmless joke.

He'd be alone here until at least one, and maybe even after. They knew that. That's why they were taking their time. That's why they were waiting. They wanted things to quiet down, they wanted other people to be asleep.

He got up every once in a while and went over to the door and listened. Nothing. The ticking of the clock in the other room was all he could hear.

Maybe if he could push the key out, and it fell real close to the door, he could pull it through to his side underneath the door. It was an old, warped door, and the crack seemed pretty wide along the floor.

It was easy to push it out. He did that with a pencil stub he had in his pocket. He heard it fall. Then he got a rusty old wire coat hanger that was in the room, and pushed that through the crack on its flat side and started to fish around with it, hoping the flat hook at the top of it would snag the key and scoop it through to him.

He could hear himself hitting it, but each time he'd ease the hanger through, the hook would come back empty. Finally he couldn't hit it any more at all, and he knew what had happened. He'd pushed it farther away, it was out of reach now entirely. He'd lost it.

The church bell sounded again. Again he counted. Eleven. Had a whole hour passed, just doing that?

Most of the lights in the back windows were out now. The last radio had stopped.

If he could last through the next hour, maybe he'd be all right. From twelve on time would be working in his favor. Mom would be on her way back, and—

He stiffened. There was a single creak, from directly overhead. From *them*. The first sound they'd made. Trying not to be heard. You could tell the person was going on tiptoe by the slow way it sounded. Cree-eak. It took about a whole half-minute to finish itself.

Then nothing more for a long time. He was afraid to move, he was afraid to breathe.

Then another kind of a sound, from a different place. Not wood, but shaky iron. Not overhead, but outside. Not a creak, but a kind of a soft clank.

His eyes flew to the window.

The shade. He should have thought about that sooner. But if there was no light on, nobody could see into the room anyway, even with it up.

He could see out a little. Not much, but just a sort of sooty dark gray color, a little bit lighter than the room itself, that was all. And now this was getting darker, right while he watched it. It was sort of blotting out, as if something was coming down from above, out there in front of the window.

He crouched back against the wall, hunched his head low between his shoulders, like a turtle trying to draw its head into its shell.

The looming shape was up close now, it covered the whole pane, like a black feather bolster. He could see something pale in the middle of it, though, like a face.

Suddenly the middle of it lit up bright silver, in a disk about the size of an egg, and a long spoke of light shot through the glass and into the room.

It started to swing around slowly, following the walls from one side all the way around to the other. It traced a white paper hoop as it went. Maybe if he got down low he could duck under it, it would miss him. He bunched himself up into a ball, head below knees now.

It arrived right over him, on the wall, and there was nothing he could push in front of him, nothing he could get behind. Suddenly it dropped. It flashed square into his squinting face, blinding him.

Then it went out, as suddenly as it had gone on. It wasn't needed any more. It had told them what they wanted to know. They knew he was in there now. They knew he was *alone* in there.

He could hear fingers fumbling about the woodwork, trying the window. It wouldn't move, the nails held it tight.

The looming black blur slowly rose upward, out of sight. The fire escape cleared. There was another creak overhead, on the ceiling. Not so slow or stealthy any more; the need for concealment was past now.

What would they do next? Would they try to get in the other way, down the front stairs? Would they give up? He knew they wouldn't; they'd gone to too much trouble, sending that phony telegram. It was now or never, they'd never have such an opportunity again.

St. Agnes' chimed the half-hour. His heart was going so fast, it was just as though he'd run a mile race top speed.

Silence for minutes. Like before thunder, like before something happens. Silence for the last time. He was breathing with his mouth open, that was the only way he could get enough air in. Even that way he couldn't, he felt as if he were going to choke.

Then a lock jigged a little. Out there, in the room past this. You could hardly hear it, but it gave off little soft turning sounds. The outside door started to open guardedly. He could hear one of the hinges whine a little as it turned. Then it closed again.

A skeleton key. They'd used a skeleton key.

The floor softly complained, here, there, the next place, coming straight over toward the door he was behind, the final door. Somebody was in there. Maybe just one. Maybe the both of them together.

They didn't put on the lights. They were afraid, maybe, they'd be seen from outside. They were up to it now, the door to where he was. He almost thought he could hear their breathing, but he wasn't sure; his own made enough noise for two.

The knob started to turn. Then it went back again to where it had been. They were trying the door. If only they didn't see that key lying there—But then he realized they didn't need that one anyway; the same skeleton key that had opened the outside door would work on this.

Maybe he could jam the lock; the pencil stub that he'd used the first time, to force the original key out. He dredged it up from his pocket. Too fast, too flurriedly. He dropped it, and he had to go feeling all over the floor for it, with slapping hands. He found it again, floundered toward the door. The door seam had gleamed a little, for a moment, as if a light were licking along it, to place the keyhole. Just as he got there, the keyhole sounded off, the key rammed into it.

Too late; the key was in, he was gone.

He looked around for something to shove up against the door, to buy a minute more. Nothing heavy enough. Only that chair he'd been sitting on, and that was no good.

The key was squirming around, catching onto the lock.

He hoisted the chair and he swung it. But the other way, away from the door. He swatted the window pane with it with all his might. It went out with a torrential crash just as the door broke away from its frame and bucked inward.

He got out through the jagged opening; so fast that his very speed was a factor in saving him. He felt his clothing catch in a couple of places, but the glass didn't touch his skin.

Heavy running steps hammered across the wooden floor in there behind him. An arm reached through and just missed him. The splintered glass kept the man back, he was too big to chance it as Buddy had.

Buddy scuttled down the fire escape for all his life. And around the turn, and down, and around another turn, and down, like a corkscrew. Then he jumped down to the ground, and ran into the basement.

It was plenty dark down there, and he knew every inch of it by heart from being in there a lot at other times. But he was afraid if he stayed in there they'd come right down after him and trap him, cut off his escape. Then eventually ferret him out, and do it down there instead, in the dark. He wanted the open, he wanted the safety of the streets, where they wouldn't dare try anything. Where there would be people around who could interfere, come to his rescue.

So he plunged straight through without stopping, and up the janitor's steps at the front to sidewalk level. Just as he gained the street, panting, the oncoming rush of his pursuer sounded warningly from the cavernous building entrance alongside him, and a moment later the man came careening out after him. He'd come down the front stairs, to try to cut him off.

Buddy turned and sped away toward the corner, racing as only the very small and the very light in weight can race. But the man had longer legs and greater windpower, and it was only a matter of minutes before the unequal pursuit would end.

Buddy made the corner and scuffed around it on the sides of his shoes. No one in sight, no one around that offered any chance of protection. The man was closing in on him remorselessly now, every long step swallowing three of Buddy's. Buddy would have had to be running three times as fast even to break even with him, and he wasn't even matching his speed. The woman had joined in the chase too, but she was far behind, unimportant to the immediate crisis.

He spotted a row of ashcans just ahead, lined up along the curb. All filled and set out waiting to be emptied. About six, making a bulwark of about ten yards or so in length. He knew he couldn't get past them, the man was within about two outstretched arms' length of him now, and already had one arm out to bridge half the span. So he ran to the end of them, caught the rim of the last one to swing himself around on—its fill held it down fast—and suddenly doubled back along the other side of them. A feat the man couldn't hope to match as quickly, as deftly, because of his greater bulk. He went flying out too far on a wasteful ellipse, had to come in again from out there. Buddy was able to keep their strung-out length between the two of them from now on. The man couldn't reach him across them the short way, all he had to do was swerve back a little out of his reach. The man couldn't overthrow them either, they were too hefty with coke and ash.

But Buddy knew he couldn't stay there long, the woman was coming up rapidly and they'd sew him up between the two of them. He stopped short and crouched warily over one of the bins. He gouged both hands into the powdery gritty ash, left them that way for an instant, buried up to the wrists. The man dove for him. Buddy's hands shot up. A landmine of the stuff exploded full into the man's face. He got more of it that way than by throwing it. The whole top layer erupted.

Buddy shot diagonally into the open for the other side, left the readymade barricade behind. The man couldn't follow him for a minute, he was too busy staggering, coughing, pawing, trying to get his eyesight back.

Buddy made the most of it. He gained another corner, tore down a new street. But it was just a postponement, not a clean-cut getaway. The man came pounding into sight again behind him after a brief time-lag, murderous now with added intensity. Again those longer legs, the deeper chest, started to get in their work.

Buddy saw a moving figure ahead, the first person he'd seen on the streets since the chase had begun. He raced up abreast of him, started to tug at his arm, too breathless to be able to do anything but pant for a minute. Pant, and point behind him, and keep jerking at his arm.

"Geddada here," the man said thickly, half-alarmed himself by the frenzied incoherent symptoms. "Warrya doing?"

"Mister, that man's trying to get me—! Mister, don't let him—!"

The man swayed unpredictably to one of Buddy's tugs, and the two of them nearly went down together in a heap.

A look of idiotic fatuousness overspread his face. "Warrsh matter, kid? Somebody trying to getcha?"

A drunk. No good to him. Hardly able to understand what he was saying to him at all.

Buddy suddenly pushed him in the path of the oncoming nemesis. He went down, and the other one sprawled over his legs. Another minute or two gained.

At the upper end of the street Buddy turned off again, into an avenue. This one had tracks, and a lighted trolley was bearing down on him just as he came around the corner. That miracle after dark, a trolley just when it was needed. Its half-hourly passing just coinciding with his arrival at the corner.

He was an old hand at cadging free rides on the backs of them; that was the way he did all his traveling back and forth. He knew just where to put his feet, he knew just where to take hold with his hands.

He turned to face the direction it was going, let it rumble by full length, took a short spurt after it, jumped, and latched on.

The man came around into view too late, saw him being borne triumphantly away. The distance began to widen, slowly but surely; legs couldn't keep up with a motor, windpower with electricity. But he wouldn't give up, he kept on running just the same, shrinking in stature now each time Buddy darted a look back.

"Stop that car!" he shouted faintly from the rear.

The conductor must have thought he merely wanted to board it himself as a fare. Buddy, peering over the rim of the rear window, saw him fling a derisive arm out in answer.

Suddenly the car started to slacken, taper off for an approaching stop. There was a huddle of figures ahead at trackside, waiting to board it. Buddy, agonized, tried to gauge the distance between pursuer, trolley, and intended passengers. The man was still about twice as far away from it, in the one direction, as they were in the other. If they'd get on quick, if it started right off again, Buddy could still make it, he'd still get away from him, even if only by the skin of his teeth.

The car ground to a stop. A friendly green light was shining offside, at the crossing. The figures, there were three, went into a hubbub. Two helped the third aboard. Then they handed up several baskets and parcels after her. Then she leaned down from the top of the step and kissed them severally.

"Goodbye. Get home all right, Aunt Tilly."

"Thank you for a lovely time."

"Give my love to Sam."

"Wait a minute! Aunt Tilly! Aunt Tilly! Your umbrella! Here's your umbrella!"

The motorman went *ding!* impatiently, with his foot.

The green light was gone now. There was nothing there in its place, just an eclipse, blackness. The car gave a nervous little start, about to go forward.

Suddenly red glowered balefully up there. Like blood, like fiery death. The death of a little boy.

The car fell obediently motionless again, static. In the silence you could hear *wap-whup, wap-whup, wap-whup,* coming up fast from behind.

Buddy dropped down to the ground, too late. The man's forked hand caught him at the back of the neck like a vise, pinned him flat and squirming against the rear end of the car.

The chase was over. The prey was caught.

"Now I've got you," his captor hissed grimly in his ear.

The treacherous trolley, now that it had undone him, withdrew, taking the shine of its lights with it, leaving the two of them alone in the middle of the darkened trackway.

Buddy was too exhausted to struggle much, the man was too winded to do much more than just hold him fast. That was all he needed to do. They stood there together, strangely passive, almost limp, for a few moments. As if taking time out, waiting for a signal to begin their struggle anew.

The woman came up presently. There was a cold business-like quality to her undertone worse than any imprecations could have been. She spoke as though she were referring to a basket of produce.

"All right, get him out of the middle of the street, Joe. Don't leave him out here."

Buddy went into a flurry of useless struggling, like a snagged pinwheel, that ended almost as soon as it began. The man twisted his arm around behind his back and held it that way, using it as a lever to force submission. The pain was too excruciating to disobey.

They remounted the sidewalk and walked along with him between them. Sandwiched between them, very close between them, so that from the front you couldn't tell he was being strongarmed. The pressure of their two bodies forced him along as well as the compulsion of his disjointed arm.

Wouldn't they meet anybody, anybody at all? Was the whole town off the streets, just tonight? Suddenly they did.

There were two men this time. Not swaying, walking straight and steady, cold sober. Men you could reason with. They'd help him, they'd have to. They were coming toward him and his captors. Otherwise the latter would have tried to avoid them. They couldn't; the men had turned the corner just before them too abruptly, catching them in full view. A retreat would have aroused suspicion.

The man Joe took a merciless extra half-turn in his already fiery arm just as a precaution. "One word out of you," he gritted, "and I'll yank it off by the roots!"

Buddy waited until the two parties were abreast of one another, mustering up strength against the pain; both present pain and the pain to come.

Then he sideswept one foot, bit its heel savagely into his captor's unprotected shinbone. The man heaved from the pavement, released Buddy's arm by reflex.

Buddy flung himself almost in a football tackle against the nearest of the two passers-by, wrapped both arms about his leg, and held on like a barnacle. "Mister, help me! Mister, don't let 'em!"

The man, hobbled, was unable to move another step. His companion halted likewise. "What the—!"

"Y'gotta listen! Y'gotta believe—!" Buddy sputtered, to get his lick in first. "They killed a man last night. Now they're gonna do the same thing to me—!"

Joe didn't do what he'd expected. He didn't grab for him, he didn't show violence, even anger. There was a sudden change of attitude that threw Buddy off key, put him at a disadvantage. The thing had become psychological instead of physical. And he wasn't so good psychologically. The line-up had turned into one of age groups before he knew how it had happened; a kid against four grownups. Grownups that gave each other the benefit of the doubt sooner than they would give it to a kid.

"His own mother and father," Joe murmured with mournful resignation.

The woman had taken a handkerchief out, was applying it effectively to her eyes.

"They're not! They're not!" Buddy howled agonizedly.

The woman turned her back and her shoulders shook.

"He doesn't mean to lie," Joe said with paternal indulgence. "He makes these things up, and then he believes it himself. His imagination is over-active."

"They're not my parents, they're not!" Buddy groaned abysmally.

"Well, tell them where you live, then," Joe said suavely.

"Yeah, kid, give us your address," one of the two strangers put in.

"20 Holt Street!" Buddy rushed in incautiously.

Joe had suddenly whipped out a billfold, held it open for the men to see some sort of corroboratory identification. "For once he admits he lives with us," he said ruefully. "Usually—"

"He stole five dollars out of my pocketbook," the woman chimed in tearfully. "My gas-bill money for this month. Then he went to the movies. He's been gone since three this afternoon, we only found him just now. This has been going on all the way home."

"They killed a man," Buddy screeched. "They cut him up with a razor."

"That was in the picture he just saw," Joe said with a disheartened shake of his head.

The woman was crouched supplicatingly before Buddy now, dabbing her handkerchief at his face in maternal solicitude, trying to clean it. "Won't you behave now? Won't you come home like a good boy?"

The two strangers had turned definitely against him. The woman's tears, the man's sorrowful forbearance, were having an effect. One man looked at the other. "Gee, I'm sure glad I never married, Mike, if this is what you get."

The other one bent over and detached Buddy none too gently. "C'mon, leggo of me," he said gruffly. "Listen to your parents, do like they tell you."

He dusted off his trouser leg where Buddy had manhandled it, in eloquent indication of having nothing more to do with the matter. They went on about their business, down the street.

The tableau remained unaltered behind them for as long as they were still within call. The woman crouched before Buddy, but her unseen hand had a vicious death grip on the front of his shirt. Joe was bending over him from behind, as if gently reasoning with him. But he had his arm out of kilter again, holding it coiled up behind his back like a mainspring.

"You—little devil!" he exhaled through tightly clenched teeth.

"Get him in a taxi, Joe. We can't keep parading him on the open street like this."

They said something between them that he didn't quite catch. "—that boarded-up place. Kids play around there a lot." Then they both nodded in malignant understanding.

A cold ripple went up his back. He didn't know what they meant, but it was something bad. They even had to whisper it to each other, it was so bad. "That boarded-up place." A place for dark, secret deeds that would never come to light again; not for years, anyway.

A cab glided up at the man's up-chopping arm, and they went into character again. "It's the last time I ever take you out with me!" the woman scolded, with one eye on the driver. "Now you get in there!"

They wrestled him into it between them, feet clear of the ground; the woman holding his flailing legs, the man his head and shoulders; his body sagging in the middle like a sack of potatoes. They dumped him on the seat, and then held him down fast between them.

"Corner of Amherst and 22nd," the man said. Then as the machine glided off, he murmured out of the corner of his mouth to the woman, "Lean over a little, get in front of us." Her body blocked Buddy from the oblivious driver's sight for a moment.

The man pulled a short, wicked punch with a foreshortened arm, straight up from below, and Buddy saw stars and his ears rang. He didn't lose his senses, but he was dazed to a passive acquiescence for a few minutes. Little gritty pieces of tooth enamel tickled his tongue, and his eyes ran water without his actually crying.

The cab stopped for a light, while he was slowly getting over the effects of the blow. Metal clashed, and a figure on the opposite side of the street closed a call box and leisurely sauntered on.

A policeman, at last! What he'd been hoping for, what he'd been praying for—

The woman's hand, handkerchief-lined, guessed his intent too late, tried to find his mouth and clamp itself tight over it. He swerved his head, sank his teeth into her finger. She recoiled with a stifled exclamation, whipped her hand away.

He tore loose with the loudest scream he could summon; it almost pulled the lining of his throat inside out. "Mr. Officer! Mr. Pleeeceman! Help me, will ya? Help me!"

The policeman turned on his course, came toward them slowly. A kid's cry for help, that wasn't the same as a grownup's cry for help, that wasn't as immediate, as crucial.

He looked in the cab window at the three of them. He even rested his forearm negligently along the rim as he did so. He wasn't on the alert; it couldn't be anything much, a kid squawking in a taxicab.

"What's up?" he said friendlily. "What's he hollering for?"

"He knows what he's going to get when we get home with him, that's what's up!" the woman said primly. "And you can holler at all the policemen you want to, young man, that won't save you!"

" 'Fraid of a licking, hunh?" the cop grinned understandingly. "A good licking never hurt any kid. My old man useta gimme enough of 'em when I was—" He chuckled appreciatively. "But that's a new one, calling the cops on your old man and lady to keep from getting a licking! I tell you, these kids nowadays—"

"He turned in a false alarm one time," the "father" complained virtuously, "to try and keep me from shellacking him!"

The cop whistled.

The cab driver turned his head and butt in, unasked. "I got two of my own, home. And if they gave me half as much trouble as this young pup's been giving these folks here since they first hailed me, I'd knock their blocks off. I'm telling you."

"They m-m-murdered a man last night, with a knife, and then they cut him up all in pieces and—" Buddy sobbed incoherently.

"What a dirty mind he's got," the cop commented disapprovingly. He took a closer look at Buddy's contorted face. "Wait a minute, don't I know you, kid?"

There was a breathless silence. Buddy's heart soared like a balloon. At last, at last—

"Sure, I remember you now. You come over with that same story and made a lot of trouble for us at the station house this morning. Wasting everybody's time. Brundage even sent somebody over to investigate, like a fool. And was his face red afterwards! A lot of hot air. You're the very one; I seen you there meself. Then one of the guys had to take you home afterwards to get rid of you. Are you the parents?''

"Do you think we'd be going through this if we weren't?'' Joe demanded bitterly.

"Well, you've sure got my sympathy.'' He waved them on disgustedly. "Take him away. You can *have* him!''

The cab glided into lethal motion again. Buddy's head went over supinely, in ultimate despair. Wasn't there anyone in the whole grown-up world believed you? Did you have to be grownup yourself before anyone would believe you, stop you from being murdered? He didn't try to holler out the window any more at the occasional chance passers-by he glimpsed flitting by. What was the use? They wouldn't help him. He was licked. Salty water coursed from his eyes, but he didn't make a sound.

"Any p'tickler number?'' the driver asked.

"The corner'll do,'' Joe said plausibly. "We live just a couple doors up the street.'' He paid him off before they got out, in order to have both hands free for Buddy once they alighted.

The cab slowed, and they emerged with him, started walking hurriedly away. His feet slithered along the ground more than they actually lifted themselves. The cab wheeled and went back the way it had come.

"Think he'll remember our faces later?'' the woman breathed worriedly.

"It's not our faces that count, it's the kid's face,'' Joe answered her. "And nobody'll ever see that again.''

As soon as the cab was safely gone, they reversed directions and went up another street entirely.

"There it is, over there,'' Joe said guardedly.

It was a derelict tenement, boarded up, condemned, but not demolished. It cast a pall of shadow, so that even while they were still outside in front of it, they could scarcely be seen. It sent forth an odor of decay. It was, Buddy knew, the place where death was.

They stopped short. "Anyone around?'' Joe said watchfully.

Then suddenly he embraced the boy; a grim sort of embrace if
there ever was one, without love in it. He wrapped his arm
around his head and clutched him to him tight, so that his hand
sealed Buddy's mouth. Buddy had no chance to bite him as he
had the woman. The pressure against his jaws was too great, he
couldn't even open them.

He carried him that way, riding on his own hip so to speak,
over to the seemingly secure boarded-up doorway. He spaded
his free hand in under this, tilted it out, wormed his way
through, and whisked Buddy after him. The woman followed
and replaced it. A pall of complete darkness descended on the
three of them. The stench was terrific in here. It wasn't just the
death of a building; it was—some other kind of death as well.
Death in two suitcases, perhaps.

"How'd you know that was open?" the woman whispered in
surprise.

"How do you suppose?" he answered with grisly meaning.

"*This* where?" was all she said.

The man had taken his torch out. It snapped whitely at a skeleton stair, went right out again; instantaneously as the lens of a
camera. "Wait here where you are; don't smoke," he warned
her. "I'm going up a ways."

Buddy could guess that he didn't knock him completely out
because that would have made him too heavy to handle; he
wanted him to get up there on his own two feet, if possible. They
started to climb, draggingly. The soundtrack went: *crunch,
crunch, skfff.* That was Buddy's feet trailing passively over the
lips of the steps.

He was too numbed with terror now to struggle much any
more. It was no use anyway. No one anywhere around outside to
hear him through the thick mouldering walls. If they hadn't
helped him outside on the street, they were never going to help
him in here.

Joe used his torch sparingly, only a wink at a time. Only when
one flight had ended and they were beginning another. He
wasn't taking any chances using it too freely. It was like a white

Morse code on black paper. Dot, dot, dot. Spelling out one word: death.

They halted at last. They must have reached the top now. There was a busted skylight somewhere just over them. It was just as black as ever, but a couple of low-wattage stars could be made out.

Joe pressed Buddy back flat against the wall, held him that way with one hand at his throat. Then he clipped his light on, left it that way this time. He wanted to see what he was doing. He set it down on the floor, left it that way, alight, trained on Buddy. Then his other hand closed in to finish the job.

A minute, maybe a minute and a half, would be all he needed. Life goes out awfully quick; even manually, which is one of the slowest ways.

"Say goodbye, kid," he murmured ironically.

You fight when you die, because—that's what everything alive does, that's what being alive *is*.

Buddy couldn't fight off the man's arms. But his legs were free. The man had left them free, so he could die standing up. Buddy knew a man's stomach is soft, the softest part of him. He couldn't kick it free-swinging, because the man was in too close. He kicked upward with his knee, rammed it home. He could feel it pillow itself into something rubbery. A flame of hot body breath was expelled against him, like those pressure things you dry yourself with.

The death collar opened and the man's hands went to his middle. Buddy knew that one such punch wasn't enough. This was death and you gave no quarter. The man had given him the space he needed. He shot his whole foot out this time, sole flat. There was almost a sucking noise, as if it had gone into a waterlogged sponge.

The man went all the way back. He must have trodden on the cylindrical light. It spun crazily around. Off Buddy, onto the man for an instant. Then off the man, onto somewhere else. You couldn't follow it with your eyes, it jittered too quick.

There was a splintering of wood. There was a strange sagging feeling, that made everything shake. Then a roaring sound, like of a lot of heavy stuff going down a chute. The light flashed across the space once, and showed nothing: no Joe, no rail, no anything. Then it pitched down into nothingness itself.

There was a curious sort of playback, that came seconds late, from somewhere far below. Like an echo, only it wasn't. Of something heavy and firm, something with bones in it, bones and a skull, smacking like a gunshot report. A woman's voice screamed "Joe!" hollowly. Then a lot of loose planks went *clat-clat, clat, clattity, bang!* The woman's voice just groaned after that, didn't scream any more. Then the groans stopped too. A lot of plaster dust came up and tickled his noise and smarted his eyes.

It was very still, and he was alone in the dark. Something told him not to move. He just stood there, pressed himself flat and stood there. Something kept telling him not to move, not to move a finger. He didn't know what it was, maybe the way his hair stood up on the back of his neck. As if his hair could see in the dark better than he could, knew something that he didn't.

It didn't last long. There were suddenly a lot of voices down there, as if people had come running in from the street, and lights winking around. Then a stronger one than the rest, a sort of thick searchlight beam, shot all the way up, and jockeyed around, and finally found him.

The whole stair structure was gone. A single plank, or maybe two, had held fast against the wall, and he was standing on them. Like on a shelf. A shelf that ended at his toes. Five floors up.

A voice came up to him through a megaphone, trying to be very calm, very friendly; shaking a little around the edges, though. "Close your eyes, kid. We'll get you down. Just don't look, keep your eyes closed. Think hard of something else. Do you know your multiplication tables?"

Buddy nodded cautiously, afraid to move his head too much.

"Start saying them. Two times two, two times three. Keep your eyes closed. You're in school and the teacher's right in front of you. But don't change your position."

He was in Six-A, didn't they know that? You got multiplication in the first grade. But he did it anyway. He finished the twos, he finished the threes. He stopped.

"Mister," he called down in a thin but clear voice. "How much longer do I have to hold out? I'm getting pins and needles in my legs, and I'm stuck at four times twenty-three."

"Do you want it fast and just a little risky, kid, or do you want it slow and safe?"

"Fast and just a little risky," he answered. "I'm getting kind of dizzy."

"All right, son," the voice boomed back. "We've got a net spread out down here. We can't show it to you, you'll have to take our word for it."

"There may be loose planks sticking out on the way down," another voice objected, in an undertone that somehow reached him.

"It'll take hours the other way, and he's been through enough already." The voice directed itself upward to him again. "Keep your arms close to your sides, keep your feet close together, open your eyes, and when I count three, jump."

"—three!"

He was never going to get there. Then he did, and he bounced, and it was over, he was safe.

He cried for a minute or two, and he didn't know why himself; it must have been left over from before, when Joe was trying to kill him. Then he got over it.

He hoped they hadn't seen him. "I wasn't crying," he said. "All that stuff got in my eyes, and stung them."

"Same here," Detective Ross, his one-time enemy, said gravely. And the funny part of it was, his eyes *were* kind of shiny too.

Joe was lying there dead, his head sticking out between two planks. They'd carried the woman out on a stretcher.

Somebody came up and joined them with a very sick look on his face. "We've pulled two valises out from under what's left of those stairs back there."

"Better not look in them just yet," Ross warned.

"I already did," he gulped, and he bolted out into the street, holding his hand clapped to his mouth.

They rode Buddy back in state, in a departmental car. In the middle of all of them, like a—like a mascot.

"Gee, thanks for saving me," he said gratefully.

"We didn't save you, son. You saved yourself. We're a great bunch. We were just a couple minutes too late. We would have caught them, all right, but we wouldn't have saved you."

"How'd you know where to come, though?"

"Picking up the trail was easy, once we got started. A cop back there remembered you, a cab driver showed where he let you out. It was just that we started so late."

"But what made you believe it now all of a sudden, when you wouldn't believe it this morning?"

"A couple little things came up," Ross said. "Little, but they counted. The Kellerman woman mentioned the exact program you were supposed to have overheard last night, by name. It sounded better that way, more plausible. It's the exact time, the exact type; it fitted in too good to waste. But by doing that she saved your life tonight. Because I happened to tune in myself tonight. Not out of suspicion, just for my own entertainment. If it was that good, I wanted to hear it myself. And it *was* that good, and even better. It's a serial, it's continued every night. Only at the end, the announcer apologized to the listeners. For *not being on the air at all last night.* Tuesday's election, and the program gave up its time to one of the candidates. And what you'd said you heard was sure no campaign speech!

"That was one thing. Then I went straight over to their flat. Pretty late, and almost as bad as never. They must have already been on the way with you. Everything in order, just like I'd seen it the first time. Only, a towel fell down from in back of the bathroom door, as I brushed past. And under it, where nobody could be blamed for overlooking it, not even the two of them themselves, there was a well-worn razor strop. The kind you use for an open blade, never a safety. With a fleck of fairly fresh soap still on it. Just a couple of things like that, that came awfully late, but that counted!

"Come on, Buddy, here's your home. I'll go in with you."

It was already getting light out, and when they knocked, Buddy said in a scared whisper, "Gee, now I'm going to get it for sure! I been out the whole night long!"

"Detectives have to be sometimes, didn't you know that?" And Ross took his own badge off and pinned it on him.

The door opened, and his father was standing there. Without a word, he swung his arm back.

Ross just reached up and held it where it was.

"Now, now, just be careful who you raise the back of your hand to around here. It's a serious matter to swat a member of the Detective Bureau, you know. Even an auxiliary, junior grade."

Ludmila

JEAN L. BACKUS

Contrary to what some may have us believe, day-to-day life behind the Iron Curtain is generally the same as it is here — the same struggles, the same fears and hungers, the same injustices; yes, and sometimes the same tragedies, too, as Jean L. Backus movingly demonstrates in this unusual story about a Russian child named Ludmila. Ms. Backus has also written a novel with a Russian setting, Dusha, about a prima ballerina. Her diverse literary talents include those of an accomplished spy novelist (Troika, Traitor's Wife, Fellow-Traveler, all under the pseudonym of David Montross); and nonfiction writer and editor (as exemplified in her acclaimed 1982 book on aviatrix Amelia Earhart, Letters from Amelia).

USUALLY Grandmother screeched at her the minute the door opened, asking why Ludmila had loitered in the woods, or if she'd been bad in school and made to stay for punishment. Sometimes the old woman didn't even say that much before flinging her pillow at Ludmila, who was always ready to jump to one side or the other. But today was different. No pillow slung at her this late afternoon. No screeching either.

"Babushka?" Risking a glance at Grandmother, she saw the old woman's thin white braids spreading from under the pillow, and the blankets pulled up high as she'd arranged them hours ago. She wanted to say, "Forgive me for this morning, Babushka. I didn't mean to be a bad girl. Do please forgive me and say something. Please."

Because if Grandmother didn't speak now, then she wouldn't say anything for days and days. Not one word. Maybe not until after it was time for snow to fly, and the hut to be crowded with Ludmila's Papa and her brothers, after they returned from harvest.

Quietly so as not to awaken Grandmother, she set a string bag of beets and cabbage and a precious sliver of salt pork on the table, and hurried to throw faggots on the fire. Babushka complained of being cold even in the hottest weather, and now finding fallen wood was harder, and Ludmila had to wander in greater circles through the forest each day. Next spring she'd ask Papa and her brothers to leave a larger wood pile for her before they went off for the summer to cut the grain. If Babushka wanted the hut kept hotter this summer than last, she'd want more heat than ever next year.

But then Ludmila would be thirteen, and surely she'd be able to cut her own wood. At least the lower branches of fir and birch which grew right up to the clearing. If she could do that, the men would be free to dig the well that someday would bring water right inside the hut, or build a shelter of some kind around the vegetables so rabbits and deer couldn't rob the garden as they had recently. Why, there was almost no food at all for this coming winter. The thought made her hungrier than usual. There were hardly any rubles left either, until Papa got home.

Careful not to look at Grandmother, who hated to be caught sleeping, Ludmila fried the pork and peeled the beets and chopped the cabbage and put them all to boil on the hearth, using the last water in the pail. Very quietly she put her shawl on again and went out across the clearing to the stream which chubbled over the rocks, sounding almost like Shura's balalaika.

If she stayed outside awhile, Babushka might sleep on, and there'd be less time for her to complain before they went to bed. Anyway, it was nicer out here alone, thinking and looking around at the shrubs and trees. It smelled better too; inside the hut it was awful.

She'd pretend when she did go in that she'd just come from school and the food store, and Grandmother could screech or throw her pillow as usual. Then they'd eat soup and go to bed, and in a day or two or a week Papa and the boys would be home. Babushka was quieter when they were around.

But as Papa said last spring, "If you were held in bed by useless legs, dear little Ludmila, you'd fret and whine and be mean too."

Since Papa said it, it must be so. Wasn't he the best father in the world? Helping with her lessons and always appearing at school on dark winter days just as she started the long lonely walk home through the woods. Comrade Varvara, the schoolteacher, said people must produce according to their ability, and reap according to their need. But Grandmother ate without producing any food. Papa said at her age that was natural; in her time she'd produced plenty.

This summer when birds and animals ate the vegetables and there was no grain or any feed for the cattle or sheep or pigs or chickens, old Nikolai at the food store said the coming winter would bring out the wolves for sure. Nobody in the village had seen one for at least three years, but everyone knew that when people died of hunger, the wolves always came.

Ludmila had never seen one either, but she'd heard them howling often enough. And Babushka was always saying that bad little girls were only good for feeding wild animals.

Ah, it would be nice when Papa and the seven brothers returned. This week probably, old Nikolai had said, shaking his bald head sadly, because early return meant bad harvest, and less food for everyone. Still Papa would keep the wolves away from the hut; he always had before.

Once they were all at home, there'd be no more dark and lonely mornings when Ludmila had to get up from beside Babushka, break ice on the pail of water left by the banked fire, and cook kasha after she pushed the pan under Grandmother.

Sometimes the old woman sat so long and fussed so about the way Ludmila fixed her blankets and fluffed her pillow afterward, she had to run all the way through the golden birches and green firs to the road and past the village houses to the collective hall where the schoolroom was. Then Comrade Varvara gave her extra homework to do by candlelight. If only Grandmother could produce candles even, or not be such a long time on the pan.

Oh, there was the first star. And others beyond it, getting brighter in spite of the rising moon, which tonight was as yellow as the birches by day. A lovely night filled with whisperings from the forest.

Last year Papa and the boys had been a month later than this, roaring with song as they tramped through the trees from where the lorries let them off in the village. Racing when they saw her waving, to see which of them reached her first. Whoever did would lift her off her feet and smother her squeals with kisses, taking his time before letting her go to the next in line. But none of them ever raced to kiss Grandmother.

How lovely to have them back early this year, if Nikolai was right. But sad about the people who'd starve this winter, maybe some from their own collective.

Which of the family might die?

Not Papa because he was healthy and strong. Nor the boys because they were young and strong. Not Babushka because if neither healthy nor young, she was the strongest of them all. Papa said so often. Every time Babushka asked him.

"Who's the strongest of us all?"

"You are, dearest little Mother."

Babushka would nod and grin, showing her shrunken gums, and the seven boys and Ludmila would laugh and cheer. Because Papa always stood where Grandmother couldn't see him, and winked as he answered to show what he truly thought.

But with all of them so strong that left only one who was weak. A bad little girl who couldn't cut her own wood, and begrudged the time Babushka spent on the pan each morning, and hated bringing her water to wash, and arranging the blankets and the pillow under the thin white braids.

Poor old woman. It was easy to hate her, hard to remember she was old and crippled. But who could love her when she smelled so and screeched so? This morning when Ludmila was already late for school, Babushka threw her pillow because it was hard and lumpy she said, and Ludmila began to cry. She'd thrown the pillow back at Grandmother, watching it fall on the old face. Minutes later she'd run as fast as she ever had to school, crying all the way.

More stars. And in the moonlight, shadows running short and long ahead of her as she left the stream and crossed the clearing to the door of the hut. She set the pail down, not wanting to go inside.

A screech or a pillow in her face? A complaint or a demand? What would happen if she screeched back? Or threw the pillow again? What if she didn't go inside, but stayed out here waiting for Papa and the boys?

When they came, she'd want to go inside. Then the hut would ring with talk and laughter, and Oleg's violin at night with Shura's balalaika and Papa's rhythmic clapping. Rodion and Vukuly and Kyril would dance a gopak, and afterward she'd waltz with all of them, counting to make sure they didn't fight over who was her next partner. They didn't have music and dancing every night because once a week the men would go to the village and drink beer and talk to their friends.

If she starved to death this winter who would they dance with? She snuffed and wiped her nose on a corner of the shawl. Dying might not be so bad. In heaven she'd know for herself what her mother looked like, although Comrade Varvara said there was no heaven. When she told Papa, he said, "That may be, but your mother was an angel." Only he couldn't remember if she'd been big or little, plain or pretty, only that she was just right for him, and he'd never find another like her.

Babushka said no woman, and certainly not her son's second wife, deserved such devotion. Anyway, he hadn't needed a second wife, not with seven fine sons already. What had the second wife ever done for anybody but produce a useless afterthought? A good thing Ludmila was the last baby, she was always so hungry. Sometimes when Babushka talked about weak little girls, bad little girls, hungry little girls, Ludmila wanted to hurt her.

Two years ago when Babushka started to get up one morning, she fell out of the bed she shared with Ludmila. Papa came running around the curtain that divided the hut, and Ludmila was so frightened she put her thumb in her mouth, something she hadn't done for a long time. Babushka lay with her eyes closed and her breathing was as loud as her snoring. When Papa knelt beside her and began to cry, Ludmila cried too.

But Grandmother finally opened her eyes and rolled them around in her head. And still later she grunted and said, "Ludmila . . . Ludmila . . . she pushed me . . ."

A doctor who came to examine her for admission to a state hospital said she'd had a stroke and would never walk again. And he said there were few enough beds for the living let alone for the dying, so there was no reason to move her. She could go any time, from a sudden shock or just because her heart stopped, or she might linger for years. But that was their problem; his concern was for those who would recover and produce again.

Ludmila had wanted to ask, What about me? because the summers were bad enough as it was, and if Grandmother had to stay in bed, next summer would be longer and harder than ever with the men away.

Two years ago, An endless time, and never a "thank you" or "please" from Babushka. Only screeching and thrown pillows except when Papa was home last winter and got angry. "Enough, old woman. You're too harsh with Ludmila. She's doing more work than you'll ever do again."

Babushka had hardly spoken all winter, she was so offended. And she took to pinching in the night, her cruel fingers finding Ludmila's arm or leg or an ear. She'd pinch and pinch until Ludmila couldn't stand it, and then she'd push Grandmother away. But the old woman never fell out of bed again.

Ludmila sighed and reached for the bucket at her feet. Opening the door, she hesitated, waiting for the pillow to come flying at her. But Grandmother lay exactly as she'd lain earlier. And the pillow was still pressed over her face from this morning.

Very carefully, Ludmila set the pail down, took the pot off the hearth, and ladled soup into her bowl. Then she took a spoon and enjoyed every mouthful. Without a glance at the bed, she got up and ladled out the rest of the soup and ate that as well.

Day for a Picnic

EDWARD D. HOCH

Among contemporary professional writers, Edward D. Hoch is that rara avis: one who makes his living almost entirely from short stories. He has published some six hundred in the past thirty years, most of them mystery and detective tales featuring a host of series characters; one, "The Oblong Room," was the recipient of the Mystery Writers of America Edgar as the Best Mystery Short Story of 1968. In addition to writing short fiction, he also edits the annual Year's Best Mystery and Suspense Stories and is a recognized authority on the mystery short story. His talents are amply demonstrated in "Day for a Picnic," one man's "nostalgic" trip into the past—to the time of his tenth year and a fateful mid-July picnic. . .

I SUPPOSE I remember it better than the other, countless other, picnics of my childhood, and I suppose the reason for that is the murder. But perhaps this day in mid-July would have stood out in my mind without the violence of sudden death. Perhaps it would have stood out simply because it was the first time I'd ever been out alone without the everwatching eyes of my mother and father to protect me. True, my grandfather was watching over me that month while my parents vacationed in Europe, but he was more a friend than a parent—a great old man with white hair and tobacco-stained teeth who never ceased the relating of fascinating tales of his own youth out west. There were stories of Indians and warfare, tales of violence in the youthful days of our nation, and at that youthful age I was fully content in believing that my grandfather was easily old enough to have fought in all those wars as he so claimed.

It was not the custom in the Thirties, as it is today, for parents to take their children along when making their first tour of Europe, and so as I've said I was left behind in grandfather's care. It was really a month of fun for me, because the life of the rural New York town is far different from the bustle of the city, even for a boy of nine or ten, and I was to spend endless days running barefoot along dusty roads in the company of boys who never — hardly ever — viewed me strangely because of my city background. The days were sunny with warmth, because it had been a warm summer even here on the shores of a cooling lake. Almost from the beginning of the month my grandfather had spoken with obvious relish of the approach of the annual picnic, and by mid-month I was looking forward to it also, thinking that here would be a new opportunity of exploring the byways of the town and meeting other boys as wild and free as I myself felt. Then too, I never seemed to mind at that time the company of adults. They were good people for the most part, and I viewed them with a proper amount of childish wonder.

[199]

There were no sidewalks in the town then, and nothing that you'd really call a street. The big touring cars and occasional late model roadsters raised endless clouds of dust as they roared (seemingly to a boy of ten) through the town at fantastic speeds unheard of in the city. This day especially, I remember the cars churning up the dust. I remember grandfather getting ready for the picnic, preparing himself with great care because this was to be a political picnic and grandfather was a very important political figure in the little town.

I remember standing in the doorway of his bedroom (leaning, really, because boys of ten never stood when they could lean), watching him knot the black string tie that made him look so much like that man in the funny movies. For a long time I watched in silence, seeing him scoop up coins for his pockets and the solid gold watch I never tired of seeing, and the little bottle he said was cough medicine even in the summer, and of course his important speech.

"You're goin' to speak, Gramps?"

"Sure am, boy. Every year I speak. Give the town's humanitarian award. It's voted on by secret ballot of all the townspeople."

"Who won it?"

"That's something no one knows but me, boy. And I don't tell till this afternoon."

"Are you like the mayor here, Gramps?"

"Sort of, boy," he said with a chuckle. "I'm what you call a selectman, and since I'm the oldest of them here I guess I have quite a lot to say about the town."

"Are you in charge of the picnic?"

"I'm in charge of the awards."

"Can we get free Coke and hot dogs?"

He chuckled at that. "We'll see, boy. We'll see."

Grandfather didn't drive, and as a result we were picked up for the picnic by Miss Pinkney and Miss Hazel, two old schoolteachers who drove a white Cord with a certain misplaced pride. Since they were already in front, the two of us piled in back, a bit crowded but happy. On the way to the picnic grounds we passed others going on foot, and grandfather waved like a prince might wave.

"What a day for a picnic!" Miss Hazel exclaimed. "Remember how it rained last year?"

The sun was indeed bright and the weather warm, but with the contrariness of the every young I remember wishing that I'd been at the rainy picnic instead. I'd never been at a rainy picnic for the very simple reason that my parents always called them off if it rained.

"It's a good day," my grandfather said. "It'll bring out the voters. They should hold elections in the summer time, and we'd win by a landslide every time."

The Fourth of July was not yet two weeks past, and as we neared the old picnic grounds we could hear the belated occasional crackling of left-over fireworks being set off by the other kids. I was more than ever anxious to join them, though I did wonder vaguely what kind of kids would ever have firecrackers unexploded and left over after the big day.

We travelled down a long and dusty road to the picnic proper, winding down a hillside to a sort of cove by the water where brown sandy bluffs rose on three sides. There was room here for some five hundred people, which is the number that might be attracted by the perfect weather, and already a few cars were parked in the makeshift parking area, disgorging there the loads of children and adults. Miss Pinkney and Miss Hazel parked next to the big touring car that belonged to Doctor Stout, and my grandfather immediately cornered the doctor on some political subject. They stood talking for some minues about — as I remember — the forthcoming primary election, and all the while I shifted from one foot to the other watching the other kids at play down by the water, watching the waves of the lake whitened by a brisk warming breeze that fanned through the trees and tall uncut grass of the bluffs.

Finally, with a nod of permission from my grandfather, I took off on the run, searching out a few of the boys I'd come to know best in these weeks of my visit. I found them finally, playing in a sort of cave on the hillside. Looking back now I realize it was probably no more than a lovers' trysting place but at the time it held for us all the excitement and mystery of a smuggler's den. I played there with the others for nearly an hour, until I heard my grandfather calling me from down near the speakers' platform.

Already as I ran back down the hill I saw that the campaign posters and patriotic bunting were in place. The picnic crowd was gradually drifting down to the platform, clutching hot dogs and bottles of soda pop and foaming mugs of beer. Over near the cars I could see the men tapping another keg of beer, and I watched as a sudden miscalculation on the part of the men sent the liquid shooting up into a fizzing fountain. "It's raining beer," shouted one of the men, standing beneath the descending stream with his mouth open. "This must be heaven!"

Frank Coons, the town's handyman and occasional black sheep, had cornered my grandfather and was asking him something. "Come on, how about some of your gin cough medicine? I been waitin' all afternoon for it!"

But my grandfather was having none of it. "None today, Frank."

"Why not? Just a drop."

"Have some beer instead. It's just as good." He moved off, away from Frank, and I followed him. There were hands to be shaken, words to be spoken, and in all of it grandfather was a past master.

"When's your speech, Gramps?" I asked him.

"Soon now, boy. Want a soda pop?"

"Sure!"

He picked a bottle of cherry-colored liquid from the red and white cooler and opened it for me. It tasted good after my running and playing in the hot dirt of the hillside. Now grandfather saw someone else he knew, a tall handsome man named Jim Tweller, whom I'd seen at the house on occasion. He had business dealings with my grandfather, and I understood that he owned much of the property in the town.

"Stay close to the platform, Jim" grandfather was saying.

"Don't tell me I won that foolish award!"

"Can't say yet, Jim. Just stay close."

I saw Miss Pinkney and Miss Hazel pass by, casting admiring glances at Jim Tweller. "Doesn't he have such a *mannish* smell about him!" Miss Pinkney whispered loudly. Tweller, I gathered even at that tender age, was much admired by the women of the town.

"Come, boy," grandfather was saying. "Bring your soda and I'll find you a seat right up in front. You can listen to my speech."

I saw that the mayor, a Mister Myerton, was already on the platform, flanked by two men and a woman I didn't know. In the very center was a big microphone hooked up to an overhead loudspeaker system borrowed from the sole local radio station. Empty beer mugs stood in front of each place. My grandfather's chair was over on the end, but right now he strode to the speaker's position, between Mayor Myerton and the woman.

"Ladies and gentlemen," he began, speaking in his best political voice. "And children, too, of course. I see a lot of you little ones here today, and that always makes me happy. It makes me aware of the fact that another generation is on the rise, a generation that will carry on the fine principles of our party in the decades to come. As many of you know, I have devoted the years since the death of my wife almost exclusively to party activities. The party has been my life-blood, as I hope it will be the life-blood of other, future generations. But enough of that for the moment. Mayor Myerton and Mrs. Finch of the school board will speak to you in due time about the battle that lies ahead of us this November. Right now, it's my always pleasant duty to announce the annual winner of the party's great humanitarian award, given to the man who has done the most for this community and its people. I should say the man or woman, because we've had a number of charming lady winners in past years. But this year it's a man, a man who has perhaps done more than any other to develop the real estate of our town to its full potential, a man who during this past year donated — yes, I said donated — the land for our new hospital building. You all know who I mean, the winner by popular vote of this year's humanitarian award — Mister Jim Tweller!''

Tweller had stayed near the speakers' stand and now he hopped up, waving to a crowd that was cheering him with some visible restraint. Young as I was, I wondered about this, wondered even as I watched grandfather yield the honored speaker's position to Tweller and take his chair at the end of the platform. Tweller waited until the scattered cheers had played themselves out in the afternoon breeze and then cheerfully cleared his throat. I noticed Frank Coons standing near the platform and saw grandfather call him over. "Get a pitcher of beer for us, Frank," he asked. "Speeches make us thirsty."

While Frank went off on his mission, Jim Tweller adjusted the wobbly microphone and began his speech of thanks and acceptance. I was just then more interested in two boys wrestling along the water's edge, tussling, kicking sand at each other. But Tweller's speech was not altogether lost on me. I remember scattered words and phrases, and even then to me they seemed the words and phrases of a political candidate rather than simply an award winner. ''. . . thank you from the bottom of my heart for this great honor . . . I realize I think more than anyone else the fact that our party needs a rebirth with new blood if it is to win again in November . . . loyal old horses turned out to pasture while the political colts run the race . . .'' I saw Mayor Myerton, a man in his sixties, flinch at these words, and I realized that the simple acceptance speech was taking a most unexpected turn.

But now my attention was caught by the sight of Frank Coons returning with the foaming pitcher of beer. He'd been gone some minutes and I figured he'd stopped long enough to have one himself, or perhaps he'd found someone else who carried gin in a cough medicine bottle. Anyway, he passed the pitcher up to the man at the end of the platform, the opposite end from my grandfather. I wondered if this was his revenge for being refused that drink earlier. The man on the end filled his glass with beer and then passed it on to the mayor who did likewise. Jim Tweller interrupted his speech a moment to accept the pitcher and fill his glass, then pass it to Mrs. Finch of the school board who was on his right. She shook her head with a temperant vigor and let it go on to the man I didn't know, sitting next to grandfather at the end of the platform.

Tweller had taken a drink of his beer and shook his head violently as if it were castor oil. "Got a bad barrel here," he told the people with a laugh. "I'm going to stick to the hard stuff after this. Or else drink milk. Anyway, before I finish I want to tell you about my plans for our community. I want to tell you a little about how . . ." He paused for another drink of the beer. ". . . about how we can push back the final remains of the depression and surge ahead into the Forties with a new prosperity, a new ve . . . agh . . ."

Something was wrong. Tweller had suddenly stopped speaking and was gripping the microphone before him. Mayor Myerton put down his own beer and started to get up. "What's wrong, man?" he whispered too near the microphone. "Are you sick?"

"I . . . gnugh . . . can't breathe . . . help me . . ." Then he toppled backward, dragging the microphone with him, upsetting his glass of beer as he fell screaming and gasping to the ground.

Somewhere behind me a woman's voice took up the scream, and I thought it might have been Miss Hazel. Already Doctor Stout had appeared at the platform and was hurrying around to comfort the stricken man. As I ran forward myself I caught a funny odor in the air near the platform, near where the beer had spilled from Jim Tweller's overturned glass. It was a new smell to me, one I couldn't identify.

Behind the platform, Doctor Stout was loosening the collar of the convulsed man as grandfather and the mayor tried to assist him. But after a moment the thrashing of arms and legs ceased, and the doctor straightened up. The bright overhead sun caught his glasses as he did so, reflecting for an instant a glare of brilliance. "There's nothing I can do," he said quietly, almost sadly. "The man is dead."

Suddenly I was bundled off with the other children to play where we would, while the adults moved in to form a solid ring of curiosity about the platform. The children were curious too, of course, but after a few minutes of playing many of the younger ones had forgotten the events with wonder at their newly found freedom. They ran and romped along the water's edge, setting off what few firecrackers still remained, wrestling and chasing each other up the brilliant brown dunes to some imagined summit. But all at once I was too old for their games of childhood, and longed to be back with the adults, back around the body of this man whom I hadn't even known a few weeks earlier.

Finally I did break away, and hurried back to the edges thinning now as women pulled their husbands away. I crept under the wooden crossbeams of the platform, became momentarily entangled in the wires of the loudspeaker system, and finally freed myself to creep even closer to the center of the excitement. A big man wearing a pistol on his belt like a cowboy had joined them now, and he appeared to be the sheriff.

"Just tell me what happened," he was saying. "One at a time, not all at once."

Mayor Myerton grunted. "If you'd been at the picnic, Gene, instead of chasing around town, you'd know what happened."

"Do you pay me to be the sheriff or to drink beer and listen to speeches?" He turned to one of the other men. "What happened, Sam?"

Sam was the man who'd been on the end of the platform, the opposite end from grandfather. "Hell, Gene, you know as much about it as I do. He was talkin' and all of a sudden he just toppled over and died."

At this point Doctor Stout interrupted. "There's no doubt in my mind that the man was poisoned. The odor of bitter almonds was very strong by the body."

"Bitter almonds?" This from Mayor Myerton. He was wiping the sweat from his forehead, though it didn't seem that hot to me.

Doctor Stout nodded. "I think someone put prussic acid in Tweller's beer. Prussic acid solution or maybe bitter almond water."

"That's impossible," the mayor insisted. "I was sitting right next to him."

Grandfather joined in the discussion now, and I ducked low to the ground so he wouldn't see me. "Maybe the whole pitcher was poisoned. I didn't get around to drinking mine."

But the mayor had drunk some of his without ill effects, as had the man on the end named Sam. Someone went for the pitcher of beer, now almost empty, and Doctor Stout sniffed it suspiciously. "Nothing here. But the odor was on the body, and up there where his glass spilled."

"Maybe he killed himself," Frank Coons suggested, and they seemed to notice him for the first time. Frank seemed to be a sort of town character, lacking the stature of the others, an outsider within the party. And — I knew they were thinking it — after all, he was the one who went for the pitcher of beer in the first place.

"Frank," the sheriff said a little too kindly, "did you have any reason to dislike Jim Tweller?"

"Who, me?"

"Don't I remember hearing something, a few years back about a house he sold you? A bum deal on a house he sold you?"

Frank Coons waved his hands airily. "That was nothing, a misunderstanding. I've always liked Jim. You don't think I could have killed him, do you?"

The sheriff named Gene said, "I think we'd all better go down to my office. Maybe I can get to the bottom of things there."

Some of them moved off then, and I saw that the undertaker's ambulance had come for Jim Tweller's body. The undertaker discussed the details of the autopsy with the sheriff, and the two of them proceeded to lift the body onto a stretcher. At that time and that place, no one worried about taking pictures of the death scene or measuring critical distances.

But I noticed that the woman from the school board, Mrs. Finch, pulled grandfather back from the rest of the group. They paused just above me, and she said, "You know what he was trying to do as well as I do. He was using the acceptance of the award to launch a political campaign of his own. All this talk about rebirth and new blood meant just one thing — he was getting to the point where he was going to run against Mayor Myerton."

"Perhaps," my grandfather said.

"Do you think it's possible that the mayor slipped the poison into his beer?"

"Let me answer that with another question, Mrs. Finch. Do you think the mayor would be carrying a fatal dose of prussic acid in his pocket for such an occasion?"

"I don't know. He was sitting next to Tweller, that's all I know."

"So were you, though, Mrs. Finch," my grandfather reminded her.

They moved off with that, and separated, and I crawled back out to mingle with the children once more. Over by the beer barrel, the man named Sam was helping himself to a drink, and I saw a couple of others still eating their lunch. But for the most part the picnic had ended with Tweller's death. Even the weather seemed suddenly to have turned coolish, and the breeze blowing off the water had an uncomfortable chill to it. Families were folding up their chairs and loading picnic baskets into the cars, and one group of boys was helpfully ripping down the big colored banners and campaign posters. Nobody stopped them, because it was no longer a very good day for a picnic. . . .

The two remaining weeks of my visit were a blur of comings and goings and frequent phone calls at my grandfather's house. I remember the first few days after the killing, when the excitement of the thing was still on everybody's lips, when no one hardly noticed the children of the town and we ran free as birds for hours on end. Frank Coons was jailed by the sheriff when they learned for certain that the beer had been poisoned, but after a few days of questioning they were forced to release him. No one could demonstrate just how he would have been able to poison only the beer poured into Jim Tweller's glass while leaving the mayor and the others unharmed.

I knew that Mrs. Finch still harbored her suspicion of the mayor, and it was very possible that he suspected her as well. All of them came to grandfather's house, and the conversations went on by the hour. The fact that no one much regretted the death of Tweller did little to pacify things in those first two weeks. The man still had his supporters outside of the political high command, all the little people of the town who'd known him not as a rising politician but only as the donor of land for a hospital. These were the people who'd voted him his humanitarian award, and these were the people who publicly mourned him now, while the top-level conferences at grandfather's house continued long into the night.

At the end of two weeks I departed, and grandfather took me down to the railroad station with what seemed a genuine sadness at my going. I stood in the back of the train waving at him as we pulled out of the station, and he seemed at that moment as always to be a man of untried greatness. His white hair caught the afternoon sunlight as he waved, and I felt a tear of genuine feeling trickle down my cheek.

If this had been a detective novel instead of a simple memoir of youth, I would have provided a neat and simple solution to the poisoning of Jim Tweller. But no such solution was ever forthcoming. I heard from my mother and father that the excitement died down within a few weeks and the life of the town went on as it had before. That November, the mayor and my grandfather and the other town officials were re-elected.

I saw my grandfather only briefly after that, at annual family reunions and his occasional visits to our home. When I was sixteen he died, quietly in his sleep, and we went up to the town once more. It hadn't changed much, really, and the people seemed much the same as I remembered them. In the cemetery, I stood between father and Mrs. Finch, who commented on how much I'd grown. The mayor was there, of course, and Doctor Stout, and even Miss Pinkney and Miss Hazel. I understood from the talk that Frank Coons no longer lived in town. He'd moved south shortly after the murder investigation.

So I said goodbye to my grandfather and his town forever, and went back to the city to grow into manhood. . . .

I said a moment ago that this was a memoir and not a mystery and as such would offer no solution to the death of Jim Tweller. And yet — I would not be honest either as a writer or a man if I failed to set down here some thoughts that came to me one evening not long ago, as I sat sipping a cocktail in the company of a particularly boring group of friends.

I suppose it was the sight of cocktails being poured from an icy pitcher that made me remember that other occasion, when the beer had passed down the line of speakers. And remembering it, as the conversation about me droned on, I went over the details of that day once more. I remembered especially that pitcher of beer, and the pouring of Tweller's drink from it. I remembered how he drank from the glass almost immediately, and commented on the bad taste. Certainly no poison was dropped into the glass *after* the beer had been poured. And yet it was just as impossible to believe that the poison had gone into the glass *with* the beer, when others had drunk unharmed from the same pitcher. No, there was only one possibility — the poison had been in the glass *before* the beer was poured in.

I imagined a liquid, colorless as water, lying in the bottom of the glass. Just a few drops perhaps, or half an ounce at most. The chances were that Jim Tweller never noticed it, or if he did he imagined it to be only water left from washing out the glass. He would pour the beer in over the waiting poison, in all likelihood, or at worst empty the glass onto the grass first. In any event, there was no danger for the poisoner, and the odds for success were in his favor.

And I remembered then who had occupied the speaker's position immediately before Tweller. I remembered grandfather with the empty glass before him, the empty beer mug with its thickness of glass to hide the few drops of liquid. I remembered grandfather with his little bottle of cough medicine, clear cough medicine that usually was gin. Remembered his reluctance that day to give Frank Coons a drink from it. Remembered that I hadn't seen the bottle again later. Remembered most of all grandfather's devotion to the party, his friendship with Tweller that must have warned him earlier than most of the man's political ambitions. Remembered, finally, that of all the people at the picnic only grandfather had known that Tweller was the winner of the award, that Tweller would be on the speaker's platform that day. Grandfather, who called out to Coons for the pitcher of beer. Grandfather, the only person with the motive and the knowledge and the opportunity. And the weapon, in a bottle that might have been cough medicine or gin — or prussic acid.

But that was a long time ago, a generation ago. And I remember him best standing at the station, waving goodbye. . . .

Carnival Day

NEDRA TYRE

Born in Georgia in 1921, Nedra Tyre has drawn upon the South and her job experience in the social services as background for her novels and short stories. Her Mouse in Eternity, which was nominated by the Mystery Writers of America as one of the best crime novels of 1952, features a social worker in Atlanta, and Hall of Death (1960) is set in a southern girls' reformatory. Nedra Tyre's excellent handling of suspense and her deft characterization are shown in such other novels as Death of an Intruder (1953), Everyone Suspect (1964), and Twice So Fair (1971), and in the short story "Carnival Day." While the story's specific location is not named, the scenes portrayed evoke a small southern town during carnival week; in them, the author leads us through a young girl's last uneasy day as a child, to the brink of her sudden—and shocking—entry into the adult world.

Betty wanted to lie in bed a little longer and look at the lowered shade that held out the sunlight except for a bright streak of it nosing through at the bottom. Then she could think about the nice things that might happen. Except that they might not.

Her mother was in the hall cleaning, doing the brisk morning work of Saturday. Betty listened to the rub of the mop, the whispering of the dust cloth. She pulled the Teddy bear from his crumpled position on the floor and placed him on the pillow beside her. His hanging button of a left eye seemed to leer; his fur was worn and in spots was missing, as if he had mange. She took his right paw, that was jerked toward his forehead in a kind of salute, and rubbed it against her face so that he caressed her.

Outside the mop made its way down the hall—the only sound in the house. Then the ringing of the telephone tore open the silence—first the ringing downstairs, then the echoing ring of the extension upstairs. Her mother would answer it, just outside Betty's door.

Betty knocked the Teddy bear so that he made a somersault and landed face down on the floor. She knew the telephone call would be the sign she had been waiting for to tell her what kind of day it would be, and she was not quite ready to learn. She grabbed her pillow and burrowed beneath it, pressing the sides tight against her ears. The feathers, the ticking, the pillow case, nothing kept the noise out. She had heard the words before they were spoken, she had dreamed them all through the night.

Her father had said weeks ago—when the first signs were pasted on the billboards, the placards set up in the drug store windows, the shoe shop, the beauty parlors—that of course they must go to the carnival together. Hadn't they gone for years? But she couldn't really believe him because everything had been so different these last months. He understood her fear, her uncertainty, and weeks ago had given her five crisp dollar bills to hide away in her desk. The money was there for her to spend at the carnival, even if he didn't get to go with her.

Betty heard her mother's voice; if her mother had been at the North Pole her voice couldn't have been colder, and yet it was so nice, so distinct, every syllable of every word sounded.

"I tried to tell Betty not to count on you. She'll be hurt. But then you seem to take pleasure in hurting us."

It wasn't fair of her mother to talk to him like that; he'd left the money; he'd made his apologies, he'd said something might come up so that he couldn't take her; and now her mother talked to him as if he had broken a solemn promise.

Her mother didn't say goodbye but Betty heard the little latching click the telephone made as it slid back into place.

The autumn wind puffed the shade so that it slapped the sill. Betty reached down for the Teddy bear and threw him across the room.

Outside there were the sounds of her mother putting away the mop in the utility cabinet, then a knock on the door.

"Good morning," her mother said, and filled the room with her briskness. "It's time you were up."

Betty kicked the sheet and made a wad of it at the foot of the bed.

"Your father telephoned to say he can't go to the carnival after all. I know how disappointed you are. But you can go with some of the other children on the street." She stooped over the Teddy bear and picked him up, regimenting him so that his legs were straight and his arms were close to his sides. "It's silly the way you hang on to this old thing. You're nearly twelve—much too old for Teddy bears. He ought to be thrown in the trash."

She was picking up clothes, straightening shoes—her mother was always, always picking up, straightening up now; she didn't used to be that way.

"Here's your robe. Go on downstairs and eat your breakfast. You'll find a glass of orange juice in the refrigerator. Take your milk from the bottle nearest the freezing unit. I'll be down in a minute to cook your egg."

"I don't want an egg," Betty said.

Betty tried to stamp as she walked down the stairs; she wanted to have the house filled with the jolting sounds of heavy footsteps and to have her mother tell her to stop, but the soft soles of her bedroom shoes sounded quieter than tiptoes.

She stood in the kitchen door looking at the neat rows of cabinets with everything stacked precisely in them, the white sink scrubbed spotless, the chairs lined up tight against the walls like shy children at a party. On the second shelf of the refrigerator she found the glass of orange juice. She held it in both hands and rubbed her nose against the film outside until she made a wobbly circle; then she started to drink the juice—but it wouldn't go down; it held back because this was the day of the carnival and her father wasn't going with her.

Her mother was coming downstairs. Betty heard her precise heels strike the steps. She wanted to gulp the orange juice but the first taste of it made her sick. Betty looked at the full glass in her hands; she couldn't listen to a lecture, not today, on the way thousands of children in foreign countries would give anything for this delicious orange juice. There just might be time to get rid of it. She ran to the sink and poured the juice down the drain.

"You must drink some milk now," her mother said, as she entered the kitchen and saw the empty glass in Betty's hand.

"I don't want any milk," Betty said, waiting for the threat to come, waiting for her mother to say she couldn't leave the house until she had drunk some milk.

"I suppose it won't hurt you to go without it this once. Anyway, you'll eat enough junk at the carnival to fill you up. Run on upstairs and bathe."

Her mother said the words but she wasn't paying attention even to herself; her mother's mind seemed to be deep inside her, digging away at other thoughts.

In the bedroom Betty played the lovely forbidden game. If her mother downstairs buzzing with the vacuum cleaner on the dining room rug knew, she'd be mad. Betty brushed her teeth and punched the brush hard on the back of her tongue so that she gagged and the little bit of orange juice that she had swallowed came up. Next she stood in the middle of the floor, holding a glass of water in her hand, and spat water into the basin, spitting like old man Robinson who could stand in a store door and hit the middle of the street, making a cascade over the sidewalk. She filled the tub half full, then stuck only her toes in the water and rubbed herself hard with the towel as if she had taken a bath all over.

She dressed and was trying to sneak out of the house without last minute admonitions from her mother. But there was no need to try to sneak out. While Betty had dawdled over dressing, her father had left his office and come home. He and her mother were talking now, then shouting; the deadly barrage of their voices was wounding them all. Betty did not matter at such a time, not even on carnival day. She didn't belong to them when they were like that. She was alone. She wasn't even born.

She darted down the hall onto the porch and jumped across the front steps.

At the corner she heard a high scream and then a noise that she had never heard before, but she did not dare stop to listen to it.

Long before she got to the huge vacant lot across the railroad tracks, the sounds of the carnival came to her, the voices jabbering, pleading, cajoling, then the music all scrambled up so there was no tune, like children yelling at each other, nothing making sense. And then she was there. It felt good to walk in the sawdust, to have it slow her down like walking in water, to have it creep inside her shoes. She made the rounds to see what she wanted to do; she might do everything; first, though, she must look things over, be cautious, the way you were careful about a new child or a new teacher or a new book before you accepted them.

Betty thought she had remembered it all, yet she hadn't; her memory had changed the carnival, but now it all came back, like a movie she was seeing for the second time—all the small booths with shelves, almost like the vegetable stalls at the Farmers'

Market, but instead of vegetables they were strewn with dolls and animals and blankets and lamps and clocks.

The shooting gallery was just ahead. She stopped, remembering last year her father had stood right there, shooting as hard as he could, yet all the ducks marched past ignoring him and his shots until he had popped off a tail. This was the first place they had gone; she closed her eyes trying to make her memory bring it all back, trying to recall what her father had worn, what she had worn; but nothing came—nothing except the emptiness of her father's absence. A man picked up a rifle and squinted, then shot, and Betty walked past him.

Above all the invitations to step this way folks, try your skill for valuable prizes, she heard someone say, "You, young lady with the pigtails, you look like someone who could win. Toss the ring on the numbered pegs and if they add up to an odd number you can pick out what you want." His smile slashed his face and he waggled his hand at her. Betty pulled the envelope her father had given her out of her skirt pocket. The five new dollars made crackling sounds as she fingered them to be sure she gave the man only one.

The man's fingers reached greedily for the dollar; they lingered in his change box. "Naturally you want more than one chance," he said. "One for a quarter or three for fifty cents."

"One," Betty said firmly.

She bumped hard against the counter as she made her first throw. The twine ring fell to the ground before it reached the target. The next one flew past the target and thumped against the thin wall of the booth; the third one looped a peg from which dangled a little placard with 16 painted on it.

"Too bad," the man said. "Sixteen is not a lucky number. But you made a good try. I'm sure you could win the next time."

"No, thank you," Betty said.

The man's smile dwindled; he erased her from his consciousness the way Miss Collins erased the arithmetic lesson in one swoop from the blackboard so that nothing was left, and was calling out, "You, young man in the corduroy jacket, come this way and try your luck at this interesting game of chance and skill.''

"One, please," Betty said and tiptoed to shove her money through the mouse trap of an opening in a ticket booth before a tent splashed with signs reading *Thrill to the Death Defying Riders. Crashes. Spills.*

The roar of the motorcycles frightened her; she leaned down and watched them making rushing-spluttering circles; a man fell off; she screamed, wanting to grab her father, to dig her hands into his arms, the way she had when they had watched the riders in the years before. The helmeted men roared past, goggled men stooping, spread over the motorcycles like frogs.

Nothing was the same without her father; she had done all the things they did together. He wasn't there and it would serve him right if she saw things they hadn't seen together. He hadn't ex- actly steered her away from them; he had mentioned shows and rides he thought they might enjoy more. Now she walked up to the platform where the girls stood in their costumes, wearing robes, then one girl unloosened her robe and showed her cos- tume. The men near Betty grinned; two whistled. The man on the platform winked and said, "Plenty more of the same on the inside."

Betty bought a ticket and sat down in a chair on the outer circle. The ground was uneven and her chair rocked back and forth. The lights went off; six girls came out on the stage and threw kisses at the audience; then a man came out and said something; hoots followed what the man said. Next to Betty a man placed his hand on the knee of a woman sitting on his right and the man and woman smiled at each other. Hoots came again from the audience—hoots full of a special and secret knowledge, shutting out everyone who didn't understand and share the knowledge; Betty looked at the upturned faces of the men sitting near her, their eyes catching strange lights from the stage; and all around, the sun sprinkled through holes in the tent and sifted through in bright dots to the ground. A woman sang a song while some girls in back of her danced, none of them doing the steps quite like any other or at the same time; then the curtain slapped to in gigantic relief that the show was over. The men around Betty got up and reached for cigarettes and they all walked out into the sunlight.

After that Betty went to the Jungle of Snakes; she looked over the canvas sides of an enclosure down to the waving bodies, the snakes writhing-twisting-squirming like all the nightmares of her life, and in the middle of their weaving a woman sat caressing them, letting them climb around her body, small ones making bracelets around her arms and anklets around her ankles; one large one twisted three times around her waist; heads darted back and forth, back and forth, their tongues licking like flames in and out of their flattened heads; then the woman picked up one from the canvas floor and held it to her, fondling it as if it were a baby, kissing it as if it were sweet. To escape her the snake wiggled down, moving in the shape of an S, then lost himself among the other twists and whorls. Fear like fire swept over Betty and she rushed out of the tent.

She stood shivering and her teeth were clamped hard together as if she were playing in snow on the coldest morning in the year, though the midday sun felt like hot August heat on her shoulders. Twice she made the circuit of the booths and shows, trying to decide which one to see next. A sign beckoned to her. *Consult Dr. Vision the Visionary, the Mystic, the Clairvoyant. He Sees All, He Knows All. Come in and Discuss Your Problems.*

Her father didn't approve of fortunetellers; he said it was much nicer to wait and see what the future brought. But her father wasn't there. Betty stood half in and half out of the tent opening, the way she did in the dentist's reception room, waiting to push the buzzer to let the dentist's assistant know she had come. There was movement within a tent and a man said, "Do you wish to seek the advice of Dr. Vision?" He wore a green satin suit, with a gold sash, and his head held up the huge burden of a turban from which a limp feather dropped like a coxcomb. His mustache was drawn on in a thin black line and his eyebrows almost filled his forehead.

She nodded. It was still like being at the dentist's, not able to deny having an appointment.

"You are speaking to Dr. Vision," the man said, pointing to a chair. She sat at a table across from him; his turbaned head seemed to sit on the crystal ball that separated them.

"The fee is one dollar," he said. Betty's hand rummaged in her pocket for money. Fifty cents bounced to the ground. Dr. Vision sat still with his hands pressed against his forehead and Betty fell to the ground hunting for the money, beating against a small rug that seemed to float on the grass and rubble beneath it. She found the money near Dr. Vision's feet and was surprised to see that he wore unlaced tennis shoes and no socks. She scrambled back to her chair and gave him an apologetic look, as if she had had to excuse herself from the table to be sick. He paid no attention and said in a voice that was a strange kind of whisper, "Do you have some special problem?"

She answered him in the same kind of whisper. "Yes, my mother—" And then she could go no further. What she was about to say had been betrayal, spreading the dark misery in her house before him, undressing her mother's hurt and her father's hurt before a stranger.

Dr. Vision looked into the crystal.

"I see," he said. "Your mother. Yes. She's been ill. She'll be all right. Don't worry about her. Is there anything else?"

Betty looked at her fingernails. There was one, just one that wasn't chewed; she had tried to leave at least one; one whole nail showed that she had some control; she held her hand tightly but the finger sprang to her mouth and she started biting the nail.

"Maybe your schoolwork is bothering you. Is that it?"

School. Miss Smith saying, until this year you did good work. What's the matter now? It's not that you aren't capable. Don't you like your teachers? Are you getting lazy? What is it?

She couldn't answer Dr. Vision any more than she could answer Miss Smith; the words stopped in her throat.

He smiled, his mustache curling around in his smile like a
cat's whiskers. "It's a little early but maybe you want advice
about love."

"No," she shouted. Her voice startled them both, so that she
dropped it back to the whisper they were using and said, "No,
no."

"Then there's just one thing left. A career. You want advice
about your career. Well, finish school first, then decide what you
want to do. I predict a successful career for you."

Betty stood up and the chair fell behind her. She expected a
banging, jolting noise but the grass caught the chair like a net
and hushed the sound of its fall. She started to run.

"Just a minute," Dr. Vision said, "You are permitted to communicate with the Secret Powers of the Universe and ask a secret
question or make a secret request. They will send you an answer,
and only you will know their answer. Look closely into the crystal and repeat your request or your question to yourself three
times." Betty walked toward the crystal and bent over it. She
made her request silently, as reverently as she said her prayers,
her hands folded and her eyes closed: *Let everything be like it
was, let everything be like it was, let everything be like it was.*

There was no noise—the whole carnival seemed quiet and
still. Then Dr. Vision said words that she didn't understand and
all the time he made huge gestures in the air. His hand moved
under the table and his thumb reached around his little finger
and he held a paper there. "This is your answer. The Powers
have spoken," he said and made a bow as if he were waiting for
applause. Betty snatched the paper from him and ran, grabbing
at the slit in the tent, feeling herself almost smothered by the
curtain as she rushed out. She couldn't look at the paper—she
didn't dare look; she had the feeling she had had one Christmas
when she had been sure that she wouldn't get anything, when
she hadn't dared go to the Christmas tree in the living room.
Only this wasn't quite like that; this was more—this wasn't being frightened over not getting presents, this was asking for

what had to be. The small piece of paper was her destiny and she wadded it in the desperate knot of her fist.

Ahead of her was the largest cluster of people she'd seen all day. Above them on a platform a man took off his coat and swept his brow; as he raised his hand a huge circle of sweat showed underneath his arm on the yellow silk of his shirt. He had the voice of all the men standing on platforms, a chant that came from the back of his nose. "Ladies and gentlemen, you have seen many remarkable things today but you have seen nothing to equal the phenomenon we are presenting. The half man, half woman. This phenomenon can be legally married in any state of our great and beloved America to either a man or woman. You will hear a scientific lecture, absolutely clean, explaining this sexual phenomenon. I urge you to buy your ticket at once. For this performance only the cost is thirty-five cents, the usual price of admission is seventy-five cents, you will be paying less than half the usual charge. Only adults allowed. No one under sixteen admitted."

People moved against Betty, crushing her, pushing her toward the tall box where a man sold tickets. She tried to move away from them, but the man kept looking down at her and saying thirty-five cents please, thirty-five cents, and the ones behind her were saying go on, what's holding us up, and she was trying to tell the man she was only eleven.

The crowd pushed Betty, shoved her, thrust her closer to the man. She felt that she was being suffocated.

"No," she cried out. "No. I don't want to see." She threw back against the rocks of their bodies and squirmed through.

She sobbed and plunged through the sawdust, her feet kicked up little storms of it; then her sorrow told her what she was searching for, longing for, what she loved most of all about the carnival. The merry-go-round. That was all she wanted now. She ran toward it and its piping tune embraced her and she saw the stiff ponies with their arched tails and prancing legs making their rounds far away. She dashed toward the merry-go-round, remembering how her father used to let her ride it for hours; how he rode a pony alongside her, and his long legs dangled, striking the floor when his pony descended; how sometimes he doubled up his legs in the stirrup so that he looked like a jockey; how sometimes they got off their ponies and sat together in a chariot. Her father would get tired at last and stand outside the merry-go-round's circle waving to her as she rode by; their waving lasted so long that one wave was not over before she was back again, passing him, waving to him again.

She reached for money to buy tickets and the paper with her destiny on it dropped to the ground. She did not even notice.

"Five," she shouted above the magic piping. "I want five tickets for the merry-go-round."

She folded the tickets and waited on the outside for the merry-go-round to slow down. Some boys leaped off before it stopped, and the younger children squatted down to jump flatfooted to the ground.

Betty found a red pony and climbed on it.

The music started, the merry-go-round began to revolve, while all the booths and shows were lined up outside, not able to touch the enchanted circle of the merry-go-round; voices were saying what they had been saying all day, but now the music blotted them out so that Betty had to strain to hear—hot dogs ten cents, hamburgers made of the finest beef twenty cents, souvenirs you'll value the rest of your life, canary birds two dollars, pennants of your favorite college fifty cents, see the half man half woman, take a chance at this interesting game of skill . . . hurry, hurry, hurry.

And then she did not hear them at all; she would not let her ears hear and she closed her eyes; she was holding on to her pony and listening only to the music, safe from everything, safe from her mother's eternal cleaning and the sad things that went on at home, the harsh voices and the harsher silences.

The merry-go-round slowed and Betty opened her eyes.

He was thoro.

Her father was just outside the circle of parents waiting for their children. And Betty's day was saved. She should have known her father would not disappoint her.

He waved at her and she saw that he was not alone. It was funny. She knew the man he was with. It was Mr. Williams the policeman—everybody in town knew Mr. Williams. They must have met each other accidentally at the carnival. Maybe Mr. Williams was waiting for someone he knew to get off the merry-go-round. Her father seemed to be pleading with him, as if he were asking permission, and Mr. Williams nodded.

The music was beginning again, the merry-go-round started its slow turning, the children scrambled on and her father leaped on and came toward her. His arms grabbed for her and his mouth seemed to have words that could not be spoken. Then the man taking the tickets came round and Betty handed him two, one for herself and one for her father. The merry-go-round was going faster and her pony started to rise; the lifting took her from her father's embrace, but his hand reached wildly for her hand and their grip was as strong as their love. The carnival around them was not yet the blur it would be when they went at full speed and Betty could still see Mr. Williams watching them, watching most of all her father, and the policeman's face was very sad.

Good Man, Bad Man

JEROME WEIDMAN

Born in 1913, Jerome Weidman was awarded a Pulitzer Prize in 1959 for his Broadway play, Fiorello. Prior to this, he met with great critical success with such novels as I Can Get It for You Wholesale (1937), What's In It for Me (1938), and The Enemy Camp (1958), a haunting story of anti-Semitism. In "Good Man, Bad Man," Weidman again touches on the theme of unreasoning prejudice—this time against a good and gentle, yet different man. Told through the eyes of the youthful protagonist grown to manhood, the confusion the boy feels initially, and the horror he feels upon understanding the injustice are as fresh in remembrance as in actuality.

ONE thing about the obituary page. It starts people talking. Men and women who for years have been afraid to open their mouths, they read a four-line item on the obituary page, and suddenly they become garrulous. I'm no exception.

Yesterday, if you had mentioned the name Jazz L. McCabe to me, I would have given you an innocent look and said, "Who?" Today, try and shut me up. This morning's *Times* reports that McCabe died last night at Mt. Sinai Hospital. A coronary at the age of seventy-three. High time.

His name was James, but down on East Fourth Street we called him Jazz because that's the way he signed his name: *Jas. L. McCabe*. The first time I saw *Jas. L. McCabe*, it was written at the bottom of a letter. The letter was typed. That threw my mother into a panic. She thought it was a *moof tzettle*, which is Yiddish for eviction notice. These were just about the only typewritten communications that arrived on East Fourth Street in those days.

"It's not from the court," I said, after studying the letter. "It has nothing to do with our rent."

"What is it, then?" my mother said.

"It's for Natie Goodman," I said.

"Then why did the letter carrier put it in our box?"

"Well, it's for Natie and me," I said. "The both of us."

This was not strictly true, but my mother was a peasant woman from a remote corner of Hungary, and she had come to America only a couple of years before I was born. Things went on in this country that she did not understand, and at the age of almost fourteen I had not yet developed any great desire to waste my time enlightening her.

Let me go back to before that letter came, to when I was only twelve.

I had a friend named Nathan Goodman. His father owned a grocery store at the corner of Lewis and Fourth streets, and the Goodmans lived two floors above us in a huge, dirty-gray tenement that faced the store. Natie was a great reader. Most kids on East Fourth Street were. A borrower's card for the Hamilton Fish Park branch of the New York Public Library was standard equipment for every kid on the block. The reason was simple. Art Acord in *The Oregon Trail* at the movie theater on Second Street cost a dime. *David Copperfield* cost nothing, not if you got to the front door of the library at nine o'clock on Saturday morning. Dickens was big stuff on East Fourth Street.

What got me involved with Jazz L. McCabe was Natie Goodman's laziness. Natie was a tough kid to get out of bed in the morning. He was late for *Nicholas Nickleby*. Some other kid got it. What Natie got was a book called *The Boy Scouts of Bob's Hill.*

My wife doesn't believe me. But I swear. There once was a book called *The Boy Scouts of Bob's Hill,* and it changed my life.

"I want you to read this," Natie said to me the day after he missed out on *Nicholas Nickleby*, and he handed me the book.

"Why?" I said. I was working my way through *Great Expectations,* and hated to be deflected.

"You wait and see," Natie said.

I didn't have to wait long. *The Boy Scouts of Bob's Hill* was a short book. It told the story of a group of boys, about the same age as Natie and me, who formed a Boy Scout troop with headquarters in a cave at a place called Bob's Hill. Don't ask me where Bob's Hill was. Probably somewhere in New England or out West, maybe even in California. Wherever it was, it was about as different from East Fourth Street as Addis Ababa is from Radio City. Furthermore, until I read this book I had never even heard of Boy Scouts. But I had never heard of London either, until I read *Martin Chuzzlewit*. The effect was the same. It was immediate, and it has lasted. I still feel about London the way Troilus felt about *Cressida*. The moment I finished reading *The Boy Scouts of Bob's Hill,* I ran down to the grocery store to find Natie Goodman. He was stacking empty cartons out in back, a chore for which his father paid him twenty-five cents a week.

"I know what you're going to say," he said, "and I'm way ahead of you. Let's start a Scout troop."

I had been going to say only that I liked *The Boy Scouts of Bob's Hill* and intended to hotfoot it right over to the library and see if maybe it was one of a series of books, because if it was, I wanted to read them all. But, as Natie had said, he was way ahead of me—and not for the first time, either.

"How can we do that?" I said.

"We write to the national headquarters," Natie said. "I looked it up in the telephone book. It's right here in New York."

Natie wrote the letter, but I helped with the phrasing, and we chipped in for the stamp. It cost two cents, and no nonsense about zones or zip codes. Two cents, no matter where you were writing to, Seattle or the Bronx. Actually, Natie and I were writing to Two Park Avenue, but the answer came from a man in New Rochelle.

It was a short, handwritten letter, and it was signed *Lester Osterweil*. Mr. Osterweil said that the National Council of the Boy Scouts of America had advised him that Master Nathan Goodman and a friend, both of East Fourth Street in New York City, had inquired about organizing a Boy Scout troop in their neighborhood, and that he, Mr. Osterweil, had been asked to pursue the matter because he worked not too far from East Fourth Street. Mr. Osterweil asked if we knew the location of the Hamilton Fish Park branch of the New York Public Library (which was like asking Gertrude Ederle if she knew the location of the English Channel), because that was where he would like to meet us the following Tuesday at 6:00 P.M., a time he hoped was convenient for us, but if it wasn't he would be pleased to make a more convenient arrangement. In the meantime he begged to remain yours for more and better Scouting, sincerely Lester Osterweil.

In those days, when life was still uncomplicated, anything that I didn't have to explain to my mother was convenient for me, and to make things convenient for himself all Natie had to do was steer clear of the grocery store in which his father and mother were trapped until almost midnight every day except Friday, when they closed at sundown.

The following Tuesday evening, Natie and I were on the front steps of the library by five thirty, and at six o'clock a tall, thin, hatless man with a sad face, wearing a dirty raincoat, came down the block and introduced himself to us.

Looking back on it now, I would guess that Mr. Osterweil was then around thirty, give or take a couple of years, but to me and Natie, who had just turned twelve, he looked as old as Calvin Coolidge. He talked like Coolidge, too. Not that I ever heard Coolidge talk, but there were a lot of jokes in those days about how rarely he opened his mouth and, when he did, how little came out.

The first thing Mr. Osterweil said was an explanation of what he'd meant when he wrote that he worked not too far from East Fourth Street. He was the manager of the F. W. Woolworth store on Avenue B between Fifth and Sixth streets, about a five-minute walk from the Hamilton Fish Park branch library. Mr. Osterweil's next words put me and Natie Goodman in his pocket forever. He asked how we'd like a couple of ice cream sodas.

Between that night, when he came into my life, and the night, about two years later, when he left it, I learned a lot about Mr. Osterweil, but I don't remember how I learned it. For example, I don't know how I learned he was a bachelor and lived with his mother in New Rochelle in the house where both of them had been born. Not that at twelve I was what you would call shy, exactly, but I can't believe I ever asked Mr. Osterweil for this piece of information.

I have a theory—which I can't prove, but which I will never stop defending—that if you feel strongly about anybody, if you really love or really hate, you pick up information about them without trying, the way a blue serge suit picks up lint, because all your pores are always open, so to speak. Maybe I don't mean pores but antennae.

Whatever I mean, this much I know: What I remember about Lester Osterweil I remember because I was crazy about him, and what I remember about Jazz L. McCabe I remember because for almost forty years, until this morning when I read his obituary in the *Times*, I have hated the bastard. He was something, Jazz L. McCabe was. Something rotten.

Lester Osterweil was just the opposite. Goodness came out of him the way hot air comes out of politicians. He didn't even have to try. Maybe that's what drew him to the Boy Scout movement. There is something simple about it. Like the Golden Rule. If you want boys to be decent, if you care about helping them grow up to be good men—why, just get them out into the open, take them on hikes, teach them to tie knots, to make fire with flint and steel, to believe that the Kingdom of Heaven is not a bull stock market but a khaki uniform that a boy wins by proving he has accepted the ludicrous belief that it is admirable to be trustworthy, loyal, helpful, friendly, courteous, kind, obedient, cheerful, thrifty, brave, clean, and reverent. Silly, of course. I shudder to think what an ass I must have been at the age of twelve to believe such stuff. I have, however, a good excuse. I was corrupted by Lester Osterweil.

Not only did Mr. Osterweil believe all this, he built his life around his belief. He had very little money. This is no reflection on the F. W. Woolworth Company. I'm sure they paid their store managers a fair wage, that Lester Osterweil was paid as much as he deserved. If the money didn't go as far as he wanted it to go, that was his fault, not Woolworth's. Lester Osterweil wanted his money to go to the boys of East Fourth Street, but he didn't have enough to go around because his mother lived in a wheelchair and earned very little by sewing for her New Rochelle neighbors. Mr. Osterweil did pretty well, though.

He helped me and Natie Goodman and a dozen other kids to buy our first Scout uniforms. Troop 224, which met every Saturday night in the downstairs reading room of the Hamilton Fish Park library, always met as a troop should meet—every member properly dressed, every member wearing the insignia to which he is entitled. I still get a kick out of remembering the day I gave Mr. Osterweil four quarters, a dime, and a nickel, the last payment I owed on the $3.50 he had advanced so I could buy a new

shirt and a merit-badge sash to wear at the troop ceremony when
I was made Senior Patrol Leader. I earned the money by taking
over Natie Goodman's job, which Natie hated, of stacking empties for his father. I wore that merit-badge sash the way King
Arthur wore Excalibur. For the man who made it possible for me
to wear it, I would have killed.

Before what happened happened, there were good times with
Mr. Osterweil. Pretty damn near a year and a half of them.

The weekly meetings. The new skills. The merit badges. The
useless knowledge picked up for the fun of it. I don't know why,
but I still enjoy knowing that the poplar *tremuloides* can also be
identified as the trembling aspen. Or that the square knot is used
for tying ropes of equal thickness. If they are of unequal thickness, you'd better use a sheet bend, and I still do. Morse code? I
can wigwag ten words a minute with a single flag, assuming
there is still anyone around who can read wigwagged Morse. If
there isn't, I can send it electronically, almost as fast as AP bulle-
tins come in on a news ticker. I haven't stopped much arterial
bleeding lately by calling on my knowledge of the proper pressure points, but not too long ago a neighbor's son, chasing a long
fly across our lawn, crashed through our kitchen window, and
when the ambulance came an intern complimented me on the
spiral reverse bandage I'd put around the kid's forearm. Just a
few of the things I learned from Mr. Osterweil.

But the best things were the Sunday hikes. That's what I remember clearest. The Sunday hikes.

Getting out of the bed I shared with my kid brother, and out of
the house without waking him or my mother, who thought Mr.
Osterweil was an American militarist working to turn me and
Natie and the other boys of Troop 224 into *pogromniks*, her word
for all people who wore uniforms, whether they worked for the
New York Sanitation Department or Czar Nicholas II. Meeting
Natie in the grocery store, which would not open officially for
another hour (we'd sneak in with a key Natie was not supposed
to have). Stuffing our knapsacks with stale rolls, a little jar of
butter scooped out of the big wooden tub in the icebox, a block

of silver-wrapped cream cheese, a can of baked beans. *No, let's take two. Baked beans are the best. . . . But what about your old man? . . . Aah, I'll push the other cans to the front of the shelf. He won't notice we took two.* I think Mr. Goodman did notice. But I also think he didn't mind. He was proud of the way Natie's merit badges kept piling up. Mr. Goodman had come to America when he was still a young man. He was not as scared as my mother.

Knapsacks loaded, there was the long walk across town to the Astor Place subway station. Except that it never seemed long, not at seven o'clock on those Sunday mornings. The streets empty and quiet, except for the sparrows screaming their heads off, their screaming somehow making it all seem even quieter. On First Avenue, the sun coming across the El, putting golden covers on the garbage cans. On Seventh Street, beyond Second Avenue, the young priest getting ready for early mass, sweeping the steps of the church, his skirts hiked up to avoid the dust. On Third Avenue, in the slatted shade from the El, the sleeping drunks looking friendly and curiously clean. And the sky, like a long wedding canopy over the tenements, smooth and blue as Waterman's ink.

Then the troop gathering slowly outside the subway kiosk. The comparison of knapsack contents. The arrival of Mr. Oster-weil. The long ride in the almost empty subway car, up to Dyck-man Street. The ferry crossing the Hudson, standing at the gate up front, catching the spray in your face when she hit a big one. On the New Jersey side, the briefing by Mr. Osterweil. Tall, skinny, his Adam's apple bobbing in and out of his khaki collar, his yellow hair blowing in the wind, his sad face looking sadder with the seriousness of his instructions. We needed flint for our fire sets; he'd heard there was quite a lot of it lying around as a result of the blasting they were doing for this new bridge, so would we keep our eyes open?

We kept our eyes open. By the time we arrived at our campsite, we were loaded down with flint. I've often wondered how they managed to get the George Washington Bridge finished without it.

Then the fires. And the cooking. And the smell of roasting hot dogs. And lying around on the grass, digesting the baked beans, while Mr. Osterweil read aloud from the Scout *Handbook*. Watching the traffic on the river. Skipping stones out toward the sailboats. And finally, the sinking sun.

I never realized I was doing anything more than having the time of my life, and then we won the annual All-Manhattan rally. All of a sudden, I was famous. Well, Troop 224 was famous. The day after I won eight of our winning forty-nine points for speed knot tying, and Natie Goodman rolled up sixteen for flint-and-steel and two-flag semaphore, a picture of Troop 224 appeared in the New York *Graphic*. All thirty-three of us, grouped around Mr. Osterweil, who looked as though he thought the cameraman was pointing a gun at him. The *Jewish Daily Forward* ran a somewhat smaller picture, but my face and Natie's were clearly visible, and the paper called Mr. Osterweil—in Yiddish, of course—"a fine influence on the young people of the neighborhood."

All this was very surprising and very pleasant. None of it was a preparation for the appearance in our lives of Jazz L. McCabe. His typewritten letter, the one that scared my mother because she thought it was a *moof tzettle*, was in our mailbox a few days after the pictures appeared in the *Graphic* and the *Forward*. The letter was addressed to me, as the troop's Senior Patrol Leader. I stared at it for a while, then took it over to the Goodmans' store, where Natie stared at it for a while.

"There's something fishy about this," he said finally.

It was the *mot juste*, all right. The letter advised me that Mr. Lester Osterweil had resigned as Scoutmaster of Troop 224, and that our new Scoutmaster would be the man whose name appeared at the bottom of the letter and who looked forward eagerly to seeing me and the other Scouts at our next weekly meeting. Jas. L. McCabe.

"Why should Mr. Osterweil resign?" I said.

"I don't know," Natie said. "Who is this Jazz L. McCabe?"

"I don't know," I said.

"Let's go find out," Natie said.

Mr. Osterweil had asked us long ago never to visit him during working hours. He did not think it was fair to his employers to devote to Scouting any of the time for which he was paid by the F. W. Woolworth Company. We had always obeyed Mr. Osterweil's rule, but Natie and I agreed that Jazz L. McCabe's letter was important enough to justify breaking it. We did not, however, get the chance. Mr. Osterweil, we learned when we got to the store, had not showed up for work that day.

But he did show up at the troop meeting the following night. When Natie and I came into the room, Mr. Osterweil was standing at the table up front, talking to a man we had never seen before. He called us over.

"This is Mr. McCabe," he said. "He says he wrote you a letter."

"Yes, sir," I said.

I pulled the letter from my pocket and handed it over. While Mr. Osterweil read it, Natie and I studied Mr. Jazz L. McCabe.

I have always had a tendency, which I'm sure is fairly common, to form mental pictures of people I have not yet met from the sound and appearance of their names. Seeing the *Jas. L. Mc-Cabe* at the bottom of his letter, my mind had at once constructed an image of a large, bluff, hearty Irishman. I was wrong.

Jas. L. McCabe, when I saw him for the first time that Saturday night, reminded me of the man pictured on the bottle of Ed. Pinaud's Eau De Cologne that stood on the marble shelf in Mr. Raffeto's barbershop on Lewis Street.

Jas. L. McCabe was small, neat, and dapper. He wore a tight double-breasted sharkskin suit and highly polished black shoes with pointed toes. A diamond stickpin in the form of a tiny horseshoe held his tightly knotted black tie in an elegant little fop's bulge under his stiff white collar. His face was round; it seemed plump because his collar was so tight that the flesh of his neck bulged. His black hair was parted in the middle and slicked back with some sort of ointment that gleamed in the glaring electric light. The sharp points of a waxed mustache gave Mr. McCabe something to do with his nervously darting hands, and he kept them busy doing it, so that he seemed to be swatting flies.

He didn't look as though he had ever heard of a sheet bend, much less knew how to tie one. Jas. L. McCabe looked as though he was ready at any moment to whip an apron over you and give you a haircut. What he gave me and Natie Goodman that night was the willies.

Mr. Osterweil's face was pale when he looked up from the letter. "This letter is a lie," he said to us. "I have not resigned as Scoutmaster of this troop."

What happened next was startling. Jas. L. McCabe stopped looking like a foolish barber. He looked suddenly like one of those Sicilian bodyguards who were always following Edward G. Robinson around in the movies.

"OK, you bastard," he said in a cold voice to Lester Osterweil. "You asked for it."

He stalked—no, he sort of hopped—furiously out of the meeting room, and slammed the door.

"Do you want this back?" Mr. Osterweil said.

A moment went by before I realized he was talking about the letter.

"No, sir," I said.

Slowly, deliberately, as though he wanted me and Natie to realize his movements held a message for us, Mr. Osterweil tore Jazz L. McCabe's letter into small pieces, and dropped them into the wastebasket.

"All right, Senior Patrol Leader," he said. "You may call the meeting to order."

I did, but it was not a success. Neither was the next day's hike. Everything was the same, and yet everything was different. Even the sky, on the long walk across town to the Astor Place subway station, did not look smooth and blue as Waterman's ink. The unexpected, troubling appearance of Jazz L. McCabe had spoiled everything, even the feel and smell of those mornings.

I did not realize how upset we were until the next day. I was in the back of the Goodman grocery store, helping Natie stack the empties, when his father asked what we were talking so noisily about. We told him about the letter from Jazz L. McCabe, and the scene that had taken place at the troop meeting.

"What kind of a name this is, a man should call himself Jazz, this I don't know," Mr. Goodman said. "But what it means, what he wants, this anybody with a head on his shoulders can see."

"What does it mean?" Natie said.

"You boys won the rally, so you got Mr. Osterweil's picture in the papers," Mr. Goodman said. "This Jazz L. McCabe, he's one of the new Democratic district leaders, and what a district leader wants is votes. You don't get votes if nobody knows who you are. But if you get your picture in the papers, that's how people learn who you are. So this Jazz L. McCabe, he figures if he gets rid of Mr. Osterweil and becomes the Scoutmaster himself, the next time you and the troop win something, the *Jewish Daily Forward* will be saying about this Jazz L. McCabe, not about Mr. Osterweil. They'll be saying it's Jazz L. McCabe who is a fine influence on the young people of the neighborhood."

Nobody ever got around to saying that. Not in my presence, anyway. Or Natie's.

Two days later I got another typewritten letter. This one was from the Manhattan Council of the Boy Scouts of America. Over a dramatically illegible signature, Natie Goodman and I were asked if we would be good enough to appear at the Manhattan Council offices uptown on Lexington Avenue on the following day at 4:00 P.M. It was a matter of the utmost urgency.

I was impressed. Not just because this was a typewritten letter. I was impressed because this was the first time I had ever seen the word "utmost" on anything but a page written by Charles Dickens.

When Natie and I got to the offices of the Manhattan Council the next day, we found Mr. Osterweil waiting on a bench in the anteroom. He looked sad. Under ordinary circumstances this would not have made an impression on me. Mr. Osterweil always looked sad. But sad in a nice way. As though the cause of his sadness was not something bad that had happened to him, but his troubled concern that something bad might happen to you. These were not, however, ordinary circumstances.

This was a man who had changed my life. He had brought something into it that I had never known existed. And I don't mean only the knowledge that the poplar *tremuloides* can also be properly called the trembling aspen. He had broken down the walls that until his arrival had always surrounded East Fourth Street. He had let in the sunlit world outside the ghetto. I did not, at the time, understand all that. But I felt it.

"Mr. Osterweil," I said, "what are we all doing here?"

"Well," he said slowly, "I'm not sure, but I think it's because Mr. McCabe wants to take over Troop 224."

"But why did they ask us to come here?" Natie said. "Not you, Mr. Osterweil. *Us*."

The Scoutmaster's Adam's apple bobbed a couple of times, and then he said, "If the boys in the troop want me to stay on as Scoutmaster, the Council will have to let me stay on."

"You mean," Natie said, "if we say the word, it's nuts to this Jazz L. McCabe?"

"Pretty much, yes," Mr. Osterweil said.

"OK," Natie said grimly. "You got nothing to worry about, sir."

For forty years, every time that I have found myself hating Jazz L. McCabe, I have also found myself hearing again the sound of Natie's voice as he uttered those words: *You got nothing to worry about, sir.* If you want to feel confidence in the power of decency and justice to direct the forces that rule the world, the best time to take a shot at it is when you're thirteen going on fourteen. After that, it's an uphill fight.

I didn't realize that, of course, when a door opened at the far side of the anteroom and a secretary said, "Mr. Osterweil, please?"

He stood up and followed her out of the room, and the door closed behind him.

"When he comes out," Natie said, "I think it would be a good idea if we talked to him for a couple of minutes before we go in."

It was an excellent idea, but when the door opened again, about a half hour later, the secretary was alone.

Natie and I both stood up, but she only wanted me. "This way, please," she said.

Wondering what had happened to Mr. Osterweil, I followed the girl into a corridor. At the far end she opened a door on the right and smiled encouragingly at me. I stepped through, and she pulled the door shut behind me.

I was in a room that reminded me of the "Closed Shelf Section" in the Hamilton Fish Park library, except that the walls were lined not with books but with pictures of men like Dan Beard and Lord Baden-Powell. But there was that same feeling of a room in which nobody lived, but which people visited for a special purpose.

At a long table between the windows sat three men. I had never seen men like these in real life, but I had seen hundreds of pictures of them in the newspapers. These were the faces, photographed by Underwood & Underwood, that appeared in the financial section of the *Times* when the corporations for which they worked appointed them to vice-presidencies and board chairmanships. They looked prosperous and well scrubbed. They were all smiling kindly at me. They all had good teeth.

"Please don't be afraid," said the man in the middle. "We just want to ask you a few questions."

"Yes, sir," I said.

"Why don't you sit down," said the man on the left, pointing to a chair facing the table.

"Thank you, sir," I said.

"It was you and Scout Goodman who were responsible for the founding of Troop 224, were you not?" said the man on the left.

"Yes, sir," I said.

"May we congratulate you on your fine showing at the recent All-Manhattan rally," said the man on the right.

"Thank you, sir."

I don't think, looking back on it, that I was usually all that polite at the age of thirteen going on fourteen. But there was that fifth point of the Scout Law, which came out squarely in favor of courtesy, and I was at that moment seated close to the heartland of the American Scout movement.

"Now, then," said the man in the middle, and even if he had not hiked himself forward in his chair and leaned across the table, I would have known the preliminaries were over. There was a mainbout sound to that "Now, then."

"We have asked you to come here today because we are faced with a very painful problem," said the man in the middle. "It has to do with Mr. Osterweil."

"Yes, sir," I said.

"Do you think he is a good Scoutmaster?"

"Yes, sir."

"Good," said the man in the middle. "We would be very sorry to hear that your troop had not been assigned a good Scoutmaster. What's that?"

I jumped slightly in my chair before I realized that the last two words had not been addressed to me. The man on the left had leaned forward and was whispering to the man in the middle.

"Right," the man in the middle said finally to the man on the left. Then he said to me, "You understand, of course, that to be a good Scoutmaster requires more than a knowledge of the various skills in which Scouts are trained. He must also be a good man in the moral sense. Do you understand what I mean?"

"Yes, sir," I said, and it is possible that I did, but I think my main concern was not to cause trouble by appearing stupid. Feeling my way without advice, so to speak, I felt the best thing I could do for Mr. Osterweil, as well as for myself and Natie, was to look calm and act as though nothing unusual had happened during all the time Mr. Osterweil had been our Scoutmaster, because, with a man like that in charge, how could anything unusual happen?

"Mr. Osterweil was assigned to your troop," the man in the middle said, "because we had every reason to believe he was a morally upright person. Otherwise, of course, he would not have been admitted to the Scout movement. However, we have received a communication from a man named McCabe. Do you know him?"

"Yes, sir," I said. "Jazz."

"What?"

I sensed I had made a mistake, so I said quickly, "It's the way he spells his name, sir."

The man on the left leaned forward again, holding out a sheet of paper and pointing to something at the bottom. The man in the middle adjusted his glasses, leaned over the sheet, peered at it for a moment, then leaned back and nodded at me.

"I see," he said. "Well, Mr. McCabe wrote to us that he had recently assumed certain political duties in your neighborhood, and that in his efforts to learn as much as he could about the people he would be serving, he had made a thorough investigation of the area. He wrote that he had discovered a number of parents were worried about the relationship between the Scoutmaster of Troop 224 and the boys in the troop. Are you aware of this?"

Of course I was aware of it. But I wasn't going to tell a man with an Underwood & Underwood face that because we wore uniforms my mother believed Mr. Osterweil was training us all to be *pogromniks*.

I said, "No, sir."

The man on the right leaned over and whispered to the man in the middle, who said, "Good point," and turned back to me. "What about your relationship with Mr. Osterweil? Is it a friendly one?"

"Yes, sir."

"How friendly, may I ask?"

I thought about what it was like—lying around the campfire on Sundays, watching the boats on the river and digesting roasted hot dogs and baked beans and listening to the sound of Mr. Osterweil's voice as he read aloud from the Scout Handbook. But I didn't know how to put all that into words. Not for those faces out of The New York Times financial section. I tried with something I felt they would understand.

"Well," I said, "Mr. Osterweil lent me three and a half dollars to buy a new shirt and a merit-badge sash."

"You say he lent you the money?"

"Yes, sir."

"You're sure he didn't give it to you as a present?"

"No, sir," I said. "I paid him back by stacking empties."

"By doing what?"

I explained about Natie's father's grocery store, and the job I'd taken over from Natie.

"Oh, I see," said the man in the middle. He seemed disappointed in my answer. "Just a moment, please."

Now both the man on the right and the man on the left leaned forward. There was a whispered conference.

"Good point," the man in the middle said finally, and the other two leaned back. "I'm now going to ask you something very important," he said to me. "Please think carefully before you answer, and please answer with complete honesty, on your honor as a Scout. Will you do that?"

"Yes, sir," I said.

"On your honor as a Scout, remember."

"Yes, sir."

"Has Mr. Osterweil ever made any attempt to molest you?"

I thought that over. Not because I didn't understand the question. I knew what the word "molest" meant. Miss Marine, my English teacher, had said more than once that I had the best vocabulary in her class. But I was here for a purpose, and that was to keep Mr. Osterweil as our Scoutmaster. Just saying no, he had never molested me, was not enough. I had to do better than that.

"No, sir, he never did," I said. "Just the opposite."

"How do you mean, just the opposite."

"Mr. Osterweil is very friendly."

"In what way?"

I knew it sounded a little silly, but I wanted to counteract that crack about molesting, which I knew had come out of that bastard McCabe's letter, so I said, "Mr. Osterweil puts his arms around us."

"He does, does he?"

"Yes, sir."

Again the heads on the left and right joined the one in the middle for a hurried conference, but this time I wasn't worried. I could tell from the excitement in the unintelligible whispers that I had given the right answer. The heads separated.

"Could you . . ." the man in the middle said, then paused and cleared his throat. "On your word of honor now, as a Scout, tell us how often—and yes, with whom, any particular boys?— does Mr. Osterweil put his arms around you?"

I thought about how proud and happy Mr. Osterweil was when any one of us did something good. Like when we won the rally. Or like when I was made Senior Patrol Leader.

"Oh, he does it a lot," I said. "All the time. He likes all of us."

They didn't bother to call Natie in; that was the end of the interview. It was also the end of Mr. Osterweil, but I didn't know that at the moment. Even when I found out, three days later, I didn't put it all together. I merely thought, through the pain that was to turn into all those years of hatred for Jazz L. McCabe, I merely thought stupidly: What a funny way to become a part of history. The Empire State Building, completed only a few months before, had just been opened to the public. Mr. Osterweil had gone up to the hundred-and-second floor and jumped from the observation deck.

Looie Follows Me

JOHN D. MacDONALD

Any number of things can happen when a tough, street-wise or-phan from the big city comes to spend a few weeks with a small-town family. The things that happen in "Looie Follows Me," however, are not the ones you might expect, for this isn't a crime story at all. Rather, it is a deceptively simple story about the prevention of a pair of crimes against children, one immediate and physical, the other far-reaching and much more subtle. Its abundant suspense is to be expected in the work of John D. Mac-Donald, one of the finest craftsmen of the suspense story for close to forty years. MacDonald is the author of several hundred short stories and more than sixty volumes of fiction and nonfic-tion. His most recent books are the twentieth Travis McGee ad-venture, Cinnamon Skin, *and the first of two collections of his best pulp magazine fiction,* The Good Old Stuff.*

I REMEMBER how it promised to be a terrible summer. I had squeaked through the fifth grade and I was going to be eleven in July and I had hoped that on my eleventh birthday my parents would come up to visit me at Camp Wah-Na-Hoo, bearing gifts.

It was our third year in the big house twelve miles from town. Dad called it "a nice commuting distance" in summer and "too rugged for a dog team" in winter.

One of the main reasons for wanting to go to Wah-Na-Hoo was on account of the Branton twins, Kim and Cam, who lived a couple of hundred yards down the road. I knew that if they went for two months and I didn't go at all, they'd make my life miserable all winter yapping about the good old days at Camp. They are twelve years old, and Dad says that he can't ever look at them without wondering when they'll be the right size for a harness and bit.

The second reason was that if I stayed home all summer, Looie, the five-year-old kid sister, would tag around after me all day with her hand in her mouth.

The big discussion came in May. I was called into the living room and told to sit down for "a little talk." While Dad took off his glasses and stowed them in his coat pocket I made a quick review of recent misdemeanors and couldn't decide which one to think up a defense for.

"Jimmy, your mother and I have been discussing the question of camp for you this summer."

I dropped defensive plans and went on the offensive. "I can hardly wait to go," I said.

Dad coughed and looked appealingly at Mother. "The fact of the matter is, Jimmy, we feel you're a little young. We think you should wait one more year."

Then they told me that I would have fun during the two weeks at the shore and I made low-voiced comments about a hotel full of old ladies and besides the Branton twins were going and I played with them and how did that make me too young.

And so after I lost the discussion, I had nothing to look forward to but mooching around our childless neighborhood all summer with the clop clop of Looie's feet behind me. My parents had been mysterious about something nice that was going to happen during the summer, but I had a heavy suspicion about things they called "nice." They even called sending me to Syracuse to visit Aunt Kate "nice."

And I was prepared to resist going to Aunt Kate's to my dying breath.

The mysterious "nice" thing arrived on the fifth of July. Its name was Johnny Wotnack from New York City. It climbed out of Mrs. Turner's blue sedan and it stood in our driveway and stared suspiciously around at the big yard, the oaks, the orchard on the hill behind the house.

Dad had stayed home from the office that day. He started outdoors, and so did I, but just as I got to the door, Mother grabbed my arm and hauled me back and said, "Now wait a minute, Jimmy. That little boy is going to stay with us for a few weeks. You are going to share everything with him. He's a Fresh Air Child and we agreed to take him in here for a while and make him feel at home. So you be nice to him. Understand?"

"Why did he come here?"

"For fresh air and sunshine and good food so he can be healthy."

"He looks plenty rugged to me."

Johnny Wotnack had a small black shiny suitcase. Dad spoke to Mrs. Turner, and she waved to Mother and drove off. Dad picked up the suitcase and said, "Glad you could come, Johnny. This is my son, Jimmy. And his mother. And the little girl is Looie."

"Please to meet you," Johnny said politely enough. But there was an air of cold disdain about him, a superior condescension. He was almost thin, and his face had a seamed grayish look like that of a midget I saw once at the sideshow. His hands were huge, with big blocky knuckles.

Johnny gave me one cool glance. "Hi, kid," he said.

"Hi," I said.

His hair was cropped short, and he wore blue jeans and a white sweat shirt. Dad took him upstairs right to my room, went inside and pointed to the extra twin bed, and said, "You'll bunk in here with Jimmy, Johnny."

I suddenly realized that the pictures I had cut out and taped to my walls looked sort of childish. I wished I had known about him so I could have taken them down. Johnny slowly surveyed the room. "This'll do okay," he said.

Mother went over to him and gently pulled his ear forward as though she were lifting a rock under which she expected to find a bug.

Johnny snatched his head away. "What's the gag?" he demanded.

Mother gave her telephone laugh. "Why I just wondered how dirty you got on the trip. Those trains are a fright. I'll start hot water running in the tub."

She hurried out of the room. Johnny said weakly, "Wait a minute, lady." But she was already gone. In a few seconds we could hear the heavy roar of water filling the tub.

The three of us stood there, uneasy.

Dad said, "Well, Johnny. Make yourself at home." He went on downstairs, leaving me there with him. Looie was with her mother.

Johnny sat on the edge of his bed. He kicked at the suitcase with his sneaker. I looked at him with fascination. There were two deep scars on the back of his right hand, and one finger was crooked. To me he was a perfect example of urbanity and sophistication. It seemed an enormous indignity that Mother should shove him into a bathtub the first minute.

I said, "It happens to me too. The baths I mean. Until they'd drive you nuts."

He looked at me without interest. "Yeah?"

"I'm going to be eleven in July. July fourteenth," I said. "How old are you?"

"About twelve, I guess."

I was horrified. "Don't you know for certain?"

"No."

That was further proof of sophistication. It was a miraculous detachment to be able to forget your own birthday, to be indifferent to it. I determined right then and there to forget my own.

When he came downstairs for lunch, his hair was damp. But his face still had that grayish, underground look. He sat silently at the table while Mother and Dad made a lot of gay conversation about how nice it was in the country.

He pushed his glass of milk aside. Mother said, "Don't you like milk?"

"Never could get used to the taste of the stuff."

"In this family," Mother said in her don't-cross-me voice, "the children eat what is placed before them. Without question. We hope you'll do the same, Johnny."

He raised one eyebrow and grinned at her almost as though humoring her. He drank the milk down and wiped his mouth on the back of the scarred hand. "I still don't like it," he said.

Dad quickly changed the subject. After lunch he said, "Now you kids run out and play."

Johnny headed for the garage. Once upon a time it was a barn. He went around it, then dug a cigarette butt out of his pocket along with a kitchen match. He lit it carefully after striking the match with his thumbnail. He took one long deep drag, huffed out the smoke, butted the cigarette, and put it back in his pocket just as Looie came around the corner of the barn, her face screwed up ready to cry if we were out of sight. She came toward us with a wide happy smile.

" 'Fraid she'd snitch," Johnny said.

"She would," I agreed.

"I'm going to get sick of this Johnny, Johnny business," he said. "The name's Stoney. Stoney Wotnack."

"Ha! Stoney!" Looie said. "Stoney, Stoney, Stoney."

"That's right, doll," he said.

I couldn't think of what to say to him. It was almost like trying to talk to Auntie Kate. He said. "What's to do around this dump, Jim?"

I said eagerly, "Well, we can climb the apple trees, and there's a crick the other side of the hill to fish in, and I'm making a cave in the crick bank and. . ."

My voice trailed off. He hadn't changed expression. There hadn't been the tiniest gleam of interest in his eyes. "What do you like to do?" I asked weakly.

He shrugged. "Depends. I get a charge out of heisting candy from the five and dime. You can sell the stuff for enough to go to the movies. You can smoke in the balcony. Or you tell a guy you watch his car he'll give you two bits. And let him know that maybe you don't get the two bits first, he gets a hole in a tire. Or at night you can go hunting in the alleys for drunks. Roll 'em for everything but their clothes."

I couldn't follow him very clearly. And I didn't want to display my ignorance by asking questions. But he had opened up new and exciting vistas of experience. I saw myself sitting debonairly in a movie balcony puffing on a cigar.

He sighed. "But you can't do that stuff here. This place is . . . empty. No noises except bugs and birds. My old man was on a prison farm once. He didn't like it."

I said, "Want to look around?"

He shrugged. All the things that had looked pretty good to me turned out to be as childish as the pictures on the walls of my room. I had been proud of our six acres, the same as Dad, but under Stoney's cold stare everything dwindled away to a horrible, insipid emptiness.

At one place he came to life. The Branton twins and I had gotten hold of a feed sack, stuffed it with sawdust, and hung it by a long rope from one of the rafters in the barn. When Stoney saw it, his shoulders went back and he strutted up to it. He went into a crouch, jabbed at it lightly and expertly with a flicking left, and thumped his right fist deep into it. He bounced around on his toes, jabbing, hooking, snuffing hard through his nose. The thump of his fist into the sawdust gave me a horridly vivid picture of how that fist would feel in my stomach.

He finished and said, "Little workout's a good thing."

"Yeah " I said, consciously imitating his cold tone.

"Another couple years and I try the geegees."

"The what?" I said.

"Golden Gloves, Kid. Golden Gloves. That's a life. Win in your division and turn pro and play it smart and you're all set. Better than lugging a shine box around in front a the Forty-Second Street Library, kid. I watch 'em work out at the gym. Look, we got to get a bigger bag and fasten it more solid. It swings too much."

"Yeah," I said coldly.

"Got any funny books?" he asked. "I feel like reading. The crime kind."

"They'll only let me have cowboy ones," I said apologetically.

"Them big fairies in the pink shirts give me the itch."

"I like Roy Rogers," I said defensively.

He stared at me and chuckled coldly. "Roy Rogers! Ha!"

We walked aimlessly around for a time. I suggested weakly, "We could pretend something."

He didn't even bother to answer that one. I went moodily back to the house alone. Looie was trudging around on the pointless walk, following Stoney. I didn't like her following me usually, but this sudden shift of allegiance annoyed me. I sat in a chair on the porch. Dad came out and said, "Where's Johnny?"

"Walking," I said.

"Can't you think up a game or something?"

"He doesn't like games."

Mother came out and heard that last part. She said to Dad, "It's quite an adjustment for the boy. I think we ought to leave him alone for a little while. Polite, isn't he?"

Stoney did not come out of his mood of chill disdain. Within three days he had settled into a pattern. He fixed the sawdust bag and spent two hours every morning "working out." Dad lined up some chores for him, and after his workout he did his chores quickly and expertly. He was silent at the table, speaking when spoken to. In the afternoon he wandered around and around, tagged by Looie. She talked to him constantly, and I never heard him say anything to her that was longer than one word.

Mother and Dad began to really work on bringing him out of what they called his "shell." As far as I was concerned, he wasn't in any shell. There just wasn't much around to interest him. Mother and Dad asked him a lot of questions to get him talking. But it didn't work. Then they took us on rides, and we went to the movies and went swimming. But nothing did any good. Stoney was obedient, clean, and reserved. And I never saw him smile.

On the eleventh day of his visit Dad had set us to work grubbing the tall grass out from around the base of the apple trees. The dogged way Stoney worked made it necessary for me to work just as hard. Looie had found a hop toad and she was urging him along by poking him with a twig.

Suddenly there was a loud neighing sound, and the Branton twins, Kim and Cam, came galloping down the hill. They are the biggest kids of their age in our school. They have long faces and bright blue eyes and not very much sense.

Stoney straightened up and looked at them and I heard him say one short word under his breath. I saw that word once, chalked on a fence. I had wondered how to say it.

They ran around us three times and pulled up, panting and snorting. They both talked at once, much too loud, and I finally got the idea that there was some kind of sickness at Camp Wah-Na-Hoo and everybody had been sent home.

Stoney stood and stared at them. Kim said, "Hey, you're from the Fund, Mom said."

"You want it drawed for you in a picture?" Stoney asked.

"Yipes, he can draw," Cam yelled. Kim jumped up and grabbed an apple tree branch. He swung his feet up and got them over the branch, let go with his hands, and hung by his knees.

Then he started a gentle swinging. At the right part in the swing, he straightened his legs and dropped, half twisting in the air so his feet hit first. He had to touch his hands to the ground for balance.

Cam stared at Stoney. "Okay, let's see you do that." Both the twins seem to be made of nothing but hard, rubbery muscle and pink skin.

Stoney gave a snort of disgust and started to work again. "Scared to try, even," Cam shouted.

Stoney straightened up. "What does it get me, pal, falling out of a tree? Once I see a guy fall out a thirty-story window. When he hit, he splashed. There you got something."

Cam and Kim went into their act. They hung onto each other and yelped. They gasped with laughter. They pounded on each other and jumped up and down and gasped about thirty-story windows. When they do that to me, I get so mad that tears run right out of my eyes. Stoney acted as if they weren't there. After a while the twins got tired. Kim snatched Looie's toad, and they went racing up through the orchard, yelling that they'd see me later. Looie was yelling about the loss of her 'hopper.'

When they were seventy feet away, Kim threw the toad back to us. We heard it hit up in one of the trees, but it didn't come down. Probably wedged up there.

Looie was screaming. Stoney said, "Pals of yours?"

"Well, they live in the next house."

He gave me a contemptuous look and took Looie's hand. "Come on, Sis, and we'll get us another hopper." She went snuffling off with him. I was about to complain because he had left me with the work, and then I noticed that he'd finished the last of his trees.

The next time I saw them, Stoney was leaning against the barn, his eyes half shut against the sun glare. Looie had a new hopper and she was hopping along behind it.

With the Branton kids back, the tempo of things stepped up. They galloped into the yard in the late afternoon. Stoney stood and watched them without expression. They separated to gallop on each side of him. Kim dropped onto his knees, and Cam gave Stoney a shove. Stoney went over hard. He got up and brushed himself off.

Cam and Kim circled and came back to stand panting in front of him. "Well?" Cam said.

"Well what?" Stoney said.

"What are you going to do about it?"

Stoney hunched his shoulders. He looked at the house and for a moment he seemed to be sniffing the air like a hound. Then the tension went out of him. "I'm not going to do anything, friend."

"Yella!" Kim yelled.

Stoney looked wryly amused. "Could be, friend. Could be."

I was disgusted with Stoney. I headed out of the yard and hollered back to the twins, "Come on, guys. Leave him with Looie."

We went over to the Branton place. I was late getting back to supper. I came in with my shirt torn because they had ganged me. They hurt my arm, but I got over it before I went home. I didn't want Stoney to see me crying.

The next morning the twins came over and used the punching bag for a tackling dummy. The rope broke and the bag split when it hit the floor. Stoney leaned against the wall and watched them moodily. I knew the way the twins operated. They were trying to get a rise out of Stoney. And once they did, it would be too bad for Stoney. The twins work as a unit. In school they cleaned up on Tom Clayden, who is fourteen and pretty big. Tom quit when Kim was holding him and Cam was hitting him.

After they had gone, I said to Stoney, "Shall we fix the bag?"

He shrugged. "I only got two more days here. Skip it."

The following afternoon I was up in the room working on my stamps. A bunch of approval items had come in the mail, and I was budgeting my allowance to cover the ones I had to have.

It was getting late. I knew that Looie was trudging around after the restless Stoney Wotnack. The sound came from afar. A thin, high screaming. I knew right away that it was Looie's built-in screech. She uses it for major catastrophies.

Dad wasn't back from the office yet. I got out in back the same time Mother did, but Mother beat me to Looie. Looie was too gone from screeching to make any specific complaints. Mother went over her, bone by bone, and dug under her blonde hair looking for scalp wounds.

All we could find were some angry-looking rope burns on her ankles and wrists and a little lump on her forehead right at the hair line.

When the screeching began to fade into words, I told Mother that she was yelling about Indians. We got her into the house, and finally she calmed down so that Mother could understand her too.

Mother said, "Oh, it was just those silly Branton twins playing Indian."

For my money, silly was a pretty lightweight word. The Brantons throw themselves into the spirit of any game they play. I got tangled in one of their Indian games the summer before, and Mr. Branton had to come over and apologize to Dad about the arrow hole in my left leg in the back. The Brantons were kept in their own yard for a week, and when they got out, they twisted my arm for telling.

Just then Stoney Wotnack came sauntering down across the lot with his hands in his pockets. He was whistling. It was the first time I had ever heard him whistle.

Mother turned on him real quick and said, "Johnny, didn't you know those big twins were picking on little Looie?"

"They quit after a while," he said idly. I could see she wanted to ask him more, but he went on into the house.

Looie's yelping had simmered down to dry sobs that were a minute apart. I could see by the expression on her face that she was thinking of something to ask for. She knew that she usually got a "Yes" answer right after she was hurt.

Mother said, "When your father comes home, I'm sending him over to the Brantons. This sort of thing has happened too often."

Dad came home a half hour later. I saw a little gleam in his eyes as Mother told him about Looie. Dad gently rubbed his hands together and said, "A decent local government would put a bounty on those two. But I couldn't go out after them. It would be too much like shooting horses, and I love horses."

"This is nothing to kid about, Sam," Mother snapped.

"Okay, okay, I'll go have words with Harvey Branton. But if they carry me home on a shutter, you'll know it went further than words. Remember, darling, he's the guy who lifted the front end of our car out of the ditch last winter."

"Just give him a piece of your mind."

Dad turned to me. "Jimmy, would you care if you weren't friends any more with the twins? I can tell Harvey to keep them off the property."

"Have I been friends with them?"

Dad stood up. "Wish me luck," he said.

Just then a car came roaring into our driveway and the car door slammed almost before the motor stopped running.

Harvey Branton came striding across the grass to our front porch. He walked with his big fists swinging and a set look around the mouth.

Twenty feet from the porch he yelled, "I want a word with you, Sam Baker!"

From the way he looked, if I were Dad, I would have headed for the storeroom in the attic. But Dad came out onto the porch and leaned against a pillar and held his lighter to his cigarette. "Just coming over to see you, Harvey."

Harvey Branton pulled up to a stop, his face a foot from Dad's. "Your're harboring a criminal in this house, Baker. This is a decent section. I won't have you bringing city riffraff up here to pick on my children."

"Pick on your children!" Dad said with surprise.

"Don't pretend you don't know anything about it, Baker. My two boys were worked over by an expert. I have the whole story from them. That gutter rat you're boarding attacked them. Kim has two black eyes, and so does Cam. Their mother has driven them down to the doctor. Kim's nose has to be set, and we think that he'll have to take stitches on the inside of Cam's lip. A man couldn't have punished them worse."

Dad said mildly, "Harvey, I was coming over to tell you that unless you could keep those two pony-sized kids of yours from picking on Looie, you could keep them off the property."

"Harmless play," Harvey rasped. "Don't change the subject. I'm talking about brutal assault, and that riffraff is your guest, so you can damn well assume the responsibility."

Mother came out onto the porch and said, "I just got the rest of the story from Looie. She wandered away from Johnny, and your two fiends jumped her and tied her to one of the saplings in the back pasture and piled brush around her legs. They had matches and they told Looie they were going to burn her alive. They were holding lighted matches by that dry brush. She said they had red paint on their faces." Mother's voice sounded funny and brittle, like icicles in the winter.

"A stupid lie," Harvey Branton said.

"Looie has never lied in her life," Dad said softly.

Harvey gave him a mean look. "I'm not saying who is a liar, Baker. I'm just saying that I know my own boys and they wouldn't do a thing like that and your wife is trying to shift the responsibility."

Stoney Wotnack came out of the hallway. He came across the porch. His hands were out of his pockets, and I saw that the big knuckles were bruised and reddened. He stopped and looked up at Harvey Branton and said, "I seen it, mister. Them two creeps you got woulda burned her. Now take back what you said about Mrs. Baker."

Harvey made a sound deep in his throat. He grabbed Stoney's arm and said, "Son, it's going to take me about ten minutes to teach you to stay the hell away from decent children." He raised his big right hand, and his lips were drawn back from his teeth.

Dad said in a voice so low that I could hardly hear it, "Branton, if you hit that kid, I'm going to try my level best to kill you."

I'd never heard Dad use that tone of voice. It made the hair on the back of my neck prickle.

Branton slowly lowered his hand. He let go of Stoney and stepped back away from the porch. He said, "I'm going to sue you, Baker."

"Go ahead," Dad said. "Maybe those two kids of yours will be put in an institution where they belong when the judge hears the case. Keep them off my property from now on."

The car door chunked shut again, and the back wheels spun on gravel as big Harvey Branton backed out into the highway.

Dad said, "Somebody better help me. When I stop leaning on this pillar, my knees are going to bend the wrong way."

Mother went to him and kissed him and slapped him lightly on the cheek. "Just like Jack Dempsey. A real killer, aren't you, darling?"

She turned and put her hand on Stoney's head. He stood rigid and uncomfortable. Dad said, "Boy, this is your home away from home. We want you back here with us every chance you can get."

"Knock it off!" Stoney said. He twisted away from Mother and went into the house. We heard his steps on the stairs.

We all talked about it at dinner. Stoney didn't say anything. Near the end of the meal he said with a faint tone of wonder, "That big monkey was really going to fix my wagon."

"How did you lick both of them?" Dad asked curiously.

"Both, three, six, who cares?" Stoney said. "They both lead with the right and swing from way back and shut their eyes when they swing. All you gotta do is stay inside the swing and bust 'em with straight rights and left hooks."

Dad stayed home from the office the next day to see Stoney off. Mrs. Turner came and got him to drive him down to the station. Dad carried the black suitcase out to the car. Stoney had a little more weight on him and he looked heavier in the shoulders, but otherwise he was exactly the same.

Mrs. Turner said, "And what do you say, little man?"

"Yeah. Thanks," Stoney mumbled.

The car drove off. "Grateful little cuss, isn't he?" Dad said.

"Maybe we're the ones to be grateful," mother said mildly.

We went back into the house. Dad was the one who, by accident, found out about the shoes. And I heard them talk and figure out together what had happened. The only way it could have happened was for Stoney Wotnack to get up in the middle of the night and put a high shine on every pair of shoes he could find. It must have taken him hours.

I saw Mother's face. She had a shiny look in her eyes, and her voice was funny, the way it gets every fall with hay fever. That seemed to me to be a pretty funny reaction to some newly shined shoes.

She shook Dad by the arm and said, "Don't you see, Sam? Don't you see? He didn't know how to do anything else."

Dad looked at me and smiled. It was that same funny-looking smile that he wears when he walks out of a sad movie.

None of it made any sense to me. All I knew was that I'd spend the rest of the summer with Looie walking one step behind me, sucking on her hand.

Here Lies Another Blackmailer

BILL PRONZINI

Bill Pronzini is the author of thirty-one novels—including a dozen in the well-known Nameless Detective series—and some 275 short stories. In these shorter works, Pronzini's excellent characterization and sharp ear for dialogue combine with an almost fiendish ability to astonish us with a twist ending. While the twist of "Here Lies Another Blackmailer" is apparent by virtue of its inclusion in this volume, the story is no less enjoyable because we are already in on the secret. In fact, observing the narrator's behavior with an informed eye makes us wonder if the difference between the child and the man is really as great as we customarily assume it to be. (M.M.)

MY Uncle Walter studied me across the massive oak desk in
his library, looking at once irascible, anxious and a little fearful.
"I have some questions to ask you, Harold," he said at length,
"and I want truthful answers, do you understand?"

"I am not in the habit of lying," I lied stiffly.

"No? To my mind your behavior has always left much to be
desired, and has been downright suspect at times. But that is not
the issue at hand, except indirectly. The issue at hand is this:
where were you at eleven-forty last evening?"

"At eleven-forty? I was in bed, of course."

"You were not," my uncle said sharply. "Elsie saw you going
downstairs at five minutes of eleven, fully dressed; she told me
about it when I questioned her this morning."

Elsie was the family maid, and much too nosy for her own
good. She was also the only person who lived on this small estate except for myself, Uncle Walter, and Aunt Pearl. I frowned
and said, "I remember now. I went for a walk."

"At eleven P.M.?"

"I couldn't sleep and I thought the fresh air might help."

"Where did you go on this walk?"

"Oh, here and there. Just walking, you know."

"Did you leave the grounds?"

"Not that I recall."

"Did you go out by the old carriage house?"

"No," I lied.

My uncle was making an obvious effort to conceal his impatience. "You *were* out by the old carriage house, weren't you?"

"I've already said I wasn't."

"I saw you there, Harold. At least, I'm fairly certain I did. You
were lurking in the oleander bushes."

"I do not lurk in bushes," I lied.

"*Somebody* was lurking in the bushes, and it couldn't have

been anyone but you. Elsie and Aunt Pearl were both here in the house.''

"May I ask a question?"

"What is it?''

"What were *you* doing out by the old carriage house at eleven-forty last night?''

Uncle Walter's face had begun to take on the unpleasant color of raw calf's liver. "What I was doing there is of no consequence. I want to know why you were there, and what you might have seen and heard.''

"Was there something to see and hear, Uncle?''

"No, of course not. I just want to know—Look here, Harold, what did you see and hear from those bushes?''

"I wasn't *in* them in the first place, so I couldn't have seen or heard anything, could I?''

Uncle Walter stood and began to pace the room, his hands folded behind his back. He looked like a pompous old lawyer, which is precisely what he was. Finally he came over to stand in front of my chair, glaring down at me. "You were not out by the carriage house at eleven-forty last night? You did not see anything and you did not hear anything at any time during your alleged walk?''

"No,'' I lied.

"I have no recourse but to accept your word, then. Actually it doesn't matter whether you were there or not, in one sense, because you refuse to admit it. I trust you will continue to refuse to admit it, to me and to anyone else.''

"I don't believe I follow that, Uncle.''

"You don't have to follow it. Very well, Harold, that's all.''

I stood up and left the library and went out to the sun porch at the rear of the house. When I was certain neither Elsie nor Aunt Pearl was about, and that my uncle had not chosen to pursue me surreptitiously, I slipped out and hurried through the land-scaped grounds to the old carriage house. The oleander bushes, where I had been lurking at eleven-forty the previous night, after following Uncle Walter from the house—I *had* gone for a short walk, and had noticed him sneaking out—were located along the southern wall of the building. I passed along parallel to them and around to the back, to the approximate spot where my uncle had stood talking to the man whom he had met there. They had spoken in low tones, of course, but in the late-evening summer stillness I had been able to hear every word. I had also been able to hear the muffled report which had abruptly terminated their conversation.

Now, what, I wondered, glancing around, *did Uncle Walter do with the body?*

The gunshot had startled me somewhat, and I had involuntarily rustled the bushes and therefore been forced to run when my uncle came to investigate. I had then hidden behind one of the privet hedges until I was certain he did not intend to search for me. Minutes later I slipped around by the carriage house again; but I had not been able to locate my uncle and I had not wanted to chance discovery by prowling through the darkness. So I returned to the privet hedge and waited, and twenty-five minutes later Uncle Walter had appeared and gone back to the house.

A half hour or so is really not very much time in which to hide a dead man, so I found the body quite easily. It was concealed among several tall eucalyptus trees some sixty yards from the carriage house, covered with leaves and strips of bark which regularly peels from the trees. A rather unimaginative hiding place, to be sure, although it was no doubt intended to be temporary. Uncle Walter had given no prior consideration to body disposal, and had therefore hidden the corpse here until he could think of something more permanent to do with it.

I uncovered the dead man and studied him for a moment. He was small and slender, with sharp features and close-set eyes. In the same way my uncle looked exactly like what he was, so did this person look like what *he* was, or had been—a criminal, naturally. In his case, a blackmailer—and not at all a clever or cautious one, to have allowed Uncle Walter to talk him into the time and place of last night's rendezvous. What excuse had my uncle given him for the unconventionality of it all? Well, no matter.

The man really had been quite stupid to have accepted such terms under any circumstances, and was now quite dead as a result.

Yet Uncle Walter was equally as stupid: first, to have put himself in a position where he could be blackmailed; and second, to have perpetrated a carelessly planned and executed homicide on his own property. My uncle, however, was impulsive, and much less bright than he seemed to most people. He also had a predilection for beautiful blonde show girls, about which my Aunt Pearl knew nothing, and about which I also had known nothing until overhearing last evening's conversation. This was the reason he had been blackmailed. He had committed murder because the extortionist wanted more money than he had been getting for his continued silence—and Uncle Walter was a notoriously tightfisted man.

It took me the better part of two hours to move the body. I am not particularly strong, and even though the dead man was small and light, it was a physical struggle to which I am not accustomed. At last, however, I had secreted the blackmailer's remains in what I considered to be quite a clever hiding place—one that was not even on my uncle's property.

Across the dry creek which formed the rear boundary line was a grove of densely-grown trees, and well into them I found a large decaying log, all that was left of a long-dead tree felled by insects or disease. At first glance it seemed to be solid, but upon careful inspection I discovered that it was hollow. I dragged the body to the log and managed to stuff it inside; then I covered all traces of the entombment. No one venturing into this grove, including my unimaginative uncle, would think of investigating a seemingly solid log.

Satisfied, I returned unobserved to the house, had a bath, and spent the remainder of the day reading in my room.

Uncle Walter was apoplectic. "What did you do with it?" he shouted at me. "What did you *do* with it?"

I looked at him innocently across his desk. It was just past eight the following morning, and he had summoned me from my room with furious poundings on the door. I was still in my robe and slippers.

"What did I do with what?" I asked.

"You know what!"

"I'm afraid I don't, Uncle."

"I know it was you, Harold, just as I knew all along it was you in the oleander bushes two nights ago. So you heard and saw everything, did you? Well, go ahead—admit it."

"I have nothing to admit."

He slapped the desk top with the palm of one hand. "Why did you move it? That's what I fail to comprehend. Why, Harold? Why did you move it?"

"The conversation seems to be going around in circles," I said. "I really don't know what you're talking about, Uncle."

"Of course you know what I'm talking about! Harold—what did you do with it?"

"With what?"

"You know—" He caught himself, and his face was an interesting color bordering on mauve. "Why do you persist in lying to me? What are you up to?"

"I'm not up to anything," I lied.

"Harold. . ."

"If you're finished with me, I would like to get dressed. This may be the middle of summer, but it's rather chilly in here."

"Yes, get dressed. And then you're coming with me."

"Where are we going?"

"Out to look for it. I want you along."

"What are we going to look for?"

He glared at me malevolently. "I'll find it," he said. "You can't have moved it far. I *will* find it, Harold!"

Of course he didn't.

I knocked on the library door late that evening and stepped inside. Uncle Walter was sitting at his desk, holding his head as if it pained him greatly; his face was gray, and I saw that there were heavy pouches under his eyes. The time, it seemed, was right.

When he saw me, the gray pallor modulated into crimson. He certainly did change color often, like a chameleon. "You," he said. "You!"

"Are you feeling all right, Uncle? You don't look very well at all."

"If you weren't a relative of mine, if you weren't—Oh, what's the use? Harold, look, just tell me what you did with it. I just want to know that it's . . . safe. Do you understand?"

"Not really," I said. I looked at him steadily. "But I seem to have the feeling that whatever it is you were looking for today *is* safe."

He brightened. "Are you sure?"

"One can never be sure about anything, can one?"

"What does that mean?"

I sat down and said, "You know, Uncle, I've been thinking. My monthly allowance is really rather small, and I wonder if you could see your way clear to raising it."

His hands gripped the edge of his desk. "So that's it."

"What's it?"

"What you're up to, why you keep lying to me and why you moved the . . . *it*. All I've done is trade one blackmailer for another, and my own nephew at that!"

"Blackmailer?" I managed to look shocked. "What a terrible thing to say, Uncle. I'm only asking for an increase in my monthly allowance. That's not the same thing at all, is it?"

His face took on a thoughtful expression, and he calmed down. "No," he said. "No, it isn't. Of course not. Very well, then, you shall have your increase. Now, where is it?"

"Where is what?" I asked.

"Now look here—"

"I still don't know what it is you're talking about," I said. "But then, if I weren't to get my increase—or if I were to get it and it should suddenly be revoked—I suppose I could find out what is going on. I could talk to Aunt Pearl, or even to the police . . ."

My uncle sighed resignedly. "You've made your point, Harold. I suppose the only important thing is that . . . *it* is safe, and you've already told me that much, haven't you? Well, how much of an increase do you want?"

"Triple the present sum, I think."

"One hundred and fifty dollars a month?"

"Yes."

"What are you going to do with that much money? You're only eleven years old!"

"I'll think of something, Uncle. I'm very clever, you know."

He closed his eyes. "All right, consider your allowance tripled, but you're never to request a single penny more. Not a single penny, Harold."

"Oh, I won't—not a single penny," I lied, and smiled inwardly. Unlike most everyone else of my age, I knew exactly what I was going to be when I grew up. . .

Morning Song

BETTY REN WRIGHT

The mind of a very young child is a fragile thing—a thing that can easily be damaged by the insensitivity, by the wickedness, of adults. This is the theme of "Morning Song," Betty Ren Wright's startling and quite poignant short-short story. A former staff member at a large midwestern juvenile publisher, Ms. Wright has been a successful writer of adult short stories and juvenile fiction for many years. Her stories have appeared in a wide range of magazines, including Redbook, The Saturday Evening Post, Ladies' Home Journal, Cosmopolitan, *and* The Colorado Quarterly. *Among her juvenile novels are* The Secret Window *(1982) and* The Dollhouse Murders *(1983).*

THE song blew into her mind unexpectedly, like hot September wind, bringing with it the smell of the kindergarten room and the feel of her plastic nap-pack warmed by the sun. She closed her eyes and pretended she was lying on the nap-pack right now, and she sang the song in a very small voice, hoping no one else would hear:

"Good morning to you,
Good morning to you.
We're all in our places
With bright shining faces.
Good morning to you,
Good morning to you."

The first day of school, Rose thought, they had learned that song the very first day. Where were the red-checked dress and white pinafore she had worn that morning? Home in the closet, probably; her mama hadn't packed any of the clothes she liked best when she sent her to this place. Rose remembered fingering the smocking on the front of the dress when Miss Williams called her name and made her stand up. Later, Miss Williams had taken off the pinafore and hung it up so it wouldn't get dirty when she played with her new friends.

All my new friends, she thought proudly, though of course they hadn't been ready to be her friends at first. They giggled because she was the only one wearing a dress, and her heart sank since she knew there were no jeans in her closet at home, just a long row of pink and red and yellow and blue dresses. They snickered because she was afraid of the teeter-totter on the playground, afraid of the slide, even afraid to play in the sandbox because sometimes naughty children threw sand. Until that first day at school she had played only with her mama, rising and falling gently on the tiny backyard teeter-totter, swinging decorously on the red plastic swing, never far from her mama's arms.

"Hey, she's singing!" A voice broke harshly into her memories. "I wouldn't believe it if I didn't hear it."

Rose clamped her lips over the third "good morning" and finished the song inside her head. She told herself she didn't care what the people here said. The song filled her with a kind of joy, as if all the happy times at school were locked up in those few short lines. Gradually, because Miss Williams had insisted, her classmates had stopped teasing her about her dainty, always-perfect clothes. During storytime she drifted with the magic of Miss Williams' voice into a land where she had a father as well as a mama. She was a princess in that land, and she had fourteen brothers and sisters, and they played together all day every day. They wore what they wanted and they never worried about being sick and they all went to the summer camp where Miss Williams was a counselor, and they went swimming and climbed trees and never had to ask permission because they were all princes and princesses and could do as they pleased.

Once she told her mama about that magic land, but it had been a mistake. She remembered a stinging slap that spun her across the room, then the comforting mother-arms around her soothing away the shock and pain.

"It's only that I hate to see you drawing away from me," her mama had said. "My darling, perfect little girl. Don't ever stop being my sweet baby, will you?"

Rose had promised. She tried very hard to drop a curtain over the magic land and all the happiness there. It was enough to be in school—to stand in a corner of the playground watching the squealing shouting others and know she might someday be part of them and they a part of her. If she did think about the magic land, she was careful not to talk about it at home. She never mentioned Miss Williams either, after the first bad time when she said, "I really love Miss Williams," and her mama's face had turned pale and cold like the face of an angel in a painting. It was two days before her mother would talk to her again, and even though things were as they had been after that, Rose never forgot those terrible two days.

"I just don't want outsiders coming between us, dear," her mother had said, finally. "I love you so much. You and I don't need anyone else."

Rose thought about that now, until footsteps in the hallway told her the man was coming to see her again.

Good morning to you. . . .

He was a nice man, and he came to see Rose at this place quite often. She never looked at him, just hugged her doll and said nothing, but she knew he was a nice man. The only trouble was that he was full of questions.

"You look different today, Rose. How do you feel?"

Don't look up. Don't talk. Nothing to say.

"I have a feeling you're remembering today, Rose. Am I right? What are you remembering?"

She touched her doll's painted-on fingernails and waited. He never stayed very long. When he was gone she would think about Miss Williams for a while and the day she had said there was someone who could help Rose stop being afraid.

"Are you thinking about school today, Rose? Are you remembering things that happened at school?"

Good morning to you! The song shrieked through her head. She looked up for just a second, startled, wondering if the man had heard it, too.

"That's a good girl, Rose. You *are* feeling better today. Tell me what you're thinking about."

She dropped her head and began to rock her doll.

"She was singing this morning," a voice said. "I heard her."

The man sighed. He reached out and took Rose's hand. "We'll talk again tomorrow," he said. "Maybe tomorrow you'll tell me about school."

When she was alone, she laid her doll gently on the bed and covered it with a towel. The doll had yellow hair like Miss Williams', but there was no blood on her bright shining face. *We're all in our places,* the song echoed in her head, and Miss Williams' place had been at the bottom of the school stairs, lying there like a doll somebody had dropped. Rose saw herself standing beside poor Miss Williams, screaming and screaming till the janitor came and then the fourth-grade teacher who was working late. They called an ambulance and Miss Williams was carried away, and the fourth-grade teacher cried. For a while no one noticed Rose at all. When they did remember her, she had already forgotten most of what had happened. It was just there, a shadow behind a curtain, like the magic land her mama had told her not to talk about. And no one but the man here at the hospital asked her to talk about it. She had never told anyone in the whole world that just before the fall her mama had been standing at the top of the stairs with Miss Williams talking talking talking. Pushing. No one else knew. No one else saw. It was a secret forever.

"Here comes your mother, silly baby," said a voice. It was a mean, jealous voice. No one else's mother came every single day.

Rose stood up. She ran to the door and into her mother's arms, as she always did. She bent down to sniff her mama's elegant scent. Her mama held her a moment and then pushed her away.

"You're going to ruin my dress, darling," she said. "Now, tell me how you are feeling today."

Rose hunched a little so she could look straight into her mama's eyes. "We're all in our places with bright shining faces," she sang happily. She had never sung for her mama before.

The Hedge Between

CHARLOTTE ARMSTRONG

An unusual whodunit, "The Hedge Between" draws upon the tradition of the plucky girl sleuth, ever curious and eager to probe into grown-up mysteries—and often very grown-up peril. These subjects were familiar ground to Charlotte Armstrong (1905-1969), who experimented with various types of writing before she found her métier as a suspense writer. A former fashion reporter who also published poetry, she had two plays produced—without marked success—on Broadway. In 1942, she published Lay On MacDuff, *the first of a series of three mystery novels about Professor MacDougal MacDuff. It was in 1946, however, that she achieved recognition with* The Unsuspected, *a controversial suspense novel which was both praised and criticized because the author revealed the murderer's identity almost immediately. Over the course of her career, Charlotte Armstrong wrote numerous short stories, television scripts, and novels.* A Dram of Poison *won the Mystery Writers of America Edgar for Best Novel of 1956.*

THE man named Russell, who happened to be a lawyer, sat full in the light of a solitary lamp. It shone upon the brown-covered composition book in his hands. A man named John Selby, a merchant in the small city, was seated in a low chair. He hung his head; his face was hidden; the light washed only his trembling head and the nervous struggle of his fingers. The Chief of Police, Barker, was seated in half shadow. And Doctor Coles loomed against the wall beside a white door that was ajar. It was 1:00 o'clock in the morning.

Doctor, Lawyer, Merchant, Chief . . .

"Well?" the Chief challenged. "Okay, Russell. You're smart, as Selby says you are. You come running when you're called, listen to five minutes' talk about this kid, and you predict there's got to be some such notebook around. Well? Now you've found it, why don't you see what it says?"

"I'm waiting for a direction," said the lawyer mildly. "It's not for me to turn this cover. Look at the big black letters. *Meredith Lee. Personal and Private.* It's not up to me to violate her privacy. But Selby's her kin. Coles is her doctor. And you are law and order in this town."

The doctor turned his head suddenly to the crack of the door.

"Any change?" the Chief asked eagerly.

"No. She's still unconscious. Go ahead, Russell. Don't be squeamish. She's a child, after all."

"See if there's anything helpful in there," the chief of police said. "See if that notebook can explain . . ."

"Explains," the lawyer mused, "how a fifteen-year-old girl solved a seven-year-old murder mystery in four days . . ."

"She didn't solve it all the way," said the Chief impatiently.

Russell ignored him. "What do you say, Selby? She's your niece. Shall we read her private notebook?"

Selby's hands came palms up, briefly. The policeman spoke again, "Read it. I intend to, if you don't. I've got to get the straight of it. My prisoner won't talk."

[272]

The doctor said pompously, "After all, it may be best for the girl."

Russell said dryly, "I'm just as curious as the rest of you." He opened the book and began to read aloud.

Meredith Lee. New Notes and jottings.

> July 23rd.
>
> Here I am at Uncle John's. The family has dumped me for two weeks while they go to New York. I don't complain. It is impossible for me to get bored, since I can always study human nature.
>
> Uncle John looks much the same. Gray hairs show. He's thirty-seven. Why didn't he marry? Mama says he's practicing to stuff a shirt. He was very Uncle-ish and hearty when I got dumped last night, but he actually has no idea what to do with me, except tell the servants to keep me clean and fed. It's a good thing I've got resources.

Russell looked up. The Chief was chewing his lip. The doctor was frankly smiling. John Selby said, painfully, "She's right about that. Fool I was . . . I *didn't* know what to do with her." His head rolled in his hands.

"Go on," the Chief prodded.

Russell continued reading.

> Went to the neighborhood drug store, first thing. Snooped down the street. I'd forgotten it, but my goodness, it's typical. Very settled. Not swank. Not poor, either. Very middle. No logic to that phrase. A thing can't be *very* middle, but it says what I feel. On the way home, a Discovery! There's a whopping big hedge between Uncle John's house and the house next door. The neighbor woman was out messing in her flower beds. Description: petite. Dark hair, with silver. Skillfully made up. Effect quite young. (N.B. Ooooh, what a bad paragraph! Choppy!)
>
> So, filled with curiosity, I leaned over her gate and introduced myself. She's a Discovery! She's a Wicked Widow and

she's *forbidden!* I didn't know that when I talked to her.
(N.B. Practice remembering dialogue accurately.)
Wicked Widow: Mr. Selby's niece, of course. I remember you, my dear. You were here as a little girl, weren't you? Wasn't the last time about seven years ago?
Meredith Lee: Yes, it was. But I don't remember you.
W.W.: Don't you? I am Josephine Corcoran. How old were you then, Meredith?
M.L.: Only eight.
W.W.: Only eight?
We came to a stop. *I wasn't going to repeat. That's a horrible speech habit. You can waste hours trying to communicate. So I looked around and remembered something.*
M.L.: I see my tree house has disintegrated.
W.W.: Your tree house? (N.B. She repeated everything I said, and with a question mark. Careless habit? Or just pace?) Oh, yes, of course. In that big maple, wasn't it?
M.L.: Mr. Jewell—you know, Uncle John's gardener?—he built it for me. I had a cot up there and a play ice-box and a million cushions. I wouldn't come down.
W.W.: Wouldn't come down? Yes, I remember. Eight years old and your Uncle used to let you spend the night—(N.B. She looked scared. Why? If I'd fallen out and killed myself seven years ago, I wouldn't be talking to her. Elders worry retroactively.)
M.L.: Oh, Uncle John had nothing to do with it. Mama's rational. She knew it was safe. Railings, and I always pulled up my rope ladder. Nobody could get up, or get me down without a lot of trouble. I was a tomboy in those days.
W.W.: Tomboy? Yes, seven years is a long time. (N.B. No snicker. She looked serious and thoughtful, just standing with the trowel in her hand, not even smiling. That's when I got the feeling I could really communicate and it's very unusual. She must be thirty. I get that feeling with really old people or people about eighteen, sometimes. But people in between, and especially thirty, usually act like Uncle John.)

Now I forget . . . her dialogue wasn't so sparkling, I guess, but she was understanding. Did I know any young people? I said No, and she politely hoped I wouldn't be lonely. I explained that I hoped to be a Writer, so I would probably always be lonely, And she said she supposed that was true. I liked that. It's not so often somebody listens. And while she may have looked surprised at a new thought, she didn't look *amused*. My object in life is not to *amuse*, and I get tired of those smiles. So I liked her.

But then, at dinner time, just as soon as I'd said I'd met her, she got forbidden.

Uncle John: (clearing his throat) Meredith, I don't think you had better . . . (He stuck. He sticks a lot.)

M.L.: Better what?

Uncle John: Er . . . (N.B. *English* spelling. Americans say uh. I am an American.) Uh . . . Mrs. Corcoran and I are not . . . uh . . . especially friendly and I'd rather you didn't . . . (Stuck again)

M.L.: Why not? Are you feuding?

Uncle John: No, no. I merely . . .

M.L.: Merely what? I think she's very nice.

Uncle John: Uh . . . (very stuffy) . . . You are hardly in a position to know anything about it. I'm afraid she is not the kind of woman your mother would . . .

M.L.: What kind is she? (You have to really pry at Uncle John.)

Uncle John: (finally) Not socially acceptable.

M.L.: What! Oh, for heaven's sakes, Uncle John! That's the stuffiest thing I *ever* heard! Why?

Uncle John: It's not stuffy, Meredith, and it's not easy to explain why. (Looks at me as if he wonders whether I understand English.) Maybe, if you knew that there was a strange business, years ago . . . Her husband was . . . uh . . . shot in rather mysterious circum. . . .

M.L.: Shot! Do you mean killed? Do you mean murdered? Really? Oh, boy! How? When? Who did it? What happened?

Now, why did Uncle John act so surprised? Did he think I'd be scared? Don't people who are thirty ever remember how they didn't used to be *scared* by interesting things? But he *was* surprised and also very sticky and stuffy for a while. But I kept prying.

And I think it's just pitiful. I don't know why Uncle John can't see how pitiful it is. Poor Mrs. Corcoran. Her husband came home late one night and as he was standing at his own front door, somebody shot him from behind. They found the gun but nothing else. He wasn't robbed. It's just a mystery. So, just because it is a mystery and nobody knows, they've treated her as if she were a murderess! I can just see how it's been and I'm ashamed of Uncle John. He sure is practicing to stuff a shirt. He lets the hedge grow, and he goes along with the stupid town. It sounds as if nobody has accepted her socially ever since. Fine thing! She is supposed to be a wicked widow, just because her husband got murdered by person or persons unknown. Probably the town thinks such a thing couldn't happen to a respectable person. But it *could*. I'm very sorry for her.

The thing I'm saving for the bottom of this page is—it's my murder! I got that out of Uncle John. What do you know! What do you know! *I* was in my tree house that very night!

I'm just faintly remembering how I got whisked out of here so fast, that time. I never did know why. Holy cats! Eight years old. I'm asleep in a tree and a murder takes place right under me! And I never even knew it! They didn't tell me! They didn't even ask me a single question! A fine thing! A real murder in my own life, and I can't remember even one thing about it!

The lawyer paused. The doctor stirred, looked through the door. Three raised heads queried him. He said, "Nothing. It may be a good while yet before she is conscious. Don't . . . worry."

Selby turned to stare blindly at the lamp. "My sister should

never—should never have left her with me. I had no business—
no business to tell her a word about it.''

"You thought she'd be scared away from the widow?''

"I suppose so.''

The Chief said, "Now, wait a minute. The girl puts down in
there that she *couldn't remember even one thing about the kill
ing*? But that makes no sense at all.''

"That's the July twenty-third entry,'' said Russell. "Here is
July twenty-fifth. Let's see.''

I couldn't stand it—I just can't think about anything else but
my murder. I had to find out more. This afternoon I had tea
with the widow. I don't think she's wicked at all. She's very
sad, actually. She was in the garden again. I just know she was
conscious of me, on Uncle John's side of the hedge, all day
yesterday. Today, finally, she spoke to me. So I went around
and leeched onto her.

(N.B. Practice getting the "saids" in)

Nervously, she said, "I hope your Uncle won't be angry.''

I said, pretending to blurt, "Oh, Mrs. Corcoran, Uncle John
told me about the awful thing that happened to your husband.
And to think I was right up in my tree house. I can't stop
thinking about it.''

"Don't think about it,'' she said, looking pretty tense.
"It was long ago, and there is no need. I'm sorry he spoke of
it.''

"Oh, I made him,'' said I. "And now when I think that for
all I know, I might have seen and heard exactly what happened, and the only trouble is, I was so little, I can't
remember—it just about makes me wild!''

She looked at me in a funny way. I thought she was going to
blurt, "Oh, if only you could remember . . .'' But actually, she
said, "If you would like more cake please help yourself.''

"It's too bad it's a mystery,'' I said (cried). "Why couldn't
they solve it? Don't you wish they could solve it? Maybe it's
not too late.''

She looked startled. (N.B. What happens to eyes, anyhow, to make the whites show more? Observe.)

"I wish you would tell me the details," I said. "Couldn't they find out *anything?*"

"No, no. My dear, I don't think we had better talk about it at all. It's not the sort of thing a sweet child ought to be brooding about," she said.

I was desperate. "Mrs. Corcoran, the other day I thought better of you. Because you didn't laugh, for instance, when I mentioned that I used to be a tomboy, years ago. Most older people would have laughed. I'll never understand why. Obviously, I'm quite different and seven years has made a big change, and why it's so *funny* if I *know* that, I cannot see." She was leaning back and feeling surprised, I judged. "So don't disappoint me, now, and think of me as an eight-year-old child," I said, "when I may have the freshest eye and be the openmindedest person around."

She nibbled her lips. She wasn't offended. I think she's very intelligent and responding.

"I'm *going* to brood and you can't stop that," I told her. "I just wish I could help. I've been thinking that maybe if I tried I *could* remember."

"Oh, no. No, my dear. Thank you," she said. "I know you would like to help. But you were only eight at that time. I don't suppose, then or now, anyone would believe you."

"And now I'm *only* fifteen," I said crossly, "and nobody will *tell* me."

She said sweetly, "You're rather an extraordinary fifteen, my dear. If I tell you about it, Meredith, and you see how hopeless it is, do you think perhaps then you can let it rest?"

I said I thought so. (What a lie!)

"Harry, my husband, was often late getting home, so that night," she said, "I wasn't at all worried. I simply went to bed, as usual, and to sleep. Something woke me. I don't know what. My window was open. It was very warm, full summer. I lay in my bed, listening. There used to be a big elm out there beside my walk. It got the disease all the elms are getting, and it had to be cut down and taken away. But that night I could see its leaf patterns on the wall, that the moon always used to make at night, and the leaves moving gently. There was a full moon, I remember, A lovely quiet summer night." (N.B. She's pretty good with a mood.)

"I had been awakened, yet I could hear nothing, until I heard the shot. It paralyzed me. I lay back stiff and scared. Harry didn't . . . cry out. I heard nothing more for a while. Then I thought I heard shrubs rustling. When I finally pulled myself to the window, your Uncle John was there." She stopped and I had to poke her up to go on.

"Your Uncle was forcing his way through the hedge, which was low, then. And I saw Harry lying on our little stoop. I ran to my bedroom door and my maid was standing in the hall, quite frightened, and we ran down. Your Uncle told me that Harry was . . . not alive. (N.B. Pretty delicate diction.) He was calling the doctor and the police from my phone. I sat down trembling on a chair in the hall. I remember, now, that as your Uncle started out of the house again, he seemed to recall where you were and went running to his garage for a ladder to get you down."

"Darn it," I said.

She knew what I meant, because she said right away, "You couldn't remember—you must have been sleepy. Perhaps you didn't really wake up."

"I suppose so," said I disgustedly. "Go on."

"Well, the police came very quickly—Chief Barker himself. And of course, Doctor Coles. They did find the gun, caught in the hedge. They never traced it. There weren't any fingerprints anywhere. And no footprints in that dry weather. So they never found out . . ." She pulled herself together. "And that, my dear, is all." She started drinking her tea, looking very severe with herself.

I said, "There never was a trial?"

"There was never anyone to try."

"Not you, Mrs. Corcoran?"

"No one accused me," she said, smiling faintly. But her eyes were so sad.

"They did, though," I said, kind of mad. "They sentenced you, too."

"Dear girl," she said very seriously, "you mustn't make a heroine of me. Chief Barker and Doctor Coles . . . and your Uncle John, too, I'm sure . . . tried as helpfully as they could to clear it all up, but they never could find out who, or even why. You see? So . . ." She was getting flustery.

"So the wind begins to blow against you," I said, mad as the dickens. "Or how come the hedge? Why does Uncle John tell me not to come here? What makes him think you're so wicked?"

"Does he?" she said. "I am not wicked, Meredith. Neither am I a saint. I'm human."

I always thought that was a corny saying. But it's effective. It makes you feel for whoever says it, as if they had admitted something just awful that you wouldn't admit, either—unless, of course, you were *trapped*.

"Harry and I were not always harmonious," she said. "Few couples are. He drank a good bit. Many men do. I suppose the neighbors noticed. Some of them, in fact, used to feel quite sorry for me. I . . ." Her face was real bitter, but she has a quick hunching way of pulling herself together. ". . . shouldn't be saying these things to you. Why do I forget you are so young? I shouldn't. Forgive me, and don't be up-set."

"Not me," I told her. "I'm pretty detached. And don't forget my eye is fresh. I can see the trouble. There isn't anybody else to suspect. You need . . ."

"No, no. No more. I had no right to talk to you. And you'd better not come again. It is not I, my dear. I like you very much. I would love to see you often. But—"

I said, "I think Uncle John is a stuffy old stinker. To bend the way the wind blows. But *I* don't have to!"

"Yes, you do," she said, kind of fixing me with her eye. "It's not nice, Meredith, to be this side of the hedge. Now, please, never question your Uncle John's behavior." She was getting very upset. "You must . . . truly, you must . . . believe me . . . when I say   I think he meant . . . to be very kind . . . at that time." She spaced it like that, taking breaths in between.

"But that mean old hedge, for the whole town to see. It makes me mad!" I said.

She fixed me, again. She said very fast almost like whispering, "Perhaps it was I, Meredith, who let the hedge grow."

Naturally, my mouth opened, but before I got anything out she said, loudly, "It was best. There, now . . ."

(N.B. Yep. I was really disappointed. How I hate it when people say, "There, now." Implying that they know a million things more than me. And I better be comforted. I'm *not*. I'm irritated. It means they want to stop talking to me, and that's all.)

"It's all so old," she continued in that phony petting-the-kitty kind of way. "And nothing will change it. Let it rest. Thank you for coming and thank you for being openminded. But go away now, Meredith, and promise me not to think about it any more."

I fixed her with *my* eye. I said, "Thank you very much for the lovely cake."

But I'm not angry. I feel too sorry for her. Besides, she let out hints enough and I should have caught on. Well, I didn't, then. But after the session I had with Uncle John . . . *Are they ever dumb!*

We had finished dinner when I decided to see what more I could pry out of him. I said, "If Harry Corcoran was a drinking man he was probably drunk the night he got shot."

Uncle John nearly knocked his coffee over. "How do you know he was a drinking man?" roared he. "Have you been gossiping with Mrs. Jewell?" (Mrs. Jewell is the housekeeper. Vocabulary about one hundred words.)

"Oh, no, I haven't. Was he?"

"Who?"

"Harry Corcoran?"

"What?"

"Drunk?"

"So they say," bites Uncle John, cracking his teeth together, "Now, Meredith—"

"Where were you at the time of the murder?" chirped I. (N.B. Nope. Got to learn to use the "saids." They're neutraller.)

"Meredith, I wish you—"

"I know what you wish, but I wish you'd tell me. Aw, come on, Uncle John. My own murder! Maybe if I had all the facts, I'd stop thinking so much about it. Don't you see that?"

(N.B. False. The more you know about anything the more interesting it gets. But he didn't notice.)

"I told you the facts," he said (muttered?), "and I wish I had kept my big mouth shut. Your mother will skin me alive. How the devil did I get into this?"

(N.B. I thought this was an improvement. He's usually so darned stuffy when he talks to me.)

"You didn't tell me any details. Please, Uncle John . . ." I really nagged him. I don't think he's had much practice defending himself, because finally, stuffy as anything, he talked.

"Very well. I'll tell you the details as far as I know them. Then I shall expect to hear no more about it."

"I know," said I. True. I knew what he expected. I didn't really promise anything. But he's not very analytical. "Okay. Pretend you're on the witness stand. Where were you at the time?"

"I was, as it happened . . . (N.B. Stuffy! Phrase adds nothing. Of course it happened.) . . . in the library that night working late on some accounts. It was nearly 1:00 in the morning, I believe . . . (N.B. Of course he believes, or he wouldn't say so) . . . when I heard Harry Corcoran whistling as he walked by in the street."

"What tune?"

"What?" (I started to repeat but he didn't need it. Lots of people make you repeat a question they heard quite well just so they can take a minute to figure out the answer.) "Oh, that Danny Boy song. Favorite of his. That's how I knew who it was. He was coming along from the end of town, past this house—"

"Was that usual?"

"It was neither usual nor unusual," said Uncle John crossly, "It's merely a detail."

"Okay. Go on."

"The next thing I noticed was the shot."

"You were paralyzed?"

"What?" He just about glared at me. "Yes, momentarily. Then I ran out my side door and pushed through the hedge and found him on his own doorstep . . . uh . . ."

"Not living," I said delicately.

He gave me another nasty look. "Now, that's all there was to it."

"That's not all! What did you do then? Didn't you even look for the murderer?"

"I saw nobody around. I realized there might be somebody concealed, of course. So I picked up his key from where it had fallen on the stoop—"

"The Corcorans' door was locked?"

"It was locked and I unlocked it and went inside to the phone. As I was phoning, Mrs. Corcoran and her maid came downstairs. I called Chief Barker and Doctor Coles."

"Yes, I know. And then you ran to get the ladder and pulled me down out of my tree. Okay. But you're leaving things out, Uncle John. You are deliberately being barren. You don't give any atmosphere at all. What was Mrs. Corcoran's emotional state?"

"I haven't the slightest idea," said Uncle John with his nose in a sniffing position, "and if I had, it would not be a fact."

I pounced. "You think she did it?"

He pulled his chin practically to the back of his neck. "I wish you would not say that. I have little right to speculate and none to make a judgment. There was no evidence."

"But you did pass judgment. You told me she was a certain kind of—"

"Meredith, I know only one fact. Your mother would not like this at all. In any case, I will not discuss Mrs. Corcoran's character with you. I must insist you take my word for it. There is no way. . . ." He kind of held his forehead.

"Uncle John, who let the hedge grow?"

"What? The hedge belongs to me."

"That ain't the way I heered it," said stupid I.

So he pounced. "Where have you been hearing things? Who told you Harry Corcoran was a drinking man? Where have you been, Meredith?"

So I confessed. No use writing down the blasting I got. It was the usual. Bunch of stuff about my elders wanting no harm to come to me, things not understood in my philosophy, mysterious evils that I wot not of, and all that sort of stuff. Why doesn't he tell me plain out that it's none of my business?

Well, I don't think it's evil. I think it's foolishness. I think that Uncle John's too sticky and stuffy to tell me . . . (Probably thinks I never heard of s-blank-x) . . . is that he used to be romantic about the pretty lady next door. Probably Uncle John saw a lot of Harry's drunken comings-home and heard plenty of the disharmonizing. Probably he is one neighbor who felt sorry for her. Wonder if they were in love and said so. I doubt it. Probably they just cast glances at each other over the hedge and said nothing. That would be just like Uncle John.

Anyhow, when somebody shoots Harry Corcoran in the back, the widow gets it into her head that Uncle John did it. After all, she heard things—rustling bushes—looked out, and there he was. But gosh, even if she felt romantic about him too, she'd draw the line at murder! But of course, Uncle John

didn't do it. He thinks *she* did. He knows she was unhappy
with Harry. But he draws the line at murder, too. So, these
dopes, what do they do? They have no "right" to pass "judgment" or "accuse" anybody. They pull themselves in, with
the hedge between. All those years, with their very own suspi-
cions proving that neither one could have done it . . . Probably if they'd had sense enough to speak out and have a big
argument, they could have got married and been happy long
ago.

Oh, how ridiculous! How pitiful! And oh, that I was born to
put it right! (N.B. Who said that?)

The lawyer put the book down. John Selby groaned. "I had no
idea . . . no idea what she had in her head. I knew she was
bright . . ."

"Bright, yes," said Doctor Coles, "but that kid's so insuffer-
ably condescending!"

"You wouldn't like it even if she guessed right," said Russell
thoughtfully. "The girl's got a hard way to go. She'll be lonely."

"Thought she was smart, all right," growled Barker. "Wasn't
as smart as she thought she was. She was wrong, I take it?"

Selby didn't answer. His gaze was fixed on the lawyer's face.

"You shouldn't blame her for being wrong," Russell murmured. "She's not yet equipped to understand a lot of things.
But she is compelled to try. There's her intelligent curiosity
fighting a way past some clichés, but the phrase 'feel romantic'
is flat, for her, and without shading."

"I still can't see what happened," Barker broke in to complain. "Never mind the shading. Go ahead—if there's more of
it."

"Yes, there's more. We come to July twenty-sixth—yesterday." Russell began to read once more.

I've figured. I know exactly how to do it. I'll say *I can remember!* I'll tell them that when I was up in my tree that night
the shot or something woke me, and I saw a stranger running
away . . .

"So she made it up! Told a story!" Chief Barker slapped his thigh. "But . . . now wait a minute . . . you believed her, Selby?"

"I believed her," her uncle sighed.

"Go on. Go on," the doctor said.

I know how to make them believe me, too. This will be neat! I'll tell Uncle John first, and I'll mix into the story I tell him all the little bits I got from her that he doesn't know I've been told. So, since they'll be true, he'll be fooled, and think I really remember. Then I'll go to her, but in the story I tell her, all I have to do is mix in the bits I got from Uncle John that she doesn't know I've been told. It'll work! Ha, they'll never catch on to the trick of it. They'll believe me! Then they can get together, if they still want to. I'm not worried about telling a kind of lie about it. If anybody official starts asking questions I can always shudder, and be too young and tender, and clam up.

Get it exactly right. Make lists.

Russell looked up. "Meredith's good at math, I suppose?"

"A plus," her uncle groaned. "She scares me."

Russell nodded and began to read again.

List No. 1. For Uncle John. Things she told me.
1. Warm night. Full moon.
2. The elm tree that used to be there.
3. The gun was found in the hedge.
4. Harry didn't yell.

Now, put all these points in. Future dialogue.

By Meredith Lee.

M.L.: Oh, Uncle John, I do remember now!

Uncle John: What?

(Whoops! Since this is in the future, I better not write his dialogue. It might confuse me.)

M.L.: I was up in my room, thinking, and I began to hum that tune. That Danny Boy. It made the whole thing come back

to me like a dream. Now I remember waking up on my cot and
hearing that whistling. I peeked out between my railings. The
moon was very bright that night. It was warm, too, real sum-
mer. I could see the elm tree by the Corcoran's walk. (Pause.
Bewildered.) Which elm tree, Uncle John? There's none there
now. *Was* there an elm tree, seven years ago?
(Ha, ha, that'll *do* it!)
I saw a man come up their walk. I must have heard the shot.
I thought somebody had a firecracker left over from Fourth of
July. I saw the man fall down but he didn't make any noise, so
I didn't think he was hurt. I thought he fell asleep.
(What a touch! Whee!)
Then I saw there was another man, down there, and he
threw something into the hedge. The hedge crackled where it
landed. Then this man jumped through their gate and ran, and
then you came out of this house . . .
(By this time the stuffing should be coming out of Uncle
John.)
I'll say I don't know who the stranger was. "But it wasn't
you, Uncle John," I'll say, "and the widow Corcoran's been
thinking so for seven years and I'm going to tell her . . ."
Then I'll run out of the house as fast as I can.
He'll follow—he'll absolutely have to!

Russell looked up. "Was it anything like that?"
"It was almost exactly like that," said John Selby, lifting his
tired, anxious face. "And I did follow. She was right about that.
I absolutely had to."
"Smart," said Chief Barker, smacking his lips, "the way she
worked that out."
"Too smart," the doctor said, and then, "Nurse? Yes?" He
went quickly through the door.
"My sister will skin me alive," said John Selby, rousing him-
self. "Kid's had me jumping through hoops. Who am I to deal
with the likes of her? Looks at me with those big brown eyes.
Can't tell whether you're talking to a baby or a woman. Every-

thing I did was a mistake. I never had the least idea what she was thinking. You're smart about people, Russell—that's why I need you. I feel as if I'd been through a wind-tunnel. Help me with Meredith. I feel terrible about the whole thing, and if she's seriously hurt and I'm responsible . . .''

"You say you don't understand young people," began Russell, "but even if you did, this young person . . ."

"You take it too hard, John," said Chief Barker impatiently. "Doc doesn't think she's hurt too seriously. And she got herself into it, after all. Listen, go on. What did she say to the widow? That's what I need to know. Is it in there?"

"It must be," said Russell. "She made another list."

List No. 2. For the widow. Things Uncle John told me.
  1. Harry was whistling Danny Boy.
  2. He came in the direction that passed this house.
  3. He was drunk.
  4. He dropped his key.
Not so good. Yes it is, too. What woke her? She doesn't know, but I do! Future dialogue:

M.L.: Oh, Mrs. Corcoran, I think I'm beginning to remember! I really think so! Listen, I think I heard a man whistling. And it was that song about Danny Boy. And he was walking from the east, past our house. Would it have been your husband?

(Ha! She's going to *have* to say Yes!)

And he . . . it seems to me that he didn't walk right. He wobbled. He wobbled up your walk and he dropped something. Maybe a key. It must have been a key because I saw him bending over to hunt for it but . . .

(Artistic pause here? I think so.)

Oh, now I remember! He straightened up. He couldn't have found it because he called out something. It was a name! It must have been . . . Oh, Mrs. Corcoran, could it have been your name, being called in the night, that woke you up?

(Betcha! Betcha!)

Well, the rest of hers goes on the same. Stranger, throws gun, runs away, just as Uncle John comes out. "So it wasn't you," I'll say, "and I can prove it! But poor Uncle John has been afraid it was."

Then what? I guess maybe I'd better start to bawl.

Yep. I think that will do it. I think that's pretty good. They're bound to believe me. Of course, the two stories are not identical, but they can't be. *They'll* never notice the trick of it. They'll just have to be convinced that it wasn't either one of them who shot Harry Corcoran. I can't wait to see what will happen. What will they *do*? What will they *say*? Oh-ho-ho, is this ever research! I better cry soft enough so I can hear and memorize.

When shall I try it? I can't wait! Now is a good time. Uncle John is in the library and she's home. I can see a light upstairs in her house. Here goes, then.

(N.B. Would I rather be an actress? Consider this. M.L.)

The lawyer closed the book. "That's all." He put his hand to his eyes but his mouth was curving tenderly.

"Some scheme," said Barker in awe. "Went to a lot of trouble to work up all that plot . . ."

"She had a powerful motive," Russell murmured.

"My romance," said Selby bitterly.

"Oh, no. Research for her," the lawyer grinned.

"Whatever the motive, this remarkable kid went and faked those stories and she had it wrong," growled Barker. "But she must have got something right. Do you realize that?" He leaned into the light. "Selby, as far as you were concerned, you believed that rigmarole of hers. You thought she *did* remember the night of the killing and she *had* seen a stranger?"

"I did," John Selby said, sounding calmer. "I was considerably shaken. I had always suspected Josephine Corcoran, for reasons of my own."

"Lots of us suspected," the Chief said dryly, "for various reasons. But never could figure how she managed, with you rushing out to the scene so fast and the maid in the upstairs hall."

"What were your reasons, John?" Russell asked.

"In particular, there was a certain oblique conversation that took place in the course of a flirtation that appalls me, now. It seemed to me, one evening, that she was thinking that the death of her husband might be desirable—and might be arranged. I can't quote her exactly, you understand, but the hint was there. She thought him stupid and cruel and intolerable, and the hint was that if he were dead and gone she'd be *clean*. The shallow, callous, self-righteous . . . the *idea*! As if her life should rightfully be cleared of him with no more compunction than if he'd been . . . well, a wart on her hand." He held his head again. "Now, how is a man going to explain to his fifteen-year-old niece just what makes him think a woman is wicked? The feeling you get, that emanates from the brain and body?" He groaned. "That little talk pulled me out of my folly, believe me. That's when I shied off and began to let the hedge grow. When you realize that not long after that he *did* die, you'll see how I've lived with the memory of that conversation for seven years. Wondering. Was I right about what she had in mind and did I perhaps not recoil enough? Had I not sufficiently discouraged the . . . the idea? There was no evidence. There was nothing. But I've had a burden close to guilt and I've stayed on my side of the hedge, believe me, and begun to study to stuff a shirt." He groaned again and shifted in the chair. "When I thought the child had really seen a stranger with that gun, I was stunned. As soon as I realized where Meredith had gone . . . ."

"You followed. You saw them through the widow's front door?" The Chief was reassembling this testimony.

"Yes. I could see them. At the top of the stairs. Mrs. Corcoran standing by the newel post and Meredith talking earnestly to her."

"You couldn't hear?"

"No, unfortunately. But if Meredith had rehearsed it, if she stuck to her script, then we must have it here."

"If it's there, I don't get it." Chief Barker passed his hand over his face. "Now, suddenly, you say—in the middle of the girl's story—the widow yelled something that you *could* hear?"

"She yelled, '*I told you to keep out of this, you nosy brat!*' And then she pushed Meredith violently enough to send her rolling down the stairs." Selby began to breathe heavily.

"And you got through the door . . ."

"By the time I got through the door, she was on the girl like a wildcat. She was frantic. She *meant* to hurt her." John Selby glared.

"So you plucked the widow off her prey and called us for help? Did Mrs. Corcoran try to explain at all?" Russell inquired.

"She put out hysterical cries. 'Poor dear! Poor darling!' But she meant to hurt Meredith. I heard. I saw. I know. And she knows that I know."

"Yes, the widow gave herself away," said Russell. "She was wicked, all right."

"So we've got her," the Chief growled, "for the assault on Meredith. Also, we know darned well she shot her husband seven years ago. But she won't talk. What I need," the Chief was anxious, "is to figure out what it was that set her off. What did the kid say that made her nerve crack? I can't see it. I just don't get it."

The doctor had been standing quietly in the door. Now he said, "Maybe Meredith can tell us. She's all right. Almost as good as new, I'd say."

John Selby was on his feet. So was Chief Barker. "Selby, you go first," the doctor advised. "No questions for the first minute or two."

The Chief turned and sighed. "Beats me."

Russell said, "One thing, Harry Corcoran never called out his wife's name in the night. Selby, who heard a whistle, would have heard such a cry."

"Do I see what you're getting at?" said Barker shrewdly. 'It shows the kid didn't get *that far* in the story or the widow would have known she was story-telling."

"She certainly didn't get as far as any guilty stranger, or the widow would have been delighted. Let's see."

"There was something. . . ."

"Was it the tune? No, that's been known. Selby told that long ago. Was it Harry's drunkenness? No, because medical evidence exists. Couldn't be that."

"For the Lord's sakes, let's *ask* her," the Chief said.

They went through the door. The nurse had effaced herself watchfully. Four men stood around the bed. Doctor, Lawyer, Merchant, Chief . . .

Young Meredith Lee looked very small, lying against the pillow with her brown hair pressed back by the bandages, her freckles sharpened by the pallor of her face, her big brown eyes round and shocked.

"How do you feel, honey?" rumbled the Chief.

"She pushed me down." Meredith's voice was a childish whimper.

Her Uncle John patted the bed and said compulsively, "There, Meredith. There now . . ."

"Don't say that," the Chief put in with a chuckle. "It just annoys her."

The girl saw her notebook in Russell's hands. She winced and for a flash her eyes narrowed and something behind the child face was busy reassessing the situation.

"Miss Lee," said the lawyer pleasantly, "My name is Russell. I'm a friend of your Uncle John's. I'm the one who ferreted out your notes. I hope you'll forgive us for reading them. Thanks to you, now we know how wicked the widow was seven years ago."

"I only pretended," said Meredith in a thin treble. "I was only eight. I don't really remember anything at all." She shrank in the bed, very young and tender.

Her uncle said, "We know how you pretended. I . . . I had no idea you were so smart."

"That was some stunt," the doctor said.

"Very clever," the lawyer said, "the two stories as you worked them out."

"You're quite a story-teller, honey," chimed in Chief Barker.

On the little girl's face something struggled and lost. Meredith gave them one wild indignant look of pure outraged intelligence before her face crumpled completely. "I am not either!" she bawled. "I'm not any good! I got it all wrong! Didn't get the plot right. Didn't get the characters right. I guess I don't know *any-thing!* I guess I might as well give up . . ." She flung herself over and sobbed bitterly.

Chief Barker said, "She's okay, isn't she? She's not in pain?"

The nurse rustled, muttering "shock." The doctor said stiffly, "Come now, Meredith. This isn't a bit good for you."

But Selby said, to the rest of them, "See? That's the way it goes. She's eight and she's eighty. She can cook up a complex stunt like that and then bawl like a baby. I give up! I don't know what you should do with her. I've wired my sister. She'll skin us both, no doubt. Meredith, please. . . ."

Meredith continued to howl.

The lawyer said sharply, "That's right, Meredith. You may as well give up trying to be a writer if you are going to cry over your first mistakes instead of trying to learn from them. Will you be grown-up for a minute and listen? We seriously want your help to convict a murderess."

"You do not," wailed Meredith. "I'm too stupid!"

"Don't be a hypocrite," snapped the lawyer. "You are not stupid. As a matter of fact, you are extremely stuffy—as this book proves to us."

Meredith choked on a sob. Then slowly she opened one brown eye.

"The average young person," hammered the lawyer, "has lit-tle or no respect for an older's experience and nothing can make him see its value until he gets some himself. But even a *beginning* writer should have a less conventional point of view."

"Now wait a minute," bristled John Selby. "Don't scold her. She's had an awful time. Listen, she meant well . . . ."

Meredith sat up and mopped her cheek with the sheet. The brown eyes withered him. "Pul-lease, Uncle John," said Meredith Lee.

So John Selby raised his head and settled his shoulders. "Okay." He forced a grin. "Maybe I'm not too old to learn. You want me to lay it on the line? All right, you *didn't* mean well. You were perfectly vain and selfish. You were going to fix up my life and Josephine Corcoran's life as a little exercise for your superior wisdom." His stern voice faltered. "Is that better?"

Meredith said, tartly, "At least, it's rational." She looked around and her voice was not a baby's. "You are all positive the widow is a murderess," she said flatly.

Chief Barker said, "Well, honey, we always did kind of think so."

"Don't talk down to her," snapped John Selby, "or she'll talk down to you. I . . . I get that much."

"Who are you, anyhow?" asked Meredith of the Chief.

He told her. "And I am here to get to the bottom of a crime. Now, young lady," the Chief was no longer speaking with any jovial look at all, "You jumped to a wrong conclusion, you know. She *was* guilty."

"I don't see *why* you've always thought so," said Meredith rebelliously.

"I guess you don't," said Barker. "Because it's a matter of experience. Of a lot of things. In the first place, I know what my routine investigation can or cannot turn up. When it turns up *no* sign of any stranger whatsoever, I tend to believe that there wasn't one."

The Chief's jaw was thrust forward. The little girl did not wince. She listened gravely.

"In the second place, as you noticed yourself, there's nobody else around here to suspect. In the third place, nine times out of ten, only a wife is close enough to a man to have a strong enough motive."

"Nine times out of ten," said Meredith scornfully.

"That's experience," said Barker, "and you scoff at the nine times because you think we forget that there can be a tenth time. You are wrong, young lady. Now, somebody shot Harry Corcoran . . ."

"Why don't you suspect Uncle John?" flashed Meredith.

"No motive," snapped Barker.

"Meredith," began her Uncle, "I'm afraid you . . ."

"Speak up," said Russell.

"Yes. Right." Selby straightened again. "Well, then, listen. I'd no more murder a man as a favor to a neighbor than I'd jump over the moon. Your whole idea—that Josephine Corcoran would think I had—is ridiculous. Whatever she is, she's too mature for that. Furthermore, I never did want to marry her. And your mother may skin me for this but so help me you'd better know, men sometimes don't and women know it." Meredith blinked. "Also, even if I had," roared her Uncle John, "Barker knows it might occur to me that there is such a thing as divorce. Just as good a way to get rid of a husband, and a lot safer than murder."

Meredith's tongue came out and licked her lip.

"Now, as to her motive, she hated Harry Corcoran bitterly . . . bitterly. She's . . . well, she's wicked. To know that is . . . is a matter of experience. You spot it. Some cold and selfish, yet hot and reckless thing. That's the best I can do."

"It's not bad," said Meredith humbly, "I mean, thank you, Uncle John. Where is she now?"

"In the hospital," said Chief Barker, "with my men keeping their eye on her."

"Was she hurt?"

The doctor cleared his throat. "She's being hysterical. That is, you see, she was startled into making a terrible mistake when she pushed you, my dear. Now, all she can think to do is fake a physical or psychic collapse. But it's strictly a phony. I can't tell you exactly how I know that . . ."

"I suppose it's experience," said Meredith solemnly. She seemed to retreat deeper into the pillow. "I was all wrong about her. The town was *right!*" She looked as if she might cry, having been forced to this concession.

Russell said briskly, "That's not enough. No good simply saying you were wrong. You need to understand what happened to you, just how you were led."

"Led?" said Meredith distastefully.

"The widow was guilty," Russell said. "Begin with that. Now look back at the time you first hung over her gate. You couldn't know she was guilty or even suspect it, because you hadn't so much as heard about the murder yet. How could you guess the fright she got, remembering that little girl in the tree? You thought it was retroactive worry—that you might have fallen. Because that is a kind of fear in your experience. Do you see, now, when you turned up, so full of vigor and intelligence, that she never felt less like smiling in her life. *Of course* she took you seriously. And you were charmed."

"Naturally," said Meredith bravely.

"I can see, and now you should be able to see, how she tried to use your impulsive sympathy. Maybe she hoped that when you tried—as you were bound to try—to remember the night, long ago, that your imagination would be biased in her favor."

"I guess it was," said Meredith bleakly.

"Probably, she tried to put suspicion of your Uncle John into your head, not from innocence, but to supply a missing suspect to the keen and much too brainy curiosity that had her terrified. Now, don't be downcast," the lawyer added, his warm smile breaking. "I'd have been fooled, too. After all, this is hindsight."

"Probably you wouldn't have been fooled," said Meredith stolidly. "Experience, huh?"

"I've met a few murderers before," said Russell gently.

"Well, I've met a murderess now," said Meredith gravely. "Boy, was I ever dumb!" She sighed.

The Chief said, "All clear? Okay. Now, what do you say we find out where you were smart? What did it? Can't we get to that?"

"Smart?" said Meredith.

"This is our question to you, young lady. What cracked Mrs. Corcoran's nerve? Where were you in that story when she flew at you and pushed you down the stairs?"

The girl was motionless.

"You see, dear," began the doctor.

"She sees," said her Uncle John ferociously.

Meredith gave him a grateful lick of the eye. "Well, I was just past the key . . ." she said. She frowned. "And then she yelled and pushed me." The brown eyes turned, bewildered.

"What were the exact words?" said Barker briskly, "Russell, read that part again."

But Russell repeated, lingeringly, "Just past the key . . .?"

"I don't get it," Barker said. "Do you?"

"I just thought she'd be glad," said Meredith in a small groan. "But she pushed me and hurt me. I got it *wrong.*" She seemed to cower. She was watching Russell.

"You got it right," said he. "Listen. And follow me. Harry Corcoran was shot in the back."

"That's right," the Chief said.

"The key was on the doorstep." The lawyer was talking to the girl.

"I picked it up," said Selby.

"All this time we've been assuming that he dropped the key *because he was shot.* But that isn't what you said, Meredith. *You* said that he dropped the key *because he was drunk.* Now, all this time we have assumed that he was shot from behind, from somewhere near the hedge. But if you got it right, when he bent over to pick up the key . . . and was shot in the back . . ." Russell waited. He didn't have to wait long.

"*She* shot him from above," said Meredith, quick as a rabbit. "*She* was upstairs."

"From *above*," said Barker, sagging. "And the widow's been waiting for seven years for some bright brain around here to think of that. Yep. Shot from a screenless window. Threw the gun out, closed the window, opened her door, faced her maid. Pretty cool. Pretty lucky. Pretty smart. And there is nothing you could call evidence, even yet." But the Chief was not discouraged or dismayed. He patted the bed covers. "Don't you worry, honey. You got her, all right. And I've made out with less. By golly, I got her method, now, and that's going to be leverage. And, by golly, one thing she's going to have to tell me, and that is *why* she pushed you down the stairs."

"She needn't have," said Meredith, in the same thin, woeful voice. "*I* didn't know . . . *I* didn't understand." Then her face changed and something was clicking in her little head. "But she still *thinks* I saw him drop the key. Couldn't I go where she is? Couldn't I . . . break her down? I could *act*." The voice trailed off. They weren't going to let her go, the four grown men.

"*I'm* going," said Selby grimly. "I'll break her down."

"Stay in bed," said the doctor, at the same time. "Nurse will be here. I may be needed with the widow."

"And I," said Russell. But still he didn't move. "Miss Lee," he said to the little girl, "may I make a prophecy? You'll go on studying the whole world, you'll get experience, and acquire insight, and you will not give up until you become a writer." He saw the brown eyes clear; the misting threat dried away. He laid the notebook on the covers. "You won't need to be there," he said gently, "because you can imagine." He held out a pencil. "Maybe you'd like to be working on an ending?" She was biting her left thumb but her right hand twitched as she took the pencil.

"Meredith," said her Uncle John, "here's one thing you can put in. You sure took the stuffing out of me. And I don't care what your mother's going to say . . .''

Meredith said, as if she were in a trance, "When is Mama coming?"

"In the morning. I wish I hadn't wired—I wish I hadn't alarmed her . . . We're going to be in for it."

"Oh, I don't know, Uncle John," said Meredith. The face was elfin now, for a mocking second of time. Then it was sober. She put the pencil into her mouth and stared at the wall. The nurse moved closer. The four men cleared their throats. Nothing happened. Meredith was gone, imagining. Soon the four grown men tiptoed away.

Meredith Lee. New notes and Jottings. July 27th.

Early to bed. Supposed to be worn out. False, but convenient for all of us.

Everybody helped manage Mama. Doctor Coles put a small pink bandage on me. Chief Barker and Mr. Russell met her train and said gloating things about the widow confessing.

But, of course, Mama had to blast us some. She was just starting to rend Uncle John when I said, "Don't be so cross with him, Mama. He is the Hero. Saved my life." That took her aback. She was about to start on me, but Uncle John jumped in. "Meredith's the Heroine, sis. She broke the case."

Well, Mama got distracted. She forgot to be mad at us any more. "What's going on with you two?" she wanted to know. Well, I guess she could see that the stuffing was out of both of us.

(N.B. Men are interesting. M.L.)

Uncle Max

PAT McMAHON

"Uncle Max" is a fitting final entry for this anthology, for reasons which will become clear when you read its concluding paragraph. The world in which this story's young protagonist lives is not, as you'll also discover, the best of all possible worlds; in fact, as far as your editors are concerned, it may well be one of the worst . . . "Pat McMahon" is a pseudonym of Edward D. Hoch, whose other fine story, "Day for a Picnic," you have already read.

OFTEN, in the summer, I went to visit Uncle Max in the big house on the hill. Though the visits were frequent, I never tired of them, and for days in advance I would imagine myself riding my bike down the great winding driveway that led from the house to the highway below. It was a place for fun, a place for growing up, and I enjoyed every minute of it.

I enjoyed Uncle Max too, despite the fact that he was often too busy to spend as much time with me as he would have liked. Uncle Max was stout and balding, and looked like a banker. He wore a Phi Beta Kappa key on his gold watch chain and smoked cigars that were longer than my arm—or seemed to be, at least. In the early days he had a habit of kissing me, but finally my twisting and squirming must have convinced him that I was too old a boy for such things.

I was eleven during that final summer of my visits, old enough to follow Uncle Max around the great house while he tended to his far-flung business matters. In one room on the third floor were the teletype machines which fed the latest world news and market reports on endless sheets of yellow paper, keeping Uncle Max in touch with his world. Then there were the visitors too, the quiet men in their long black chauffeur-driven cars. They came, spoke with Uncle Max behind the closed doors of the second-floor study, and then departed with pursed lips and thoughtful eyes.

All this I saw, and much more I felt, playing around the big house. There was the fun of the unknown every day, the waiting to see the long cars draw up—sometimes coming dangerously close to me as I coasted down the curving driveway on my bike. There was the bustle of activity with each occasional ringing of the alarm bell on the teletype, the thrill of anticipation when the frequent long distance calls came in from far-off places.

But most of all, there were the few precious moments with Uncle Max himself. "What are you doing today, boy?" he'd ask over breakfast, sometimes winking at his big-boned wife who sat opposite him across the marble-topped patio table. "Playing cops and robbers?"

The maid would appear with orange juice and bacon and eggs and toast, and the big glass of milk for me because I was too young for coffee. "Not today," I'd stammer, because the truth was there was no fun playing cops and robbers by yourself. "Maybe I'll just ride my bike."

"Be careful of the cars," Aunt Rita cautioned, as she always did. "And don't go beyond the wall."

It was the last regulation that effectively cut me off from whatever other children might have been found in the sparsely settled suburban community. I often wondered about it, but not too hard, because as I've said the house and grounds and visitors were enough to fully fascinate any eleven-year-old boy. I had all the rest of the year to be with kids my own age, while these summer visits were my only entry into the exciting adult world about which I knew so little.

Sometimes when Uncle Max was busy, Aunt Rita would stay with me, giving a poor imitation of playing ball on the back lawn. "I guess I'll never make a pitcher," she said with a sigh one day, after a particularly lengthy session. "I'm too old for this sort of thing, Jimmy."

"Will Uncle Max be busy all day?"

She nodded, looking up at the big house. "Some important men have come all the way from Chicago to see him."

"How come Uncle Max never goes to the office like my dad?"

"He has his office here at home, Jimmy. Your uncle is important enough so that people come to see him." She shielded her eyes from the sun, staring intently at a taxi bringing the latest arrival. "Come on—feel like some lemonade?"

"Sure!"

Around the back of the house, beyond the patio, was an oval swimming pool that seemed like a small lake to me. I couldn't really swim very good, but I enjoyed splashing around in the shallow end, watching the sleek tanned women and the flabby men with their hairy chests. There was always a crowd at the pool on those hot summer days when people drove out from the city to see Uncle Max. I often wondered if they really came to see him or only to cool off in the big oval pool.

This day Uncle Max himself poured my lemonade for me. He took little interest in the swimming and I was surprised to see him at the pool at all. He watched a blonde girl make a perfect dive without a thought for her uncovered hair, and then turned to me. "Boy, I'm leaving you in charge. Watch over my pool and keep the lemonade pitcher filled."

"Where you going, Uncle Max?"

"To work on my roses. These people are too young for me. I don't know them."

He often puttered around among the myriad rose bushes that surrounded the big house. It was the only real work I ever saw him do, the only task he did not trust to the half-dozen servants who seemed constantly underfoot.

It was hot in the sun, and after he'd gone I busied myself with the lemonade, drinking two tall glasses before Aunt Rita reappeared with the latest arrivals. The slim blonde girl who'd been swimming came up to me and asked, "Are those Daiquiris, I hope?"

"Just lemonade," I told her.

"Oh. And who are you?"

"Jimmy. My mother is Aunt Rita's sister."

"Oh. They leave you up here alone?"

"I like it here," I answered defensively. "I like Uncle Max."

"Everybody likes Max." She gave a short laugh and padded away across the damp concrete.

Two men who had just arrived went to speak with Uncle Max in the rose garden, and I could see them talking excitedly. Finally Uncle Max brought them over for drinks, trying to calm them with his beautifully placid voice. "Now, now, we don't worry about those things until they happen," he said. "Have a drink and you'll feel better, both of you. Want a swim?"

But both men shook their heads. When they were settled

down with their drinks, I deserted my lemonade post and went in search of Uncle Max among the roses. "Uncle Max?"

"Yes, boy?"

"Who are all these people, anyway? Why do they come here all the time?"

"They're business associates, free-loaders, friends, just people, boy."

"Who's that lady with the blonde hair? The one in swimming."

"She's something of an actress, I suppose."

"What kind of business are you in, Uncle Max?"

"The business of making people happy, boy. The most important business in the world. Come—let's walk a bit and I'll tell you about it. You see, boy, the world today is a terrible place. There are wars and rumors of war, riots in the street and corruption in high places. The average man needs to get away from these things, to escape into a sort of dream world. I help him escape, boy. I help make him happy, just for a little bit. And don't ever let anybody tell you that's bad, to make people happy."

"Could you make me happy, Uncle Max?"

"Don't I, boy? Don't I make you happy every day you're here?"

"Is that how you make other people happy—by inviting them up here to your house and your swimming pool?"

"Not all of them, boy. I couldn't invite all of them up here."

Someone called his name, and Uncle Max turned. It was Aunt Rita, running to catch up with us. "Max, that lawyer from Chicago is on the phone. He says it's about Duncan!"

Uncle Max let out a long sigh. "I just talked to two men about Duncan. Why is everybody so excited, anyway?"

"Talk to him, Max. I'm worried."

"For you, Rita, I'll talk to him."

We headed back toward the house, with Aunt Rita very much in the lead. I'd never seen her quite so upset, and it was reflected in the rapid pace she set across the close-cropped lawn. They hardly noticed me when I tagged along up to Uncle Max's private office and stood by his desk while he picked up the phone.

"Max here. . . . Yes, I know all that. . . . Yes, yes. . . . Well, can't you stop him? . . . All right, keep me informed."

He hung up and sat somberly at the desk for a moment. Aunt Rita came up and put her long arms about his shoulders. "How bad is it, Max?"

"Duncan's going before the grand jury this afternoon."

"Do you think he'll . . .?"

"Who knows what he'll do?" Uncle Max stood up and began pacing. For the first time he seemed really disturbed. "Clear those people out of the pool," he said finally. "Send them all home."

Aunt Rita went off on her mission, seemingly pleased to have a task assigned her. I stayed, hovering at my uncle's side, and presently he noticed me. "Well, boy, you still here?"

"Yes, Uncle Max."

"You should be home with your mother. This is no place for a growing boy." He said the words firmly, but not unkindly.

"I want to stay with you, Uncle Max."

He smiled down at me. "You're a good boy. Stay, but keep out of the way."

He pushed a buzzer on his desk, and after a moment the butler arrived. "Yes, sir?"

"Go up to the newsroom and keep an eye on the AP and UPI tickers. It'll be a story out of either Chicago or Washington."

"Yes sir."

When we were alone again, Uncle Max unlocked one of his filing cabinets and started going through it. I stood very still watching him, and I knew that he'd forgotten my presence once again. I went to the front window and looked out at the winding black driveway, but suddenly it was no longer a place for fun and frolic. As the last of the visitors' cars curved down the ribbon of asphalt to the highway, a blanket of gloom seemed to slowly settle in place.

For the next three hours, hardly anyone spoke. Even the servants seemed caught up in the tension of waiting for something unknown to happen. Twice Uncle Max made long distance calls to New York, but the conversations seemed only to deepen the somber lines on his brow. He looked through the files on his desk again, and finally went upstairs to the room with the tele-type machines.

The butler, still at his post, turned and said, "I think something's coming through now, sir. From Chicago."

Uncle Max grasped the sheet of yellow paper and read the words as fast as they were printed. After a moment he tore the sheet free and crumpled it into a ball. "Bad news, sir?" the butler asked.

"The worst." And then, to Aunt Rita as she appeared in the doorway behind me, "Duncan's talked. He's told them everything."

"What will you do, Max?"

Her question was interrupted by the jangle of the house phone. The butler answered it and listened intently. "There's a car at the gate, sir. Four men in it. They insist on seeing you."

"Already?" Uncle Max stared out at the changing sky. "They must have been parked down the road with their warrants, just waiting."

"If you'll pardon me, sir, some resistance could be offered."

But Uncle Max waved an arm. "We're still civilized people. I don't want them running all over the place, trampling my roses."

"Max . . ." Aunt Rita touched his arm. "Max, was it so bad?"

He looked around him. "All this? I don't think so." And then he seemed to remember me again. "I told you, boy. Just this afternoon I told you. No matter what you hear, no matter what they might tell you . . ."

From somewhere below, the door chimes started their familiar message. Uncle Max turned away from us for just a moment, and I heard Aunt Rita scream.

"*Max! No!*"

Then there was the cough of a muffled shot, and he started to crumple. I got just a glimpse of the small automatic he'd pressed against his heart, and then the butler hustled me out. Moments later, when the tall man showed a legal-looking document and asked for Uncle Max, the butler simply shook his head and said, "You're a bit too late, sir."

And I knew Uncle Max was dead. Forever.

Later, after they'd taken away the body, I slipped out of my room and went back to the room on the third floor. There were still a few spots of blood on the rug, and I tried not to look at them. Instead, I found the crumpled ball of yellow paper where Uncle Max had tossed it, and spread it carefully between my hands. It was the news bulletin he'd watched being typed out.

CHICAGO, AUGUST 3, 2008—FOLLOWING TESTIMONY BEFORE A GRAND JURY HERE TODAY, FEDERAL AGENTS MOVED SWIFTLY TO ARREST MAX QUIRE, IDENTIFIED AS THE SECRET PUBLISHER OF OUTLAWED DETECTIVE STORIES. SINCE THE BAN IMPOSED ON SUCH LITERATURE IN 2006, AUTHORITIES HAVE BEEN ATTEMPTING TO GATHER EVIDENCE AGAINST QUIRE, DESCRIBED AS THE LAST IMPORTANT DETECTIVE STORY PUBLISHER STILL AT LARGE.